"There was a fire

from the electrical fixtures inside the tunnel. I guess after the initial impact of the trains, your train hit an electrical box of some sort, and then maybe the ceiling of the tunnel. The fire burned most of the first car but they got it out before it spread to your car." As Cala reported her findings, I recalled the impact, the pain and the noises, assigning a new meaning to the sounds.

"Get some rest. I'll be back in an hour to wake you."

"Thanks, Cala." It was in times like this where my sister's maternal ways came in handy.

Cala smiled a sympathetic grin, and lightly closed the door.

Orange, angry flames flashed inside my closed eyes. I heard the yells, the smashing of the cars, remembered the pull of my rescuer into Hell. Brown smoke, more yells, filled my anxious mind. Hot fire. Cold water.

Opening my eyes wide, I allowed them to adjust to the darkness as I had done in the tunnel. Light trickled in from under the door. I inhaled, remembering the smells; I remembered his cologne, his laugh, his smile, his body rolling over the seat. I was used to losing things, but I had never misplaced a whole person before. Inexplicably, I was overcome with an urge to find him. I *needed* to find him. Perhaps it was our chemistry. Perhaps it was just a need to make sure he was okay. My wallet had survived, I had survived—Magic 8 ball had survived—I was certain he had as well. I wanted, I needed, to finish our ride.

Praise for Lori M. Jones
Silver medal winner of Readers' Favorites

"Jones' writing is lyrical. Her stories are beautifully written with intricate plots, and descriptions that sing in harmony. *LATE FOR FATE* touches a chord in every person who has struggled to defy the odds."
~N. J. Hammer, Author

~*~

"Jones is a gifted author with a talent for sharp, fast-paced prose that keeps the pages turning."
~Kathleen Shoop, Author

~*~

"She's quickly establishing herself as a leader in the women's fiction space."
~Carolyn Menke, Author of Return to Me

Late for Fate

by

Lori M. Jones

This is a work of fiction. Names, characters, places, and incidents are either the product of the author's imagination or are used fictitiously, and any resemblance to actual persons living or dead, business establishments, events, or locales, is entirely coincidental.

Late for Fate

COPYRIGHT © 2016 by Lori M. Jones

All rights reserved. No part of this book may be used or reproduced in any manner whatsoever without written permission of the author or The Wild Rose Press, Inc. except in the case of brief quotations embodied in critical articles or reviews.
Contact Information: info@thewildrosepress.com

Cover Art by *Kim Mendoza*

The Wild Rose Press, Inc.
PO Box 708
Adams Basin, NY 14410-0708
Visit us at www.thewildrosepress.com

Publishing History
First Crimson Rose Edition, 2016
Print ISBN 978-1-5092-0830-2
Digital ISBN 978-1-5092-0831-9

Published in the United States of America

Dedication

To my mom & dad
for sending me off on the right track

"Each man is the architect of his own fate."
~Appius Claudius
~*~
"Every action of our lives touches on some chord that will vibrate in eternity."
~Edwin Hubbel Chapin

Chapter 1

After leaving my office, my chest fluttered after I asked my tiny Magic 8 ball if I'd meet my dream guy soon. When the elevator door opened, the little ball answered with an emphatic-pressed-clearly-against-the-window, *YES*. It was ridiculous for a grown woman to think that a toy could predict the future, but I put an unhealthy amount of stock in the tiny ball that dangled from my keychain. Since no one manufactured real crystal balls, this was the next best thing. It was all in good fun, really.

Heading into the world of harried D.C. commuters, I descended the escalator into the metro station. It was the end of cherry blossom season, a glorious spectacle around the Jefferson Memorial, but pressed inside the influx of tourists riding the Metro, the view was not as pretty. The tourists were easy to spot—holding maps and cameras and disobeying the unwritten rules of Metro etiquette.

My pump bit into my heel and I twisted my ankle for what had to be the tenth time in the last ten minutes. My poor shoe choice was an attempt to keep my best friend off my case about sprucing up to attract the opposite sex. If Carolyn and I were fonts, she'd be fancy cursive, but I'd be block lettering—maybe the long, skinny boring kind like Arial with perhaps an unexpected Wingding. Carolyn's goal was to add a bit of swirl to my lettering.

I surrendered to the pleas of my feet and sat on a cement bench, applying a Band-Aid to my reddened skin. I sent the typical 'sorry for my tardiness' text to Carolyn, blaming the attorney bosses for the delayed start to our dinner plans. She wouldn't be surprised.

The headlights of the redline train, along with a thunderous roar, emerged through the tunnel. I moved forward. The wind from the train's speed tossed my curls across my face and over my shoulders. Like well-trained animals, the masses pulled toward the edge of the ceramic tiled stage.

Eyeing the crowd through the cars' passing windows, I ignored my screaming bandaged blister and fought the human current like a salmon swimming upstream, making a strategic move closer to the front of the slowing train. My chances of getting a seat increased if I positioned myself closer to the front. I stopped short of the first car. The bandaged-blister had won.

The doors slid open. The familiar scent of the aging orange leather seats mixed with unfresh commuter bodies baked by the humid spring day greeted me. An available aisle seat beckoned, so I squeezed my body between the final obstacles, and slid my long legs into the seat, habitually pulling a file from my briefcase. The Metro ride to Rockville had become a good place to log some billable time.

The sweet aroma of cologne cut through the Metro's more unsavory odors. When I was lucky enough to score a seat during rush hour, it was usually next to someone who did not practice the application of deodorants, so this was a pleasant surprise.

My glance drifted to the leg an inch from mine, and I perused the suited man's physique. Tall, I surmised. Since I was always on the lookout for men who could complement my tall frame, my eyes connected with his. When his eyes fell to the papers on my lap, I slipped them into my briefcase, fearing I had breached attorney-client privilege.

"Hi," I said, closing my briefcase.

"Lawyer?" he asked in a rich, deep voice.

"Paralegal."

"So, you work for Harrington & Paulson? They're one of the largest firms nationally, right?"

"Number three."

"What department?"

"Employment Law," I said, glancing down at his well-manicured hands. Examining his left ring finger, I spied a slight indentation. Evidence, I hoped, of a marriage no longer in existence.

"I'm Kirk, by the way, nice to meet you."

"Jezebel." I took his extended hand in mine. I smiled at his touch. My face flushed with heat. *Thank you, Magic 8.*

"Interesting name, Jezebel."

I shook my head, adding an embarrassed scoff. "I get that a lot. My mom chose controversial names with negative connotations, raising us to be the opposite, proving their reputations to be wrong." I rattled off my rehearsed explanation, hand gestures galore. "My sister's name is Calamity. Cala, as she goes by, has successfully achieved the goal of being the opposite. And there's my brother Damian, as in the movie The Omen, but he likes his name and is very un-Satan like. My parents smoked a lot of weed."

He chuckled at the story, moving his leg closer to me. Frequently on the Metro, I had experienced creepy seatmates who tried to get intimate, but this time I was perfectly content to let it happen.

"Jezebel was some evil, sexually pervasive queen from the Bible, if I remember correctly."

"Hmm, yeah, it was the pot. A lot of pot."

"Well, I think you won the best name by your mother's standards." He smiled, and with a nudge of his arm against mine, he added, "I had some crazy parents, too. And not to make you feel bad or anything, but Kirk means church in German."

"I do feel a little inadequate now. Thanks." I smiled. "So, what do you do?"

"Sales and marketing for Westlaw. Ms. Paralegal, I'm sure you've used us for legal research."

"Of course. I'm a frequent Westlaw user."

"So, do you have any desire to go to law school?" he asked, cocking his head with interest.

"No, I have no desire to go back to school and work the grueling hours the associates put in. It doesn't make me sound like an overachiever, but I'm happy with my job." I had a prepared defense to this, since it was my sister's favorite nag. I calmed my tone, realizing Kirk was simply making conversation. "The paralegal job is as vital to the workings of a firm, like a nurse is vital to a hospital."

Time to stop my diatribe.

"I think that's great. I only asked because I get that question all the time. A law firm would crumble without your profession—and mine," he said with passion.

"Yeah, we're important, darn it!" I mused, louder

than intended.

He shifted to face me, pausing for a moment. "Anyone ever tell you your eyes are a fascinating shade of blue, or are they gray?"

Embarrassed, I looked down. "Thanks. I think they are both colors actually. So, where are you headed?"

"Home to North Bethesda."

"Married?" I asked boldly.

"No, separated."

"Sorry to hear that." I really wasn't.

"Thanks. What about you? Where are you headed?"

"Rockville. I usually get off at the Twinbrook stop but I'm meeting an old college roommate for dinner." I had a surprising urge to explain to him I was meeting a female and not a male. "I'm running late, as usual."

"I'm glad you were late. I wouldn't have met you if you were on time."

I laughed, bashfully looking down, still feeling his stare.

"I'm glad I'm not a punctual person either—"

A flash of light. A flash of blackness. Crushing metal, screeching brakes, and screams ended our conversation. Piercing pain racked my body as an unknown force slammed me into the seat in front of me. The seat compressed the air from my lungs, transforming it into a loud groan. Like a stuffed animal being tossed away by an angry child, my body flew out of the seat, the back of my head slamming against the Metro floor.

Inside the darkness, panicked bodies surrounded me, one rolling on top of me. I inhaled smoke. My strained voice joined in the chorus of screams. Rolling onto my belly, I attempted to crawl, not knowing where to go. I'd aim for the door connecting the train cars. Legs, shoes, and a large bag blocked my escape. I coughed and stopped moving. Feeling light-headed and weak, I no longer felt like fleeing, but craved sleep.

My blouse constricted around my chest as my body peeled off the ground. A stranger's hand dragged me toward an open side door.

"I got this door open, get up. Let's go," a voice commanded. The young man's face was an inch from mine, but his words seemed distant. My head swirled. My body tried to faint, but I refused to lose control. I prayed for adrenaline to keep me conscious.

The stranger yanked me onto a narrow walkway between the Metro car and the tunnel's wall. Water sprayed my face, distracting my body from fainting. A burst of orange flames danced to my right providing light to the dark tunnel. Suffocated by smoke-filled air, I pulled the top of my blouse over my mouth and tried to breathe. We had entered Hell, I was sure. I grabbed the young man's t-shirt in front of me as he guided me away from the inferno; he was now my life preserver, my savior, and I would not let go. A hand attached itself to the back of my jacket, while a female voice whimpered behind me. I reached back and grabbed the woman's hand, pulling her along. Ceiling sprinklers soaked my hair, my blouse, my suit jacket.

Shouts and cries reverberated from the tunnel's walls. I had no idea how deep into the tunnel the train had traveled before it met its demise. *Just walk and you'll be fine*, I told myself.

I wondered if this was a crash or an act of terrorism. Since 9/11, there had been rumors and fears of suicide bombers carrying out an act on the Metro. I trembled even more at the thought.

There had to be fatalities. I couldn't imagine anyone escaping the car ahead of me. I thought of Kirk. I could not be sure, but I thought I sensed his body rolling over the seat in front of us. My last memory of him was foggy because in a millisecond, I had hit the ground.

My throbbing shoulder captured my mind's attention. Was my difficulty breathing from the smoke, the airless tunnel, or a broken rib? I felt dizzy again. I ignored my body's aches, its screams to surrender, and I forged ahead, my hand still attached to my savior's back.

I strained to peer inside the Metro windows to see if others were escaping through the emergency doors, moving toward safety. My eyes adjusted to the darkness and made out the silhouettes of a few people moving in one direction and fluorescent stripes from fire fighters' suits walking the opposite way. I remembered a coworker telling me he carried a small tool in his briefcase that shatters glass in case of a Metro terrorist attack. I wondered if any of my coworkers or friends were on this train, too.

On the tiny sidewalk, I looked down onto the dark track. One of the tracks could electrocute on contact. More reason not to pass out.

Light peeked through the darkness ahead, beckoning us to move toward it. My feet ached and my head pulsated with a sharp pain.

I had no phone, no keys, no wallet, no Magic 8 ball; all was left inside a burning Metro. I still had my life, however, and my shoes. The shoes that caused me to pause long enough on the platform and stopped me from reaching the front car, the car that seemed to have met the worst fate.

I heard a rush of water. Killing flames, perhaps.

We reached the end of the train where others were being helped out its rear door. Rescue workers pulled passengers off the track while two firefighters took over as the leaders of the tunnel sidewalk procession. Relief washed over me when our journey ended inside a lit station. Where were we? I spotted a sign: Medical Center. Two stops before my final destination.

A stocky woman in a blue paramedic uniform clasped my arm with a rubber-gloved hand and guided me to sit on a concrete bench where she swaddled me in a blanket. Beyond the paramedic's shoulder, I watched my stranger-savior move with another paramedic away from me. I never got to thank him. Two people thrust together during the scariest moment of my life and I would never see him again, never know his name. All I knew was that his t-shirt bore the name of an unrecognizable rock band.

Smoke seeped into the station while rescue personnel evacuated victims with precision. My eyes searched for Kirk, scanning the crowd for a tall, attractive man. His chiseled features etched in my memory, but I found no one close to my mental picture. Bloodied faces, shocked expressions, and soiled business suits swept by me. A man cried. The place smelled of melting plastic and burnt rubber. Sirens sounded and stern voices shouted commands to those trained to handle a catastrophe. There was organization inside the chaos. A disaster plan created in calmer times was being executed all around me.

"Are you hurt?" the paramedic asked.

"My head and my shoulder," I answered without thinking, touching each body part like a child with a trembling hand. I hadn't even realized how much I'd been shaking. My body seemed to be catching up with the terror my mind had recorded. I coughed. It hurt.

Absorbing the scene around me, I watched a stretcher cruise by. The female paramedic conducted a brief exam of my eyes, searching for signs of a concussion. "You're code yellow and will be assigned to Bethesda Medical Center. They'll check you out in the E.R," the woman instructed, handing me a yellow card and guiding me to an escalator. "Take this to the paramedic at the top and show him your yellow tag."

I climbed the idle escalator, my legs feeling foreign, like heavy mannequin parts. The idea of a hospital trip nauseated me. I just wanted to find Carolyn in the restaurant two stops away and continue as if nothing had happened.

At the top of the escalator, I stepped into the smoke-free air under a blue sky with its sun sitting low. Daylight. How grateful I felt for daylight and fresh air in those moments before entering the ambulance.

"Miss, what's your name and age? And what car were you riding in, do you remember?"

"Jezebel Stone. I'm twenty-eight. The second one, the one behind the car…that was on fire." He scribbled some words across his clipboard.

"Okay, climb inside here. This ambulance is taking you and the others to Bethesda Medical Center. Good luck, Miss." The ambulance doors shut behind me.

Another paramedic guided me to a bench and took my vitals without speaking. I glanced at two other

Metro riders, soiled, wearing spots of blood on their business attire.

"This damn commute just keeps getting longer, huh?" asked the smiling plump man, possibly in his mid-fifties, seated next me. His yellow short-sleeved shirt was blood-stained, ironically right under his pocket protector. He chuckled softly.

I nodded, allowing a smile to fill my face, bringing a release to my embattled body. "Yeah, what's worse, the beltway or the Metro?"

"Well, we're alive at least. Survivors of what just might be the worst crash in Metro history." His serious words made me feel tense again. I was grateful to be a survivor but selfishly missed my phone and my now charred belongings. I imagined Carolyn sitting alone at our table, checking her phone impatiently. I couldn't even remember my best friend's phone number. Although dialed a million times, the number was hidden away on my cell phone's speed dial.

At the hospital, the E.R. doctor told me I had a mild concussion and gave me a sling for my sprained shoulder. The doctor instructed me on what to do and advised me to not sleep alone and to call for a ride. I used the hospital's phone to call the restaurant where I was supposed to meet my friend. A waiter promised to find Carolyn.

"Jezebel, are you okay? You were on that train!? Holy God!"

I pulled the phone away from my ear as my friend's shrill tone hurt my head. "Yeah, I was. I'm okay. Just freaked out a little. All my stuff's on the Metro. My wallet. My keys. My phone." All of these things I had lost before, even repeatedly, but picturing them all burning was distressing. I tried to do a mental inventory of the documents inside my briefcase.

"I'll be right there. Where are you?"

I told her and she promised to be there in minutes. At least I would soon see a familiar face. I would figure out how to get into my locked apartment later.

Needing to be in the fresh spring air, I exited the hospital, glad to inhale the pollen saturated air. My allergies flaring up didn't seem so serious anymore. With a plastic bag full of damaged clothes in my hand, I leaned against the warm brick exterior. Instead of meeting my fashionable friend in my well-planned outfit, I waited for Carolyn in my hospital-issued sweats.

My head throbbed and my shoulder ached, and the pain forced a reflection on the evening's events. Had I left the office when I had planned, saying no to an associate's plea for help, I would now be sitting at dinner, laughing with my friend over a shared dessert. But, I was grateful I didn't make it to the first car. I thanked my blister, the Band Aid, and the bench. Part of me wished I had stayed in my original position in the center of the platform that would have placed me on a car further from the wreckage. Maybe the impact would not have been so severe. I wondered again about Kirk's fate. A chill shook my body.

"Jez!" Carolyn yelled, running toward me, a long silver chain bounced across her silky teal blouse. "I parked illegally around the corner. Are you okay?" Carolyn pulled me in to a gentle hug. "Oh, you smell like smoke, dear God."

"I think I'm still a little stunned actually, and I just realized I'm starving. Did they say what happened?"

Carolyn hesitated, and then shared the information. "The latest news report said it wasn't terrorism. One train hit the rear of another, maybe from a failed signaling circuit that alerts the driver to a stopped train ahead. They think at least fifteen, maybe more, are dead, including the driver. Terrible."

I felt a pang of relief the disaster was not caused by someone's vengeful hand, but then again, what did it matter? People were dead.

Carolyn continued speaking, guiding my arm toward her car. "I hope you don't mind, but I called your sister to tell her you were okay, in case she was worried. Anyway, Cala said your mom was freaking out so it's a good thing I called. Your sister said she has your spare key but wants you to stay with her tonight." Carolyn helped me into the passenger seat and ran around, jumping into the driver's seat.

"Thanks. I feel like taking a long, hot bath and sleeping alone in my own bed tonight, but I guess with the concussion thing, it's probably a good idea to stay with her."

"You're welcome at my place too, but my two crazy munchkins wouldn't give you a whole lot of peace and quiet."

"I'm not sure my sister is going to give me that much peace and quiet either." I rubbed my head and noticed the muscles along my back were beginning to ache and tighten.

Carolyn drove up the busy city street and asked, "Jez, you want something for pain?"

The doctor had given me a Percocet prescription, but because of what happened to my father many years ago, I never took prescription painkillers. My shoulder begged me to reconsider.

"I'd love a burger and some Tylenol."

While keeping her eyes on the road, Carolyn reached over and pulled a small container of Tylenol from her purse and handed me a bottle of water from the cup holder. Her multi-tasking was a result of honed parenting skills, she often boasted.

"Nothing ever makes you lose your appetite, does it?"

Carolyn pulled into a fast food drive-thru and ordered. We sat in the car and ate a dinner drastically different than the one we had planned. While sharing tales of her children's Brazilian au pair, Carolyn never stopped assisting me with my food and beverage difficulties. During our brief meal, I allowed the tragedy to slip to the back of my mind temporarily. Carolyn shut off the radio when the D.J. announced there were sixteen confirmed dead. The burger threatened to return.

"I'm a little dizzy. I think I need to go to bed," I announced.

Carolyn chauffeured me through the tree-lined neighborhood leading past large bricked homes belonging to the capital's lawyers, politicians, and other wealthy suburban residents. Curving around the cul-de-sac, we pulled into Cala's long driveway. The manicured lawn was illuminated by professionally positioned lighting.

We walked to the front door and before we could reach for the doorbell, the large wooden door whipped open.

"Jezzie, thank God you're okay! You need to stay here, you look awful. Get in here and sit down," my sister commanded, pulling my sling-free arm toward the formal living room. I kicked off my shoes before stepping on the plush, white carpet coated with fresh vacuum tracks.

After sending Carolyn on her way, Cala closed the door and began to share her well thought-out plan. "So, I took tomorrow off. I assume you will, too. I'll drive you to your bank to get a new banking card and then to the DMV to get you a license and then to the mall to get you a briefcase and probably a phone as well." Cala spoke while stroking my frazzled locks into place.

I knew not to protest or alter my sister's plans in any way. "Thanks, Cala. That sounds like a good plan. I need to get some rest."

"The guest room is ready. I set my alarm so I can wake you every hour to check on you, as I'm sure the doctor instructed."

I acknowledged that Cala had my best interest at heart. However, my sister's intensity elevated the level of anxiety in any situation. Tonight, I yearned for peace.

After our father had died when I was twelve, our mother fell into a deep depression. Sixteen-year-old Cala stepped in as the maternal and paternal leader. Even after our mother pulled herself together and rejoined life, Cala never relinquished her motherly role. Cala carried those same leadership qualities with her throughout life. I loved my sister, but felt less accomplished in her presence. Cala's dissatisfaction with our brother's unpredictable career as a musician was even harder for her to disguise.

I closed the door of the spacious guest suite and showered in the marble bathroom. After slipping into the nightgown my sister had spread at the foot of the bed, I smiled and rolled my eyes at the Lenox vase full of tulips recently snipped from the backyard garden, sitting on the nightstand.

As I pushed back the fluffy floral comforter, an urgent knock sounded against the door.

"Jez, can I come in?"

"Yeah, sure," I answered uselessly since Cala had already entered.

Cala had tilted her head around the semi-open door and announced, smiling, "I called around to a few police stations and they recovered your briefcase. Your train car never burned, but it did get wet. We'll head down there in the morning."

"Thanks, Cala. I didn't even think to call about it. I assumed it burned." *Typical Cala*, I thought, *always taking the extra step*.

"There was a fire from the electrical fixtures inside the tunnel. I guess after the initial impact of the trains, your train hit an electrical box of some sort, and then maybe the ceiling of the tunnel. The fire burned most of the first car but they got it out before it spread to your car." As Cala reported her findings, I recalled the impact, the pain and the noises, assigning a new meaning to the sounds.

"Get some rest. I'll be back in an hour to wake you."

"Thanks, Cala." It was in times like this where my sister's maternal ways came in handy.

Cala smiled a sympathetic grin, and lightly closed the door.

Orange, angry flames flashed inside my closed eyes. I heard the yells, the smashing of the cars, remembered the pull of my rescuer into Hell. Brown smoke, more yells, filled my anxious mind. Hot fire. Cold water.

Opening my eyes wide, I allowed them to adjust to the darkness as I had done in the tunnel. Light trickled in from under the door. I inhaled, remembering the smells; I remembered his cologne, his laugh, his smile, his body rolling over the seat. I was used to losing things, but I had never misplaced a whole person before. Inexplicably, I was overcome with an urge to find him. I *needed* to find him. Perhaps it was our chemistry. Perhaps it was just a need to make sure he was okay. My wallet had survived, I had survived—Magic 8 ball had survived—I was certain he had as well. I wanted, I needed, to finish our ride.

Chapter 2

"Good morning, Miss Stone, are you late for something?" The head of the Employment Law Department greeted me as I stepped inside the elevator, a Starbucks coffee clutched in his hand. I could never quite tell if he was being sarcastic or not.

"Driving to work makes for a tougher commute, Jon." I really did need to start trusting the Metro again.

Since the crash two weeks ago, I'd driven to work after taking a few days off to recover. Although my commute time hadn't changed, I was now without my relaxing moments on the train to read the newspaper, apply makeup, and eavesdrop on my fellow commuters' conversations. At least I was done wearing the arm sling, so driving was easier.

"Well, the work's not going anywhere, so relax." The advice to relax seemed comical coming from the man who still insisted on wearing bow ties and suit coats in spite of a business casual dress code policy.

Tossing my briefcase on my office floor, I sighed at the briefs on my chair requiring my review. After grabbing a coffee, I continued with my morning routine, which included popping my head into the billing manager's office for a quick conversation to start my day with a smile.

Ken's office was my escape from attorneys and from work in general. He could transform the negative into refreshing comedy and possessed a talent for turning every coworker into a cartoon or television character.

"Morning, my favorite coworker." I collapsed into his only guest chair. His room resembled a large walk-in closet as opposed to a full sized office.

"Right back at ya, Jezzie. Whoa, your hair is particularly wild today, young lady!"

"Humidity is a cruel thing, Kenny. Toss me a rubber band. Hey, do you think I need counseling, like real honest to goodness therapy to get myself back on that damn train again? I hate driving into work," I mumbled, harnessing my thick curls into a truss.

"Girl, you could use real honest to goodness counseling for more than just Post Traumatic Stress Disorder." We laughed, and I added a snort.

"Our health plan covers six weeks. I'm thinking of doing it. Carolyn thinks I should."

"Hell, bill the firm, baby. This place has caused you to lose your marbles plenty of times. Maybe all the paralegals here could get a group rate?" His deep green eyes glanced at the ceiling, feigning intense thought.

"So true. Hey, how was your date with the Navy dude?"

"He's so hot, Jez. I'll pull up his Facebook page and you can have a looksee yourself." Ken did and I agreed, as usual. He had the ability to land hotter men than I could. He reported date details before becoming distracted by my hairdo. "Oh, your hair looks so cute pulled back, shows off that pretty freckled face. What a hot tall drink of water you are, girl." He snickered as an associate entered his office, my cue to leave. This particular attorney Ken had dubbed Charlie in the Box, the character from "Rudolph the Red-Nosed Reindeer." Ken got a lot of his material from the Island of Misfit Toys.

"Why can't you be straight, sweetheart?" I whispered, enjoying our daily game, then disappeared into the hall.

I'd found a quiet moment and made a phone call to the nearby therapist's office. When the receptionist suggested a noon visit due to a cancellation, my palms prickled with perspiration. Making the appointment sent nervous flutters to my belly and a feeling of failure deflated me a bit. Why couldn't I fix this on my own? I had survived traumas in the past, like losing my father at a young age and breaking up with my soul mate, so why couldn't I get over an incident that had disrupted a mere thirty minutes of my life?

Well, that's what I'd need a counselor for, I concluded.

Before filing a pleading with Superior Court, I had to stop by Justin's office for a signature. I rounded the corner and braced myself for whatever demeanor he presented to me this visit.

"Good morning, Justin, I just need your signature." Smiling, I entered with a self-assured strut. My entrance didn't stop him from picking up the receiver of his phone and dialing as I walked toward his desk. As he attached the receiver to his ear, he motioned for me to come over to him.

"Hello, David, Justin Moorehead here. How are you? Just checking to see if you had time to review that pleading I sent last night…" He signed my document, sliding it back to me, talking loudly to the client on the other end of the phone, but barely acknowledging this human being before him. He returned to his call with an exaggerated laugh, pushing himself back into his large leather chair, spinning it to face the window.

Justin was a fourth year associate, certainly no reason to be arrogant, but I knew it was his way of showing me that my presence had no ill effects on him. A typical game he played ever since our awkward post office holiday party rendezvous.

Shaking off the Justin encounter, I stopped by my secretary's desk. The legal secretaries usually were assigned to one partner, two associates and a paralegal or a summer intern. The paralegal's work always took lower precedence after those with law degrees. Since I had a friendship with Vanessa outside of the office, she always made it a point to treat me as an equal to her associates.

"Hey baby girl, whatcha up to?" Vanessa sang, her appearance always pristine, makeup radiant over her flawless skin, no matter what time of day, or night. Her peach blouse held snugly against her large breasts, and as hard as I tried, I found my eyes drawn downward to envy Vanessa's appealing cleavage.

"Just checking to see if the Carrington brief came back."

"No, not yet. Hey, why did you take the health plan directory—you need a doctor, sweetie?"

"Well," I said, adjusting my voice into a whisper, "I made an appointment with a therapist to get over this fear of the Metro thing. They fit me in today. Stop looking at me again like I'm crazy."

"Oh, sorry. Well, that accident was a scary deal for you, I get it, sweetie. I've been praying for you, I have been, really. Maybe it's a good idea to see someone."

"Thanks, but the prayers haven't been helping."

"How do you know? Maybe my praying got you to call the counselor. And have you even tried to ride it again?" Vanessa questioned tilting her head, emphasizing it with a firm hand placement on her hip.

"Two days ago, I walked onto the platform, broke out into a cold sweat, and got back in my car and drove away."

"Why don't you say a prayer yourself, Jez? Might give you courage to talk to the Lord on the way there."

As a devout Baptist, Vanessa's answer to everything was to "pray to the Lord." It didn't offend or bother me. In fact it was comforting to know someone was praying for me. Although I did believe in God, I never felt comfortable talking to Him. Even at the scariest moments in the blackened Metro, although muttering, "Oh my God" repeatedly, I never appealed to a higher power for real help. I just crawled, and cried, and gasped for air. Why didn't God stop the train or cause the sensor on the tracks to alert the drivers of a train ahead? I knew all the details of the crash, the cause, and the aftermath. But couldn't really see God in all that mess.

In the week following the crash, I had become obsessed with the news coverage. I read all sixteen obituaries of those who perished. Ten had been on my train, just one car ahead of me, and six were in the last car of the train we hit. I cried at stories of the newly created widows and widowers. An elderly couple from New England died who had been touring D.C. for the first time since they married here 52 years ago. I read the transcript from the NTSB's initial press conference. I had watched doctors at Washington Hospital Center speak to reporters on the conditions of those in critical condition in their burn unit.

Carolyn had diagnosed my constant gnawing ache in my gut as survivor's guilt. Guilt because my seemingly innocuous decisions that day had placed me among the living and not in the Washington Post's obituaries. Yet another issue to discuss with Dr. Dennison.

Missing lunch hour with my work friends was a necessary sacrifice in order to fit in a session with the psychologist. As I settled into the decaying leather cab seat, I looked forward to spilling my soul to a stranger. But recounting the accident might send me in the other direction. Would I mention Kirk to the therapist? Would I tell the therapist how he appeared in my dreams and caused me to conjure up the most erotic fantasies I ever had in my life? Probably not, since mysterious-hot-guy-on-Metro had no relevance to my fear of returning to the scene of the accident. If anything, he was a motivation to return.

I would focus on my fears and not my fantasies, for now. At least I knew, after reading the names of the crash victims, he was alive. I knew I could call the Westlaw offices to track down a man named Kirk, but something held me back. I couldn't quite face him yet, not until I worked a little longer with my therapist. Mysterious-hot-guy would remain a fantasy, saved for relaxing me into a peaceful sleep.

My stomach grew tight on the elevator's upward ride to the sixth floor. I checked in with the receptionist seated behind the sliding glass window and took a seat in the tranquil waiting area.

"Jezebel Stone?" the slight, professionally dressed

woman called from inside her office doorway.

"Yes," I answered and stood, my face washed with embarrassment. Without revealing even a single detail of my life, I was already ashamed in front of this woman. What was worse: being naked in front of a gynecologist or bearing my soul to a psychologist? As I followed the woman to her office, I longed to be in the stirrups.

"I'm Dr. Dennison. Please have a seat."

I sat across from the suited, well-accessorized woman, relaxing inside the leather wing-backed chair. I decided to enjoy this hour of therapy.

"What brings you here, Jezebel?"

"I was on the Metro that crashed two weeks ago. In the second car, behind the one where people died. I can't get back on it. I sweat on the platform. The sounds of the trains on the tracks make me sick. I've had nightmares. I've been driving to work, but it's stressful. I want to get back on the train and not remember the crash. Can you hypnotize me or something?" I asked as I watched the woman cross her legs and make a tiny circle in the air with her booted foot, as if loosening her ankle for a race.

"Jezebel, what you're experiencing is completely normal. That was quite a significant crash. So first of all, don't beat yourself up for being afraid or not wanting to go back. That's normal."

"I feel frustrated that I just can't get over it. It's not just mental, it's…physical."

"They typically go hand in hand. I think you'd be a good candidate for Prolonged Exposure Therapy. It's commonly used for those who were in an accident, or a disaster. Even soldiers and rape victims have had success with it. We are going to relive and remember everything from the event, engaging with, rather than avoiding triggers and reminders. Over time, you will see that you've desensitized yourself from the event. You will want to get back on that train."

The same treatment for those raped or at war? Good grief. This was just public transportation.

"Okay," I agreed.

I relived the day of the crash with the doctor, the walk to the Metro, the clothing I wore, the shoes that gave me blisters, my anxiety of being late to meet my friend, the cement bench that held me for a moment—before and after the crash. I discussed the crowds, the smells, the heat inside the train. That heat I felt from sitting next to the sweet smelling man who made me smile before my concussion. Saying his name aloud to the therapist made me blush and glance down at my lap, just as I had done before the crash.

I told her about the fall to the floor and being pulled from the train. The long walk through the tunnel and the paramedics. Out loud, I relived every feeling along the way—the pain, the dread, the desire to be seated at a table with Carolyn following a Metro ride which had departed fifteen minutes before the train I had ridden.

Most of my bad feelings, the feelings that made my chest constrict, came days after. In the quiet moments alone in my apartment, in the moments before I dozed off, was when I experienced a gripping fear. I would tremble when the flames rushed in my mind. I shook when I tried to recall if the deceased elderly couple had passed me on their way to the front car.

The one thing that would calm me and push me

past the flames and ease me into sleep was my fantasy of seeing Kirk again. How we'd reunite someday in a D.C. park and he'd kiss me. He would push away my hair from my face, pull my waist toward his, and heat my body with a deep kiss. He'd pull away, breathing heavily, hypnotized by our passion. He would tell me how he almost succumbed to the thick smoke, but it was his desire to rescue me that had made him pull himself off of the floor. He would tell me I had rescued him, and as he played with my hair and studied my face, he would whisper his gratitude for my tardiness. He would whisper to me how I had been his savior.

After fifty-five minutes, I said goodbye. Feeling drained, I meandered through the city blocks to my office building. My body felt like I had crashed again, minus the shoulder and head pain. I wanted to go home and sleep, but the call of the work piling on my desk was too strong to ignore.

Inside the office hallway I saw a smiling face, but I moved swiftly to avoid conversation. "Hey, Vanessa," I mumbled.

"Hey, girl, Justin's looking for you. Just a warning."

"Thanks for that."

I rounded the corner into my office, exhaling at the sight of the red message light on my phone. More work. The voice coming through my receiver pushed me into my seat. My breathing halted. My heart raced.

"Hi there, Jezebel. Luckily there is only one Jezebel working for Harrington & Paulson. It's Kirk. From the train. Hope you don't think this is weird that I'm calling. I just had the urge to speak to you again. Unfinished business I guess. Want to see if you're okay. Sorry it took me so long, I've been in Atlanta on business. Still here actually. I'll call again when I get back. Maybe we can finish our train ride to Rockville."

Chapter 3

The thing that Kirk remembered most vividly from the crash was the chubby, yellow-shirted man. His body glowed—even in the blackened car—like an orb. And he'd never forget that pocket protector clinging to the man's chest.

When the crash happened, Kirk's body had flown over the seat ahead of him, knocking a woman out of her seat, and slamming them onto the floor beside a door. He tried to pry open the door with the help of the yellow-shirted guy, but it wouldn't budge. His next goal was to get to the emergency doors that connected the train cars. He yanked the yellow-shirted man toward the back of the car as smoke choked them, and they tripped over strewn debris. A side door had been opened, but that path was clogged.

His eyes darted around in a quick search for Jezebel, hoping she was searching for him, but he didn't see her.

He stumbled through the first set of connecting doors and hurried along to the final car that opened onto the tracks. Firefighters helped them all into the tunnel. The sounds of women crying irritated him, though, he felt like crying himself.

They walked through the tunnel and another set of firefighters guided them up a ladder onto the platform inside the Medical Center station. The blood left his head, his body went clammy and he started to pant. A male paramedic grabbed Kirk's arm and asked him to sit. Instead, he rested his hands on his knees, bending over, suffocating. It had been a full-blown panic attack.

Kirk took off, dashing past the medic, pushing a few stunned-faced crash victims out of his way. He hurried up the escalator steps like he'd suddenly been given super powers. Sunlight. Fresh air. His breathing relaxed.

Thoughts of Jezebel rushed through his buzzing mind. Her stunning eyes still seared in his memory.

The chubby orb guy had followed him and tried to take him with him into an ambulance. Kirk stared at the man's bloodied yellow shirt and pocket protector. His only thought was how the blood would be just as hard to get out of that shirt as ink.

When another paramedic spoke, he bolted from the chaotic mess. Ran up Rockville Pike and ducked into a coffee shop.

That was when he phoned his wife to pick him up.

That night, he used his near death experience and some wine to get her into their bed and out of the guest room. They didn't make love, in fact, he couldn't remember the last time their sexual encounters were tender and giving. As of late, in addition to being rare, they were raw and rough, like two animals seeking to quench a physical need, while ascertaining dominance over the other. In an effort to tap into her softer nurturing side, he exaggerated his injuries, but his attempts were in vain. Nicole took what she needed with complete disregard for his damaged body and, as always, his busted heart.

In spite of the lawsuit against her boss, Kirk knew

she continued to be obsessed with him. She underestimated his intelligence.

While in his hotel room in Atlanta, he found his thoughts drifting to Jezebel. She had chosen the seat next to him right in the middle of his feeling-sorry-for-himself moment. His wife's cold attitude early that morning had painted a cloud across his day's mood, but as soon as Jezebel flopped down beside him, his spirits lifted a bit. Of course he noticed her bordering-on-hot body, but it was something else that caught his eye: the papers she placed on her lap. She worked for Harrington & Paulson.

The case she was working on: D'Angelo v. Winston. His wife, Nicole, versus Nicole's ex-boss.

Luck. Pure luck. Or, a gift.

And since Nicole had refused to take his last name, unable to depart with her Italian heritage, Jezebel would never connect him to the plaintiff in her case.

It seemed his plan started at the moment he told Jezebel he was separated. Leaving his wedding ring in his gym bag was—again—pure luck. Or, perhaps it was a sign that this was the way to win back his wife's affections.

Jezebel—the fallen queen—would get the little male attention she craved and Nicole would get the kind of man who excited her.

Chapter 4

As soon as Nicole entered the break room for her morning coffee, the chatter stopped. "Carry on, ladies. Don't let me stop your conversation," she smirked and poured her coffee.

"Good morning, Nicole." One brave voice broke the obvious tension. "We were just talking about going to the movies next weekend. You're invited, if you want to join us."

Great, a pity invite from Dana, the office's syrupy sweet social organizer. Nicole used to enjoy hanging out with the secretaries, when she felt superior. But ever since her demotion from working for the firm's top attorney, Jack Winston, to working for two associates, she sensed the condescension in their stares.

After word spread like a bad cancer that she was suing Jack, the catty chatter increased. She decided it was time to reestablish herself as the queen bee around the office.

"Thanks, girls. I think I will do that. Email me the deets." Smiling as if someone was focusing a camera on her, she tossed the coffee stirrer into the trash and left the kitchen. She was certain Dana stared with envy at her firm ass as the door closed behind her.

The first time Nicole sensed a divide between her and the other secretaries was two and half years ago when she was chosen to work for Jack. She had clocked in seven years working for multiple associates at Crosby & Miller, ran the summer intern program, and took every overtime hour available. Then good old Betsy Walters and her collection of Talbot's cardigans had retired and the hot topic in the break rooms was whom Jack would pick as Betsy's replacement. Sure, there were others who had served more time at Crosby & Miller, but the senior partner called Nicole into his office one snowy afternoon.

He had just returned from the gym, the tips of his wavy brown hair still damp from the shower. She'd always thought of him as attractive, but up close, behind his closed door was the first time her body reacted to the scent of him. As a newlywed of six months, she shouldn't have felt that so easily, and certainly not with someone thirteen years older.

"Ms. D'Angelo, have a seat, please." He smiled, holding his tie against him as he sat behind a massive desk. He rolled up the sleeves of his white dress shirt, exposing his platinum watch. His skin glowed from his workout. Later, she would find excuses to come into his office just as he returned from the gym.

"Thank you, Mr. Winston." Nicole sat, crossing her legs.

"Please call me Jack. I brought you in here today because I would like you to consider taking the position as my secretary. As you know, I work for many high profile clients and have quite the busy schedule. I need someone who I can rely on, who I can trust. This could require me calling you in on the weekends and in the evenings. Would you be up for that, Nicole?" He leaned against the back of his leather chair, running his fingers along his temples, across the sporadic gray hairs that looked like they were carefully added with a paintbrush.

"Absolutely, Mr., ah, Jack. You could certainly trust me. I'd be honored to work for you, sir." She lost the ability to suppress her excitement.

Jack's specialty was White Collar Crime. His clients, some famous, some infamous, would certainly make work exciting. He represented politicians and well-known business executives. As the son of Jonathon Herbert "Herb" Winston II, the retired conservative U.S. Representative from Norfolk, Virginia, it was no secret Jack had political aspirations of his own. He was practically a celebrity in this town. And if she said the word, she'd be his assistant.

"You have an impressive employment record here at the firm and outstanding evaluations. I think we'd make a good team." He leaned forward with his elbows on the desk, smiling a grin he frequently wore at the firm. His jade eyes glistened, and she couldn't help but smile back. Some of the other secretaries found him slightly pompous, but she thought he exuded an intimidating confidence. She recognized this same trait in herself.

"Yes, Jack, I do believe we will." She stood and shook his hand. While her hand was still in his, he brought his other hand and rested it on the back of Nicole's. Jack possessed the type of magnetic personality that could dazzle juries and judges, and could make each of his clients feel special. With a booming laugh, a twinkling eye, and that white-toothed grin, he could render anyone helpless beneath his hypnotic power. So, was it any surprise that Jack would cast a spell on Nicole, too?

From that day forward, the secretaries at Crosby & Miller treated her differently. As a former Redskins cheerleader, she'd grown accustomed to women rolling their eyes as their husbands gawked. Women had always envied her looks, but now, they envied her position as Jack's secretary.

Jack and Nicole made a dynamic team, and kept things professional for the first year. Then the accidental stray touch turned into a purposeful caress, the innocent joke turned into a flirt, and graduated into a sexual innuendo or two. His hand closing the door behind her, would linger, his body not moving out of the way as quickly as it should have. The pauses as their bodies passed each other created a hot tension that after some time could no longer be ignored. The fantasies could no longer be denied. Their first kiss was behind the closed door of that very office where he offered her the job. And, it was the same door that she slammed shut just a few months ago, after she overheard him flirting with an attorney from Boeing, Rebecca Snyder. It was that flirting that caused Nicole to melt down, Jack to demote her, and her self-proclaimed depression to escalate.

Her depression caused things to deteriorate even further with Kirk. Managing their marriage and her time with Jack went perfectly well until everything blew up. Of course she felt guilty for cheating on Kirk, but she was able to compartmentalize her work life and her home life. And it worked. Kirk provided stability at home, but Jack provided excitement. Divorce wasn't something she would choose, but if Jack had left his wife, she would have divorced Kirk in a minute.

Things seemed a bit out of control, but this lawsuit

was pure genius. Jack was upset with her, but he'd come around and realize he needed her. He'd especially need her during his Senate campaign. She'd planned a beautiful fundraiser for him already. In due time, she'd get Jack to admit he still loved her. And Kirk would provide comfort when she needed it.

She would consider herself a failure if she ended up without Kirk, without Jack, and without her old job back. She knew what excited Jack and she'd give him exactly the excitement he enjoyed. She had no doubt she'd get everything she wanted. Everything.

Chapter 5

Kirk's message managed to paralyze all my other thoughts. I had to call Carolyn, so I could function again. "Guess who left me a message? The hot train guy from the crash." I answered my own question, along with a giggle.

"Get out! What'd he say?"

I told her.

"That's great. Did you get a last name? Any more information on him?"

"None. He didn't say a whole lot." I bit my nail. My attempt to grow long nails had ended in the days after the crash.

"How in the hell are you going to finish your ride when you can't even get back on the Metro?"

"Therapy's working. I'm on my way to being cured. Maybe I'll stall him until I finish my sessions. Or, maybe he'll meet me somewhere else first." A park, I fantasized, just like in my daydreams. My stomach tingled at the possibilities that lay ahead.

In a brief moment between ending the call and delving into my pile of work for the afternoon, I reflected on my pathetic love life. Since Kirk said he was separated and not divorced, I knew I was getting ahead of myself fantasizing about us as a couple. Just harmless fantasies. With full confidence, I knew I had not inherited the hopeless romantic gene my parents seemed to have carried. My mother would share, with a far off look and a dreamy smile, endless stories of her and my father's fairytale love. Her tiny ballerina body would flit about as she practically sang their anecdotes. Cala and I joked it was all pot-induced love.

I had dated casually through high school and college. A few times I had fallen in love, but the feelings hadn't been returned. Finally after graduation, working as a waitress in a diner, I met the man I thought would be "the one." Michael Zolowski swept me off my feet, literally, since he was the diner's bus boy and I had tripped over his push broom. He picked me up off the ground, and to make it up to me, took me to dinner that night in Bethesda. We shared a powerful, almost animal-like attraction. We made love seventeen times before I learned Michael's middle name or his birthday. We dated, engaging in loads of orgasmic-filled sex, for nineteen months when it ended as passionately as it had begun. He had a temper, and I discovered I had one too, and after a massive tearful fight that climaxed into a shoving match, we called it quits.

The next time I felt an urgent magnetic attraction was with Justin, the associate from my department. We joked, teased, and flirted until others in the office sensed the sexual tension. Ken called me out repeatedly. After too many drinks at this past year's office holiday party, we continued our own party upstairs at the Mayflower Hotel. Unfortunately, while Justin was rounding second base and attempting to slide into third, I stopped the encounter and fled the room. It hadn't felt right, so I stopped it. Justin attempted to start a relationship in the following weeks, but I used the "I don't want to ruin our friendship or work relationship" excuse. Things remained tense, awkward, and out of sync with him to this day.

Thoughts of Justin reminded me I had a meeting with him in five minutes. I needed to focus on our clients' problems and not our own.

****

That night, the flames reemerged behind my eyelids as I longed for sleep. I replayed Kirk's message in my mind, using his words like a fire extinguisher to erase my visions of fire. The memory of his voice made me smile, and with a giddy excitement, I rolled over on my side and snuggled into my comforter, drifting off to sleep.

The next morning, I toyed with the idea of driving to the Metro parking lot and taking the death-train into work. But what if I got on the train and panicked? Instead, I drove through the Friday morning traffic, singing along to my favorite radio station, looking forward to my noon appointment with Dr. Dennison. Magic 8 had grown tired of my 'will I ride the metro soon?' questions, answering me with only apathetic maybes.

At my therapy session with Dr. Dennison, I once again described the fear, terror, dread, that were the constant feelings flooding my body. Well, along with blasting pain. But those five minutes before the impact I had felt hope, excitement, and sexual attraction. I shared that first.

After the appointment, I stopped at the entrance to the station I had entered weeks ago. I watched people engaging in the simple exercise of participating in public transportation. Men wearing dress shirts and neckties walked together laughing and talking, discussing business or where to go for lunch. Young and middle-aged professionally dressed women passed me with a Friday afternoon lightness as they made their way through town for some lunchtime shopping or socializing. I watched bodies moving down the escalator and saw bodies emerging from the top of the escalator. Bodies unsoiled by smoke or blood. Faces passed by, content, not plastered with fear. Families hurried past in vacation attire continuing along their sightseeing tours. Life carried on. I saw no one pausing to think of the dead or to remember the tragedy. No one passing me was sweating in panic. I sighed, felt a tinge of pathetic failure, and went back to my office.

****

After work, I headed to my mother's fifty-ninth birthday celebration. My mother's boyfriend, Joe, had invited the whole family to a barbeque in their backyard. Joe had gradually moved into my mother's house over the last year.

I drove down the Gaithersburg street lined with a canopy of mature trees. I had traveled down this street a million times. It was where I had ridden my first bike, and where I had driven my first car. I parked in the driveway of the modest brick three bedroom Cape Cod. It was the house where I could recall vivid memories of my father.

I walked around the side of the house onto the back patio where Cala, my brother-in-law, Rob, and Damian gathered, conversing.

"Hey, Jez," Damian called. My brother came forward on his chair that had been tipped back on its back two legs. After two wide strides in his leather flip-flops, he yanked me into a hug with his chilly beer bottle touching my exposed shoulder. "You're looking good, Sis."

"Thanks, Damian." I kissed his cheek, and then reached to hug my sister and Rob. After my hug with my brother-in-law, I knew his cologne would cling to me for the next hour. I laughed to myself thinking Rob was the only man I knew who was comfortable wearing the color peach.

My mother emerged from the sliding glass kitchen door, carrying a stack of plates. The same Corelle dishes we used growing up. She did not believe in replacing anything until it broke and Corelle rarely broke.

Joe followed behind my mother, hauling a tray of marinated meat and smiled widely at me, yelling out a "hey" along with a jolly chuckle.

"Oh, Jez, they let you out of that office. I'm so glad you're here, baby," my mother squealed and kissed my cheek and placed the plates on the table. Her floor-length tie-dyed skirt swayed along with her necklace of turquoise beads. A long brown and gray braid rested along the back of her tank top. Although fifty-nine, my mother's firm body could pass for thirty. Yoga and meditation were her secret, she would humbly insist. Her toned arms, although slightly wrinkled from years of unprotected tanning, still exhibited evidence of their ballerina past.

"Happy Birthday, Mom," I sang, handing her a floral gift bag.

"Oh, thanks, baby, but I don't need any gifts. The only gift I want is a grandchild. Jezzie, your sister had an appointment about IVF treatment today."

"Oh, that's right, Cala, how'd it go?" I asked my sister as I accepted the bottle of beer my brother offered.

Cala flashed my mother the same, uncomfortable expression she used at her chronic openness with information.

"Good. I can start the drugs next cycle and then they can start the process," Cala answered, with an obvious twinge of angst. For the past twelve months, Cala and Rob had tried to get pregnant using labeled calendars, temperature charts and ovulation testing kits. When the calendar cycled exactly one year, Cala sought intervention. My sister's plan for children did not factor in a year of delay with inconvenient infertility issues. If Cala could have her way, she would probably have several treatments going simultaneously with adoption papers filed.

"I'm sure it's going to work." I sent a wave of positive energy toward my sister with a confident nod and a smile.

"You know what I always say is the best way to get knocked up? A good old fashioned shot of tequila and a bottle of cheap red wine." We all laughed at Joe's joke, but Cala responded with only a polite, snipped laugh. There was nothing cheap in Cala's home, especially the wine.

Joe continued to laugh at his joke while looking down at the grill through the billowing smoke. He bobbed his head, making his thick silver mullet bounce along with him. I was impressed that Joe had chosen a white pressed collared golf shirt and khaki shorts, a detour from his usual rock band t-shirts with ripped sleeves revealing his faded bicep's tattoo of a rose. As the owner of the local Harley Davidson shop, he frequently donned motorcycle apparel as well. His hair was neatly brushed and he had left the do-rag at home tonight. His leathery face smiled. Today, Joe looked handsome.

My mother had met Joe at a widows and widowers support group almost sixteen years ago. Joe had lost his wife to breast cancer, leaving him alone with two young daughters. The two became instant friends but hadn't started to seriously date until a few years ago.

Joe interrupted the table's circle of chatter with a plate of sizzling meat. My mother insisted we hold hands around the table while she led a short prayer of thanks.

"Dig in!" Joe announced when she was done, passing the meat plate. I enjoyed watching my former vegetarian mother chomp on a hot dog, one of the changes she had made during her relationship with Joe. The most notable change was her new passion for riding motorcycles.

"Jezebel, any new interesting cases at the firm?" Rob asked, cutting into a piece of barbecued chicken. Rob worked for Lockheed Martin as a program finance manager on government contracts. He often retold the story how he had been accepted to Law School at Georgetown, but weeks before the semester was to start, he changed his mind and went for his Masters in Finance. Rob considered this to be his one spontaneous rebellious act in his otherwise well-structured, conservative life.

"We got a new sexual discrimination case about a month ago that seems pretty juicy. Legal secretary from another big law firm in town suing the partner she worked for. I'm still spending most of my time on the age discrimination class action, though."

"I'm gonna guess that partner is guilty of sexually harassing the secretary." Joe laughed, bouncing his short mullet again.

"Probably not. I'm gonna guess she's out for cash." I smiled with a mouthful of food, leaning back against my chair.

"Always loyal to your defendants, Jez," Rob quipped, popping a piece of watermelon into his mouth.

"You have no idea how many crazies are out there," I said before biting into my hot dog.

"Plaintiffs or attorneys?" Rob snorted.

"Both." I glanced at my sister who was noticeably quiet, and flashed her a quick smile. Cala returned the smile, but I could tell her mind was elsewhere, thinking about ripening eggs and IVF drugs, most likely.

"How was your therapy session today, Jez, honey?" Now it was my turn to cringe at my mother's openness.

"Nice transition, Mom, from the crazies to me. It went well."

"Oh, I didn't mean that. Your job is stressful enough and you don't need your commute to be stressful too." My mother looked at me while placing a piece of fruit into her mouth.

"I'll be cured in no time, Mom."

"The Metro's safe, Jez," Rob commented. "You have to trust that."

"See, Jez, and you always knock my motorcycles for being dangerous. Then, the train goes and screws you up," Joe commented.

"I suppose it all depends on who's driving…and

who's designing the safety system," I replied.

"Accidents happen. Just not with Lockheed Martin's aircraft." Rob smiled, pleased with his contribution to the conversation.

"I suppose I could be in a car accident on the beltway, too," I said softly.

"One hundred and fifteen people die every day on the highways. Less than thirty have died total in Metro history. You're safer on the Metro." Rob rattled off the statistics with ease. The man was the exemplification of the word 'nerd'.

Joe, chomping on his chicken breast, interjected, pointing his fork at Rob, "I was delivering a motorcycle in Arlington the day that Florida plane crashed into the Fourteenth Street Bridge. That same day the Metro derailed and people died on that. Crazy, crazy day. There was a snowstorm and I didn't get home until ten o'clock that night. I'll never forget it." Shaking his head, he stared down at his plate as if images of the Fourteenth Street Bridge were displayed there.

"Three died on the Metro that day," Rob stated, dabbing a piece of meat into a pool of barbeque sauce. I was not surprised he knew this fact as well.

"Not sure I want to fly again either," I said with a smile, pulling my hair in front of my shoulder. "Look, I know it defies logic, but I just can't shake it. I want to get back on. I'm trying to get back on. I will. I have to…" My voice hushed as my mind drifted to Kirk. I was thankful the conversation shifted back to motorcycles and government contracts for defense aircraft.

When most of the plates had emptied, Joe stood, pulling all eyes toward him. "Before we sing happy birthday to Juliana, can I have everyone's attention, please?" he commanded as his words quivered.

"Juliana, I wanted to do this in front of your children. I hope you don't mind." He looked at my mom and grabbed her hand as he knelt down next to her. She covered her mouth as tears budded in her eyes. "You came into my life at its lowest point when I never thought I would be able to be happy again. Losing my wife was rough. I went to that support group meeting on that fateful day but couldn't go into the room so I turned around, and headed back to my car. You were coming in the building but I was looking down, so you touched my arm and asked me my name. You pulled me in the meeting with you. I didn't find the second love of my life that day, but I found a friendship that saved my life. Then three years ago, I discovered I was in love with you. God gave me a second chance at true love, but I was just too stupid to realize it for thirteen years. So, will you, Juliana Marie Stone, do me the incredible honor of being my wife?" He pulled a ring from a large pocket on the side of his cargo shorts and slid it on her trembling finger.

"You are my second chance at true love too, Joseph Brian Atler. And yes, I would love to be your wife!" She leapt off the ground and into Joe's muscular arms.

We all jumped to our feet and cheered, pushing away tears and pounding our hands together. I smiled. I had wished on life's dark days, like the day of my father's drug overdose, that the heartbroken would be granted a glimpse into a crystal ball. Not the Magic 8, but a real crystal ball. One peek at a brighter day that lay ahead, like this scene I was witnessing now. Maybe that crystal ball was called faith. Or hope.

Damian grabbed his guitar and began to strum one of his original songs, written for a past love. Contently, we relaxed in aging lawn furniture and watched Joe and my mom dance, inside an unpretentious yard bordered by overgrown shrubs. Joe spun his fiancée around and pulled her into him. Two people brought together by tragedy, now reveling in the pure joy of a shared love and friendship.

"How about a summer wedding? What do you think?" Joe asked my mom loud enough for all of us to hear.

"The sooner the better." My mom kissed her future groom.

After chocolate cake and wedding planning conversation, fireflies emerged, flickering throughout the yard. I wondered if we had that crystal ball right now, would it show Cala's children running around their Grandma's yard, capturing the bugs in old peanut butter jars? Would the crystal ball show a man next to my side, perhaps a man I had met once upon a fateful day aboard a subway train?

Chapter 6

A week passed and in spite of another therapy session, I could still not call myself a metro passenger. After fighting the traffic home once again, I grabbed my favorite Chinese food. Inside my building, I pushed button number seven on the elevator panel, and the doors creaked and closed as the aging elevator lifted me toward my apartment. I looked at the word Westinghouse embossed below the buttons, and wondered if the engineers at Westinghouse Electric had created a safe machine. Were the cables sturdy and strong, guaranteed not to snap and plummet me to a painful death? What if the elevator installer had a bad day and neglected to secure a few bolts and screws? I shook my head to dislodge the crazy voices, the ones determined to turn me into a hermit or a pedestrian terrified of all forms of transportation. I refused to let my fears control me.

My loyal cat, Furry, greeted me at the door. I pulled her into my chest with one arm, using the other arm to rest my dinner on the kitchen counter. Since I was expecting an assignment from a senior partner, I checked my work messages. I released Furry, perhaps a little rougher than I intended, as soon as I heard his voice.

"Jezebel, it's me, Kirk. I'm heading to New York for a few days, but next Monday, I'll be commuting again on the Metro and I thought we could finish our ride and then celebrate with a drink in Bethesda. I'll call you after my trip. Hope you are well. Bye."

I replayed it three more times. Strange and mysterious, indeed. This inspired me to do the exercise my therapist had assigned. If writing out the accident in detail would help cure me, then I would do it.

****

The next day, I went directly to Ken's office. "You are not going to believe this," I announced and fell into Ken's guest chair, still carrying my briefcase.

He kept his eyes on his computer screen as his fingers continued to fly across the keyboard. "Do tell, my friend. Share with Kenny." He directed his full attention toward me, resting his chin in his hand, flashing a wide grin.

"Train Guy called me again but he still didn't leave his cell number."

"Get. Out." He threw his hands in the air, pushing against the back of his seat.

I described the call in detail.

"I have to admit, my Creep Radar just went off a bit…ping, ping." Ken made the high-pitched noise as he flicked his forefinger against his thumb.

"It's strange, but I don't think it's creepy."

"Hmm. Why doesn't he ask you to call him back? Did he leave a last name?"

"Don't know and no."

"Maybe he's still married and he doesn't want you calling him when the wifey is nearby and only calls you when she's not around?"

"Nah, he told me he's separated and living in his own condo."

"And I tell guys I was in the Peace Corps and a retired Air Force Pilot. People lie."

"Yeah, but what's his motivation? This guy is gorgeous and he could have anyone he wanted. Why randomly lie to a frazzled paralegal on a Metro during rush hour?"

"You gave off a sexy vibe, maybe? Not that I would know." Ken pretended to check me out.

"Well, he certainly set off my Sexy Vibe Radar... ping, ping. I can't stop thinking about him. Major attraction."

"Your attraction mechanism has been known to malfunction, my dear. Michael, and then Justin, and then the cashier dude at Panera..."

"Michael was the real-deal. Panera dude flirted heavily and I had no way of knowing he was gay. You win with Justin. You gotta see Kirk, Ken. He's hot."

"A dude can be hot *and* creepy," Ken declared, arranging his pencils in their holder.

"In person, he was not creepy at all. Plus, Magic 8 said he's not a stalker." Checking the time, I turned toward the hallway, waving over my shoulder. "I better go."

"Later, sexy-thang," Ken said with a loud laugh.

As I rounded my desk, my phone rang. I leapt toward the receiver without checking Caller ID. It was Justin.

"Jez, do you have time to cite-check a short pleading for me?"

"Sure, I'll come by."

"No, I'll bring it by."

Justin entered my office moments later with a smile, holding the pleading. "How are you doing?" he asked after dropping the document in front of me. His tone indicated it wasn't a rhetorical question.

"I'm good, thanks," I answered, flipping through the document.

"Headaches all gone?"

I looked at him, pausing and wondering why he cared. "Yes, actually, they are. No more side effects from the concussion. Thanks for asking, Justin."

"I heard from Vanessa that you're not taking the Metro. You know I live in Bethesda, so if you want me to ride to Rockville with you someday, I can."

Shocked, I blushed. "That is super sweet, Justin. Thank you. I'm getting some counseling, but I may take you up on it after a few more sessions."

He paused and a pleasant silence rested between us, void of our usual awkwardness. "Okay, Jez, thanks for your help. Also, some documents from our discovery request are coming in today for the Winston sexual discrimination case. They're coming to you."

"Oh, I could use a steamy sexual harassment case for some entertainment."

Looking relieved that I made a joke, he smiled and said, "I think you're going to love this case, Jez."

I smiled at my computer screen. "Oh, no doubt."

****

A few days later, I relaxed in the leather chair inside my new haven.

"Tell me, Jezebel, in detail about the man that pulled you from the train," Dr. Dennison's mellow words instructed.

"Well, I remember being pulled off the ground by the back of my suit jacket." I watched the raindrops drip down the giant glass office window, trying to recreate the image of the man who saved me. "At first, it was hard to see him. But I remember the graphic of a guitar on his black tee. He was skinny, and had brown bangs that swung down across his eyes when he spoke to me." I acted out the scene with my moving hands accenting each word. "I still can't figure out how that skinny guy got that door open, but he said, 'I got this door open, come on.'"

I continued describing the ball of nausea that hit my gut and how the sounds around me softened. With a flash of flame, I told her how I noticed his baggy jeans, and remembered thinking they were stylish. An odd thing to think at the moment, but I was sharing it all.

The therapist requested I replay the rescue again, but this time I was to discuss my feelings, acknowledging every single thing I had felt, the entire way in the tunnel. For the first time, I acknowledged an additional feeling—guilt. Why hadn't I tried to rescue anyone? The people inside my train car had made it out, but at the time I didn't know they would. My rescuer took time out of his escape to pluck me from the ground, but my journey had been self-centered. Sure, I spoke kindly to the woman behind me and held her hand, but I hadn't changed my course, interceded in that woman's fate, or anyone's fate. Maybe had I been truly brave, I would have gone the other way in the tunnel, and pulled someone from the flames. I inhaled with that thought and paused, digesting the event through ruthless recollections, unable to change a thing.

****

My weighty fears made me feel like a failure. I was ready to prove I was no longer weak. That evening, I met Carolyn for dinner at our favorite Rockville restaurant—the one we had intended to dine at on the evening of the crash. Afterward, I walked with broad, unhesitant strides past my parked car and toward the Metro Station. The escalator was out of order, so I hiked down the concrete stairs to the platform. The sound of the train rushing into the station dampened my palms and twisted my stomach. I planted myself on a cement bench that faced the tracks. Two redline trains passed before I stood at the edge of the platform. I stared down onto the unoccupied tracks, focusing on the rail that held the power to electrocute on contact.

Danger lurked all around me. My heart hammered, trying to break free of its cage. My body swayed like a skyscraper being rocked by high winds. Next to me, a pleasant smelling man in a suit snapped open a newspaper, pulling my eyes off the death rail.

I had gone far enough. This was a huge accomplishment. When Kirk called again, I could tell him I would meet him on the train. I was excited to share my accomplishment with Dr. Dennison at our next session.

First, I would share my news with my cat. I entered my apartment, swept Furry into my arms. With a nagging curiosity, I checked my work messages. Sure enough, he had called after I left the office.

"Hey Jezebel, stalker Kirk again. I'm home from New York. I'll be on the train all next week if you happen to be traveling to Rockville. I usually reach your Farragut North Station around 6:00. I'll jump off and see if you're on the platform. If you are, we can jump on the next train. If you're not, I'll assume you're not interested. No pressure. Hope to see you next week."

"You've got to be kidding me," I yelled to the ceiling. Still no last name and no number. Ken's voice whispered, "ping, ping" in my mind, but I ignored it and only entertained the giddy excitement in my belly.

That night, I fantasized about our upcoming encounter. What would I wear? Would I have a panic attack and sweat all over Kirk, or would we pick up where we had left off, easing into laughter and a flowing conversation. Whatever the outcome, I had embarked on an adventure that was a welcome distraction from my current mundane routine. When a tinge of nervousness caused me to inhale, I longed once again for the ability to take a glimpse into a crystal ball.

Chapter 7

"Hey, Vanessa." I greeted the smiling secretary before reaching my office.

"Hey, baby girl. Still driving? Whoa, you look yummy todaaay and on a Mondaaay," she sang, sliding a pencil behind her ear.

"Oh, I'm meeting someone after work. My brother-in-law had a meeting downtown so he drove me in today. I'm going to ride the Metro home though!" I announced with a lilt in my voice.

"So proud of you!"

"You can share that news with Justin, since you like to talk about me to him so much," I teased and nudged her plump arm.

"Hey, he was the one prying, all up in my face inquiring about you, young lady. If you ask me, he still likes you, even though you broke his poor heart." Vanessa swung her hands about in lively animation.

"I didn't break his heart. It just wasn't there for me."

"Drunken make-outs never work, girl. I have a hard time believing someone like Justin, the way he moves that fine booty, woulda been a dud in the sack. You shoulda gone all the way. Mmmmm," she said as if she'd just taken a bite of her favorite dessert.

"Can we please stop talking about having sex with Justin?"

"Who's having sex with me?" Justin poked his blond head around the partial wall of Vanessa's cubicle.

My face boiled. "I was just leaving, excuse me."

I tried to pry my body from the tight space and slide past Justin, but the hands on his hips blocked my way. Our eyes connected in a brief, intense moment, and he smiled at me with a low chuckle, allowing me to pass. Vanessa laughed and handed Justin a stack of collated documents, as I slipped away.

****

I gasped when I opened my email. The senior partner on the Winston case had called a meeting at five o'clock. My plan was to leave the office by 5:45 to meet Kirk. I could not be late for my second chance at fate. If recreating fate could be considered fate.

Before the meeting, I prepared my briefcase for a seamless departure, fluffed my hair and touched up my makeup. As expected, the meeting dragged past my planned departure time. I hustled toward the elevator, arriving in the lobby in minutes.

"Jez, wait up!" Justin's voice called behind me.

Waiting was not in my plan, but I stopped and looked at Justin as he jogged toward me. "Are you metro-ing this evening?"

"Maybe, but I'm trying to meet someone first and I'm late." I panted, wiping a few beads of sweat from my upper lip.

"Oh, sorry, okay, I'm on my way to the bookstore. Remember, if you need me to ride with you someday, I can." He flashed a boyish, white-toothed grin, but I had no time to play our off and on flirting game right now.

I pushed through the glass doors toward the street, calling over my shoulder, "Thanks so much, Justin. I'll talk to you tomorrow."

I rounded the corner of the building. I held my briefcase behind me to make myself thinner in order to penetrate through the hoard of pedestrians. Then disaster struck.

"Ah," I shrieked as my body flew to the side, my ankle twisting with pain.

"Shit!" I yelled, picking up my broken shoe's heel off the ground. "You've *got* to be kidding me," I called to the sky, holding my shoe in two parts.

Taking a deep breath, I removed my healthy shoe, and then tossed all pieces of shoe debris into my briefcase. I would have to finish my journey barefoot. Bolting across the street, I saw the Farragut Metro Station ahead. I could not even look at my phone to check the time. The escalator was still out of order, so I slipped past slower walkers with a disgusted sigh and darted down the concrete stairs.

I stopped on the platform, scanning the bodies passing by, and peeked over heads, searching for Kirk. After pacing the platform the entire length three times, I finally stopped, acknowledging defeat. Okay, I thought, this was simply a dry run. Tomorrow I'd be here early and would complete my mission successfully. Maybe this was a good thing. I didn't want to appear overly eager. And tomorrow, I'd be wearing shoes.

Breathless, I stopped at the edge of the platform. I studied the strangers' faces surrounding me in a way I hadn't on the day of the crash. These people had lives, had missions, perhaps even close encounters with death or even close encounters with love. What would their obituaries say in the morning if this Metro crashed and burned? Which person here would deviate from his or her escape to yank me off the ground toward safety?

A crowd engulfed me as the doors whisked open. "Farragut North," the automated female voice announced from the speakers on the packed train. Bodies spilled through the doors and between the parted opening created by my fellow commuters. I curled in my toes to avoid being trampled. The bodies then collapsed around the doorway and pushed their way into the train car, nudging me along. Still thinking of obituaries and studying strangers' faces, my body naturally moved onto the orange patterned carpet inside the car.

"Bing, bing," the chimes sounded announcing the impending closure of the doors.

I was on the Metro.

Motionless, I faced the sliding doors. Planning to jump back onto the station platform, I took a step. The rubber rims of both doors kissed, sealing me inside a tomb. I had no escape. I grabbed a metal pole as the train slid forward on the tracks. Sweat formed a barrier between the pole and my trembling hand. Nausea filled my gut, bile climbed in my throat, and a ringing deafened my hearing.

"I'm going to pass out," I mumbled, swaying from side to side. Heat, and then a cold sensation filled my face and head. I saw nothing but black as I attempted in vain to force my eyes open. My head rocked violently backward as the sickness that filled my body had triumphed. I imagined I was falling backward on top of my soft mattress of my queen-sized bed, the fluffy comforter catching and surrounding me.

"Miss, miss, can you hear me?" A deep, male voice broke through my silenced darkness.

A halo of heads, just like in the movies when the unconscious awakens, circled above me. Realizing I was lying on the dirty Metro floor, I snapped my head up, trying to stand, self-conscious of the scene I knew I must have caused. Being barefoot didn't seem so embarrassing anymore.

The man placed his hand under my head and guided me to a standing position, taking my elbow in his other hand. A woman took my other arm and together they led me toward an abandoned seat. The mass of commuters parted, making way for me, like a bride parading down an aisle. My clothing clung to every part of my body, perspiration covering every inch of my skin.

A young man stuck a bottle of water in my face and I gratefully accepted his offer with a timid smile. I guzzled and nodded my head at those asking if I was okay. I heard an elderly woman say to another passenger, "I bet she's pregnant." This made me laugh to myself.

"Are you feeling okay now, Miss?" the same soothing deep male voice that brought me to consciousness, questioned from the seat next to me.

"Yes, much better. And I'm really riding the Metro. I did it!"

"Well, that was certainly a dramatic way to start off your trip."

"Ah, yeah, how awful." I looked down to make sure I had my briefcase.

"Oh my, your shoes are gone," my fifty-something year old seatmate proclaimed.

"They're in my briefcase. One broke on the way here, so I tossed both in here." Wow, this man must really think I'm one hot mess. "Thank you for helping me. I really do feel a thousand times better now." I let out a quick laugh and guzzled the rest of the water. Tears of joy filled my eyes. The hot mess continued.

"Would you like me to walk you to the hospital at the Medical Center stop or call someone for you? Perhaps get you a ride home?"

"No, really, I'm fine, but thank you. You don't understand. I know it doesn't look like it, but I'm great. I've been afraid to ride this Metro and I did it." I stopped, realizing how crazy I sounded and not wanting to discuss the crash. I had moved forward, significantly forward, and I wanted to celebrate this moment.

I did wonder if I hit my head hard when I fell, giving myself another concussion. Maybe that's why I felt so good right now, I was officially brain damaged.

As if reading my thoughts, today's designated guardian angel asked, "Is your head okay?"

"I think. I recently had a mild concussion, but I feel good, no pain, no dizziness."

"My goodness. Do you pass out often?" The kind man's eyes widened, and then his eyebrows pressed toward each other.

I laughed and said, "No, no, well, I did pass out giving blood at a college blood drive once, but this is a first on public transportation." I remembered the tall orange chair the Red Cross nurse had put me in, wheeling me toward a cot, right past the group of hot Delta Chi brothers. That had been more embarrassing than Metro-fainting. "I got my concussion during the Metro crash."

"Well, that explains your anxiety coming on the Metro. My son was in that crash but didn't get hurt."

"Oh my. What car was he on?"

"I'm not sure. He really doesn't want to talk about the accident."

"I'm sorry to hear that. I actually went to therapy and it helped a great deal. Maybe he could do that?"

"I've been suggesting he see someone for awhile, even before the crash. I'm sure he'll work through it. He's young. He needs to go back to school. That would fix his problems." The long and lean pristinely dressed man stared ahead, lost in thought. He straightened his tie and pursed his lips.

I suddenly felt guilty for hearing about intimate details about this man's son, whom I didn't know.

I changed topics. "Do you work downtown?"

"Not exactly. I'm a pastor of a big church in Rockville, Community Life Church. The big one on route 355. I was visiting a sick member in the hospital."

"Oh, okay. I know your church. It's huge." I laughed to myself and thought of Vanessa's prayers. Had Vanessa ordered a nice pastor to take care of me on my first post-crash Metro ride? I'd have to thank her, I thought with a smile.

"Do you attend a church...I'm sorry, I didn't ask your name."

"Jezzie, and no, I currently do not attend church. I did for a while after my father died and my mom threw herself into religion. And then that stopped. She's spiritual, but she doesn't go to church. So, no I don't." My giddy babbling could not be halted.

"I'm Pastor Stevens. Jessie, I would love for you to attend my service some Sunday. It's contemporary, with a band. You'd like it. I promise."

I did not correct him on calling me the wrong

name. Explaining the whole Jezebel name-origin thing would surely make me appear even loonier, or perhaps destined for sin.

"I'll keep you in mind." I smiled, thinking I had never been invited to attend a church service before, not even by Vanessa.

"Great, well, I'm jumping off here to make a stop at another hospital. Nice meeting you, and take care. Hope to see you soon."

"Yes, nice meeting you, too, Pastor Stevens, and thank you so much for saving me from the Metro floor." I smiled widely, and he returned with a grin and a chuckle.

He waved again as he left the train at the Medical Center stop, the same stop where I ended my tunnel walk after the crash. What a nice man, I thought, as I stared out the window and into the dark tunnel. Today the tunnel was empty of smoke, of fire, and of injured passengers. It was at this exact point where the Metro crashed. The train on this trip flew along the tracks unimpeded. I held my breath, finally exhaling at the sight of sunlight. The train reached the above ground station without issue.

"Bing, bing," the opening doors chimed. "Grosvenor-Strathmore Station. Doors opening," the automated voice announced.

I smiled as I glanced at my bare feet, wiggling my liberated toes. This trip had not gone as I had imagined, but it was a successful trip nonetheless. As the train brought me to the final stop, I wondered if any trip really goes as planned. And maybe, I thought stepping through the open doors into the humid air, that was a good thing.

Chapter 8

Kirk saw her on the platform. Jezebel was ahead of him, but when she turned, he ducked away, slipping between two tall men. She looked prettier than he had remembered. Her hair bounced when she walked. He wanted to call to her but couldn't. He let her go.

His breathing increased, his heart raced, so he sat on a concrete bench near a garbage can and leaned against it. He refused to believe his reluctance to yell out her name was rooted in any form of guilt. His wife had been cold this morning, and nothing would have pleased him more than for her to have seen a strange number appear on his cell phone's screen, for her to wonder if he was being unfaithful, for her belly to fill with a disgusted nausea, and her mind to fill with dread. Just the way he felt many times when Nicole stayed late at the office or her boss would call her cell phone on the weekend.

He wanted to believe her when she'd say nothing ever happened with Winston. Call it denial or stupidity, but he chose to believe her. With Winston's plans to run for Senate, it was possible he kept things professional. But, the way her eyes would sparkle when she talked to him or about him, made Kirk ill. Infidelity of the heart seemed more brutal than infidelity of the body.

After her demotion, he'd asked her to find another

job, but she claimed she'd put in too many years at Crosby & Miller and didn't want to leave. He agreed that a lawsuit would be the answer. It would be nice to bring Winston down off his high horse, and they could use the money. He wanted to get this case behind them so they could move on. So they could concentrate on fixing their marriage. If he could help her in some way to win this lawsuit, she would appreciate him even more. How lucky that he sat right next to Winston's attorney's paralegal the day of the crash?

Tomorrow he'd find Jezebel again and call out her name. They'd meet and continue their ride, as planned.

Chapter 9

The day after my return to public transportation, I glided from the elevator, wearing a confident smile. I breezed past my secretary's desk, pleased to make my announcement. "I rode the Metro today and it was easy." Since I was running late, I didn't pause to talk, but could hear Vanessa's voice throughout the hallway.

"Yes, baby girl. That's what I'm talkin' 'bout. Way to go!"

I'd fill her in on yesterday's metro saga at lunch. I dropped my briefcase on my office floor and checked all my messages before sitting, exhaling in relief that no late day meetings were planned for today. I relaxed.

"Jez-e-bel-icous! You are looking hot again today! What gives?" Ken blurted out within a second of me coming into his view.

I rested into my usual guest chair inside my friend's office, sipped my coffee, crossed my legs, and with a sigh, explained, "Well, for starters, I actually applied mascara two days in a row. And, the hot train guy chase is on again."

"So no contact last night? I figured when I didn't get a text from you that either you didn't see him, you were having a night of passionate love, or he kidnapped you." Ken laughed at his own comment.

"Well, thank you for calling 9-1-1 and filing a missing person's report, dear old friend."

"You weren't missing long enough for that, and truth is, I was having my own fun last night with Navy guy. But, enough about me, what happened with you?" Ken gestured his hand toward me, leaning back in his chair.

"The usual—got out of here late, broke a shoe, ran for blocks barefoot and missed my window of opportunity, got on the train, and passed out. Yep, fainted on the Metro floor." My hands spread out slowly, mimicking my body splayed along the floor.

"What? Oh, Jez, I'm sorry to laugh, but this would only happen to you. Well, you survived and you rode the train right?"

"Well, yes, a nice pastor plucked me off the ground as horrified passengers gawked and offered me their seats and water. It actually was a great trip, though. And, at least I didn't faint in front of Kirk."

"Yes, probably a good idea to remain conscious around the kidnapping stalker."

"Oh stop, he's not a stalker or a kidnapper. I have a feeling he's a really nice guy."

"Ted Bundy was a nice guy. Jeffrey Dahmer—also nice. Bay City Strangler…"

"Okay, okay, you've made your point."

And our morning conversation ended when an associate popped his head in the door. We smiled at each other with laughing eyes, knowing we would continue the Kirk analysis at lunch.

****

Success. The day ended at the time I had hoped. I planned to grab my briefcase and slip into the elevator unnoticed. As I began to execute my plan, standing in the threshold of my office door, my phone rang. Justin was calling me. He probably was calling to see if I wanted to ride the Metro with him. I let it go to voicemail and bolted toward the elevator. Like a coordinated, athletic woman, I breezed down the city streets.

I arrived on the Metro platform wearing the original shoes I had left my apartment with that morning and surprisingly felt somewhat relaxed. All sense of calmness left my body as I moved toward the edge of the platform and the train rushed into the station. My heart thumped in my chest as wildly as my hair danced inside the burst of wind. Was this train carrying Kirk from the Metro Center station into my station and back into my life? It was.

He exited the second car, the same one we rode the day of the fire. Our eyes locked. He smiled. My face bathed in heat, I moved toward him around the other commuters, never disconnecting eyes with Kirk.

"Hey there, Jezebel."

He was more handsome than I had remembered. I wished I had applied more makeup.

"Kirk, so good to see you again," I called out with enthusiasm, my natural blush taking over my face.

"You're alive." He joked, reaching for me with his left hand, holding a briefcase in the other.

I slipped my right hand into his left and we both squeezed. Awkwardly, we leaned in toward each other and exchanged a quick hug. He smelled as good as I had remembered.

"So, you got my messages and didn't think I was crazy. This is great…great." He nodded, sounding somewhat flustered.

"Yeah, no, didn't think you were crazy. Relieved

actually to bring closure to our disaster. It's good... good to see you again," I repeated with a smile, still feeling a burn in my cheeks.

"Shall we ride?" Kirk motioned gallantly toward the open Metro doors.

"Yes, definitely."

We crossed the threshold, and as if reserved for us, the second seat on the left side remained unoccupied. Fate, I thought.

He gestured for me to sit first. I slid toward the window, opposite of how we sat on our inaugural ride. *Stay conscious, Jezebel*, I heard Ken beg.

Once situated inside our tiny orange booth, I asked, "So, were you hurt that day?"

"Um, a little bruised on my right shoulder from the tumble over the seat, but nothing a little Advil couldn't cure. How about you?" After rubbing his shoulder, he then turned his body toward me.

"Sprained my shoulder and got a mild concussion."

"Wow. I tried to find you, but it was so dark."

"Some guy pulled me out a side door that he somehow pried open. I looked for you when I got to the platform, but obviously, no luck."

"Well, we're survivors and for that we should be thankful."

A pause, as if we were observing a moment of silence for the dead, fell between us.

Kirk slapped his hand on his leg. "Let's change the subject. How's the law firm doing?"

"It's doing very well, lots of unhappy people suing away. And I suppose this makes you happy, Mr. Westlaw?"

"Yes, business is good for me, too. Lots of

traveling, but I like it. It's a great company. Any interesting cases?"

"Well, in employment law there are always some interesting cases. Just started on a new one with a secretary suing her boss. Pretty common. Those ones usually settle. We're thinking we can win this one on Summary Judgment, though. The guy being sued is pretty well known in DC and wants to fight it hard. There is a class action case I'm working on that takes up most of my time—"

"So what law firm are they from? The well-known attorney that's getting sued? I'm wondering if their law firm is a client of mine."

"Oh, I'd rather not say, attorney client privilege thing, you know."

"So, this secretary, what's she saying the boss did?"

"The typical, lewd comments, inappropriate touching, got reassigned to another partner because she wouldn't sleep with him, so she lost status, blah blah blah...typical stuff. Anyway, if I talk anymore about this case I'll have to bill the client. Let's talk about something other than work... Like, where would you like to stop for a drink?"

"How about the Bethesda stop, let's say, the Blackfinn on Fairmont?" He chose a stop before the site of the crash.

"Perfect."

My nerves rattled, causing my stomach to stir. I couldn't decipher between the feelings of nervousness and excitement, but I knew I was feeling them both. Attraction between us was evident. After a joke, he laughed, quickly touching my leg with this hand, sending a sensation throughout my body I welcomed.

At the conclusion of my third post-crash Metro trip, I internally celebrated my graduation from Dr. Dennison's therapy sessions and couldn't wait to let her know I would no longer need her services.

Sauntering up the busy Wisconsin Avenue, we rounded a corner toward our destination. A chilly late spring breeze moved my hair in front of my face. I pushed it behind my ear, smiling and giggling at Kirk's story, feeling peaceful and unaffected by the clamor of rush hour traffic around me.

Kirk held the large wooden door open, allowing a gush of noise out of the pub. I passed in front of him, guiding my briefcase along with me. We chose a high-walled, secluded booth. For some reason, inside the mahogany stall, I felt safe. My mind wandered to Ken's warning of being lured by a serial killer, and I dismissed it with a smile and a flirtatious giggle. Our hands met at the center of the table for a quick touch. Kirk pulled his hands back onto his lap as he sat upright placing his back against his seat.

"Well, Jezebel Stone, I'm glad you decided to meet me tonight."

I didn't remember telling him my last name.

"Yes, I'm glad you decided to hunt me down." I smiled and looked away from his silent stare. I got the feeling he was deep in thought while smiling at me. Was he thinking of his ex-wife? He was only separated, so I couldn't even add the ex part yet.

"I still find your eyes fascinating, by the way." He smiled, appearing a bit embarrassed.

"Thank you." I turned to look for the waitress, trying to avoid his eyes.

We ordered drinks: he a lager from the tap and I a glass of white wine. He loosened his tie as he leaned to the side slightly, becoming more comfortable in the booth.

We discussed some current events, all safe topics. I played with my hair, pulling it all over my right shoulder, letting the curls spill across my breast. Flashing him a smile, I batted my eyes. I typically felt unskilled in the art of flirting, but right now it seemed natural.

Kirk pulled his elbows on top of the table, folding his hands under his chin. "So," he said commanding my attention, "If you had died on the Metro that day, what would you have regretted not ever doing?"

I rested back into the leather seat, biting my lip and looking off in thought. "I think if I had to pick one thing, I would've regretted not visiting all the places that I had planned to travel to."

"Huh, that is exactly my answer. I love baseball and I've wanted to see a game in every stadium. I've only crossed eleven off my list."

"Interesting. That's a fun goal." I nodded, studying his perfect and pleasant features.

"Where would you like to travel to?" he asked.

"Well, I've toured Europe and I've been to Asia, so it's nothing too extravagant. Just Niagara Falls. I've never been to Niagara Falls. Simple, easy to get to, but I've just never taken the trip yet. There are a lot of other spots I plan to travel to, but if I had died on that Metro, I would have been mad at myself for not taking the easy trips."

"Right, I've made it to Dodger stadium all the way in Los Angeles, but I've never taken the short drive to

PNC Park in Pittsburgh." He paused and ran his fingers through his hair. "So, you wouldn't have regretted not marrying or having children?"

"I suppose, yes, but I only gave you my number one regret. And, how about for you, on the children thing?"

"I have a fear of being a lousy father. Never had a great relationship with my own father. But I guess it would be on my list somewhere."

I tipped my glass back finishing the final sip of wine. "I guess I haven't given it much thought. My focus right now is, well, primarily surviving the Metro and then maybe finding an easy relationship."

"Had some rough relationships in the past?"

"I've met some great guys, but if it gets difficult, I end it. My dad's most over-used line was 'don't force it, you'll break it'. He'd say it whenever we were trying to force things together or pull something apart. I think that applies to relationships, too." My voice trailed off, as my eyes looked off again in thought.

"That's a good philosophy. Well, you did achieve surviving the Metro, so perhaps an easy relationship is on the horizon."

I smiled, crossing my legs. "So, did you read about the people who died on the train that day?" I asked, losing my smile.

"A little, but it freaked me out."

"Yeah, me too, but I became obsessed with finding out everything about them."

"Hmm, wonder what they regret? That is, if you get to regret things on the other side."

"So, you believe there's an afterlife?" I asked.

"I do. I do believe there's more after this life.

You?"

"My father passed away, so I've always believed he's off somewhere happy, watching over us. I hope he is unable to have regrets, though. I hope it's nothing but peace on the other side," I said.

"Yeah, well if that's the case, don't worry about missing out on seeing the Falls." He smiled.

"Good point. I have one survivor's regret from that day, however. I keep wishing I had done more to save someone, help someone. That man who pulled me from the car didn't need to take the time to do that, but he did. Maybe had I tried to go toward the flames, I could have rescued someone. I don't know. I can't change it, but that's something that still bothers me."

Kirk wasted no time in responding, "No one can predict how they're going to react in a disaster and you certainly can't fault yourself for running away from danger. I remember the heat and the smoke and the chaos. Human instinct is to run in the opposite direction."

"I know. It's just one of those thoughts I can't control. But, it's nice to talk to someone about this who understands."

He reached across the table again, leaning forward, his hand searching for mine. I splayed my fingers out and slid them to the middle of the table, inviting him to touch me. He did, and I found it difficult to not smile with obvious pleasure. My eyes glanced down when an unexpected wave of shyness hit me. Breaking our peaceful moment, his cell phone sounded from his briefcase. He glanced toward it.

I pulled my hand back. "You can take that call, I don't mind." I lied, I would mind.

"No, no, I'll let it go to voicemail."

After a few more minutes of light conversation, he peeked at his phone inside his briefcase. I did the same, as not to appear I was bothered by his distraction.

"Well, I probably should get going," he announced. "I have a busy day tomorrow, but I have enjoyed our time together."

"Oh, yeah, I have to get moving, too." Flipping my hand, I indicated our departure was no big deal.

He motioned for the waitress to bring the bill. When she did, he offered the young eager server his credit card along with a charming grin. The blonde returned with an equal amount of charm, tossing her ponytail over her shoulder as she turned away on her toes with zest. Probably a former cheerleader, I thought.

"Thank you, you didn't have to pay for me..." I said bashfully.

We pulled ourselves out of the booth, fumbling for briefcases. "You're welcome. You can pay next time." He smiled, the same grin he had just delivered to the cheerleader-waitress, placing his hand on my upper back.

My belly tingled.

We entered the cool late evening air, closing the pub's door behind us. "Will you Metro back to Rockville or would you like to share a cab?" he asked, stopping mid-sidewalk.

"A cab sounds great." I smiled, relieved to not have to test out my Metro riding readiness again.

A cab slipped along the curb and he held the door as I slid across the seat. I enjoyed his body next to mine. He touched my knee and asked, "So where's your apartment?"

A paranoid thought entered my mind narrated by Ken warning me not to give the stalker my home address. I thought about Kirk's company's search technology and realized he could find my address if he wished. And then I told the narrating-Ken voice that I hoped Kirk would indeed stalk me.

"Off Rockville Pike, the Congressional Towers."

"Oh wow, I lived there before I got married."

"So where do you live now?"

"Grosvenor Towers."

"Wow, those look very nice."

"Yeah, they are."

"Where does your wife live now?" I questioned boldly.

He glanced out his side window, pausing, "Ah, she's staying with her cousin in Silver Spring, for now."

"Oh," I responded, sensing a tension fill the cab's backseat.

An uneasy sensation clenched my gut when I heard Ken commentating in my mind again that the guy was probably still married. I wanted to ask him how long they'd been separated, but I decided against it, instead, changing the topic to work. He laughed at my humorous tale about Vanessa, and again lightly touched my knee.

The cab pulled up to the front of my building and I handed a twenty-dollar bill to the driver. Kirk stopped my hand with his. "No, don't bother. I'll settle it when he drops me off. Your money is no good here." He laughed, and opened his door. I thanked the cab driver and followed Kirk.

"Well, I'm glad this trip ended better than our

first." He smiled an electric grin that weakened my legs, his eyes luring me into a spell.

"Yes. I'm quite pleased with our accomplishment." I looked down as he leaned in for a hug. My face brushed against his lapel and I inhaled his sweet scent mixed with a lingering pub aroma. At the end of the hug, his left hand took the back of my head and he softly kissed my cheek. To fill the silence, I said, "Have a safe trip home. That's not a cliché for us anymore, right?"

"Right. Good night, Jezebel," he said, sitting back inside the cab.

I waved and returned to my building. Inside the elevator, I typed out a text to Ken: I'm home and I'm not murdered or kidnapped. Had a nice time!

Ken replied instantly: Good news, Jez. Any action?

I replied, exiting the elevator, smiling: Just a goodnight cheek kiss. Very sweet and un-stalker like.

Ken: Make sure your cat is still alive! Just kidding! Sweet dreams my love xoxo

I laughed and replied for him to do the same.

I entered my silent apartment and swept Furry—my very much alive cat—up into my arms. She purred and I too felt a similar peaceful purr inside me. Unlike Cala's philosophies on achieving lofty goals, I felt proud of my simple achievement: completing my Metro ride with Kirk. Kicking off my heeled shoes and pulling my curls into a hair tie, I thought how life was all about just surviving the simple trips. And finishing a trip with unbroken shoes was even better. I sat at my computer, and Furry leapt onto my lap. I pulled up a travel website and typed in: Niagara Falls.

Chapter 10

Nicole thought it was very un-Kirk like that he didn't answer his phone when she called. When he got home, he claimed to have stopped after work to grab a quick drink with a client, but he didn't make eye contact. She couldn't imagine he'd cheat, but the pang in her gut said otherwise. He smiled smugly as he strutted into the bedroom.

She followed him and watched him take off his tie and coat. Maybe it was the thought of him cheating that excited her, but she was intensely attracted to him. She needed to keep him close, to keep his passion for her alive. He had been so easy to manipulate.

They'd met by chance in her law firm library five years ago. She was returning a few books for an associate, and Kirk was leaving a Westlaw meeting with the librarian. From the second he saw her next to the collection of Code of Federal Regulations, she knew she'd successfully captivated him with her charms.

She could still use those same powers to make sure he knew he belonged to her. Her body slid between him and his closet. She never looked into his eyes as she unbuttoned the top few buttons of his shirt and his chest heaved with a deep breath.

"What are you doing, Nicole?"

"Hush," she commanded, and worked on completing the unbuttoning mission. When she popped open the last button, she slid her hands along his smooth abdomen. She'd always been a fan of his body. His insecurity that she had wandering eyes made him a regular at the gym.

Her fingers teased as they caressed the skin under his waistband. He stood there, staring at her. Probably shocked at her timing, but he was no doubt enjoying it.

His mouth touched her shoulder as he pulled her waist toward his. He reached down, yanked up her skirt and tugged at her panties, as she unexpectedly gasped at his forcefulness. With equal fervor, she tore into his belt and pants. He shoved her down onto the bed and wasted no time pressing his body on top of hers. She tried to remove his dress shirt from his shoulders, but it clung to his biceps. His hands shoved her arms against the mattress, and then his hand finished forcing her shirt up to her neck and with one swift movement, unfastened her bra.

Void of tenderness, the encounter was a quest for instant gratification. He rolled off of her without saying a word and retreated to the bathroom for a shower.

She turned onto her side, relaxed but conflicted. Again, she wished she could let go of thoughts of Jack, but she couldn't. He'd become an intricate part of her being. He appeared to hate her now, but she knew he was just consumed with fear at her sabotaging his political career and his marriage. This lawsuit was an ingenious way to win Jack back. And, she wasn't lying or committing perjury, since he did demote her over sex.

She wished she could return to being true to her marriage vows, but the demon that was the memory of Jack, lurked inside her. Love isn't a sin. It wasn't her fault she loved two men.

Nicole used to fantasize that after she became the senator's secretary, becoming his wife would soon follow. She'd find a way as the senator's wife to organize tons of charity events and make up for the sin of divorcing Kirk.

In retrospect, she shouldn't have flown off the handle over Rebecca Snyder, but she was humiliated. She thought he might settle quickly and, as part of the settlement, restore her position as his secretary.

But, one day shortly after filing the suit, he cornered her in the hallway outside of the restroom and hissed, "I'm gonna fight this hard, Nicole. Don't look for a settlement from me either, that would make me look guilty. I'll win and make you look like a fool. A crazy, gold-digging bitch. Or should I call you Paula Jones?" His body standing closely and his hot breath in her ear terrified and thrilled her all at the same time. He was arrogant enough to equate himself with a former president. It was such a turn-on.

Before Kirk got out of the shower, Nicole crawled under the covers of the guest room bed. She said a prayer, thinking it would help.

But it never did. Did God even listen?

The smell of Kirk remained on her, and in some way, she still loved him. Since she was in a little pain, she decided to go back and spend the night next to him.

Chapter 11

On the sticky Saturday morning of Memorial Day weekend, I met my mother and Cala at our favorite diner in Silver Spring. Our mother had asked for a mother-daughter meeting to solicit our assistance in wedding planning.

"So, Joe and I were thinking that we want the ceremony to start around noon."

"Jez, that's 11:30 to you." Cala smiled, pointing at me with her pen before she returned to scribbling notes in her leather-bound notepad.

"Ha ha. I won't be late to my mother's wedding!" I rolled my eyes. It was the standard Stone family joke.

"Mom, you know you can use my backyard to hold the ceremony. By late July the gardens will be spectacular. We could rent a big tent in case it rains," Cala suggested with enthusiasm, scooping up a piece of omelet with her fork. I wondered if showcasing her home was Cala's main goal or if she truly was intent on making a memorable wedding for our mother.

"That is a beautiful thought, Cala. It would eliminate having to find a church and all. Yes, I think Joe will love the idea as well. Let's do it," she declared, pounding her fist lightly on the table. She adjusted her colorful tapestry headband and rested her hands back on top of her faded flora skirt, a skirt she owned for at least two decades.

"We could have the reception near the pool or I'll have the furniture moved downstairs, and round tables and flowers brought in, if you're worried about rain. I know a wonderful caterer who makes the most exquisite salmon dish. We used them for the Cystic Fibrosis fundraiser last fall." Cala's left hand gestured with her every word, while she stabbed her fork into her fruit cup with the other.

"Oh, Cala, that is a generous offer, but far too much work for you. Plus, Joe and I like things simple. Maybe chicken instead of salmon?"

"We have time to settle on a menu, Mother, but let me call Phyllis now and see what weekends she'd be available." Chewing a piece of cantaloupe, Cala crossed her legs. She rested against the back of the booth, pulling up her contact list on her phone. Before waiting for Mother's agreement on the caterer, she spoke loudly to Phyllis.

As she made opening-conversation small talk with the caterer, I turned to my mother and asked, "So, what do you plan to wear on your big day?"

"Oh, I'm picturing something simple. Maybe a long, cream, cotton sundress."

I refocused on my sister, whose voice had entered authoritative-planning mode. "Oh, the last weekend of July sounds great, oh, yeah, the first weekend of August would work, too. The hydrangeas would be in full bloom, but the azaleas would be gone, but that's okay." Turning toward our mother, Cala asked, "Mom, last weekend of July?"

"Okay, let's do it. I suppose if Joe has a problem, we can switch it. Have her send us a price sheet, Cala, before we commit, though," she whispered, leaning closer to Cala.

"Great, Phyllis, book us for the last weekend of July. I'll send you a check. Thanks so much." Cala hung up with a triumphant smile, resting her phone on the table with determination. "Done. Mom, I'll send the deposit. Don't worry about the price. The caterer will be our wedding gift to you." She grinned wider, folding her arms in a 'my work here is done' gesture.

I couldn't come up with a gift as wonderful as a caterer, but I could try. "And Mom, I'll buy your dress."

"Oh, you two are so generous. Thank you, but you really don't need to. Joe's bike shop is doing quite well…" Tears welled in her eyes, and she quickly dabbed them with her napkin.

"Mom, we are both happy you found someone to grow old with. Joe's a great guy." I smiled, rubbing my mom's shoulder.

"He's a damn good guy!" She laughed, trying to turn off her tears. "And maybe Damian could play his guitar during the ceremony."

"Oh, Mom, I'll just hire a string quartet or something like that," Cala insisted.

"So, enough about me. Cala, how are the fertility treatments going?" my mom inquired.

"Oh, well, I'm gaining weight, if you haven't noticed. The drugs are wreaking havoc on my body. But, the good news is, they should be able to retrieve eggs at the end of this week."

"Oh, that's wonderful, Cala sweetie, you'll be pregnant in no time, maybe even for the wedding." My mother's hand gesturing caused my eyes to focus on the sparkling diamond waving in the air. It would take some time to get used to seeing a diamond on her hand. While married to my father, my mother had only worn a plain thin gold band.

"So I shouldn't pick out my dress today?" Cala said, looking down. She refolded the napkin on her lap.

"I'm praying all goes well for you, Cay." I sent a sincere smile and sentiment across the table to my sister.

"Thanks, sis." Cala winked.

I enjoyed these times when Cala seemed vulnerable and on an equal playing field instead of assuming a holier-than-thou persona. I winked back and decided to share my Kirk encounter. "So, I met a guy. The day the Metro crashed, I was riding with this hot guy, but never saw him after the crash. Well, he contacted me and we met for drinks earlier in the week." I smiled slyly.

"Was it the same guy that pulled you out the door?" Cala asked.

"No, this was the guy seated next to me."

"So he's hot and single?" Cala asked with wide eyes.

"Well, he's separated but we had a great time. It was nice to talk to someone who had been through the ordeal with me." I purposely looked at my mother to avoid Cala's judging eyes.

"Well, maybe Jezzie will have a date to my wedding, huh?" my mother asked with hope and prying eyes.

"I don't know about that. We haven't exactly arranged a second date yet," I said with confidence but my stomach twinged with disappointment. "I was thinking I'd make the next move. He likes baseball, so maybe I'll invite him to a Nationals' game?" I smiled, looking off, pleased with my new idea.

"Just be careful, Jez. Getting involved with a guy who's not quite divorced yet might not be such a superb idea." Sipping her coffee without making eye contact, Cala had reassumed her motherly role, and this slightly irritated me.

"It's just a baseball game," I said.

"Be careful, sweetie." My mother gently caressed my arm.

"Well, do some digging at least and find out why he's divorcing," Cala suggested. She always seemed to have a suggestion.

"Why don't we pay the bill and hit some dress shops?" I proposed, bringing an end to the Kirk discussion. Although inside, I continued to think of him, like I did every day and every night.

We entered a small strip-mall bridal shop, even though my mother doubted she would find a simple sundress inside. A crisply suited woman approached us with an exaggerated grin. "Well, hello, you must be the future bride," she unclasped her hands, gesturing toward me.

Embarrassed, I stammered, "Oh, no, my mother here is the bride-to-be." I pulled my mother in front of me. "This is Juliana."

The saleswoman unabashedly eyed my mother from head to toe with her grin fading. "Oh, well, what do you have in mind, Juliana, for your...second wedding, I assume?" She touched her heavily hair sprayed blonde bob, forcing a smile, looking disappointed.

"Yes, something simple. Off-white," my mother announced, unaffected by the saleswoman's arrogance.

"Of course, right this way." The saleswoman's face lost its feigned animation at the word "simple." I made up my mind that I did not like this woman at all.

"Here, have a seat and I'll select a few and get you a dressing room." The saleswoman disappeared.

"Mom, I'm not sure this store has what you have in mind," I whispered in my mother's ear.

"I know it doesn't, but let's try some on for fun and waste Ms. Snooty's time," my mom whispered back to me followed by a playfully evil giggle. "Get her hopes up for a nice commission and then leave."

"Oh, mother, behave yourself!" Cala disciplined with a smile.

Pulling my mother into the dressing room, I whispered, "Have fun, Mom."

I sat next to Cala in a viewing area surrounded by mirrors and tiny, carpeted platforms. My mind took a sentimental trip to the framed photo on my mother's antique dining room buffet. It was the only wedding picture of my parents that my mother had displayed. They were barefoot on a beach in Virginia. My mother held a bouquet of wildflowers, holding the bottom of her long pink flowered dress with the same hand. My mother's eyes were closed, her head tilted back and her mouth opened in a burst of laughter. My father looked at his bride with a wide smile and adoring eyes. It was a picture of joy, of love, of perfect contentment. I hoped my mother could relive those feelings this coming July in Cala's backyard.

The future Mrs. Atler exited the dressing room, grinning in a pearled and sequenced gown. Although the cut was plain, the dress was anything but simple.

"You are beautiful, Mom!" Cala yelped, clapping

her hands.

"I think I need a long flowing veil. Do older second-time brides wear veils?" my mom asked the saleswoman with feigned excitement.

"Why, yes. I'm sure that would be just lovely. I'll fetch a few." Again, the saleswoman disappeared and we snickered.

"Oh, and some spiky pumps, too!" my mom yelled to the saleswoman's back.

"This is kind of fun," Cala admitted.

"Mom's a riot."

I jumped as my phone buzzed in my purse.

As Cala rattled off the names of her favorite bakeries that could handle the wedding cake, I retrieved my phone. I stopped listening as I read the text from Kirk: Hey Jez, I got out of my plans this evening. Want to meet at our pub for a drink around 8?

I instantly typed back: Yes. Sounds great!

Before hitting send, I changed the exclamation point to a period.

A wide smile crossed my face as my mother exited the dressing room. The smile was not for the beaded A-line dress she was presenting but at the thought of seeing Kirk again. I decided I would keep my date to myself since the first discussion about Kirk had not gone so well.

After we ended our fun with the snobby saleswoman, we headed out into the warm overcast day. Rain threatened, but it did not deter us from walking to a nearby bakery. Cala and I linked arms with our mother and laughed together, reliving our prank.

"You know, I really don't care what I wear, girls. I could wear this old thing I'm wearing now and be perfectly happy."

"We know, Mom, but we want to create some pretty pictures for you two to cherish forever. You need to feel special," Cala insisted.

I had no doubt that Cala's wedding plans would be spectacular. But the moments our mother would cherish could not be orchestrated, that was not how she functioned. She would certainly feel special on her wedding day, but that feeling would come from Joe loving her. He'd smile at her with adoring eyes, while his wife reeled her head backward in a burst of heart-felt laughter. Probably because a waiter dropped a tray or a swarm of bees attacked the wedding cake. Something unexpected would happen and our mom would detect the outrageous joy in it. And at that moment, I would snap a picture.

Chapter 12

Kirk walked into the bathroom as Nicole coated her lashes with thick mascara, prepping for a girls' night out. "Can we go to counseling? Can we try to be a real married couple again?"

She sighed with a dismissive disgust. "Kirk, just be patient. I need space. I'm working through some things. I don't want to see some stupid counselor."

And that was the end of the conversation.

After Nicole left, he looked forward to sharing another drink with Jezebel. The past months had been full of tense banter and petty bickering. He had to tiptoe around Nicole's fragile moods, or depression, as she indulgently liked to label it. His plan seemed to be working. After he'd returned from his first meeting with Jezebel, his wife had thrown herself at him. Perhaps his evasiveness as to his whereabouts had caused Nicole to worry, like she had done to him so many times in the past.

So, keeping the plan alive, he took a cab to the Bethesda pub, selecting a booth close to the one they'd shared their first night. He scanned the place, hoping to not see anyone he knew.

His phone buzzed with a text from Jezebel: Running a little late, on my way. Sorry!

He ordered a beer and watched the baseball game on the television above the bar. The refreshing beer slid down easily. A slight buzz filled his head after half of the beer hit his empty stomach. There was not a hint of guilt inside of him.

"Kirk." He heard Jezebel's voice next to him. "Sorry I'm late. I had a hard time getting a cab for some reason…"

He stood and smiled at her. "No problem. I'm enjoying a beer and the baseball game. Glad you joined me."

She had on form-fitting dark jeans with a loose low cut pink t-shirt. She looked sexy, at ease. Inside their hug, her hair smelled freshly washed as it brushed along his cheek. When she separated from their embrace, she stepped backward, into a passing waitress. The waitress's tray wobbled, spilling a drink.

"Oh, I'm so sorry!" Jezebel gushed, trying to steady the tray.

"No, it was my fault. Sit down, please, what can I bring you to drink?" The waitress smiled, trying to nonchalantly wipe the liquid off of her arm.

"Miller Lite, and again, I'm really sorry. So, how are you, Kirk?" she asked with sincerity and lightness as she slid into the booth, tossing her long curls behind her shoulder as if the moment of chaos with the waitress had never happened. He deduced that Jezebel was well versed in disaster recovery. She smiled and he smiled back.

"I'm well, and you? Did you get anything on you?" he asked.

"Oh no, I'm great. I had a really good day. My mom is getting remarried, so my sister and I took her dress and cake shopping."

"Good for her. So this is her second marriage? I

remember you saying your father had passed away."

"That's right. She met Joe at a widower's support group."

They continued with more wedding discussion and shared tales of their equally crazy relatives, ordering some burgers and finishing off some more beers.

"So, if you don't mind me asking, how did your father pass away?"

"Oh, I don't mind. He was in a car accident that injured his back pretty badly. Then, he became addicted to painkillers. He overdosed one day, slipped into a coma, and died two days later." She looked down and slid a French fry through ketchup. She continued, "So, I knew my parents had been pot smokers, but my mom told us many years later that she knew that he was having trouble kicking the painkillers. He kept telling her he'd quit and she believed him, so she just let him go. She had a hard time after his death, losing him was rough but her guilt ate at her. She still regrets she didn't do more to help him."

"Wow, that's a hard thing to go through, for all of you. I'm sorry. But it wasn't her responsibility."

"She knows that now, but she wishes she'd forced him to get help instead of waiting."

He needed to lighten the mood. "So, that's the second time you mentioned their pot smoking. You weren't kidding last time." Kirk smiled, amused, as he picked up a French fry.

"Nope. No joke," she said with French fry inside her cheek. "When most kids my age had yuppies for parents, I had the hippies." A smile returned to her face.

Jezebel leaned back and crossed her legs, speaking after she finished chewing a bite of her burger. "So, when I got home after we met last, I booked a trip to Niagara Falls. I'm going to head there at the end of August."

"Oh, that's great!" His gut reaction was to tell her he'd like to join her. But he stopped himself, realizing their little relationship most likely would have run its course by then. "That's terrific, Jezebel. You've inspired me. I'll go book a trip to PNC Park in Pittsburgh."

"You should. Will that complete our post-crash bucket list?"

"That ought to do it. Love, I guess we can still try to find love." He paused, hoping she would help bring the woman he loved back to him.

Snapping him back to reality, Jezebel pointed at him. "Guitar lessons. I've wanted to learn to play the guitar and my brother has always said he'd teach me. So guitar lessons is on my bucket list." She slapped the table, making her statement official. Their glasses wobbled, and he used both hands to steady them.

"Good, learn to play guitar has moved up in front of finding love."

"Most definitely. My brother has wooed plenty of women with his guitar." She smiled playfully, batting her eyes and exaggerating a hair toss.

"Chicks are suckers for musicians, but I'm not sure if that works the other way around," he teased, enjoying the frivolity of their discussion.

"Do you need to be coordinated to play the guitar? Come to think of it, might not work for me."

"It does require two hands doing two different things, and reading music. So yeah, coordination seems important."

"I'm screwed. That means ice skating lessons should be removed from the list as well." Jezebel smiled, squinting her eyes and tapping her finger on her lips in jest, as if pondering her list deeply.

Kirk laughed. The laugh released a tension he'd unknowingly held in his shoulders. He realized he hadn't genuinely laughed in awhile.

"So how's your paralegaling going?"

"Oh just dandy! How's life at Westlaw?"

"Dandy as well. So how's the legal secretary lawsuit progressing?" He squirmed as a guilty pang nudged his belly.

"Okay. Just reviewing documents and getting ready for depositions. Nothing exciting yet. I'll let you know when I discover the smoking gun."

"Yes, I'd love to hear about it. Who will you depose?"

"Um, obviously the plaintiff first and they'll depose the defendant first. Human Resources is usually next."

"What about friends of the plaintiff?"

"Sometimes the husband if they're alleging problems at home were caused by the situation, severe emotional distress, etc. Coworkers are deposed if they were witnesses to behavior. But, I think that concludes your employment law lesson for the night."

"Okay, I'll stop talking about work."

"So, since you got personal with the father question, mind if I get a little personal?" she asked, tilting her head feigning shyness.

He cringed, knowing where the conversation was headed. "Sure, go ahead, shoot." He sipped his beer, readjusting himself in the booth.

"Well, I was wondering where things stand with your wife? How long have you been separated?"

"Ah, we started having problems about a year ago. She pulled away, and didn't want to fix our relationship. I felt her giving up. I think she was, probably is, in love with someone else." He'd successfully answered her truthfully without directly answering the question.

"Oh, my, so she cheated on you?"

"I did suspect that, but she denied it."

"So, she didn't want to fix things?"

"She's not interested in counseling."

"If she wanted to, would you?"

"Objection! You've gone over your allotted number of personal questions for the evening, Miss Stone—"

"Not fair, you just made up that rule. Answer the question honestly, and I'll switch topics."

"Honestly, probably. If she sincerely wanted to fix things, then yes, I would. I would try to fix things with her." The beer and his comfort in her presence made his lips loose.

Jezebel nodded and looked down into her beer, picked it up and finished the last sip. "Well, it's a shame she gave up so easily."

"Yes it is, but I don't see her making any moves to fix things. She claims our passion is gone. I thought I was a pretty darn good husband. But, what can you do when your wife becomes obsessed with another guy?" He threw his hands up in the air.

"So who was the other guy? Did you know him?"

"Uh, you promised to switch topics, Miss Stone."

"When's your birthday?" she asked, not skipping a

beat.

"August 18th."

"Ew, a stubborn Leo, huh? You are actually my sign's opposite."

"And your sign is...let me guess, the ever-dreamy aloof Aquarius?"

"Very impressive, Mr. Flynn. The 29th of January. My moon sign is actually Leo."

"Learned to love astrology through your hippie parents, I see."

A burst of female laughter a few tables behind him, caused him to jerk and look over his shoulder. His heart raced wondering if Nicole and her crew had arrived at one of their favorite hangouts.

"Those ladies are well on their way to a hangover," Jezebel said.

"Yes, it definitely sounds that way," he replied as he watched the one woman in the loud group throw back a shot. Disappointment filled him. He had enjoyed the brief adrenaline rush at the thought of Nicole seeing him with another woman. *Maybe some other time*, he thought, turning his attention back to Jezebel. "Want to head out?"

"Sure. Dinner is my treat this time, remember? And, I need to give that waitress a big tip." She insisted, handing her credit card to the waitress when she approached the table.

"Thank you." Kirk smiled.

"Want to share a cab again?" Jezebel asked, checking her phone.

"Sounds good. And that's my treat." He checked his phone. As expected, no texts or calls from his wife.

They moved out of the booth and he let her pass in

front of him. He leaned in and whispered in her ear, close enough to smell her hair again. "Just don't run over any waitresses on the way out."

She laughed hard, seeming to enjoy their closeness. "Very funny. I'll try not to embarrass you, but I can't guarantee it."

He placed his hand on the small of her back, guiding her past the loud table of women. He fantasized that Nicole was seated there, dumbfounded and silenced as she watched them together. He would have pretended not to notice her.

They slid into the backseat of the cab. Their voices raised in chatter, as if still talking over the noise in the pub. He felt childish with Jezebel, full of a sense of reckless abandon. Perhaps it was the alcohol, or perhaps it was just this woman seated next to him, singing slightly off-key to the seventies music coming from the cab radio, who made him feel like singing off-key too.

He touched her leg without even thinking. She placed her hand on top of his.

Outside of her apartment building, he told the cab to wait. He held the door for Jezebel and closed it behind her. He clasped her hand, again without thinking, and walked her to the front door of her building.

"Would you like to come up for a little bit?" she offered, tempting him. He remembered how many beers he had had, and reminded himself to behave.

"No, I better not. I should get home. But can we do this again?"

"Sure, that would be great," she answered, stepping toward him, leaving not much space between them.

Again, without much thought, he placed his hands

on her shoulders and brought her into a hug.

As she took a step back, she whispered, "Thanks, Kirk, I look forward to next time…"

"Me too," he said as he turned toward the cab. He knew he should get inside, but instead he walked back to her. She was in the same spot, watching him. She smiled. He smiled and placed his hand on her warm cheek and slid it under her hair.

He kissed her with just a soft, respectful peck. But he wanted more, so he kissed her again with one slow kiss. He took in a breath as her eyes opened. Guilt welled up in his gut and he tried to erase his wife's face from in front of his mind.

"Good night, Jez."

"Good night, Kirk. Call me." She reached for the door and disappeared inside the building.

When he got home, he fell on the leather couch without even changing his clothes. He put his feet up on the coffee table and found a movie on HBO. His thoughts bounced from Jezebel to Nicole.

The door opened, and Nicole seemed startled to see him still awake.

"Hey," she said.

"Hey, how was your night?" he asked, not looking at her.

"Fun. A lot of fun. Did you go out?" She sat on the couch, far enough away that a whole other body could have fit between them.

"I did."

"With whom?"

"A friend from work."

"Oh, who?" she asked with heightened interest.

"Nicole, you know what? You get to pick and

choose what and when you share things with me, like our bed for instance, so I'm choosing not to share with you tonight," he said without taking his eyes from the television.

"Okay, fair enough." She slipped closer to him and rested her hand on his belly, moving it downward. She began to undo his belt.

He took her hand and placed it on her own leg, with his eyes still glued to the movie. He chuckled at a funny line.

She stood and marched to the guest room, slamming the door. His plan was working.

He grabbed his phone and sent Jezebel a text: Great time! Talk to you soon.

She responded: I had fun, too! Looking forward to the next time.

He purposefully left Jezebel's text displayed on his phone. He placed the phone face-up on the coffee table and went to bed.

Chapter 13

Nicole was convinced that Kirk had to be getting sex somewhere else since he turned her down. She'd kill the woman if she figured out who it was.

She hadn't planned for her night to end as it did, but it ended perfectly. She'd met a group of the secretaries for a movie and dinner, and after two glasses of wine, she was feeling good. They were laughing, eating, and having a decent time. Sometime after nine o'clock, she started to feel low. This feeling plus wine usually equaled desperate. So she went to the bathroom and sent Jack a text. She wrote: Can we talk? Things are out of hand and I'd just like to talk privately with you.

Nicole waited in the bathroom for a few minutes until she got a response: The W at 10:00.

Her heart pounded and she let a small squeal escape. She fixed her makeup and returned to the table with a pretend headache. Dana left too, wanting to ride the Metro together, but Nicole told her she needed a quiet cab ride alone because she sensed a migraine was coming. She then hailed a cab to The W Hotel in Northwest Washington. The air was chilly, but her body flushed with warmth.

They'd met only two times at The W and those times were before their first sexual encounter. It made her sad he hadn't suggested their old rendezvous location. Was that a hint to his mood?

The elevator delivered Nicole to the top of The W and inside the busy POV Lounge. She selected a secluded table that held a breathtaking view of the city. The large windows displayed the White House and the Washington Monument at their best. She blew out a stress-relieving sigh, staring at the blinking hypnotic light atop the tallest monument. The country's power rested before her.

She wasn't sure exactly what she'd accomplish, but she needed to see him again. Soften him again, and maybe even kiss him again. She asked God to forgive her.

"Nicole." Jack's voice was stern as he slid into the seat in front of her. Before making eye contact, his eyes darted around the room. He folded his hands on top of the table, never removing his jacket.

"It's good to see you, Jack," she said, wanting to reach across and touch him. When they used to meet during happier times, he never allowed any public affection. It made the trip to the hotel room later all the more heated.

"I think we can skip the small talk. What's this all about?"

"Well, I've just been feeling, well, sad. Sad and regretful. I'm sorry this whole lawsuit thing is happening—"

"Then drop it, Nicole. Drop the fucking suit," he whispered, appearing to restrain himself from exploding. His lips pressed together, making them go white. His beautiful eyes scanned the room again. He was irritable when he wasn't getting some good sex, so it pleased her that he was in need.

"Are you still seeing Rebecca?"

"No. I was never 'seeing' Rebecca, Nic," he huffed, glancing toward the elevators.

"Are you seeing anyone other than your wife?"

"Nicole, this is ridiculous. What's this got to do with the lawsuit?" He stared into her eyes with a hatred that made her blood rush. Completely turned her on.

"It's just, well, I'll drop the suit, forget about it, if you, if you'll give me my job back. I miss working for you..." She surprised herself. Her hands were shaking, so she squeezed them between her crossed legs.

"I give you your job back and you drop the suit, and pretend our little affair never happened? Never." He cocked his head, leaning as close as he could with the table there.

"Give me my job back and when you run for office, I'll work the campaign and when you're elected, you make me your secretary. Obviously I'd have a vested interest and I'll keep my mouth shut about the affair. I want my marriage to work too, so obviously I wouldn't say anything or Kirk will leave me..." She spoke with a surprising confidence.

"This is nuts, Nicole. This is extortion, black mail." The more he scolded, the more she wanted to kiss him.

"It's not. We both get something and you lose nothing. You gain a very devoted campaign worker and a very devoted secretary, Mr. Senator." She tried to speak as if she was in control and calm, but her insides were a muddled mess.

"Here's the deal, my dear. You drop the suit, but keep your current secretary position with your associates. When the campaign starts, you bust your ass and keep your mouth shut about us. If I win, and if you prove your loyalty, then you can have a position as a Senator's secretary."

"But if I drop the suit, and you go back on your word, then I've lost everything. After I dismiss the suit, people will assume I had been a little crazy to sue you. So I can't blab about the affair because you'll just claim I'm a whack-job. No, I want a little more insurance from you now. I'm not dropping the suit quite yet—"

"Nicole! You're pissing me off. I'm out of here. I'm sick of your games and I'm gonna win this suit regardless of what you do, and I may even counter-sue for defamation." He stood with a burst of rage and walked toward the elevator.

She took a different elevator to race him to the lobby. He would hate to cause a scene in a hotel lobby, so it was safe to follow him. The doors opened and Nicole jogged to catch him, trying in vain to silence her clicking heels on the marble floor.

He threw open a set of glass doors and entered a small empty vestibule. Before he reached the second set of doors that led outside, she called his name. They both stopped inside the small area, alone.

He turned, breathing heavily.

"I've missed you, Jack. I'm sorry this has gotten so ugly, but I miss you, desperately miss you." She touched his arm, glancing through the glass doors. No one was approaching the hideaway.

With a force that possibly bruised the back of her neck, he grabbed the base of her skull, drawing her face against his. His kiss hurt but healed her at the same time. It was hungry and angry. Yanking her away by her hair, he already clenched in his hands and forced her away. Out of the grasp of his kiss, she wanted more of him. Still holding her head, he pressed his hot lips against her ear. Their severe breathing was in sync. "I miss you, too. You need to stop screwing with me, Nicole. Drop the suit."

She knew he took that last moment to breathe in her scent. He then discarded her like she was soiling his hands, and disappeared through the second set of doors.

She removed the smeared lipstick from her chin and smoothed her hair, regulated her breathing, and smiled.

He missed me. He still missed me, she thought. She held the power right now. A lot of power. "Jesus," she whispered to herself. "Forgive me."

Chapter 14

"So, Jez, based on the documents you've seen so far, what do you think?" Justin slipped comfortably inside my small office's guest chair. Resting his ankle on top of his left knee, he grabbed onto his right knee, appearing ready to hear my thoughts. Before the holiday party incident, his visits had started off work related and then would morph into trivial discussions mixed with flirting and laughter. Recently, his visits were quick and business-like and he would never help himself to a seat. So, seeing him at ease inside my office was comforting. Perhaps working together on this new case would mend our friendship.

"Well, her employee file is spotless, exemplary, really. There is so much evidence of Winston raving about D'Angelo's work and they seemed to have had a great working relationship. His reason for moving her does seem abrupt." I slid my candy dish toward him. He took a piece of chocolate and smiled.

I continued, "His claims that she began to have feelings for him and began acting unprofessionally are not documented. She did report to HR that he had been harassing her, but it was after he had her position changed. HR did address Winston so that's good and their conversation is documented. He, of course, denied any wrong-doing. Just said it was time for a change and he suspected she had unprofessional feelings. Some of the emails from Winston to D'Angelo could be interpreted as unprofessional though."

"Any social media?"

"Nothing. If she had any accounts, she deleted them."

"Did you listen to the voicemail recording?"

"She recorded two of his voicemails, and I read the transcripts of them, but haven't listened to them yet. They are damaging to his defense. It's possible she was obsessed and in love with him and he's telling the truth. Or, he wanted to sleep with her and she refused. Or they slept together, he regretted it and wants to get rid of her so he can run for the Senate."

"But based on what you saw…"

"It's 50-50. We need him to explain a few of those emails and somehow explain the voicemail, maybe they had a playful, flirty relationship, but he meant no harm. In our favor, in addition to not complaining to HR prior to the position move, they produced no documents showing she complained to anyone. And she never sought therapy for her 'emotional distress.' She was never even seen crying at work by anyone, as far as we know. She's going to have to produce some witnesses if she wants to win. Sorry, you just asked me about the documents."

Justin slapped his leg and smiled. "Okay, well, as long as you saw nothing that said, 'hey, gorgeous, sleep with me or you'll lose your job.'"

"What did I just interrupt?" Vanessa sauntered in, placing a document in my inbox.

"You always have impeccable timing, Vanessa." I laughed.

"You know it, girl. Justin, Mr. Tenley called, he

left you a voicemail."

"Thanks, Vanessa," Justin said, sitting upright in his seat, as Vanessa left the office, leaving her perfume behind. "So, Jez, how's Metro riding going?" He stood in front of my desk, fiddling with the lid of my candy dish.

"Great, I'm cured. No more panic attacks, fainting, nightmares, nothing. Cured!"

"Good. I'm glad. Well, my offer still stands to ride with you if you have any set-backs." He strummed his fingers on my desk, then turned and walked to the doorway.

"Thanks, Justin. I appreciate your support," I said, watching him leave.

I was still smiling from my conversation with Justin when the phone rang. It was Kirk, who I hadn't spoken to since Saturday. He invited me to lunch at the Corner Bakery.

Since I couldn't find any bit of makeup in my purse, I decided to raid Vanessa's stash.

I slipped behind Vanessa's desk. "Vanessa, I need to borrow some makeup for a lunch date."

My secretary giggled, never removing her eyes from her computer screen, fingernails clicking on her keyboard. "Ah, ha, I knew you and Justin were getting cozy this morning. You're gonna have to mix my blush with my powder for that pale complexion of yours. Go on, hit my makeup stash and go pretty yourself up, girl." She chuckled again, never averting her eyes from her screen.

"It's not with Justin. It's with hot train guy," I explained, opening Vanessa's desk drawer.

"Shut-up, woman! Woo-hoo, I need a name for this

hot train guy."

"Kirk."

"Yummy Kirky," she said, pivoting in her chair to face me. "Eek! Oh good Lord, girl, borrow a hair band from someone too while you're at it." Vanessa waved her index finger in the air, as if it were a magic wand, painting my hair into place.

"Thanks for the make-over advice."

"Someone say 'make-over'?" Ken entered the cubicle, placing a large stack of papers in Vanessa's inbox.

"Kenny, our girl has a lunch date and look at her hair." Vanessa directed him to the disaster area.

"Mother Mary, full of grace." Ken grinned, covering his mouth with his hand, pretending to withhold laughter.

"Very funny, people. I was in a hurry and didn't have proper hair-blowing time this morning. I just found out about the date. Help me."

"Okay, sweetie, come hither." Ken pulled a rubber band off of his wrist and wrestled my hair up into a high ponytail. "There, you're gorgeous, my love."

Vanessa slapped her thigh and exclaimed, "Oh Kenny, your hands do work magic. Now with a little make-up, you'll be ready to dazzle the train guy."

"Now, tell Vanessa what you told me about the red flag and all from Saturday night." Ken swept his hand from me toward Vanessa, giving me the stage.

I shot Ken a look of a disapproval, but did as he instructed, explaining Kirk's willingness to seek marital counseling if his wife requested.

"Hmm, separated but not divorced and still has feelings for her. Yeah, that's red-flag worthy. Just be careful, girl. I'll yell out a prayer to the Lord for your soon-to-be-broken heart."

"Relax people. We're keeping things casual."

Before heading out to meet my lunch date, I tied up some final loose ends. Upon pushing the button for the elevator, I heard my name and turned to face Justin. "Hey Justin. What do you need?"

"Nothing. You look good. You changed your hair from this morning."

"I'm meeting someone for lunch and didn't want to scare him." I hit the button four or five more times in a futile effort to make the elevator arrive sooner.

"Oh, it's a him, huh? Well, have a good lunch date."

"Thanks," I said as the elevator doors shut between us. I dismissed the idea that I sensed jealousy in Justin's words and shook my head at the thought of Justin still harboring any interest in me.

I jogged a few blocks, hoping I wouldn't sweat too much. K Street sped by in a blur, knowing I was already five minutes late. Finally, I burst through the glass doors of the Corner Bakery. Kirk's eyes met mine through the crowd. He looked good in his dark blue suit.

"Hello, Jez." He smiled, taking my frazzled body into a hug.

"Hey there. Sorry I'm a little late." I took a deep breath. "Thanks for calling me. I haven't been to Corner Bakery in a long time."

"Hope it wasn't too far for you?"

"No, no, I needed the exercise." I pushed my bangs aside and regulated my breathing, forcing myself to appear calm and together. We grabbed trays and silverware and ordered our meals.

"Working hard?" Kirk asked, gently touching my arm and looking into my eyes before I was forced to turn to look at the restaurant employee handing me a plate of food.

"I am working hard, but that's nothing new."

"It's good to see you. I've been busy too, but I missed you. I'm glad you could make it last minute." He led us to a small table in the corner while he spoke.

"Yeah, I missed you too." My body tensed in embarrassment at our intimate words contrasted against the busy lunchtime restaurant environment.

We sat, adjusted ourselves in our seats, exhaled together, and held a gaze for an uncomfortable moment.

Breaking the silence, I tapped my straw on the table to release it from the wrapper. "So, any weekend plans?" I asked.

"Well, I'm going to a big family gathering at my brother's house tomorrow afternoon for my nephew's first birthday party. Should be full of drama, as all family gatherings are. How about you?"

"Well, I bought two baseball tickets to the Nationals' game tomorrow night, and the friend who planned to go can't now. Would you be interested in joining me if the birthday party ends early?"

"Hmm, well, okay, my brother lives in Annapolis, so I'll have to call you and let you know. Maybe I can meet you there?"

"Great. Sounds good. If you can't make it, let me know. My brother is always my last minute date for things, so I'm sure he'll be happy to use the other ticket," I said. Embarrassed, I avoided eye contact and raked a fork through my salad. Pleased with myself for asking him to the game, but now I had to produce two tickets.

Plates emptied and iced tea glasses drained. Lunchtime expired.

"Well, Kirk, I should be heading back to the office. Are you going back to your office or do you have another law firm to visit?"

"Actually, I'm heading to Skadden Arps, near the White House. So, yes, let's get out of here. The time went fast, but it was good seeing you again."

"Yeah, well I hope to see you tomorrow night." I moved in front of him in order to walk through the crowd efficiently. His hand touched the small of my back and his breath stroked my cheek as he spoke into my ear from behind.

"I will try my best to escape. I'll text you tomorrow." He moved his body around mine and grabbed the door for me. We departed the air-conditioned restaurant and entered the hot air. Kirk spoke, looking at his phone, "My meeting at Skadden Arps is actually at 2:00, so I have some time. Mind if I walk you back to your office?"

"Oh, that would be great." We walked closely, bumping arms occasionally. I had an urge to grab his hand, but decided to let him make that move first.

As we rounded the corner, entering K Street, I noticed a tall blonde woman who was passing in the other direction. She stopped in her tracks and looked at Kirk.

"Kirk," the attractive woman said, stunned to see him.

"Hey, Nic, hey…" Kirk stammered and halted his stride.

"Hi, I'm Nicole. Kirk's wife. And you are?" She held out her hand with boldness, darting her eyes from Kirk to me.

"Hi, I'm Jezebel Stone—"

"Nic, this is a friend of mine and a Westlaw client."

"Oh, what firm do you work for? Jezebel, is it?" she asked, releasing our grip, dragging out the syllables of my name as if they tasted sour.

"Ah, Nic, we're in a hurry. I have a meeting and so does Jezebel."

"I work for Harrington & Paulson," I answered Nicole's question.

"Oh, really? I know that firm very well. Big firm." Her eyes widened and darted to Kirk.

I could not ignore her obvious glare. It was painful to look at. Like a D.C. monument, the awkwardness stood in the center of us. Impenetrable, looming, cold.

"Gotta run, Nic. Good to see you," Kirk announced. He stepped away, attaching his hand to my elbow, guiding me along with him.

"Nice meeting you, Nicole," I said over my shoulder as we walked. I lied.

"Yeah, super great meeting you too," Nicole hissed, disappearing behind us into a group of suited bodies.

Kirk remained silent, guiding me forward.

Breaking the strained silence, I spoke, "So, that was weird. Does she work down here?"

"Um, sorry about that. She's an interesting one, isn't she? Um, yeah, she's a secretary for a small boutique firm, Kemp & Thatcher. Her office is in the building there on the corner."

"Haven't heard of them. We have a client in that building," I said. "She seemed irritated with you."

"She's pretty much irritated with me twenty-four seven. Sorry to put you in such an awkward position. She's got a nasty jealous streak so that's why I said you were a client. I didn't want to tell her your firm name, because she's so crazy she might track you down. I'm trying to keep things civil between us."

"Well, sorry if I complicated things for you."

"No, don't be sorry. She's the one who's complicated my life, not you."

As we walked, I felt a nauseous grumble in my belly that was more than my lunch disagreeing with me. A brilliant crimson flag waved before my eyes. Was I in the middle of something unfinished and was my fateful ride not so fateful after all?

He took control of the door and followed me inside the small area before reaching the lobby.

"Thanks for lunch, Kirk."

"You're welcome and sorry for the wife run-in," he apologized with sincerity. He moved in front of me without hesitation, swept his hand along the back of my neck, resting it under my ponytail. Wasting no time, he kissed me twice on the lips and released me. "I'll call you tomorrow." He winked, moved around me, and grabbed the door from someone coming into the building. He breezed out of sight. My hand was on my mouth and I realized it had been several seconds since I'd inhaled.

In a daze, I made my way back to my desk. I pulled up the D.C. law firm listing on the Internet and typed, "Kemp & Thatcher." No firm by that name appeared. Perhaps I misheard him. I slammed down my mouse and closed the Internet browser.

Collapsing into the back of my chair, I processed in stillness all that had happened in the last hour. Why had he lied about something so simple? What else had he lied about? I then remembered I had two baseball tickets to purchase. I guess I had lied with ease as well.

Unlike our original Metro ride that crashed without warning, this ride was announcing its demise. I should exit.

My phone buzzed with an incoming text. It was from Kirk: Thinking of you. Wanting another kiss.

My body screamed to hang on and stay aboard. I picked up the phone off my desk and typed a reply: Me too.

Chapter 15

Kirk's phone buzzed, as expected, on his way to the Skadden meeting. Nicole. He let it go to voicemail. He felt awful for lying. But, the sick feeling in his gut was not remorse for lying to Nicole, but to Jezebel. He wanted Nicole to see them together, but when it happened, he could barely handle it. The fantasy was much more satisfying than reality.

To alleviate some guilt, he sent Jezebel a text, and he meant every word of it.

Her response made him smile.

What in the hell was he doing, he wondered, pushing his fingers through his hair.

Kirk got home that evening fully aware his night would not be pleasant.

During their first year of marriage, they'd coordinated their trips home from town, riding the Metro and driving home from the parking lot together. Over the past year, their schedules became harder to coordinate and Nicole insisted on driving to work alone. She claimed she could always find a parking space on her street, a spot with a broken meter. And she asserted, like earning them a free upgraded lighting package in their condo, her charm could always get her free parking. She considered this a gift, as if she was a concert pianist, or something.

Kirk arrived at their condo before Nicole. She blew

in shortly after he did like the Metro flying into the station with an attention-grabbing gust of energy. She threw her briefcase on the floor and began her apparent pre-planned speech.

"Thanks for ignoring my calls, Kirk! First off, what the hell are you doing having lunch dates with a single woman? I checked out her ring finger—I'm not stupid, Kirk. Second, why in the hell would you eat with someone from the firm that is representing Jack, and third, you said today she was a client, and you told me Harrington & Paulson were not in your territory. You've got some explaining to do, Kirk. I'm furious." She paced around the dining room as he stood in front of the couch in the adjoining living room.

"They're not my client, Dave has that firm. I lied about the client thing because I wanted to avoid a confrontation, like we're having right now, over something so innocent. Jezebel was on the train with me the day the Metro crashed. Before it crashed, we had had a pleasant conversation over work stuff. When it crashed, we separated. She looked me up at Westlaw at the suggestion of her therapist to see if I was okay. She wanted to meet for lunch, so we met. It's a coincidence that she works for Harrington, but I think we can use this to get information on Winston."

Nicole walked toward him, sweeping her hair out of her face. She seemed to have swallowed some of her fury. "Well, now you've got my attention, Kirk." She pointed her finger at his face. "You just better not screw things up for me, Kirk, I mean it. But, if you can get me information—"

"Relax, Nic, Jezebel's pretty tight lipped on the matter. But I'll see what I can do."

"Does she like you? Before our little sidewalk meeting, did she know you were married? You're always leaving your ring in your stupid gym bag. Kirk, was she the person you went out with on Saturday? If you're cheating on me, so help me I'll freakin' kill you and her with my bare hands." She stormed toward the dining room. On the dining room wall, a large picture of them, posing in front of the altar on their wedding day, ironically provided the backdrop for her performance. She twisted her body back toward him in a dramatic Nicole-like display.

She slammed a dining room chair against the table.

"Calm down, Nicole. And what if she is interested in me, so what? Like you give a crap about me right now. You're so wrapped up in your own little world you wouldn't even notice if I were having an affair right under your nose. You're living in the guest room. We're practically separated, barely married anyway."

"Good God. You are sleeping with her, aren't you?" She rushed at him, stopping short of striking him in the chest.

Kirk grabbed her forearms, squeezing them hard. Seeing his plan unfold created a pleasant rush. In a low, forced whisper, he breathed into her face, "I never said that. You just asked if she was interested in me."

"Listen to me." Whipping her arms out of his hold, she pointed her freshly manicured finger at his face. "Keep Miss Olive Oyl out of your pants, you hear me? And don't mess up my lawsuit."

"I wouldn't dream of messing up this battle with your boyfriend."

"He's not my boyfriend and I'm sick of explaining it to you. And don't forget, you were just as into this lawsuit idea as I was. You know what, the more I think about this, I think you will mess this up. Break things off with Olive Oyl." She drove her hand again through her hair. "I'm not sure how much she'd help me, so just end this now. This little arrangement is stressing me out."

"Fine. I'll end contact with Jezebel, if you can swear to me on the Holy Bible that you never slept with Winston." He pointed at her face this time.

"We've been over this, Kirk. We never slept together. I'm telling you the truth." She paused and whispered, "on the Holy Bible." She crossed her arms like a four year old as her eyes welled with tears.

He believed her. He wanted to believe her.

"I need to be close to you right now. I'm hurting..." Nicole cried. Even when he knew she was crying to purposely manipulate, it still weakened him to see her in tears.

She could use the weapon of tears as fiercely as she used her beauty.

He couldn't help but move toward her and hold her. Her crying stopped, but her breathing increased. She kissed his neck and pressed her waist against his. He didn't stop her when she unbuckled his belt with determination. She unbuttoned his shirt and ran her hands all over. He didn't kiss her back.

His pants fell to the floor with well-rehearsed ease. He tore at her blouse, and may even have caused a button or two to pop off. They tumbled onto the couch and he forced his way into her as she shrieked in another dramatic Nicole-like display.

For a brief moment, he saw Jezebel's eyes and could swear he smelled her shampooed hair. When he finished, it was Jez's name he wanted to say, but instead he just breathed into Nicole's neck, suffocating any emotion.

They dressed in silence. Nicole disappeared for a while, reappearing in her "going-out" clothes. The room filled with the scent of her perfume. Kirk's eyes were drawn to her cleavage, her breasts heaved at the top of her tank top, letting him know she was wearing his favorite push-up bra of hers. Her skinny jeans hugged her hips and her waist looked tiny beneath the black leather belt.

She pushed her styled bleached-white hair over her shoulder as she dug through her purse.

"Where are you going?" he asked, trying to hide disappointment.

"I told you yesterday, Kirk, that I'm going out with my cousin tonight," she huffed in her usual irritated tone.

"Nic, what the hell is this? Are we just casual roommates who screw every now and then? Who don't talk, but just scream at each other?"

"What do you want from me, Kirk?" She whipped her face in his direction, seemingly annoyed that she had to pull her attention away from organizing her purse.

"I want a wife, dammit, a real wife who enjoys spending time with me. Who actually wants to make love, not just screw, and who maybe wants to go out to dinner with me?"

"I can't be Mrs. Cleaver right now, Kirk. I'm working through some issues. This isn't the kind of marriage I want either, you know. Maybe I should leave and move out, how about that?"

"Fine. Do it."

"Oh, so you can be free to date Olive Oyl? No way. On second thought, I'm staying. We're married and we're staying married."

"This isn't married."

"I need to work through things."

"So then I should just wait around for you to figure everything out, never knowing when or if that will happen? I think we should officially separate."

"No! How will that look? I don't want to have to tell everyone we're separated and then everyone will be all in our business."

"Right, God forbid you look bad, Nicole. God forbid you put me and our marriage first."

"Shut up. Just shut up! I give you sex, I cook you nice meals, I clean your condo, just get off my back."

"What about love, Nicole, what about that part, huh?"

"I love you, Kirk, I do."

"No. I don't need your patronizing words, I need the real thing. Go stay at your cousin's tonight. I want you out of here."

"No. This is my place, you leave," Nicole insisted.

"No way. You schedule marriage counseling, or you get out."

"I'll finish out this suit and then we'll get counseling."

"Get your ass out of here now. You figure out what you want without me having to see you every day, wondering if today will be the day that you decide to fix things," Kirk said.

"What about tomorrow? Your whole family will be at your brother's. I don't want your family hating me and thinking I'm the bad guy here!"

"God forbid. Okay, fine, go to the party, act the part of the sweet and loving wife, and then get the hell out."

"Fine. Don't say anything to your family. I'll stay with my cousin for a few days until you calm your ass down. But this is no real separation. You better stay faithful to me, Kirk. If you cheat, I'll kill you."

"I'm not promising any such thing. You come home when you're ready to make this marriage work and you want to see a real counselor and you want to put me first."

"Fine. As long as you stay away from my lawsuit and that freaky-eyed Olive Oyl. Maybe it's better if we're not together—my lawyers could say the stress of my work situation affected my marriage..." Her eyes glanced off, appearing to further contemplate her strategy.

"Maybe you need some counseling on your own." He stormed past her, grabbed his keys, and left to get some take-out. Mrs. Cleaver obviously wasn't doing any cooking tonight.

Chapter 16

It was noon and I had not heard a word from Kirk. My brother had agreed to be my date to the Nationals' game—if I got ditched, he had said with a chuckle. And he said I could uninvite him, if Kirk decided to call.

During lunch with Carolyn, I checked my phone constantly for texts. It was unlike me to act so desperate and pathetic. A seed of distrust had been planted and normally the smallest hint of a red flag would make me run for the hills, but for some reason it was not happening this time.

"Jez, I've never seen you like this over a guy before. What's up? You're jittery and distracted."

"Just hoping he makes our date." My eyes floated upward, above Carolyn's head.

"And?"

"And, I met his wife yesterday."

"What?"

"On the street after our lunch. The Barbie doll ran right into us. And, she was wearing her ring."

"Oh..." Carolyn's face contorted, clearly showing her disgust. She appeared to be searching for words that usually came easy to her. "Well, was it a big rock? Maybe she doesn't want to say goodbye to the diamond yet?" She wiped her napkin across her mouth, looking into her lap.

"Yeah, maybe."

Carolyn looked into my eyes. "I think you need to ask this guy more questions. Look, Jez, you need to listen to your gut, hon. What's your gut saying?"

"My gut is bipolar. One minute it says, run from Train Guy. Then it yells, kiss Train Guy. Run, kiss, run, kiss!" I exclaimed, tossing my hands from side to side.

"Good grief. Well, what's Magic 8 say?" One side of Carolyn's mouth lifted upward in the beginning of a smile.

"Oddly, he's bipolar too."

We laughed together and didn't mention Train Guy again.

Late afternoon, I visited the mall alone in search of some baseball-fan attire and found a figure-flattering red Nationals' t-shirt. Ken always said I looked good in red. Now, I just needed a text from Kirk agreeing to meet me so I could ditch my sweet brother.

As I stood in the checkout line, my phone rang. I gasped and dropped the t-shirt, fumbling for my phone. It was Cala.

"Hey, Cay, what's up?" I asked, disappointed to not be talking to Kirk.

"Got some bad news. The first round of IVF didn't work."

"Oh, Cala, I'm so sorry. How terrible," I said, feeling guilty at my own trivial disappointments.

"It's okay. We got the go-ahead to try again next cycle. These things take time I suppose…" Cala's voice drifted off. I knew she was forcing self-imposed patience, attempting to allow things to happen outside of her control.

I showered my sister with encouragement, wishing I could hug her. After hanging up, I decided to buy her a little gift, before completing my own shopping goals.

Pleased with all my purchases, I headed to my car. My phone buzzed and my heart leapt along with it. Kirk's text said: My car died. Still at my brother's. Go to the game with Damian. Can I meet you after for a drink? So sorry.

With a smirk, I yelled to the sky, "Oh, you've got to be kidding me. Dead battery? Really?" Was he lying again? The fact that I heard this question ringing in my head should have caused me to turn down his drink offer. But admitting I was weak and bipolar, I replied I would meet him at 10:30 inside our pub.

****

My brother lifted me off the ground inside a hug. "Thanks for coming, Dame."

"Hey, my pleasure." He reached around my shoulder, pulling me close to his side as we walked into the stadium.

He strolled with me in harmony along the interior cement walkway. With his hands now tucked in the pockets of his worn out favorite cargo shorts, his flip-flops clapped beneath him.

I had always been in awe of Damian's Zen-like, self-assured demeanor. With the exception of two heartbreaks, Damian had the enviable ability to let nothing frazzle him or extinguish his sincere contentment with simply being alive. His boyish good looks mixed with a touch of hipster flair aided in his natural ability to flirt with just his eyes at every young woman who walked by.

Ascending the sticky cement steps, through the smells of popcorn and perspiration, we found our seats and joined the crowd in all the baseball game traditions.

Sometime after the seventh inning stretch, Damian nudged me out of a daydream.

"More peanuts?"

"No thanks, I'm good."

"Hey, what gives? Are you that disappointed that train-crash dude couldn't make it? He's meeting you later, right?"

Unlike times with my sister, I could fully relax around my brother. He advised without condescension and judgment. "I'm sorry. I'm having a good time with you, I am. And I'm looking forward to seeing him. It's just, well, I think, I think he might be lying to me. I caught him in one lie, so now I'm thinking this whole car breaking down thing may also be a lie."

"I did wonder why he didn't have jumper cables…"

"I'm not fully convinced he's really separated…"

"The Jezebel I know would have said 'get lost bucko' and dropped him fast." He snapped his fingers in the air, imitating my voice.

"I know. What's wrong with me? What am I doing? Maybe it's this whole Metro crash thing and the fact that he's gorgeous. I feel we have this bond and I was hoping we were meant to be together. I'm trying to make it into a fairy tale ending."

"Don't force it—"

"You'll break it." I finished his predicted statement. "Maybe the crash was my fate. Fate separated us and I am forcing us together. No, no, I picked that car for a reason…"

"You're over-thinking this, Sis. Get off the metaphorical Metro and dump the guy."

"That's what my head is saying, but—"

"But your hormones are saying otherwise?"

"Yep! Darn it."

"Why don't you ask to go back to his place tonight? If he's still with this wife, he won't want you coming around, right?"

"Yeah, I thought of that. But, I also don't want to sleep with him if he's a snake."

"Just text him and say you're tired, go home and give yourself more time to think this through."

"Yeah, that's what I'll do," I said softly. My mouth said what I should do but my heart and body screamed otherwise.

Crack. The crowd collectively gasped and rose, reeling our heads to follow the soaring baseball arching high. It crossed the warning track with ease, landing in the stands over the wall. Cheers and fireworks rocked Nationals Park. I high-fived my brother as the stadium celebrated the three-run homer.

I grabbed my phone from my back jean pocket, ready to text Kirk informing him I couldn't meet him. When I looked down at my phone, a text from him appeared on the screen. With the crowd's excitement, I had not heard it arrive.

He said: I feel terrible that I'm not at the game with you. Nice homerun! I replaced the car battery. I am looking forward to our date.

I replied: Me too.

We made our way out of the stadium through the happy crowd.

"Are you sure you don't want a ride to Bethesda?" Damian asked.

"No, you head downtown to meet your friends, I'll metro."

"Okay, but I'm walking you to the platform. And for the record, I'm protesting you meeting this dude tonight."

"Thanks for your concern, but it'll be okay. I'll find out why he lied."

"Where there's one lie, there are usually more…"

"And you know this because?"

"Just do. And no, I usually don't lie to chicks."

"I'm a chick and you just lied to me!"

"Okay, so maybe I have lied a little to women in the past, but not to the ones I cared about. Present company excluded."

"Hmmm, good point. Okay, I promise, any more red flags, I'm running." I stopped in front of a vendor's table of Nationals' gear, pulling my brother with me. "And that doesn't count," I said, pointing to a red Nationals' pennant flapping in the breeze above the vendor's stand. "I want to buy a t-shirt."

"Hmm, you're taking train-crash dude a gift, aren't you?"

"Maybe."

He shook his head with a chuckle. "Yeah, I don't see you 'running' from this guy anytime soon, Jez. You're so far gone. Across the warning track and over the wall gone."

I playfully slapped my brother's hard bicep. "You just hush now. Did I mention he's gorgeous?"

"Once or twice." Damian laughed again, squeezing my shoulder.

I paid the vendor and shoved the t-shirt inside my purse. "Now, to the Metro, Dame." I grinned, interlocking arms with my brother, as if we were heading off to see the Wizard.

Inside the Navy Yard station, I pulled out my Metro pass and hugged Damian goodbye.

"Jez, thanks for the ticket and be careful—on the Metro *and* with Train Crash dude." Damian kissed my cheek. I smiled at him, as he pushed his wavy locks out of his face.

I entered the Green Line train along with other baseball fans, thinking of Kirk. What would the next stop on this crazy ride bring? I wondered.

Transferring onto the Red Line at Gallery Place station, I was pleased to be close to making our arranged date time. I rushed up the street through the warm night air that was tinged with the typical D.C. humidity. Before reaching for the door, I heard my name.

"Hey gray-eyed girl," Kirk called. Hands in his pockets, he smiled while casually leaning against the pub's brick exterior wall.

"Kirk, oh, hey! Have you been waiting long?"

"Nope, just got here." He pushed his backside off the wall, still smiling. Unhurried, he walked toward me with his hands still in his khaki pants. I couldn't tell if it was his smile or the shade of his blue golf shirt that made his eyes glisten. Whatever it was, I got lost in it. His dirty blond hair shimmered as well, perhaps with a hint of gel or whatever a man puts in his hair to make it look that good. He kissed my cheek.

We slid into our usual booth. The waitress recognized us from one of our previous visits, confirming this was now "our place," as Kirk joked.

"So, how was the party, other than your car breaking down?"

"Okay. The family was tolerable and my nephew

enjoyed pounding his cake into oblivion." We laughed together.

"Oh, I got you something." I reached into my purse, pulling out the t-shirt.

"Nice. Thank you." He tugged it over his head and over his blue shirt. He looked good in red, too.

"I'm sure you have a bunch already."

"Not this style. I love it. Thanks for getting me a gift even though I ditched you. Sorry about that, by the way."

"It's okay, really. Sorry about your car."

"Yeah, and I was all ready to text you and say I was on my way, put the keys in, and dead. Nothing."

We shared a basket of fries and a second drink.

"So, I have to admit that the little wife encounter on Friday did throw me for a loop. I just have a feeling that things are pretty unsettled between you."

He exhaled loudly and looked off through the bar. "Yeah, that didn't go as planned—"

"Planned?"

"I mean, it didn't go as I would have liked...you know, her attitude was a bit hostile and it flustered me a bit. I apologize. She's the one that left the marriage and she's still territorial with me. It'll get better. I hope."

My mind swarmed with thoughts that eroded my buzz. A feeling of being the third wheel smacked me hard. Well, I was here with him right now and told myself to enjoy the evening. I packaged up one of the red flags, rationalizing that Kirk probably lied because he was flustered and didn't want his worlds to collide.

"Hey, your pretty eyes look worried. Have another drink." He lifted his beer mug, gesturing a toast.

"Wanna get out of here?" I asked, not sure what the

question would lead to.

"Interested in showing me your place?" he asked.

"Sure, or you can show me yours?" I asked bravely, sliding from the booth.

"I want to meet this cat, Furry. Let's go to your place."

"Okay, just don't stereotype me as a crazy cat lady. I'm sensitive about that with the whole 'old maid' status looming on the horizon."

"Sure, whatever you say." He winked with a grin, sliding out of the booth.

We left our hangout, his arm around my shoulders. I leaned into him, but didn't want to relax too much. On guard for the next red flag, I held my ground.

After we exited the cab, I laughed at Kirk imitating the driver's accent. His hand moved from my shoulder to the side of my neck, pulling my ear to his mouth. "Does Furry bite?"

"Only if you bite me."

"Darn it. I was hoping to sneak a little nibble of the cat lady, but I'll behave—don't want to piss off her cat." He laughed as I elbowed him, releasing me to hit the elevator button.

Inside the elevator, I leaned against the wall and smiled at Kirk. He grinned, his eyes burrowing into mine. I liked knowing he found my eyes pretty, so I batted my eyelashes a bit. I held onto my breath as he moved toward me. Stopping an inch from me, he looked down at our feet.

As the seals of the doors fastened together, Kirk disclosed, "I haven't made out with anyone in a very long time."

A vision of the pretty blonde ex-wife flashed

across my mind like the fireworks at Nationals Park. There was no room for a third wheel right now, so I chased away the picture and replied, "It's okay. I don't bite either."

Gradually he moved his eyes up my body and met my eyes. He lifted one side of his mouth into a half smile. Taking my neck in both of his hands, he tilted his head. As his thumbs rested on my jaw, his eyes closed and I closed mine. This kiss was much different than our previous platonic pecks. He kissed me with an energy that made me move closer to him and awaken parts of my body that hadn't been aroused in a while. I glided my hands up his back, regretting my gift—because now two shirts stood between us. I enjoyed the taste of him.

A screeching jolt rocked us off balance.

"Oh no. The elevator stopped. Something's wrong." I snapped back to reality.

We listened. We waited. We braced against the wall.

"Are we stuck? What floor are we on?" Kirk asked, looking around the elevator.

"I think four? Three floors short." My eyes wide in panic, I hit the number seven button and then stabbed at the open door button several times. Nothing happened. "You've got to be kidding me!" I exclaimed to the ceiling. "Is this a sign?" I asked in an exasperated gasp.

"A sign that we're not supposed to make out in an elevator?"

I thought how another form of transportation caused an interruption to our encounter. My mind whirled. Would I smell fire soon? Would we need to be rescued again?

He rubbed his hand along my shoulder, attempting to calm me. "Relax. It may just be a small hiccup and start right up any second now. Any second now..." He spoke to the door as if he knew the magic words to make it start.

"We're cursed."

He laughed. "We're not cursed. Just somewhat unlucky with electronic transportation is all."

Electric, fuel, battery powered...

Screech. Jolt. The elevator moved upward toward the seventh floor as if nothing had gone awry. The doors opened with a sounding "bing." We looked at each other, smiling in relief to be stepping onto solid ground.

"Okay, that was weird. My apartment is this way." I pointed to the left. He followed close behind me as I found my key and led him inside.

Furry greeted us and rubbed her body against Kirk's leg. "She likes me."

I placed my purse on the kitchen counter and flicked on the lights. Kirk stood across from the kitchen in front of my small round dining room table, glancing around my apartment. "Don't take this the wrong way, but I pegged you as having a messy apartment, and this place is immaculate."

"Thank you and I agree. I keep my apartment and office surprisingly tidy. Must be nature's balance—so when I lose my keys, my phone, my brush, important documents, I'm not wasting the whole day searching through piles of clutter. Can't be a total disaster, right?"

"Nothing's a total disaster." He glanced down at my table at the only clutter in the 800 square foot space. "Hey, what are you working on?"

"Oh, that's just work stuff. I was drafting some deposition questions for the plaintiff in the sex case I told you about, based on my review of the documents."

"Oh, find anything interesting in the documents?" Kirk asked, starring down at the table.

"Nothing earth shattering. I'm predicting they had a fling and now he or both of them regret it. Just a hunch."

"Interesting. What makes you think they had a fling?"

"No real proof yet, just a gut feeling. The guy's running for public office soon. They're both married. Probably an affair that got out of hand. I'm totally violating attorney client privilege here. I better clean this up." I stepped between Kirk and the table and stuck the documents and my notes back in my briefcase. "Probably nothing here that won't end up in public record eventually."

"So, maybe one of them is hoping the other gives up first?"

"Something like that, I'm sure. You're not an aspiring politician are you?" I asked, moving closer to him, placing my hands on the sides of his waist.

"No, ma'am. Never. They're all snakes. All of them. Watch your defendant, probably a snake."

"I don't know. He seems like a nice guy."

"They all seem nice."

He held onto my waist and leaned down to meet my lips, ending our discussion. I kissed him back with a matched fervor, edging closer to him. When standing and kissing became awkward, we moved with urgency toward the couch. He led me to sit. We kissed.

He pulled his head back, "Are you okay?"

Breathless and surprised, I answered, "Yeah, why? You're not?"

He paused, sighed, and turned his head to the side. He looked back at me and kissed my cheek. "Maybe we should cool things off a little here before I'm unable to stop."

"Stop?"

"I'm sorry, I want to…I really want to. It's just I'm not sure this is a good time. We shouldn't rush this."

"Oh, yeah, I agree. I'm sure it's a little weird for you."

Resting his arm on the back of the couch behind me, he smiled, and said, "I enjoyed kissing you. A lot."

"I didn't mind it either." I smiled back at him.

I heard his phone vibrate on the dining room table. He ignored it and leaned back in and stole a kiss. "Thanks for understanding. I shouldn't have invited myself up here if I didn't intend—"

"Stop. I'm fine. Really, I'm not quite ready yet either." I lied. I was.

"Okay, well I should get out of here before I go back on what I said. And, while Furry still approves of me." He stood and smoothed his pants with his hands and straightened a couch pillow.

"I'll call you a cab." I picked up my cell phone and hit the pre-programmed number to the cab company. As I rattled off my address into my phone, I noticed Kirk reading, but not replying to the text that had arrived a few minutes before.

At the elevator, I hit the down button for him. We boarded the car and were seamlessly delivered to the ground floor.

In front of the lobby's glass doors, he brushed his

hand along my arm, looking down with shyness. "I want to take you somewhere other than our usual hangout next time. I'll pick a nice restaurant."

"Sounds great. I'll look forward to it."

He placed his index finger under my chin and effortlessly seized my breath with a simple goodnight kiss.

Alone, I walked back to the elevator and hit the up button. Like a crazy person, I mumbled to the elevator door, "What were you trying to tell me, little elevator car? Were you sending me a message earlier?"

"Bing," it answered with an opening door.

"I'll take that as a 'yes', my elevator friend." I grinned, feeling suddenly giddy. Oh, to have that crystal ball.

As the doors shut, I shook my head, still smiling. This mysterious ride was entertaining in a way I had never experienced and couldn't quite describe. For now, disembarking was not an option. I wondered, with the same giddiness, what restaurant Kirk would select for our next date?

Chapter 17

Nicole had planned an outfit she knew would keep Kirk's eyes on her during his nephew's party. Her plan was to get him to drink a few beers and regret his decision to have her move out. In a clever last minute decision, she left her car door slightly ajar, which she knew would drain his battery. His battery had been dying a lot, so she simply helped it along. Once the battery was deemed dead, her plan included suggesting they spend the night at his brother's house on the water, maybe a ride on his brother's boat, and then they'd sleep together in the guest room. But, it didn't quite happen that way.

Kirk had seemed distracted at the party. He barely made eye contact with her and never even glanced at her cleavage or her legs, unlike his brother. Then Kirk flipped out when he discovered the battery had died. It couldn't be jump-started, he needed a new one. He had insisted they call AAA and take care of it immediately instead of staying over, like his brother suggested so she helped herself to more wine to make the additional time with his whole family tolerable.

When the car was finally fixed, they drove home. The silence was unbearable. She felt the burn of his hate next to her.

"Kirk, have you changed your mind on me moving out yet?"

"Have you changed your mind on going to counseling and working on our marriage?"

"Kirk, I'm not ready to do that yet. Can't you be patient with me?"

"I've lost all patience with you, Nicole."

She released a few tears, but he didn't budge. So, she tried another route. "I'll sleep in our bed. I won't sleep in the guest room anymore."

"You just don't get it, do you?" He hit the steering wheel, shaking his head. His lips were pressed together and she noticed his biceps bulge beneath his short-sleeved shirt as he gripped the steering wheel. The tendons on the tops of his tanned forearms flexed.

She touched his arm in an attempt to calm him. She moved her hand to his thigh and said, "Calm down, you're going to wreck the car."

He tossed her hand from his leg and snapped. "You need to move your stuff out when we get home."

"Whatever, Kirk. Way to keep our marriage vows intact." She squeezed out a few more tears.

At their condo, Kirk told her he was going for a long walk and she'd better be gone when he got back. So, she packed up a few suitcases and headed to her cousin's, but not before leaving a lacey red bra hanging in the bathroom. She left a few wedding pictures in the top drawer of his dresser, too.

She dumped her suitcases in her cousin Gina's guest room. Gina was out on a date, but had left a note for Nicole to make herself at home. She felt anxious and seriously lonely. After pouring herself a glass of wine, she sent Jack a text: Do you want to meet tonight?

It was an agonizing fifteen minute wait, but he

responded: Meet at the George- 10:00.

She regretted leaving her best bra with Kirk, but put on the black push-up that Jack loved. She slipped on her tight black short dress that she used to wear to the office hidden under a suit jacket. Jack would love to close his office door and peel off the jacket. They'd tease each other with inappropriate touches, and then she would slink back to her desk.

This meeting might be detrimental to the lawsuit, but she was in desperate need of Jack's touch.

Since she had been drinking wine all day, she called a cab. Kirk used to believe her stories that she was meeting a friend in need when she'd sneak away to meet Jack. Usually their encounters would happen when Kirk was out of town.

When she jumped into the dirty cab, she thought back to the times Jack had sent a black town car to pick her up. She would relax inside the luxury and pretend she was wealthy, fantasizing he was already Senator and she was his girlfriend. Ignoring the unpleasant cab odors, she closed her eyes and let her mind go back to that comfortable fantasy, washing away the ugliness of a lawsuit, of being forced out of her apartment by Kirk, and being shunned by Jack. Her eyes shot open with a tiny burst of anxiety of not knowing where Kirk was tonight. She sent him a text but got no response. She hoped he was at a bar with his friends, drinking his face off because she had moved out, and hoped he wasn't out with the skanky paralegal.

An excitement welled inside of her when the cab glided to a stop in front of the hotel. She paid and hurried inside, passing through the contemporary marble foyer to the back bar. She was early. A small table with high backed leather chairs was open, one of their usual tables. She ordered a drink, but let it sit on the tiny round table between the chairs. She wouldn't be able to touch him easily, but she was sure he'd feel nostalgic and remember the times they'd sat across from each other. The heat between them would become unbearable and then he'd gaze around the room and say, "Upstairs?"

Jack had a lifelong friend who was one of the general managers of The George. This friend had received some nice legal favors from Jack, so in turn this friend would have a room prepared for him that they'd use for an hour, something unheard of in this swanky hotel. Due to the hotel's close proximity to Capitol Hill, and its long list of congressional patrons, she'd wondered if it was really that unheard of.

Jack knew what to say to the bartender and a key to their usual room on the sixth floor would appear tucked under the bar bill. He'd slip it to her. She'd stand up and shake Jack's hand and pretend to leave the lounge, in case anyone was watching. She'd head to the sixth floor and wait for Jack.

After a long day of acting professional at the office, sharing a drink at a table where she could only touch him with a handshake, and riding alone in an elevator in anticipation of making love to him, she'd nearly combust. He would too. The rewards on the other side of the hotel door were so intoxicating, she became like a cocaine addict needing her next line, a gambler needing her bookie. It was all she thought about and sometimes felt like she couldn't inhale a complete breath until she saw him again.

"Nicole," Jack's voice jolted her from the walk

down memory lane. The reality of their current situation hit her with the smack of his icy stare.

"Jack, hi, sit down," she instructed with a quiver in her voice. "I ordered you a gin and tonic."

"So, what prompted this little meeting, Nicole?" He lingered on her name.

She picked up her drink, averting eye contact. "Do you remember our little meetings here, Jack? How we would disappear upstairs?" She sipped slowly, teasing him with a deliberate crossing of her legs.

The waitress placed a drink in front of him on the low tiny table and he thanked her. He stared at Nicole while taking a long sip. He removed his phone from his pocket to check a text, and said, "Of course I do, Nicole." His voice softened. He placed the phone and his drink on the table and continued, "And I also recall you completely enjoying it, unlike what you're claiming in your little lawsuit, my dear." With breathy words, he leaned toward her resting his elbows on his knees. His eyes pierced into hers.

She took in a long breath, enjoying the pleasure his words sent through her body. If he wouldn't agree tonight to quench their escalating heat, then she surely would combust. She had to reel it in.

She readjusted herself in the seat, and spoke, "Okay, so I had to lie a bit to get my point across and squeeze this into the legal parameters of a sexual harassment claim. The point is, you made me switch jobs and demoted me—over sex. So I blurred some legal lines, I'm still entitled to sue you. You hurt me."

"Yes, I suppose in your warped mind you are, but in the real world you are actually breaking the law." He leaned closer and she could smell his cologne. His eyes canvassed the room to make sure no one was watching. He touched her leg with the tips of his fingers as his eyes followed them. "But Nicole, before we had to separate, did I ever do anything to you that you did not enjoy?"

The fire inside her cooled temporarily by the goose bumps growing on her leg under his touch. "No, you know I loved you, Jack."

"I know, Nicole, I know you fell in love with me. But we had to stay professional so I had to move you, do you understand that, Nic?" He stroked her knee with the back of his hand, and flashed a softened look, like the plea of a puppy asking to play.

"Yes, but it hurt. It hurt so much. You gave me no choice. I needed to get back at you in some way and I needed to show you how deeply it hurt and how much I love you. I still love you, Jack and I will do anything to get you back in my life." She stopped the pathetic rant. He could always bring out her weak side. She stuffed it back inside, deep inside.

He picked up his phone and checked it and said, "Nic, I need to make a call to my wife and let her know I'll be later than I thought. Hold on here a minute." He winked and raised his finger like he was telling his dog to "stay."

She smiled to let him know she'd wait. With her eyes attached to the back of him, he walked toward the bar to make his call. The only woman she'd ever envied in her thirty-two years of life was Mrs. Jack Winston. She was certainly not more attractive, but Nicole considered her a rival. Dara, like her husband, was well-connected in the District of Columbia. Doctor Dara Kennedy-Winston loved to name-drop at the office holiday parties. Her sorority sister bond with the First Lady was her favorite brag, and she was not related to the famous Kennedy family, she just let people believe she was. Dara perfected ways to slip into every conversation how she had "just been at the White House." She relished the role of supportive wife, but every move she orchestrated was more about the picture she painted of herself, and had nothing to do with Jack.

Nicole had been the one who was there for him during the stressful times during his day, and whenever else he needed her. Every October, Jack ran the D.C. Marine Corp Marathon. Nicole would stand at mile sixteen and cheer for him, giving him a needed boost at a crucial juncture for him. His wife would wait at the finish line, dressed in Dolce Gabbana, sipping a mimosa on a blanket.

Jack returned from his phone call, and with his usual glance around the room, said, "Do you want to get out of here, my dear, and talk somewhere privately?"

She wanted to scream and jump into his arms with a resounding "yes," but played it cool. "Maybe, but can we finish our drinks here first? Does your wife expect you home soon?"

He sat down and picked up his drink. "No, I told her I was having a drink with one of the partners, so she's fine."

"Good."

He spun the ice around his drink and finished it with one gulp. "You look good tonight, Nic." He set the glass on the table and leaned back, crossing his legs in an authoritative fashion. From his oxford to his loafers, he never slacked on any detail. His eyes perused the room as if memorizing all the faces in the lounge. She wished she could captivate him enough to hold his gaze. She was never able to achieve that with him, but she hadn't given up.

"Thank you. You always did like this dress." She brushed her hand along her leg, enjoying how his eyes followed.

Still not making eye contact with her, he smiled and said, "You'd always cover it up with a jacket, though. Used to drive me nuts."

The waitress placed a second round of drinks between them.

He looked at her and said, "I ordered us more drinks. I was hoping we would take them upstairs with us."

Her insides burned with arousal, causing a hum inside her ears. She played along. He liked to be teased. "Let's drink here. We have some catching up to do."

"Okay, but that means less time upstairs." He smiled, glancing to the side.

She ignored him. "So, how are your daughters?"

"Good. Jenny finished up her second year at Emory and is spending the summer with her sorority sisters at the beach. Megan is touring Europe before she heads back home."

"And your wife? How is she?"

"Huh, like you care, but she's fine."

"Still doing her little charity work?"

"Yes, she's on the medical advisory board of a 'little charity' and she's still teaching at Georgetown." He smoothed out his pants with both hands as he uncrossed his legs. "And she's into her painting and vacationing with her friends and has little time for me these days."

"Still hanging with the First Lady?"

"Yes, that too." He smirked.

"Feeling neglected, Jack?" She took another slow drink, cradling her glass with two hands. She used every gesture to flirt.

"Perhaps. I've got a lot to keep me busy, though." He leaned forward resting his elbows on his knees. "So, Nic, when are you going to take care of old neglected Jack? This small talk thing is getting mighty dull."

"Aren't you going to ask about me, Jack?"

He huffed, smiled, and leaned back in his seat, bringing his glass with him. "Okay, I see we're playing a little game here, as usual. How's your husband, Nic? Kirk the salesman? Are you still living in that cramped apartment in Rockville or has he bought you the big house you deserve." He smiled at the contents of his glass. He knew exactly what would push her buttons.

"Our condo is in North Bethesda. He's fine but he kicked me out because I won't go to marriage counseling. I'm living with my cousin, Gina, starting tonight. But, I'm sure he'll take me back soon. Men can't stay away from me. Perhaps a nice little lawsuit settlement will help me with a down payment on a house I deserve. What do you say, Jack?"

He laughed. "Well, if it's a settlement you want, maybe you should have your lawyers talk to mine."

"I just don't want some measly settlement. I want a nice settlement."

"Well, my attorneys seem to think we have this thing in the bag. So I'm sure a small settlement is all you'll get your greedy little hands on at this point."

"It's just, the better the settlement, the quieter I

stay on our little visits here. That's all I'm saying, Jack." She smiled into her drink. "So, these attorneys of yours, are they any good?"

"The best, the best in employment law, Nicole. You shouldn't be surprised I hired the best."

"Just heard a rumor that the firm you hired got into trouble in the past with violating attorney client privilege and some staff got fired and things got ugly for a client. Just make sure the whole staff is on the up and up, is all I'm saying. But I'm sure they're completely professional, just like you like things to be, Mr. Winston." She licked her lips and uncrossed her legs.

"Upstairs?" he asked, slamming his drink down on the table.

She stood, her cleavage at his eye level, and extended her hand. He shook it. "It was nice meeting you tonight, Mr. Winston."

"Always a pleasure, Ms. D'Angelo." He stood and winked.

She turned and sauntered to the elevator, walking slowly so he could enjoy a good look at her backside. Once the elevator door closed, she exhaled with force. She'd played with fire before, but the flames had never been quite this intense. The possible repercussions of this meeting didn't bother her. All she focused on was reconnecting with Jack and reminding him of what he had thrown away. Her plan was working.

God, thank you for bringing him back to me. This is not infidelity. I love him and he loves me.

She exited the elevator and panicked, remembering he didn't slide her the key, like usual. She paced in front of the doors. With him out of her sight, she felt a sudden pang of doubt. What if he didn't join her?

Bing.

She turned, forgetting her flirty confidence, her eyes glared at the opening doors. A couple emerged, nicely dressed, giggling, drunk, in love. The sight of them, arms entwined, with a mutual destination of a shared room—for the whole night and not just one hour—made her queasy with jealousy. She pictured Jack with his wife. She pictured Kirk finding a new love. She checked her phone to see if Kirk had called or texted. He had not.

She paced some more, twisting her hair around her finger, feeling foolish. What if he left her in the hotel to humiliate her? Maybe his lawyers did assure him a win, leaving her with nothing.

Bing.

She stopped, placing her hand on the wall for support, she didn't turn around to watch the elevator open. She froze and listened to the footsteps coming toward her. They stopped behind her. She could smell him. Then she felt his body behind her. He touched her right arm and spoke into her left ear. "Do you want to do this, Nic?"

She almost collapsed. "Of course I do, Jack."

"We got our usual room. Coast is clear."

They walked side by side to room 615 without a touch, never looking at each other. She turned and faced their room's door. He held his body behind hers and reached around, forcing the card key into the slot, slowly pulling it out. He took the card and brushed her hair off her left shoulder and kissed it. She was sure his eyes were checking the hallway, confirming he was still safe, before focusing on her.

"Who else have you brought here, Jack?" She reached back and caressed his cheek.

"Just you, my dear. Only you, Nic."

She grabbed the handle and opened the door. The door clicking closed behind them released the memories of previous visits here, the same way the smell of an evergreen can trigger intense recollections of Christmases past.

She leaned her back against the door when he faced her, inches away. His hands pressed against the door next to the sides of her head as if he was holding it shut to prevent her escape. She couldn't look into his eyes but whispered, "Did you miss me, Jack?"

"I have. You're a beautiful woman, Nic. I'd be stupid to stay away from this." His chin brushed along her forehead. "Just remember, Nic, you ended it, not me." His lips pressed into her neck. His hands moved up over her hips, along her sides, and rested between her shoulder blades and the door. His belt buckle hurt as it sank into her belly.

Abruptly, she stopped running her fingers through his hair. "You ended it when you slept with Rebecca. I loved you, Jack." Her hands moved urgently to touch him again.

This time, he was the one who stopped. He looked into her eyes, breathing hard. "I had a meaningless fling with Rebecca. You flipped out and gave me no choice but to reassign you. You ended us. You threatened to ruin my aspirations to be Senator. I had no choice."

"*I* had no choice."

He released her, allowing her body to fall back against the door. He placed one hand on his hip and used his free hand to comb through his hair, and then returned it to his other hip. "I'll admit that it made me even more attracted to you when you filed the suit. Didn't think you had it in you to fight. It was ballsy, Nic. You're hot, in more ways than one, my dear." He grabbed her waist and raked his eyes along her body, stopping at her lips. "Drop the suit and let's resume this…"

"I don't trust you, yet." She placed her hands on his chest as if she would push him away.

The force of his kiss slammed her head into the door, her hands falling to her side like windsocks after a diminished breeze. His whole body surged against hers. Her spine, she was sure, left an indentation in the door. She ignored the pain of his full weight, and got lost in his all-consuming kiss. No man's kiss had ever had the kind of power over her as his did, arousing every nerve in her entire body. She lifted her knee to the side and slid it up to his hip, losing a shoe. He lifted her so that no part of her touched the ground. His strength sustained her.

Both of her feet back on the ground, he kissed her neck. "What don't you trust about me, Nic?" His hands never stopped exploring.

"I think this is a ploy to get everything you want." She drove her hips against him to release some of his weight from her.

"It is. I want you back. I want your loyalty. I want to be Senator." He thrust his pelvis back into her, shoving her back into the door.

"When I'm working at my old desk and you're sleeping with me, then all my loyalty will be yours again," she hissed.

His eyes penetrated hers as he yanked her away

from the door. He tugged the zipper down along her back, over the top of her hose, and downward. He kept his eyes locked on hers as he peeled the shoulders of her dress down along her forearms, over her hips. In one move, he unfastened her bra and tossed it to the side, delivering an intense pleasure that she hadn't felt in months.

She pushed him away and jerked his shirt out of his pants. He watched her unbutton his shirt and toss it to the floor.

His hands behind her, his thumbs slipped into the tops of her hose. He tried in vain to yank them down. She pinned herself against the door, stopping his attempt. Giving up, he moved his hands to his own pants, undoing them himself while his mouth overpowered hers. She wanted him to carry her to the bed and make love, but he continued to undress her without her help.

His hand slid in between her legs and she clamped them closed. He begged, panting, "Come on, Nic, you're driving me insane."

There was nothing she wanted more, than to let him in. But in those few moments, she held the power. She relished his desperate fight.

He pulled her to the floor. She surrendered to him, wanting him to take control. She tasted his chest's perspiration as it covered her face until he slid down pressing their chests together. He took a moment to look into her eyes and kissed her with a tender patience. She felt his love in those kisses. Every moment connected to him propelled her into a state of elation. Like a runner crossing a finish line, it was also coated in triumphant relief.

Afterward, she wished they could snuggle under the crisp white sheets on the bed a few feet away. Instead, she stood with the same amount of dignity as a prostitute at the end of a job, and gathered her clothes. She wanted a shower and a fluffy hotel robe, but instead she covered up with her wrinkled dress. Jack pulled up her zipper over her brush-burned back. He took her head in his hands and kissed her sweetly.

"That was amazing, my dear. Gonna consider dropping the frivolous suit now? Huh, then we can do this more often?"

She kissed him and brushed her hands across his cheeks and ears. "I'll think about it, Jack. Thanks for screwing me on the floor." She kissed him again, delivering a smirk. He had no response.

She escaped into the elevator. The doors shut. She covered her face, wanting to cry, but composed herself in order to maintain some dignity for her walk through the lobby. She stood on the sidewalk, feeling dirty.

A bellhop approached her. "Ma'am, are you Anna Lewis?"

She was about to say, "No," but remembered that was one of Jack's code names. "Yes, I'm Anna."

"My manager said there's a town car on the way for you to take you home. Just wait here."

She smiled. Jack loved her, she knew it. Would she drop the suit? Hell no. Her plan was working.

Her feeling of filth disappeared as she relaxed against town car's leather seat. She chuckled at the sight of the mighty white rotunda of the Capitol building contrasted against the black sky. Would Senator Winston and his secretary be happy there one day? Whisking past the other majestic monuments aglow, she sat upright basking in the feeling of power all around her. This was the nation's capital and she just had sex with a man who had the ability to be president of it.

Reeling in confidence, she sent Kirk a text: Miss me yet?

Chapter 18

"That's right. It's D'Angelo v. Winston, et al.," I said into the phone to the court reporting company, "Great, see you at the deposition." I hung up the phone, grabbing my hair, pulling it over my right shoulder. I turned my attention to Justin who stood smiling, leaning against my doorframe.

"So, all set for our big deposition?" Justin asked, moving to sit in my guest chair. He placed a document on my desk.

"From my end, anyway, how about you?"

"Yeah, looks good. Can't wait to get her in here."

"It's gonna be interesting, that's for sure. Bet she's quite a character."

"Aren't they all? Are you gonna sit in on it?" Resting his calf on top of his opposite knee, he sank into the seat.

"No, I usually don't. I will have to peek in and get a good look at her, though."

"Yeah, Jon said she's hot."

"I'm sure she is." I smirked, rolling my eyes.

"So, can you do a quick cite-check of this pleading here that needs filed tomorrow?" he asked, pointing to the paper he had laid on my desk.

"Sure."

"And, would you like to grab lunch with me later?" he asked with a grin.

"Okay," I answered, with a suspicious tone and a smile.

"Just as a thank you. You've been working hard and I want to treat you to a sandwich outside of the office. You've been eating at your desk far too much lately."

"Thanks," I said, drawing out the word with the same hint of suspicion.

"And, I want you to go to New York with me in a few weeks…"

"Excuse me?"

"I know, you're gonna hate me for this. It's for the Boeing case. Document review. Boring shit, but I need to take a paralegal and I was hoping you'd say yes?" He smiled with pleading eyes.

"Okay, but you better take me somewhere nice for dinner."

"Um, two dinners, we'll be there for two nights. They said they'll probably have a meeting room full of boxes for us."

"When?"

"I'll let you know. Our co-counsel in New York is getting back to me. Just wanted to make sure I had a document-review partner." Justin walked back to the doorway.

"Okay, but no drinking on this trip. That gets the two of us in trouble." I blushed, and noticed Justin's face had flushed as well.

He laughed nervously, and turned to leave. "See you at noon for our lunch date, Jezebel." He tapped his Georgetown class ring against the metal doorframe as he made his exit.

I cringed at the word "date," but told myself to not

read into it. Hearing the word did make me think of upcoming dinner with Kirk. He'd been traveling a lot, but we were finally able to make plans for this Friday. As promised, he would take me somewhere nice.

With time to spare before my paralegal meeting, I decided to pay a quick visit to Ken, since I had arrived late this morning and missed my usual morning coffee with him. He motioned me in as he typed away, and I instantly shared a piece of law firm gossip I had just gathered.

He stopped me from moving onto another story with a wave of his hand. "Enough about our coworker freaks. I have important info."

"By the way, nice shirt."

Ken brushed his hand down his chest. "You like? This color of gray would look good with your eyes, by the way. No changing topics, we need to discuss Metro Man." His index fingers pointed to the ceiling and danced, indicating an incoming song. "Metro, Metro man, yeah, I want to be a Metrooo man…" Everything could be transformed into a song lyric, according to Ken.

I attempted to ignore his Village People imitation and launched into my tale. "Metro Man is fine. We have plans Friday. He just texted me, actually, that we have reservations at Morton's in Bethesda. Maybe I can talk him into meeting me on our roof top for the fireworks on Sunday." I tilted my head and smiled at Ken, bracing for a jibe.

"Nice. Well, listen to this. I got a call from this woman named Natalya, she's a billing manager at Jones Day. She had a question about a client's bill. We got to talking. She had mentioned, in passing, a firm called

Kemp & Thatcher—the firm Metro Man told you his ex worked for. That firm did exist, but was absorbed by Jones Day a few years back. So, maybe your stalker-boyfriend's ex used to work for them. But why lie about it?"

"Do you think she works for Jones Day now?"

"Detective Kenny asked her if there was a Nicole Flynn working at Jones. She checked the directory, but there was no one there by that name."

"Well, either way, it was still a lie. I just need to get past it."

"I don't think you should just 'get past' a lie, Jez. I've got a bad feeling about this, my love."

"He's just going through a separation and talking about his wife is not something he's comfortable doing in front of me. That's all."

"Okay, but if you end up in a missing person's report, I'm telling the cops to go after Flynn!"

"Probably more likely that Mrs. Flynn will be disposing of my body. Hey, so Justin asked me to have lunch with him today."

"Ooooh, nice! I knew he was into you again. I called it." Ken slammed his hand on a stack of paper. "Ping ping, my love radar just went off."

"Stop it." I stood and flashed Ken my palm. "I'm done with you and your radars, Kenneth!"

"Ah, huh, whatever. My radar tells me Justin's a much better catch than liar-liar-pants-on-fire Metro Man. See, this little Crosby case brought you back to working nicely with each other. I bet next he'll be taking you on a business trip or something smooth like that," Ken said, focusing on his computer screen.

My breath caught in my throat, halting my ability

to make a quick comeback. His fortune telling was getting annoying. "Whatever. See you later, Kenneth."

"Bye, my love."

I hurried from Ken's office. I had been thrilled in recent weeks that Justin and I had regained a civil working relationship. The thought of having to reject him again, made my stomach "ping ping" with nausea. Justin wouldn't try again, would he?

After a trip to the firm's library, I stepped inside my office, my mind revisiting Ken's pinging. The sight of Justin sitting behind my desk startled me.

"Shut your door and have a seat, Jez," he demanded with a grin.

"You scared me," I scolded, pressing my hand into my chest. I shut the door and sat in my guest chair.

"Sorry." Justin sat up and leaned his elbows on my desk, speaking in a hushed voice, "just big happenings in the Winston case."

"What?" I smiled and sat forward. He had my full attention.

"Well, Green had a hush-hush meeting with Winston early this morning and just filled me in briefly on the details. He wants me to do some legal research to figure out how we'll proceed. So, apparently Winston met with D'Angelo recently at a hotel. Needless to say, Green isn't thrilled and Winston isn't forthcoming with exactly why this meeting took place. But, he claims during their little meeting, he recorded her talking on his iPhone and she admitted she basically lied and forced her case into a sexual harassment suit and really it was because she was in love with him. She wants him back and will do anything to get him back."

"What? That's crazy! So, okay, then the case is

over. Can we get the judge to throw it out now?"

"Well, the tape is admissible, since in D.C. only single party consent is needed. Here's where things get tricky, Winston isn't willing to do anything yet or let her know about the tape. He doesn't want the other side to know yet, he wants to see what we can get her to say in the deposition. Of course she won't admit to anything, but we can at least allude to the fact we know they had a meeting at her request. This will hopefully trip her up. He's not ready to enter the tape into evidence. Maybe if the deposition goes poorly, she'll be more willing to settle, for a small amount. Personally, I think Winston isn't willing to use this and go to a judge right now or use this in any way in the depo, tells me there's more to the story. He just wanted to talk to Green. He wants us to ask about meeting with Winston and what her goals were. See if she breaks."

"Interesting. Very interesting."

"Yeah. I think Winston knows that once D'Angelo discovers his betrayal, she's gonna snap. He just wants to play his cards right."

"Oh my. Things are going to get ugly."

"Do you want to have a listen?"

"Of course, I'll transcribe it, if you didn't already?"

"That would be great. I'll send it to you. But here, listen." Justin played the recording on his phone. He sat in the guest chair and I took my seat, preparing to type the words. I felt edgy as if I were actually eavesdropping on a private conversation at that moment, feeling embarrassed for the female speaking. I couldn't make out D'Angelo's first few mumbles.

After a scraping sound and a tap, I heard Winston's booming voice clearly. "Of course I do, Nicole." A loud clinking sound stunned me. Perhaps he had placed the phone down on a glass table. "And I also recall you completely enjoying it, unlike what you're claiming in your little lawsuit, my dear." Justin fiddled with my pen holder, eyes wide with curiosity.

A soft feminine voice spoke, "Okay, so I have to lie a bit to get my point across and squeeze this into the legal parameters of a sexual harassment claim. The point is, you made me switch jobs and demoted me—over sex. So I blurred some legal lines, I'm still entitled to sue you. You hurt me."

I glanced at Justin as we listened intently to more back forth banter, my fingers flying across the keyboard. I realized I was smiling, as if enjoying a soap opera. My gut told me this was an affair that went terribly wrong. Do any go well? I wondered.

"I loved working for you, Jack, why—"

I typed Winston's response, anxious for the next comment.

"Yes, but it hurt. It hurt so much. You gave me no choice. I needed to get back at you in some way and I needed to show you how deeply it hurt and how much I love you. I still love you, Jack and I will do anything to get you back in my life." A few more rustling sounds followed and the recording ended. How did people find themselves in such messed up situations? I thought, shaking my head.

"Wow," said Justin, grinning.

"Yeah. Wow."

"Hey, I have to jump on a conference call. Come down when you're ready to go to lunch and we'll discuss this mess." Justin stood and moved toward the door. "Oh the things that happen when love goes awry."

He snickered and tapped his class ring twice on the door frame as he exited, joyful as if he were the one who had discovered the smoking gun.

I finished working on Justin's pleading, and took it, along with a copy of the transcript, to his office. He was laughing into his phone, but motioned for me to come in and wait. I slipped into his guest chair, noticing the plant on his desk was in desperate need of attention. As I poured the remains of my bottle of water into the dirt, Justin smiled at me.

"Okay, sir, thank you very much. I'll talk to you soon." He hung up, without taking his eyes off me and grinned. "So, that was an interesting recording, huh?"

"Interesting, yes." I handed him the pleading along with a transcript of the recording. He moved from behind his desk and sat in the empty guest chair next to me.

"Huh, yeah, he completely set her up."

"Yeah, she had no clue he was recording her."

"Well, this can sink her case, slam dunk. But it could implicate him, meeting in a hotel sounds affair-ish to me. What woman tells her boss she's in love with him and would do anything if she wasn't getting something from him?"

"A crazy woman?"

"Well, we definitely have a little of that." He asserted, smacking the paper lightly with the back of his hand.

"Do you think they slept together?"

"Ah, yes. Maybe just once, or maybe they just made out after an office party and they both regretted it after." He blushed again and stood from his chair.

"Yeah, I'm sure it was something appalling like

that. Unfortunately, one of them in this case fell in love with the other."

"Yeah...this is definitely more appalling," Justin commented, sighing.

"But why doesn't he just sink her? He could survive the senator thing and save his marriage with the explanation of crazy stalker, right?"

"Well, maybe there are unresolved feelings on both their parts. Both want to hang on to each other, but they just don't know how to do that—the sane normal way, anyway. So, ready to go grab a sandwich?"

"Yes, I'm starving. We are spending way too much time discussing these people as if they have any effect on our real lives."

"Yep, let's leave work here and escape for a bit."

We walked through the hot blast of summertime into the cool air conditioning of a nearby deli, ordered sandwiches and carried our trays to a table for two.

"So what are your Fourth of July plans? Seeing that guy you're dating at all?"

"Yes, we're having dinner Friday night. I'm going to see if he wants to watch fireworks on our rooftop on Sunday. How about you? Are you dating anyone?"

"Um, well, I was seeing this girl but things fizzled out. So, no, not currently. I am meeting two buddies down on the Mall, hanging out all day in front of the Lincoln Memorial and watching the fireworks. Of course, I'll probably have to hit the office over the weekend, too."

"So, let me know how Green decides to handle the questions about the recording."

"Maybe something like 'So, D'Angelo, did you bang Winston at the George Hotel a few weeks ago?'

That should frazzle her a bit."

I laughed and wiped my mouth with a napkin. "I would love to hear Green use the word 'bang'. Wonder if D'Angelo will cry? Oh, this is going to be entertaining…"

"Sad, isn't it? Us making a mockery of another person's pathetic life."

"She chose the life and she pulled us into her life, as far as I see it. We're just enjoying our jobs."

"But we said we'd leave the job behind and enjoy our escape. So, this guy you're dating, things serious yet?" Justin asked, leaning forward.

"Ah, no, he's in the middle of a divorce so we are taking things slow."

"Good. I mean, that's smart. Don't want to jump into anything too quickly with a semi-married guy. May I suggest that you keep playing the field?"

"Oh, we'll see. It's not like I'm getting any other offers or anything." I began to feel uncomfortable so I changed the topic. "So, any word yet when we leave for New York?"

"Yes, Monday after the deposition. That work?"

"Sure, as long as I'm back for the big wedding. My mom is getting married at the end of the month."

"Oh that's right. So are you taking this guy to the wedding?"

I covered my mouth with my napkin, not sure why embarrassment was flooding me. "Um, I'm not really sure… I haven't exactly asked him yet." Searching my mind for another topic change, my nervous mouth spewed, "I don't even have a dress yet. I need to do that soon, before our trip, or maybe I can find a dress in New York? No, that would be cutting it close and you'll probably keep me holed up in the conference room the whole time." My spilling words attempted to drown out the awkwardness and delay another Justin comment on my dating life.

"I might be able to schedule us some fun time. I'll shop with you. I have three sisters so I'm used to sitting outside department store dressing rooms."

"Oh…okay, well we'll see if I come up with a dress before then. Thanks, Justin."

****

Ken's face popped into my office, his body hidden behind the office wall. "So, how was your date-disguised-as-a-thank-you, Ms. Jezzie-bell?"

"Awkward. Good, but awkward. Ken, it's your fault with all your flipping pinging and radar crap. I kept thinking that he was hitting on me, and he wasn't, but you polluted my mind, you little demon you." I huffed, crossed my arms over my belly, and fell against the back of the chair.

"I'm so perceptive. And, my genius did not pollute, it simply enlightened you, my friend. Cheer up, sweets. Justin is a hottie."

"Train Guy is a hottie and I'm dating Train Guy, not Justin. So not Justin."

"Okay, okay, whatever you say. Don't go all Tyra Banks-crazy on me." Ken laughed.

Ken whisked away as swiftly as he had breezed in. Still staring at my doorway, I decided to send Kirk a text. I found my phone and wrote: Looking forward to tomorrow night.

A minute passed before he responded: Me too. I'm picking you up, so you can't be late! Ha ha.

I smiled, planning to relax and enjoy the upcoming

holiday weekend, refusing to feel bogged down by red flags and pinging radars. There was a strong wave of intuition running through me telling me this was meant to be, and I was traveling on a course toward eventual happiness.

I straightened the papers on my desk. As I labeled a new file folder "D'Angelo/Winston Hotel Meeting Transcript" and placed it on top of the pile of other deposition notes, I shook my head envisioning this couple's clandestine meeting. See, I thought, my life was calm and uneventful compared to some.

Chapter 19

Minutes before Kirk left to pick up Jezebel, his front door opened.

"Nicole, don't you think it would be nice if you knocked first, since you don't live here anymore?" he asked, sliding his arms into his dinner jacket.

Nicole slammed the door, making her over-styled hair bounce. "It's still my place and you never took my key. My, don't we look spiffy this evening? Big date?" she hissed, while moving close to him and fingering the lapel of his jacket.

"Yes, I do and I was getting ready to leave." He tried to maneuver around her but she stepped in front of him, pushing her hands against his chest.

"Oh, you smell good too, Kirk. So, who is she?"

"None of your business. Why are you here?"

Kirk braced himself, inhaling a jagged breath. She moved her hands down from his chest to his belly. He pushed them away.

"Hope it's not Olive Oyl, Kirk, or I'll go ballistic." She stalked through the kitchen, her heels clicking along the ceramic with her perfume trailing behind her. "I want my cappuccino maker." She opened a cabinet and pulled out the appliance.

"Okay, you got it, now please leave. I need to lock up." Holding the door open, he swept his hand toward the hallway.

"Wait. Don't you have a minute for your wife, Kirk? I'd like to talk to you. Your date can wait." She posed with her hand on her hip and placed her other hand firmly on the counter next to her cappuccino maker, as if staking her claim.

Her exhaustive powers sucked the life from him. He slammed the door. "What do you wish to discuss?" He put his hands in his pockets, trying to appear calm and collected.

"Us. I've been thinking that maybe you're right. Maybe after my deposition and the discovery phase of this lawsuit wraps up, maybe we should go to counseling together. I do miss you, Kirk." She slinked through the galley kitchen, and stopped a foot away.

"Are you playing a game right now because I have a date?"

"No, Kirk, I had every intention of coming here to tell you this. Look, I dressed up for you, not my girlfriends, or a date, but for you, Kirk."

He couldn't help but feel a twinge of elation. This is what he'd hoped for, but a tiny voice deep inside him, peeked out, and told him not to trust her. He ignored it.

"Okay, fine. When you reach a comfortable place in your life, where you can make time for me, then we will go to counseling."

"Great. What do you say you cancel your little date and we hang out tonight, here, just you and me, like old times?" she cocked her head.

His eyes glanced at her cleavage. He inhaled, pausing. "Nope."

She squinted her eyes. "So, Kirk, did you give any thought to what might happen if Olive Oyl sits in on my deposition? Or, if I should happen to run into her in the hallway of the firm? Something for you to think about on your little date tonight." She grinned and brushed his cheek with her hand.

He waited a few minutes to ensure the elevator had delivered her to the street level and then left his apartment. Nicole did make a good point that at any moment, this thing with Jezebel could end badly. A brief stab of pain hit his chest along with a wave of sadness. Maybe it would be fine. It didn't have to end. He could lie his way out of it, explain away the coincidence.

Alone in the elevator car, he smiled. He had started to win Nicole back with the threat of another woman. But did he really want her back or did he simply want to win a game? Well, for once, he was winning at something.

****

"Sorry, I'm a little late. I got a visitor as I was leaving." Kirk leaned against Jezebel's doorframe and flashed her his most charming grin.

"No problem. Payback for the times I've made you wait. Come in." She motioned for him to come in. He smelled the familiar scent of her perfume as she walked past her. "So, who was your visitor?"

"Nikky. She wanted her cappuccino machine."

"Oh…okay. Well, you look nice."

"So do you. You look pretty." He thought her dress looked perfect and he quickly forgot about Nicole and her visit. He bent over to pet Furry. "Are you ready to go?"

They boarded the elevator and Jezebel joked about them getting trapped again. He stood next to her and reached his arm behind her shoulders and spoke in her ear, "I think we are all done with mechanical failures. Smooth sailing from here on out."

"I like your confidence." The doors opened, and Jezebel smiled. "You have been right so far, anyway."

Dinner was uneventful and the conversation pleasant. He found himself thinking of Nicole occasionally and enjoyed the light feeling it brought. Hope, it was the feeling of hope.

Then he asked, "So, how's that sexual harassment case going? Did the slimy boss settle yet?"

Jezebel swallowed a mouthful of wine, and grinned. "Actually, things are heating up. Deposing the plaintiff at our office week after next."

A rush of panic hit him. "Oh, do you attend those?"

"No, I usually just read the transcript later."

Relief.

"So what questions will they ask her?"

"All the usual stuff, pretty much go through her complaint and pull the details from her. Question her on documents, typical stuff."

He could tell Jezebel, well into her second glass of wine, was relaxed as her words seemed to spill easily. He wasn't sure what he'd learn, but kept asking questions.

"Any smoking guns?"

"Yes, actually, but we can't use it yet. I should not be talking about this." She slammed her hand on the table, laughing.

"It's just me. I'm not going to tell anyone, Jezebel." He slid his hand across the table to grab her hand, delivering another charming grin. "My job is boring. Give me some juicy law firm tidbits. Come on."

He winked.

She finished another gulp of wine and leaned in, whispering, "Okay, I'll give you a little nugget and then we switch topics, okay?"

"Deal. Now dish."

"Okay, well, the defendant, you know, the partner being accused of the alleged misbehavior, met with our attorneys this morning." She fingered air quotes around the word alleged and became theatrical in her telling of the tale, as if it were happening to a fictional character and not a real person. "Apparently, the defendant met the plaintiff at a downtown hotel recently. Okay, there's your tidbit."

"What? You can't leave me hanging with just that." His face burned. What the hell was Nicole up to? He forced himself to stay calm.

"Did they try to work out a settlement?"

"No. Well, we all think they got a room and, you know, but that's just speculation."

His insides were anything but calm. "So why'd Winston tell his lawyers?"

"Winston? I told you his name? Oh great, I'm really going to get fired. He's just wanting to fluster her with info at the deposition."

His guess was that Nicole was trying to get money out of him and settle the suit. Perhaps she really did want their marriage to work and wanted the lawsuit to go away.

"Well, that certainly is interesting," Kirk commented, placing his napkin on the table.

"Okay, I'm all done sharing. Attorney Client Privilege is blown through the roof and I'm officially fired. More wine?" she asked him, raising her finger to the waiter.

"No, I'm driving, but you go right ahead."

"Maybe I should stop, too?"

"No, please, I'm enjoying this. Have another glass."

She ordered another merlot. Smiling, she asked, "So, any plans for Sunday?"

"Um, I'm stopping by my mom's for an afternoon picnic. You?"

"A picnic at my sister's in the afternoon. Well, not your traditional Fourth of July picnic. She's having us sample all the food that the caterer is preparing for my mom's wedding. Knowing Joe, he'll bring along a pack of hot dogs, just to fluster Cala. She wants my mom and Joe's opinion on where they want the ceremony. Well, she'll pretend to ask their opinion but then passively aggressively suggest where she wants it. And, she'll drone on and on about her garden, as if she tends to it herself."

"Sounds like you and your sister don't get along very well."

"I guess I was being a bit harsh. Must be the wine. Actually we do, I just know her well and know her flaws. Our personalities can clash, but we do love each other."

"So, any plans for Sunday evening?" he asked, attempting to bring her thoughts back to him.

"Actually, I was going to watch the fireworks from my office building's roof. Would you like to join me?" she asked shyly, cocking her head.

"Okay. Can I get a tour of your office?"

"Sure. Maybe we could metro together for old time's sake."

****

On their ride home, Kirk's mind was completely distracted by thoughts of Nicole. He tortured himself with imaginings of what happened at the hotel meeting. He chastised himself for slipping and using Winston's name with Jezebel.

As they approached Jezebel's apartment, he wondered where he would take this relationship with Jezebel. He guessed he'd play the gentleman card and tell her he didn't want to rush things.

As much as he looked forward to spending time with her on the fourth, he was even more eager to get a good look inside her office.

"That was a great dinner, Kirk, thanks so much."

"You're welcome. I enjoyed the company."

"Me too. Would you like to come upstairs for a bit?" she asked.

He rubbed his temple. "Actually, the wine gave me a bit of a headache. Mind if I take a rain check?" He reached across and placed his arm around her shoulder and smiled. He kissed her forehead, and then her lips, so she would know he wasn't giving her the shaft.

"I'm a little tired from the wine myself. Rain check issued. Meet you at the Grosvenor Metro on Sunday?"

"Sounds great." He leaned his face into hers and kissed her again. Their kissing continued longer than he'd planned and the intensity built more than he anticipated.

He didn't want to stop.

She pulled away first. "Wow, the headache had no impact on your kissing."

"Yeah, forgot about the headache for a minute or two." He kissed her one more time and released his arm from their embrace.

****

The next day, he sent Nicole a text asking her to meet for coffee. He had to ask her about the Winston meeting, and he needed to read her reactions.

She breezed into the Bethesda Starbucks wearing tight work out clothes that clung to her body in all the right places. The jacket's zipper was open to just below her breasts, revealing a white lacy tank top. He kept telling himself to not look at her inviting cleavage.

"So, Kirk, I was thrilled to get your text so early. I suppose that means your date didn't spend the night."

"Well, that's none of your business, Nic. How was your night?"

"Good. Stayed in with Gina and her boyfriend and watched a movie."

"After the movie? Any secret meetings with anyone, Nic?"

"What are you talking about?"

"No meetings at a hotel with Winston?"

"No. What are referring to?"

"I just happen to know that you met with Winston in a hotel recently."

She smoothed the sides of her head as if her ponytail was disheveled. She inhaled and pulled her body up and against the table, resting her breasts on top of her folded arms on top of the table. "Kirk, are you having me followed? That would be so like you to have me followed. My God." She leaned her forehead into her hand as if it were his behavior that was appalling.

"No, I wouldn't waste someone's time or my money on having you followed. I just have a source."

"Okay, enough of your little game. How do you

know I met Winston?"

"Let's just say, he told his lawyers about you requesting a meeting and your little bad decision is about to impact your lawsuit."

"For the love of God, Kirk, you did see Olive Oyl last night. I think I'm going to be sick. Have you no standards? Morals?"

"For the love of God, Nicole," he said, matching her tone, "have you?"

Had they been in their condo, their voices would have continued to increase in volume. But she took a deep breath and then spoke in a controlled tone and volume. "Look, Kirk, he contacted me and asked if I would meet him to talk. I was feeling rather lonely and dejected that night, thanks to you evicting me, so I agreed. I was hoping to discuss a settlement and put this nightmare behind me. I am tired of fighting and I'm tired of conflicts." She covered her face with her hands. Then came the tears.

He looked around the coffee shop and pleaded, "Nic, get a grip. I'm tired of you acting like the victim. It's his story that you contacted him."

"Did you sleep with Olive Oyl?"

"Did you sleep with Winston?"

"No."

"Same here. Did he agree to a settlement?"

"Not yet. But I'm getting closer. And damn you for not ending things with Olive Oyl."

"How about a 'thank you, Kirk, for giving me a heads-up on information'?"

She looked around dragging her pointer fingers under her eyes to insure her makeup hadn't left its assigned location. "Fine. Thank you, Kirk. Do they plan to use this in my deposition?"

"Yep. Way to go, Nicole."

"He's lying. He contacted me. I was set up."

"Well, now you know about it so you can plan how you'll handle it when they ask you about it."

"Do you have feelings for her or are you using her to help me, Kirk?"

He sighed, giving her half of a grin as he rested back in the small wooden chair. In a deliberate move, he watched his latte cup as he pulled it to his mouth. He swallowed, licked his lips and stared at her until she fidgeted in her chair. "I don't know, Nicole. But you are my wife. My loyalty rests with you."

A relieved smile crossed her face. "Glad to hear it. She's not all that pretty, Kirk, so I figured you were using her to help me. Thanks so much, babe."

"Anytime…babe." He finished his latte and stood. "Okay, Nicole, I'm done with you. Stay away from Winston and finish this case. Preferably with a big pile of money."

"That's my plan."

Chapter 20

Nicole needed to see Jack and do a little damage control. Tonight. Why had he told his lawyers about their meeting? She was certain he hadn't told them about screwing her on a hotel floor and sending her away in a town car he paid for.

Like a dog snatching a treat from her hand, he agreed to a meeting. He told her he'd pick her up a block from her cousin's on the corner—like she was a hooker—at ten o'clock.

In typical over-the-top Jack-style, he arrived late in a black limo. It glided along the curb and stopped in front of her. A door popped open. She slowly slipped inside.

"Nice wheels, Jack. Thanks for picking me up on the street corner."

"You look pretty, Nicole. New perfume?"

"Yes, my husband bought it for me for my birthday." She didn't look at him, but stared straight ahead at the glass partition separating them from the driver. She could feel his heat, his magnetic pull, but didn't need to look at him.

"It's lovely, my dear, just like you," he said as his fingers teased the side of her thigh.

She breathed and steeled herself. "Aren't you sweet."

"So, why the meeting request and icy vibe?"

"Just wanted to see where we stand. My deposition is coming up. I'm getting a feeling, or maybe a message from a little birdie, that you might be trying to screw me. And not in your typical fashion—"

"Interesting. You are the one suing, yet you think I'm trying to screw you? No, my dear, I'm defending myself. Care to tell me what your birdie told you?"

"No. And maybe it's not a true birdie, but an intuition."

"Like I said, I will do whatever it takes to defend myself. Not sure what you're referring to, but my legal team is coming at you hard, Nicole. Just be ready."

"Oh, I'm more than ready. More ready than you know, Jack. You should be ready too. I have some recordings of conversations between you and Rebecca that I am keeping in my back pocket."

"Nicole, I know you're bluffing."

"Well, looks like you'll never know. Might not serve me well in this case, but the Washington Post or your wife would enjoy hearing them…"

"Again, my dear, I don't believe you for a second."

"Again, Jack, I guess you'll never know. Or, at least not until it's too late to do anything about it."

Her head snapped back. She gasped as he yanked her ponytail into the back of the seat. He slid close to her, his breath rushing against her ear and neck. "Listen, Nicole, and you listen carefully. You have no idea how far reaching my connections are. I will win this little nuisance case, win the Senate seat, and I have a network of people who have vested interests in me winning and this network has ways of guaranteeing I succeed. Within this network, my dear, are some friends who know some pretty crooked people who wouldn't think twice at doing me a favor and securing your body to the bottom of the Potomac. Get it, Nicole? I care about you a lot and that's why I haven't taken that route yet. But, don't push me. Do not push me... My dear, Nicole. You are far too beautiful to become fish food. Understand?"

Hyperventilating and in pain, she was completely turned on. "I get it, Jack." She pushed against his shoulder. "You're hurting me!"

He softened his hold and pressed his mouth against hers. Her body rose to meet his. His mouth moved along her cheek to her ear. "Sorry, my love, I just want you to realize who you're dealing with." She could feel her hair sliding out of her ponytail, falling limp, like her body.

He unbuttoned her blouse as he led her down onto the long leather seat. She could feel her skirt rising up to her hips.

"I used to work for you, Jack. I have a pretty good idea how connected you are." She breathed into his ear. Not sure if he heard her over his panting. She used every ounce of strength to push his chest off of her and wriggled out from under him. She tugged the sides of her shirt together. "Jack, you just threatened my life, and now you want to screw me?"

"Isn't that our game?"

"You've never threatened to kill me, Jack. I'm a little freaked out right now."

"Sorry, but I just want you to be careful what you threaten me with. Remember my dear, I can always strike back harder."

Looking down at her trembling hands buttoning her blouse, she whispered, "As warped as it is, I'm addicted to you. I need you, Jack." She wished to die at the bottom of the river if she couldn't have him.

His hand turned her chin toward him, forcing their eyes to meet. "Well, I'm a little freaked out, too, that there could be someone else betraying my trust acting as 'your little birdie'. Are you sleeping with one of my lawyers, Nicole? You wouldn't stoop that low would you? Would someone be willing to blow their career over you, Nicole? Huh, come to think of it, I know the answer to that question."

"With that worry planted firmly in your mind, why don't you drop me off?"

"Fine. When this case wraps up, we will finish what we just started." With his left hand on her thigh, he picked up a phone with his right and instructed the driver to return to her corner.

"I guess we'll see how things go."

She imagined what she must look like to anyone who saw her emerging from the black limo, ponytail pressed down along the back of her neck, makeup smeared. She didn't care enough to fix any of it. She just wanted to get home, climb into bed, and have a good cry. It had been a day of battles but she'd gained the upper hand in both situations. Drained and weary, she had two men right where she wanted them. Maybe there was even room to add a third man into her fold. Would a fresh young attorney be willing to take a risk? She chuckled, knowing she could get whatever it was she wanted.

Chapter 21

I parked along the curb bordering my sister's front lawn, avoiding the driveway so I could have a clear path of escape once her picnic was over. My brother's car pulled in behind me. After shutting my car door, I caught the first glimpse of Damian's date, or his "girlfriend of the month." The lanky blonde matched Damian's description to a tee—"a young, slightly anorexic Christie Brinkley."

"Hi Dame," I called out to my brother as I waved and smiled at the skinny faux-Christie. Only Damian could look cool in a short-sleeved plaid button down.

"Hey, sis, this is Paula. Paula, this is Jezebel," he introduced as we all converged at the end of the concrete driveway.

Paula took an awkward step, almost a bounce, toward me and extended a frail, limp hand to me. "Hi, your brother told me lots about you, Jezzie." Her high-octave pitch, matched her frame.

"Nice to meet you too, Paula." I smiled politely and motioned her to walk toward the lavish home.

The front door flew open, and Cala called out to us as we meandered up her path, "Hi all, just keep your shoes on, we're heading out to the back patio." Rob obediently shadowed his wife, waving and smiling. Unlike Damian, he did not look cool in a plaid shirt.

Parading through the pristinely-appointed kitchen

while wearing shoes felt like a violation, but we did as instructed and followed Cala through the French patio doors. Through a blast of heat, we entered Cala's stage. My mother immediately put down a plate of appetizers and squealed in delight. She hugged us all, squeezing Paula with the same fervor she did her children. Joe followed, smiling, mimicking his fiancée's every move.

Cala guided everyone to the food table, while Rob took drink orders. She proudly recalled the names of each food displayed, giving credit to the caterer who would be handling the wedding. Cala instructed each of us to fill a plate. We sat together at an oblong wrought-iron table beneath two tall ostentatious floral centerpieces.

"Cala, everything is delicious!" my mother exclaimed, accenting each of her syllables with her fingertips, tapping the air as if she were dotting an 'i.' "Really fantastic, Cala!"

Cala grinned as if she had prepared the dishes herself.

"This really is good stuff, Cay," I added while chewing.

"Thanks, and these centerpieces were sent over by the florist. These look very similar to the ones they're doing for the wedding. After we finish, I'll walk you up to the spot in the garden where we'll hold the ceremony. I'm just thrilled with the rose bushes this year, and the hydrangeas and crape myrtles are glorious. The landscaper is doing an outstanding job. He's working extra hours this month to make sure it is all perfect!"

"It will all be wonderful, dear. Joe and I appreciate all that you're doing for our big day."

Joe wiped his mouth, and leaned back in his chair, smirking. "Cala, sweetie, where might the perfect keg location be?" He smacked his thigh and laughed loudly. We all joined him, except for Cala.

"Well, the bar will be set up on one side of the pool, over there. We'll have waiters walking around serving champagne and taking drink orders. On the other side of the pool will be the D.J."

"D.J.? Why not a band? Come on Cala. D.J. doesn't sound like a Cala party standard," Damian teased.

"We have a budget, Damian." Cala sneered.

"Oh, you could have fooled me." He smiled, looking up at the towering bouquet in front of him. "I know a band that does weddings and they do a little of everything. Mom, Joe, my treat? What do you say?"

"Sounds fun! Maybe they'll let me join them for a tune on my electric guitar. Jezebel can join me on the harmonica," Joe said while my mom nodded and smiled in agreement.

I grinned at Joe, but said nothing. My eyes focused on my sister's serious stare. This was something off of the list, outside of the plan. The picture in Cala's mind was altered, creating a palpable tension. I held my breath, waiting to see how Cala would handle it.

Cala spoke with slight hesitation. "Well, I suppose if they are available and you're paying and Mom and Joe agree, then I could cancel the D.J.," she said, but then her voice took on the stern command, and the reaction I expected surfaced. "But Damian, I need to talk to them and make sure they are fully committed and will show up. Some of your musician friends are not the most reliable people, you know."

"These guys are friends of friends and they are very professional. But of course, Queen Cala, they will answer to you." Damian bowed his head at our sister, smiled and continued, "I'll call them and put you in touch with them. Okay?"

"Okay. I want to hear them play, too. Have them send me a demo CD."

"So," my mother interrupted, refocusing the discussion, "Jezzie, how are things going with the guy you're seeing?"

"Great. I'm meeting him tonight for fireworks downtown. I like him. Really like him." I tried to reel in my true excitement, but a bit of it slipped out. My mind had been saturated with thoughts of Kirk all day. I felt a growing giddiness in my belly when I spoke of him.

"I'm glad things are going well with you two," Damian said, appearing uncomfortable. I looked into my brother's eyes. I could tell he was not pleased with me, but was respectful enough to not debate it in front of the family. A lot could be read from Damian's gregarious expressions and gestures, but his lack of them were even more telling.

"He seems like a good guy. I'm not going to overthink it. I'm too quick to find the flaws and give up on men. They all have flaws, right?" Kirk's kisses, his lips, his body, I thought, were certainly not on the flaw list.

"Jezebel, do tell, what are train-guy's flaws?" Cala inquired with an enthusiasm that made me squirm. I knew my sister would gladly lecture me in front of a table of guests.

I fed my sister a tidbit about my worries of dating a not-yet-divorced man, and then refocused on my meal.

"Hmmm, trust your instincts." Cala passed around

a tray of sliced cake for us to sample.

After taking a bite, my mother said, "Jez, your sister's right, sweetie, be super careful. Meditate on it."

"I'm not marrying him, just dating him. And, I'm bringing him to the wedding so you can all scrutinize him in person." I hadn't even asked Kirk yet, but I was feeling attacked and had to counter.

"Jez feels bonded to this Kirk-guy because they shared a near-death experience together on the burning Metro in April." Cala shared with Paula.

"What?" Paula's eyes bulged from her fair, narrow face, her hand covered her mouth. "My God, Jezebel, my mom's cousin, Sandy, died on that train." She looked down and visibly choked back a mouthful of emotion. Damian reached his arm around his date's shoulder.

I wasn't sure if I responded, or anyone else at the table responded verbally, but I sensed the energy on the patio evaporate all around me. I felt encased in a plastic bubble, alone inside a dome full of ugly feelings. I was back on the floor of the Metro, smelling the smells, hearing the screams and feeling the heat—a heat a thousand times more intense than the temperature on this July holiday. I knew I had read Sandy's obituary since I had read them all, several times. Could I have saved Sandy? Did I see Sandy walk past me on the train platform? Guilt hit my gut and pushed the air from my lungs, like being hit with an errant basketball flying through a playground. I was reminded again of my regret of not turning around on the tunnel's sidewalk and walking toward the burning train to help someone off.

"I—I don't know what to say, Paula, I'm so sorry.

That crash was—" I swallowed my words and spared Paula the details of the horror surrounding her relative's final moments. "I'm so sorry, Paula." I stood and walked past my brother's seat to Paula and leaned toward her, wrapping her in a hug. When I read about the victims, I had wished I could console the grieving. Now I had the chance.

"Thank you, Jezebel." We smiled at each other. I returned to my seat and turned toward Paula, who continued, "Our family is finally recovering from the shock of it all. She wasn't married, so she used to spend a lot of time at my parents' house. My mom and she were very close. Sandy had traveled down that afternoon to meet a friend at the tidal basin to check out the cherry blossoms. She was on her way home. I'm sorry you were there too, Jezebel. Did you get hurt? What car were you on?" Paula pushed her thin blonde hair behind her ears and looked at me with intent, completely immersed in our conversation.

"The second car, behind the car that, that... I hurt my shoulder and suffered a minor concussion but nothing bad. The guy I was riding with flipped over the seat in front of him and I went into the aisle, so in the chaos we separated. He looked me up at the law firm I work for and we met a few weeks later." Tears burned at the backs of my eyes, but I blinked to push them away.

With an apparent lump in her throat, Paula spoke, "That's a wonderful story, Jezebel, to come out of a tragedy. It is fate that you're together. That's special. You should give the relationship a try." Paula looked down at the slice of pearl-frosted cake sitting in front of her.

Damian smiled at me, and I was sure he was suppressing an urge to comment. Probably with a "don't force it" remark again, but he must have decided to be kind to Paula and drop it.

Because Sandy was robbed of the chance to ever 'give anything a try,' I supposed I owed it to her to take chances, to not over-think things. For her, I would try.

****

I trudged through the thick air up Rockville Pike, a trickle of moisture rolling down my spine. The soft cooler, carrying a six-pack of Miller Lite bottles, beat against my hipbone as I bounded down the escalator steps into the Metro station. I refused to be late, but also wanted some morsel of makeup and deodorant to remain faithful to my body.

The sound of the train rushing into the station in the distance plunged my thoughts back to Sandy. Sandy had perhaps followed a similar path that day: an escalator took her to a ceramic tiled walkway, a ticket had been sucked from her fingers into a slot, an automatic turnstile opened, leading her past a round kiosk manned by a Metro worker. Sandy had possibly smiled, recalling a funny thing her friend had said. Perhaps she scrolled through the pictures she had just taken of the cherry blossom trees on her phone. Why hadn't a blister caused Sandy to rest on a cement bench? Instead, she had moved into a crowd as the train pulled along the walkway. Sandy had walked into the train car, perhaps exchanging small talk with a stranger. Maybe, her conversation was interrupted by the sounds of crushing metal.

I blocked out everything around me, mouth agape as I tried to picture the face of a woman I had never met. I attempted to recall the pictures that had accompanied the Washington Post obituaries. Again, I wept inside for the victims and their families.

Somehow, I arrived on the platform and stared into the pit containing the tracks. I fantasized about having had rescued Sandy from the flames. Powerless to the events of that day, I told myself it was Sandy's fate to die that day and it was my own fate to survive. Nothing could have changed it. It had happened exactly how it was meant to happen. Why couldn't I just let it go? I struggled again with this gnawing thought. Maybe there was something I could do to make sure no one forgot the victims. But what?

"Jezebel," Kirk called.

"Oh, Kirk. Hey," I said with an unintentional lack of enthusiasm, looking at the man who shared my fate as a survivor.

"I was calling your name for awhile. You look like you saw a ghost. Are you okay?" His hands took hold of my shoulders and he tilted his head trying to gain my focus.

"Oh, yeah, I was distracted by something I just learned. Sorry."

"What? What did you learn? Work related or something with your family?"

"Us, actually. Just thinking about us..." My voice drifted off as I looked back to the empty tracks to our left.

As I looked back at him, Kirk's face reddened and his eyes widened. "What exactly did you hear?" he asked, his voice taking on an urgent tone

"Oh, I'm sorry to worry you. It's just... I just met a woman, Paula, who is dating my brother and she said her mother's cousin died in the Metro crash. How awful, right?"

Kirk's face softened. "Oh. That is awful. You had me worried that something was wrong with us... That is horrible for Paula, though." He pulled me into a hug and kissed my forehead.

"More horrible for Sandy..."

"Let's celebrate our country's birth and try to forget about death. What do you say?"

"Sounds good to me. I brought us a six-pack." I held up my cooler, trying to balance as Kirk pulled me against his side and began to walk.

Motioning to his backpack slung over his shoulder, he said, "And I packed our dinner. Hope you like ham sandwiches."

"Sounds perfect. And I see you're wearing the Nationals t-shirt I got you. Nice."

"It's red, it's festive, and it makes me think of you."

"And here's our ride," I said as a train rushed next to us, obscuring my words.

We took the first seat inside the door and adjusted ourselves and our gear. "More leg room in this front seat for those like us with long legs," Kirk said, stretching out in front of him, but leaving enough room for the summer-clad passengers who were boarding and standing around us. He tucked his hands inside the pockets of his tan cargo shorts, appearing relaxed. The red t-shirt fell against his firm abdomen.

"It also provides a quick escape in case of an emergency." I smiled, leaning into him.

"Stop. No emergencies this trip. And if we do crash, I'm holding onto you this time," he said, squeezing my hand.

The sweet scent of summer clutching to the bodies around us lingered inside the air conditioned train. A cacophony of conversations and laughter floated through the Metro car. People dressed in various renditions of the American flag phoned friends, organizing meeting places inside the nation's capital.

After dwelling on thoughts of death, questioning Kirk's marital status did not seem so daunting. "So, Kirk, what's going on with your divorce?"

"Um, well, you have to be separated for a year before you can file for divorce, and we're in that waiting period now."

"So, when did that officially start?"

"Oh, a couple months ago. I'm not really sure...exactly. Why are we talking about my wife? This is a downer." He squeezed my hand again and his face took on the same wide-eyed look as it had when he greeted me on the platform a short time ago.

He didn't know exactly when he separated from his wife? My mind screamed and my brow furrowed. I wished he had referred to Nikky as "ex-wife" and not "wife." My stomach tossed, my heart hurt, but my hand loved being held in his. I caressed his forearm with my free hand.

Don't force it, said Damian.

Be careful, said my mother.

Trust your instincts, said Cala.

Don't over-think it, I thought. "So, since you're in the middle of a divorce, would it be weird for you to attend a wedding?" I looked up into his eyes.

"What are you asking, Jezebel Stone?" He tilted his head and delivered a playful grin, bringing his face close to mine.

"I'm asking if you'll be my date to my mother's wedding at the end of the month. What do you say?" I asked and blushed.

"Sounds like you officially have a date and a dancing partner!"

"Dancing? I'm not sure you want to subject your poor feet to that. I'm not the most coordinated creature on the dance floor."

"I'll take my chances and I'll lead."

"Lead? Sounds professional. Tell me you didn't take lessons."

"Actually, the wife and I did. She was a dancer, former Redskins Cheerleader. She made me take ballroom dancing lessons with her."

Great, the wife, not ex-wife, was a beautiful, coordinated, dancing, prancing, perky professional ex-cheerleader, I thought.

"Wow. I'm not intimidated or anything. Not at all," I said with a sarcastic lilt.

"Don't be. I'm really not that good. The wife criticized me heavily on my technique. But we just might be great together."

Great together, I thought.

Arms linked, hands pressed together, we smiled, turning our faces toward each other. As if we were alone on the crowded train, he kissed me. Soft at first, inhaling together, he held his lips to mine. Unlocking lips, he softly spoke, "Your lips are pretty coordinated."

"Did I mention I play the harmonica?" I whispered, my eyes focused on his mouth.

"You are just full of surprises, Jezebel Stone."

I hoped, however, that he was not.

Chapter 22

Kirk suggested they enjoy their picnic at Lafayette Park, across from the White House. Jezebel agreed, so they exited the train at the Farragut North station, and walked hand in hand toward their destination.

He was surprised at how he could compartmentalize these two women that were now in his life. He knew in the long run, he wanted to be with Nicole, to continue through their life as originally planned. But in Jezebel's presence, he felt an odd calmness, a comfort, so to speak.

When he touched Jezebel, or kissed her, he did feel a stronger pang of guilt over betraying Nicole than he felt for lying to Jezebel. This told him he really must care for Nicole. But she was not here right now, and Jezebel was. He would enjoy his time with her and try not to think of Nicole. He had no plans to sleep with Jezebel. He could come up with enough excuses to keep her at bay a while longer, so he would not have to deal with that guilt as well. Right now, he had everything under control and leading in the direction he had intended. He could relax and have fun.

"Kirk, how about this bench? Good spot to eat?"

"Yes, this is the perfect view of the White House, a camp of protestors, and a few homeless men. God bless America." He laughed, sat, and pulled out their sandwiches.

She sat next to him and crossed her long legs, making her short tan skirt slide up mid-thigh. They were nice legs, toned, not muscular, flawless except for some freckles. He touched her leg above her knee and she placed her free hand over his. She dangled her flip-flop from her red-polished toes and bounced her foot.

Still chewing a bite of ham sandwich, she asked, "You seem far off in thought. What are you thinking about?"

"Well, I was just thinking that you have nice legs and I was also wondering what would possess someone to devote their life to camping out in front of the White House and protest taxes? Can't think of anything that would make me live in a tent on concrete."

In an apparent gesture of modesty, she tugged at her skirt. "Oh, well thank you for the leg compliment. And, I think I could think of something you'd protest. What if the government was about to sign into law a bill banning professional baseball?"

"Far-fetched, but…nah, still wouldn't pitch a tent on concrete. How about you?"

"Nope, nothing I can think of. I like my mattress and warm apartment. Speaking of which, this might seem a little bold of me, but you're invited back to my place after fireworks if you'd like." She looked away.

He looked at a homeless man peeking into a garbage can and leaned back against the bench. He popped his last bite of sandwich into his mouth and swallowed. "Let's just play it by ear. See where the night takes us." He caressed her back and gave her a smile. She smiled back but looked worried.

"Okay. And no problem if you don't want to. Just be honest. I'll understand." She sighed, touching his leg. She was an easy going soul, but he could tell he had caused her some angst.

Kirk grabbed her around her shoulder, bringing her close. She nuzzled into his side and he took his opposite hand, turning her chin to face him. "Hey, whatever decision I make, has nothing to do with you. I'm new at this and just learning how to cope as an almost-divorcé."

She smiled and her eyes glanced down at his lips. In a deliberate and slow movement, he kissed her. It wasn't just for show, his whole body wanted her. Seeing her smile at the end of the kiss sent an unexpected sensation through him. She created a lightness in him. At that moment, he wanted to grab her hand and run through the park. Ridiculous. He needed to stay in control. He'd gotten lost in all those feelings that were the opposite of what Nicole created—that giant weight pulling him down, suffocating him. For one moment, it had lifted.

"I like the bandana around your ponytail." He tugged on it.

"Thanks."

After eating, they crossed Pennsylvania Avenue and made their way closer to the White House. Jezebel didn't just walk, but occasionally skipped, turning sideways to face him when she had something to say. Her child-like joy was contagious. He grabbed her hand as they strolled along the black iron fence bordering the White House lawn. A guard motioned for them to stop as the driveway gate opened, allowing two vehicles to enter the grounds.

"Hmm, how do we get invited to their party?" he jested.

"Guess it's all in who you know or who you've slept with."

"Right. We are just losers on the outside forced to celebrate with the common folk."

She laughed and squeezed his hand. They headed toward the Washington Monument, past lines of white trailers selling souvenirs.

Jezebel pointed to one of the trailers. "There is a guy who bought one of these little trailers and goes from corner to corner selling burritos. They are the best. He was a former attorney who quit to sell burritos. Can you believe it?"

"I know who you mean. I've had his burritos before. On Tuesdays, I try to catch him on the corner of I and 18th street. They're fantastic." He interrupted her, shocking himself at his giddy enthusiasm.

"I tease the attorneys I work for that one day I'm going to quit and be his assistant. I'll be his para-burrito girl."

"He needs a para-burrito girl because his lines get way too long." He laughed.

"There's no stress in filling burritos. I see why he left law firm life. I envy his gumption."

"I envy people like that, too, who know what they want and go after it. Quit complaining about your life and change it, I always say, but could I actually do it?"

"I'm sure you could."

They walked for a long time through throngs of others celebrating the country's holiday. They ended up on Constitution Avenue and strolled down toward the Lincoln Memorial. The mall area was covered with picnickers camped out for the day, waiting for the night's sky show.

They ordered ice cream cones from a vendor and devoured them before they melted, giving themselves a brutal brain freeze. After they finished, they re-clasped their sticky hands together. He felt younger than he had felt in months, years.

Under the shade of a cherry tree, they stopped and watched a brave squirrel take a piece of bread from a passerby. The city squirrels had lost all fear of humans and the tourists found their antics amusing. Jezebel shared a story, but he wasn't fully listening. He turned and interrupted her with a kiss. His hand held the back of her neck under her ponytail as he tasted sweat and ice cream on her upper lip. She lost her balance slightly, but steadied herself by grabbing onto his arm. For a moment, he wished he was sharing this day, this feeling, with his wife. But in his very next thought, he was glad it was Jezebel. Could Nicole have made him feel this good?

"Jez!" A voice called out from beside him.

"Hey, Justin. I never thought I'd find you in this huge crowd! Are you having fun with your friends?" Jezebel turned toward a decent looking guy, wearing a blue tank top that revealed two thin, but muscular arms. One arm balanced a football and the other arm reached out and hugged Jezebel. A pang of jealousy pierced Kirk's gut.

"Hi, you must be Kirk." The guy with beer breath extended a hand toward him shaking it with fervor. His smile was smaller than the one he delivered to Jezebel.

"Kirk, this is Justin. He's one of the attorneys I work for."

"With me. Not for me," Justin corrected with a smile.

"Oh, well, nice to meet you, Justin," Kirk said.

"Hey, we have a couple blankets set out over there with a ton of food and drinks if you'd like to hang out and watch the fireworks with us. We've been here since two." His eyes lingered on Jezebel.

The invitation, he was certain, was not intended for him. He interjected before Jezebel had a chance to accept his offer. "Thanks, but Jezebel invited me to watch from your office rooftop."

"Thanks, Justin, but we're heading to the office now." She touched the guy's arm.

"Okay, have fun. Nice meeting you, Kirk," Justin said, with a lack of sincerity. "Don't do any work, Jez," Justin joked while jogging backward toward his group of friends, juggling the ball between his hands.

Kirk feigned a laugh and held up his hand in a fake wave. He wondered if Jezebel had been looking for him. The lightness he felt a moment ago, dissipated. He had no claim on Jezebel and she was free to meet and hug whomever she pleased.

"Wow, it's already eight o'clock. We should head toward my office building."

"Let's do it."

They walked north and weaved through the streets between the twelve and thirteen-story buildings. When they arrived at her building, she reached inside the tiny cooler and pulled out a small purse, removing her building's security pass. She swiped the card over the sensor and opened the door.

They both expressed their gratefulness for the air conditioning, and walked along the shiny marble floor, past a fountain and ficus trees, to the elevator bank.

"So, Justin seems fun. Work with him long?" he

asked with a smirk.

"Yeah, five years. He was a summer associate when I started working here. We're in the same department," she answered, not acknowledging his smirk. "I thought I'd show you my office and you could leave your backpack there, if you want, and then we could head to the roof."

"Okay, sounds like a plan. I'd love to see your office."

"Don't get your hopes up. It's not that impressive. No window and it's only slightly bigger than a closet." She bounced off the elevator.

They walked down the hall as he studied the nameplates outside of the doors, looking to see how close Justin's office was to Jezebel's.

"Here it is. My lovely jail cell."

"Oh, it's fantastic. Nicer than my cubicle. And, it's much neater than I expected," he said, glancing at the stack of folders on the right side of her desk. He sat in her seat.

"Beer?" She twisted off the cap before he could answer her, splashing a few drops on her shirt. She handed him the bottle and he accepted, taking a swig.

She opened one for herself and sat in her guest chair, placing her feet up against the front of her desk. She tugged again at the bottom of her skirt.

He finished another large gulp and sat forward in the chair, resting his elbows on her desk, smiling. He enjoyed the feeling of the beer's effects on his body and his dry mouth.

"You look good at my desk, Kirk."

"Maybe I'll apply for your job when you get promoted to para-burrito." He laughed and looked down at her desk. The label "D'Angelo/Winston Hotel Conversation" caught his eye. His stomach burned. He panicked and turned his eyes back toward her. His mind froze and he couldn't think of anything to say. He took another sip of the lukewarm beer.

His mind tried to focus on the story Jezebel started to share, but it remained on what could be inside that file. He wanted to read it right then. He was sad, he was angry, he was curious. He pictured Nicole sitting across from Winston, showing him her legs, not caring that her skirt drifted up to her mid-thigh. She wouldn't have tugged at the bottom of it, but she would've kept it there and enjoyed his eyes on her. A sickness churned inside of him.

He concentrated on Jezebel. He watched her hands gesturing and listened to her giggle. Her ponytail swayed behind her head. She was cute, maybe klutzy and scattered and not glamorous, but she was cute. He'd never thought of his wife as being cute. His wife was sexy and gorgeous, but he wouldn't describe her as cute. Cute came from within.

They finished their beers, grabbed Jezebel's soft cooler, and headed to the rooftop, back into the warm, humid dusk air. The view was breathtaking and he spun in a circle to take it all in.

The roof area contained wooden tables and a gazebo. An unoccupied bar had been erected at one end, possibly used for office parties and happy hours. Well-maintained plants and flowers adorned the edges of the roof. A few groups of people occupied some of the tables. They claimed one for themselves, sitting on the top of the table, and resting their feet on the bench below. Jezebel opened their second round of beers.

"Cheers! Here's to a fun day." She held out her beer for a toast.

"Cheers. To a fun day, indeed." He clinked his beer bottle against hers.

Someone at a nearby table turned up the volume to their radio. A station broadcasted the patriotic tunes that would accompany the fireworks. Jezebel slid closer and slipped her hand into his. He smiled at her, kissing her quickly on her nose. She hummed a soft content hum, letting him know she liked his gesture.

The first explosion rang out in the sky as applause sounded in the distance. The patient crowds were finally being given their reward.

"Jezebel, I really did have a great time with you today. Thanks for bringing me up here. I think we definitely have the best spot in the city," he said to her while keeping his eyes on the sky.

"You're welcome. Thanks for coming with me. Oh, wow, nice one!" She commented on the cascade of red sparkles showering down in front of them. "You're a Grand Old Flag" rang from the radio nearby.

"We're pretty lucky to work in this city. It's beautiful and powerful all at the same time," he said.

"I agree. Transportation and traffic aside, it's a spectacular city."

"That nasty transportation brought us together."

"Oh, look, a flag," Jezebel squealed, pointing to the fireworks' formation. They uttered the obligatory "oooh" as it faded from its black backdrop.

As much as he was enjoying Jezebel, his mind shifted against its will to Nicole. He wondered where she was and who she was spending the holiday with—probably with her obnoxious family at her parents' house. He had dodged that bullet this year. He wondered what she had told them about their separation. Surely, she had blamed him.

Silence followed the deafening blasts of the grand finale and a roar from crowds of pleased observers rang out around them. They gathered their empty beer bottles and stuffed them into the cooler. Kirk took the cooler from Jezebel and slung it over his shoulder. Placing his hand on her lower back, he let her take the lead to the elevator.

Inside the elevator, Jezebel moved close and faced Kirk, placing her hands on his hips. When she looked up and smiled, he kissed her. The doors opened and they walked into the hall leading to her office.

Inside her office, she asked, "Hey, can you hang out here while I visit the ladies' room?"

Bingo. This was his chance to read the file. "Take your time," he answered calmly.

Without wasting a minute, he stood behind her desk and opened the file. Beads of sweat formed on his forehead when he saw the typed line:

Winston: And I also recall you completely enjoying it…

Then, he read a line that made bile creep up into his throat: So, I had to lie…

The paper shook in his hands. His eyes, wide in terror, were reading the words, but his mind had a difficult time absorbing them. A cold sickness surged and a sharp stab punctured his chest as he read the words typed after his wife's name: You know I loved you, Jack.

He read it three times.

Humiliation ripped through him and he kept

reading: I know you fell in love with me, Nicole.

Kirk hated her. A blazing rage consumed him. A white anger rocked him as he spit out the word, "bitch!" after he read the final blow: I needed to show you how deeply it hurt and how much I love you. I still love you, Jack and I will do anything to get you back in my life.

Kirk's knees buckled from under him and he collapsed into Jezebel's chair.

His wife had loved, and was still in love with another man. He had suspected a crush, but here in black and white print, recorded during a clandestine hotel meeting, her love for him was confirmed. Kirk was certain she had slept with him. He had been a fool to believe her when she said she hadn't. She probably had sex with him after this very recording. His hands shook. His heart burned.

He shoved the documentation of his disgrace back into the folder, placing the file back where he found it. He wanted to thrust the papers off of the desk and slam them into the wall. With footsteps approaching, he attempted to regain composure, to hide his mood, and put his anger in a safe place where Jezebel couldn't find it.

Chapter 23

I walked through the hallway toward my office, slightly buzzed from the beer, but admonishing myself for having invited Kirk to my apartment so early in our date. Embarrassment knocked around inside me at my boldness. I would play it cool from here on out. Even if he wanted to come back to my apartment, I would advise against it.

I entered my office and found Kirk leaning back in my chair. His face looked flushed, possibly sunburned from the day's intense sun. He didn't smile at first. Perhaps, I feared, he had been preparing to tell me he wanted to go home. Maybe he would use the headache excuse again. Another spasm of embarrassment struck me.

He adjusted his eyes on me, as if he hadn't seen me when I first entered the office.

"Hey, you okay?" I asked.

"Oh...yes. Just waiting for you." He stood, looking embarrassed himself. He walked toward me and brought me to his chest, lingering in a quiet embrace for a moment.

"Are you sure you're okay? You seem...different."

"No, I'm good. Great in fact. Had a great time today and I was thinking that I'd like to come back to your place." He kissed my forehead.

"Hey, I'm sorry about bringing that up earlier.

Truly, it won't bother me in the least if you don't want to come. In fact, I think you shouldn't come back to my place."

"Okay, then it's set," he announced.

"Um," I said, slightly disappointed at his eagerness to not come to my apartment.

He placed an assertive peck on my lips. "You are coming to my place."

"Well, great. That sounds great."

"Furry will survive until morning?"

"Yes." I was still a bit flustered at his behavior. "Sure, Furry will be fine. But, are you sure—"

He grabbed my hand and pulled me away from my office. "I'm very sure. Let's get out of here."

Along with every other occupant of the District of Columbia, we entered the Metro station.

"Everyone's leaving D.C. at the same time. Looks like we'll need some patience," I whispered.

"It's gonna be tough. I want to get you home."

"Anxious to show me your condo?" I asked, simulating naivety.

"You could say that." He pulled me against him, looking off into the tunnel for a train.

The train rushed along the platform, inviting people to move toward its doors. I grabbed Kirk's arm and led him to the center of the train. "Sorry, but I prefer riding on the middle car these days."

"You're the boss."

We moved into a train car, pressed inside a wall of bodies. Our hands took hold of the same silver pole. Facing each other, we smiled. The train lurched forward and shook us from side to side.

"So, I'm giving you permission at anytime on this

trip to bail and I'll be okay with it." I offered.

"What makes you think I want to bail?"

The train stopped, knocking us forward in sync. Kirk reached and steadied me with one hand. His phone buzzed. Removing his hand from my shoulder, he pulled his phone from his pocket, grimacing at the screen. He hit a button and stuck the phone back in his pocket. "Sorry. My phone won't interrupt us again. So, what makes you think I'll bail?"

"Just unsure if there're any lingering wife feelings…" My eyes shot toward his pocket containing his phone.

"We're through. I'm done, completely done with her. Over."

"Okay. Okay, but you still seem angry, Kirk." I tried to speak evenly without sounding accusatory. The train moved forward making us both grip the pole tighter.

He blew air through his lips and looked to the ceiling. "I am angry, Jezebel. I'm hurt and angry, but you know what?" He looked back down at me with a half smile. "When I'm with you, I'm not angry. So, can we not mention her anymore?"

I paused, digested, and asked, "Did the Nationals play today?"

"No, tomorrow at home and thank you. For changing the subject."

"Want to go? We can try to find tickets online in the morning?"

Without pause, he answered, "Yes, I'd love to. My treat."

With our eyes connected, I felt him relax.

****

We strolled through the dark summer night toward Kirk's condo. The disappearance of the sun had not provided much relief in the temperature or the thick humidity. We held hands, enjoying inconsequential conversation. Asking each other silly questions and laughing at the answers, pausing a few times for a quick peck on the lips. Kirk held the glass door open, inviting me into the lobby.

I stood in front of the elevators. "Last chance to bail, Kirk. When I hit this button, you're committed."

He reached in front of me and hit the up button.

I smiled.

We crossed the threshold and entered the empty car together. Kirk didn't speak but moved his body in front of me. Not asking or waiting for permission, he pressed his mouth against mine, slipping a hand along my back. To let him know I welcomed his boldness, I moved toward him and tasted the salty reminders of the hot day on his mouth. Sweat and sweetness mixed with a faint smell of his cologne. A hint of his five o'clock shadow rubbed on my energetic lips. His one hand teased my belly with light caresses, sending hot excitement through my body.

The elevator stopped. Our mouths separated but our eyes stayed transfixed on each other as we moved through the open door. My flip-flop caught in the gap between the car and the floor, and in an attempt to regain my balance, I rolled my opposite ankle. My body hit the ground causing an unsexy grunt to escape. I looked to the ceiling and whispered, "You've got to be kidding me."

"Are you okay?" Kirk leaned over me, his arms surrounding me as if protecting me from falling debris.

At this point, I would not be surprised if the ceiling collapsed on us.

I rubbed my ankle and then tried to gather a bit of dignity, rising to my feet. I covered a wince with a quick smile.

"Here, let me help." Kirk reached his one arm under my legs and the other behind my back and hoisted me off the ground.

"Sorry…for ruining the moment," I said, burying my head into his shoulder.

"Oh, I don't know that you ruined anything. This is kinda fun. But, I need to set you down to get my keys out of my backpack." He gently placed me down and pulled keys from his bag. With one hand, he opened the door, steadying me with the other. "Welcome."

He tossed his bag inside the door, took my cooler and pitched it alongside his backpack. I took a clumsy step forward and he pulled me back. "Wait, let me do this…" He lifted me again off of the floor, carried me inside, and placed me on the kitchen counter. "Let me get you some ice."

"This is a really nice condo, Kirk," I said, glancing down at the granite counter tops. I tugged at the bottom of my skirt, embarrassed to be sitting on the counter like a child who just got a boo-boo on the playground.

"Thank you. Let me see that ankle."

"Thanks," I said as he placed a bag of frozen peas on my ankle, resting the bottom of my bare foot against his thigh.

"Doesn't look swollen yet," he said, examining my foot and circling my ankle with his fingertips.

Again, I pulled at my skirt, self-conscious of my outfit choice.

"Yeah, these poor ankles are used to it—they've had a lot of experience rolling and twisting. Heels and I don't get along very well."

"Flip-flops too?"

"I guess gravity in general." We laughed together.

"You're cute—a total klutz—but cute."

"Cute? I haven't been called cute since I was nine. Can you maybe come up with something better?" I asked, flirting and batting my eyes.

He continued to hold my ankle and his eyes watched his other hand caress my leg, traveling upward toward my knee.

"How about funny?" he asked with a smile.

"My brother calls me funny…keep going." I smacked him on his bicep.

Circling his fingers around my knee, he said, "Hmm, how about…pretty?"

"Better…but keep going." I closed my eyes for a moment and smiled, enjoying his touch and the warmth tingling through my body.

He gazed down at my injury and slid his hand up my leg, letting the peas fall to the floor. I placed my leg down in its natural position. He reached behind my head and removed the bandana circling my ponytail. His quiet methodical movements were hypnotic. I leaned closer enjoying the closeness of his neck. He released my hair from my ponytail and pulled back slightly to look at my face.

"Your eyes, you know I love those eyes…"

I tucked my hair behind my ear, averting my gaze from his. He pushed my hands away from the bottom of my skirt and rested his hands on my upper thighs. I reached for his face and we kissed, slowly and deeply. I curled my injured leg around his backside, scooting my body closer to the edge of the counter. Skirt modesty was now a thing of the past.

He slid his hand down along my leg, behind him, and lightly touched my injured ankle. "And how does sexy sound?" He kissed my neck, stroking his hand back up my leg.

"Mmm, even better."

He moved back to my mouth, kissing with purpose. He released for a second, "How about graceful?"

"Now I know you're lying just to get me into bed..." We laughed, returning to our kiss.

His lips brushed along my neck while his hands slid under my skirt and rested on my hips.

In between kisses, he whispered with a vulnerability that brought me a wave of excitement. "Thanks for taking away all the ugliness inside me." He pulled me against him and pressed his mouth into my shoulder.

With my hand in his hair, I suppressed an urge to ask him one more time if he really wanted to do this. Not that I was receiving any indication from him that he wasn't into me, but I knew he couldn't be completely rid of *her*. I also couldn't stop the pesky Ken-voice from occasionally creeping back into my mind. But with Kirk kissing my neck and touching me in thrilling ways, it wasn't hard to block that voice and focus on the building fire. Was I falling in love or was my need for physical attention blinding me? I certainly intended to keep enjoying this journey and find out what destination was ahead.

He breathed into my ear as I kissed his neck, and asked, "How's the ankle?"

"What ankle?" I answered through labored breaths.

He lifted me off the counter while my lips were still on his neck, and carried me through the dining area, passing a giant wedding portrait of Kirk and his bride. I glanced at the portrait, swallowed hard, and returned to Kirk's neck. Why was that still hanging on the wall? I cringed.

We moved several feet into the living area. He asked, "Can you stand?"

"Yeah."

He placed my feet gently on the ground, and we simultaneously began removing each other's clothes. When his hands were free from yanking his t-shirt over his head, he held my shirtless body with fervor and brought it against his firm chest. I kissed his bulging pecs as his hands slid up my back beneath my hair and released my bra after one attempt. He gently guided my body backward toward the couch.

Letting out another unsexy grunt, my body hit the couch and Kirk's body planted on top of mine. My hands moved along his back, through his hair, and back down again. He paused, looking into my eyes. I smiled, indicating more than just my pleasure. He smiled back. His mouth moved downward, traveling the new territory with enthusiasm.

Our mouths joined again, tasting, teasing. And like swimmers readying themselves for the next few strokes underwater, we breathed, and then kissed again. Our bodies molded together without awkwardness and glided in a harmonious tempo. It had been a long time since I had experienced such primal pleasure, and I let Kirk know—repeatedly.

Red flags, Ken voices, and a swollen ankle ceased

to exist inside Kirk's embrace. My body relaxed as he concluded. Eyes closed, I savored my body's final waves of gratification.

Kirk kissed my cheek, my forehead, and then my lips. "Are you okay?"

"Yeah, great, you?"

"Great." He released a loud breath into my shoulder as we remained pressed together. Before pulling away, he kissed me one final time. "But I'd like to get you in the shower and then into my bed."

We fumbled around each other, grabbing a few articles of clothing, and made our way to the bathroom. Kirk turned on the shower, and then kissed my forehead. "You get started. I'll join you in a few minutes."

He grabbed a towel from the rack and wrapped it around his waist. He smiled over his shoulder as he exited the bathroom, closing the door behind him.

I stepped into the shower, welcoming the warm flow of water across and down my long body. I smiled as I turned and let the water hit my scalp, pushing my hair behind me. Instead of dwelling on why Kirk's shower still had peach scented Herbal Essence shampoo/conditioner combo in it, I thought instead of the scenes from our holiday celebration. Where was this all heading? I wondered with a smile. We had begun our relationship with a fire, but now we were finally able to enjoy the fireworks.

Chapter 24

Nicole was seething with anger and hoped Kirk had a good reason for not answering her text or calls—like he was hospitalized.

The elevator's lack of speed didn't help. "Go faster you stupid car!" She pounded the wall with the side of her fist. And before the door slid fully open, she squeezed herself into the hallway. She paused in front of their apartment door, applied some lipstick, and fluffed her hair. She decided not to knock. If he wasn't home yet, she'd just wait for him. She unlocked and opened the door.

A foot from the doorway, Kirk stood dressed in nothing but a towel. "Nicole! What the hell are you doing here?" His faced reddened. He had just taken their wedding portrait off the wall and had placed it on the floor, their smiling faces turned against the wall.

"You weren't answering your phone, Kirk, and I was worried about you. What the hell are doing with that? And why the hell are you whispering? Who's here?"

"Lower your voice. I have a guest. And you need to get the hell out of here. This isn't your place anymore."

"I won't lower my voice. Is it skanky Olive Oyl, Kirk? Good God, Kirk!"

He pointed at her face. "Listen, I actually had a fun

day without drama, without being lied to, and without being miserable. Don't ruin it, Nicole. Leave. Now."

"You had sex with that skinny whore. You violated our marriage vow. What about our plans for counseling, Kirk? You are such a liar."

He moved closer, and then stopped and took a long breath. He seemed angry, but she knew he still wanted her. "Nicole, you violated our vows first, you are the liar, and I'm not going to any counseling with you. You need counseling by yourself. You need to leave before I do or say something I'll regret."

"What the hell are you talking about? I'm no liar, Kirk. I love you and you promised to go to counseling with me."

"Get out. I never want to see you again. I've learned some things today and I can't even see straight when I look at you. Leave before I...hurt you."

He had the audacity to say these horrible things and then turn away. However, she thought, he did look good in that towel.

"Leave, Nicole." He faced her again with the veins in his forehead bulging.

"Wait. I don't know what you 'learned today' but it's got to be some big lie Olive Oyl told you that her stupid lawyers cooked up to screw me. Don't, Kirk... Kirk." She ran around the opposite side of the dining room table and blocked him, positioning her body close to his. She was instantly aroused.

He looked up at the ceiling with his hands on his hips. She knew he wanted her, too. She wove her arms through his arms and hugged him. "I'm sorry for making you miserable, Kirk, but you know I make you happy too..."

He grabbed her shoulders and shoved her backward, causing her to lose her balance. Her mouth hung open.

His face lit up with anger. "Get. Out. Now. Or I'll call the police. And give me your key, now."

"Kirk, are you joining me?" a voice called from the shower.

"I'll be right there. Don't move." Reducing his voice to a low hiss, he snapped. "Now, Nicole." His fingers burrowed into her shoulder and he drove her body past the dining table and toward the door.

"Fine. Stop hurting me." She shook his hand off my shoulder. "I'll call the police on you."

Whipping open the door, she knew she had one more chance. Nicole attempted to make her face as sweet and pathetic looking as possible. "Kirk, we can work through anything, okay? Please, can we talk at another time?"

"Fine, we'll talk later." He slammed the door behind her.

Success. He still wanted to talk. She waited in the hall for a few minutes with an ear held against the door, but couldn't hear anything. She had to wipe away the horrific image of him on top of the bony paralegal. Actually, she felt a little bit sorry for Kirk. He must be in need of some attention, if he had to settle for *her*.

After a few minutes of silence, she slipped the key back into the keyhole and opened the door. If he caught her, she'd tell him she was just leaving the key as he requested. Since he violently pushed her away, she didn't have time to leave it.

Without a sound, she closed the door behind her. A bag inside the door had been begging for her inspection.

Inside the tacky cooler was a small no-brand-name wristlet purse. Nicole peered inside and saw Olive Oyl's security pass. Bad picture. Had the girl never heard of hair straightening products? She held it in her hand, smiling as if she held the winning lottery ticket. Without another thought, she tucked it into her purse. The voices coming from the shower disgusted her and she had to get out fast before she heard something she didn't want to hear. Before leaving, she reached over and pushed their wedding picture backward and let it hit the carpet, so their smiling faces would be looking up.

Nicole practically skipped to her car. The pass in her pocket distracted her from any thoughts of Olive in her bed.

She stopped by Gina's place and picked up a beach hat to hide her hair and face if any cameras recorded her. Although she despised the Metro, she took it in case security cameras captured any parked cars outside of the skank's office building.

Inside her destination, she strutted across the dimly lit lobby. Adrenaline filled every part of her. One drowsy-looking security guy manned the desk, holding a Clancy novel in one hand and a mug in the other.

"Happy Fourth of July," Nicole said and then she treated him to a nice view of her backside.

"Same to you, Miss."

The elevator responded to Olive's card, and nervousness shot through her as the doors opened. She hoped the hall would be clear.

Move fast, Nic!

Without hesitation, she scanned the nameplates along the hallway looking for Jezebel's office. A paralegal would only have an interior one, probably near the room full of copy machines. Jezebel's office was in the first hall she selected. She closed the door behind her.

Olive Oyl's office was pathetically small so it didn't take long to go through it. Nicole spotted a file marked, "D'Angelo/Winston Hotel Conversation." That bastard. Really, this was a whole file? She read the words, "Transcribed from iPhone Recording."

Holy shit, Jack recorded their conversation. He had set her up. She read further to see what he had captured of their conversation. Not surprisingly, nothing to damage his reputation. Was this what Olive had shared with Kirk? It's no surprise that Kirk slept with her. He must have been distraught.

She shut the file and opened Jezebel's desk drawers, searching for anything she could use. She flipped through all the Winston case files to see if there were any more secrets waiting. One file was marked, "D'Angelo Deposition." There were the planned questions prepared by Justin Moorehead and Olive. A file marked, "Deposition Exhibits" had the documents they planned to use. She flipped through them quickly since she'd seen them all before. No surprises, but it was good to see the questions they had planned. She snapped pictures of the questions with her phone.

This Justin Moorehead had signed some of the smaller motions and pleadings, as well. This was probably the guy Jack had mentioned. She scrawled his name and bar number on the palm of her hand. Before leaving, she read a note stuck to Olive's computer screen. It said, "Jez. Hope you enjoyed the day off. If you want to do coffee with me, I'll be at Au Bon Pain

Tues morning, text me. -Justin"

Could this attorney also have a thing for Olive? What was it with this woman? Well, good, maybe he'd distract her from Kirk. Feeling fearless, she cruised down another hall and found Justin's office. She slipped inside and saw his business cards displayed on his desk. She snagged one since she might just need his cell phone number. She now had a mission for tomorrow.

****

Late Monday morning, in her tightest and sexiest t-shirt and jeans, Nicole headed to Justin's apartment building.

"Please," she said out loud in the car, "when I look in the mirror and see my own ass in these jeans, even I fall in love with myself. Justin, you're screwed."

She parked in the Starbucks parking lot next to Justin's apartment building, hoping he'd be home since offices were closed. After some sleuthing, she acquired his address and memorized his picture from his Facebook page. She thought she'd make a great private detective when she finished with this secretary thing.

She checked her makeup in the mirror—perfect. She dialed his number. Justin answered. She hung up. She tossed her phone onto the passenger's seat, along with her keys. Before hitting the lock button on the inside of the door, she checked to make sure the magnetic key was still attached to the undercarriage of the car, just in case her plan failed.

Nicole strutted to the front door of the coffee shop. "Excuse me, sir?" She—or, perhaps it was her cleavage—had gained the attention of a man entering Starbucks. "I locked my keys and my phone in my car.

May I please borrow your phone to call a friend? I'm so sorry to bother you, but I don't know what to do. I'm so stupid for hitting the lock button with all my stuff on the seat! Oh..." She wiped her brow, and traced her hand from her neck to her cleavage.

"Here, take your time, Miss. I'm just grabbing a coffee. You can give it to me when you're finished." He smiled and left her alone with his phone. Too easy.

"Thank you so much." She was sure her eyes were sparkling.

Nicole dialed Justin's number again, sending a nervous flutter into her belly. When it went to voicemail, she said, "Hi, this is a courier. There's a package for you at your building's security desk."

She tossed Justin's business card into a trashcan, returning the man's phone with a flirtatious touch.

In front of the apartment building doors, she paced, turned around, and passed the doors again, watching the security desk through the glass doors. If this worked, she may just need to go into acting as well.

Proving once again that God intended for her to be happy, she saw Justin approach the desk. He was certainly yummy looking, in a sweet sort of way—well groomed with a boyish appeal.

She watched a confused-looking security man shake his head, and then Justin put his hands on his hips as his eyes scanned the desk. Nicole decided to make her grand entrance.

"Excuse me," she said the security man, "I locked my keys and my phone in my car." She made her voice quiver. "I'm not sure what to do. I had just stopped to grab a coffee at this Starbucks. I'm such a blonde." She did the brow wipe and trace-hand-to-the-cleavage move again. It never failed her.

And as easy as stealing candy from the proverbial baby, Justin said, "Is there any way I can help you?"

For starters, you can tell me what Jack Winston has up his sleeve and you could fall in love with me in order to make Jack and Kirk jealous. Pissing off Olive Oyl would be an added bonus.

"Yes, thank you!" She began walking toward the door to eliminate the security guard from helping. "Um, do you know a locksmith?"

"No, but I can certainly find one for you." He searched for a locksmith on his phone.

"Can I buy you a coffee? It's the least I can do for you being so nice to me."

His broad smile relayed his pleasure. "Sure, a courier must have taken my package to the wrong building, it's happened before. They'll call me when it makes its way back. Oh, I'm Justin by the way." He extended his hand.

She took it and smiled. "Nicky Jones. Nice to meet you, Justin. And, I just realized I can't buy. My wallet is in my car."

"My treat." His eyes gazed downward at her chest. *That was your treat, Justin.*

Their eyes locked and they smiled at each other as he opened the Starbucks' door. She passed in front of him.

After ordering two Frappuccinos, they found a table for two. The surge of excitement she felt equaled the feeling of sneaking into Olive Oyl's office. She fed Justin some compliments and sprinkled the conversation with a few necessary lies. She told him she was a legal secretary, but for a small boutique firm.

Since they had time to kill before the locksmith arrived, they went for a walk around the block. She probed into his job a bit, knowing men loved to talk about themselves. To her, this was almost as exciting as meeting Jack in a limo under a street light.

After the locksmith unlocked her car, Nicole made a sad face to Justin, as if not wanting him to say goodbye.

He took the bait. "I know this great restaurant nearby that has an outdoor patio. Wanna grab some lunch?"

"Well, okay, I do owe you for treating me to coffee and being so sweet." With a hand on her waist, she rocked her hips from side to side. "My treat."

He smiled and tucked his hands into the pockets of his shorts. He appeared a bit nervous, like a freshman who'd just been hit on by a hot senior.

They strolled the two blocks to the restaurant and snatched the patio's last table.

Before Justin had a chance to order his own drink, she told the waitress to bring them two large draft beers. The foam from the beer's head coated her upper lip and she performed a deliberate drag of her tongue along its trail while Justin watched.

After a discussion on law firm life, they dug into some burgers and she decided to dig right into Justin's brain. "So, Mr. Lawyer, I have a legal question for you. I just read an article about a couple that was in a hot divorce dispute. The husband recorded her during their phone conversation, allegedly confessing to some things. Then the guy used it against her in court. Is that legal? Can you really tape someone without them knowing and then use it?"

"That's funny, we actually have a similar thing going on in one of my cases. Depends on the state, but in D.C. you only need single consent—just one of the parties needs to know the conversation is being taped."

"Well, Mr. Defense attorney, what could she use to defend herself here?"

"Tape him saying things, I suppose. Divorces are ugly, I'm glad I'm not a divorce attorney."

"Love does get complicated, that's for sure. So what if what had been recorded isn't pertinent to the case, but makes the guy look bad?"

"You just have to ring the bell. Get it out there to the jury or judge before the objections sound. Even if the judge determines it's inadmissible, you can't un-ring the bell. So much of the legal system is playing the game and messing with the jurors' heads. Manipulation, really." Justin leaned forward, seeming eager to share his legal knowledge or to just get closer.

"Interesting. So what did the guy tape in your case?" she asked.

"It's different, not a divorce case. The case could be thrown out with this recording, but for some reason our client is not wanting to use it yet." He emptied the beer mug into his mouth. Folding his arms in front of him, he leaned on the table and smiled.

Thank you, sunshine and early afternoon beer for giving Justin a buzz.

She grinned, but her mind flashed to Jack. What was he doing not wanting to end the case yet? Either he was afraid of her, or he still loved her. No, he wanted to win at all costs. He wanted to win at everything: win the case, win her, and win the Senate seat. He was a smart man to play his cards just right.

"What do you say we get out of here and check to see if your package arrived?" She fluffed her hair with one hand. She didn't want him dumping her before she got what she needed.

Justin took his wallet out of his pocket and slammed his credit card down on the table. Good, he forgot she had offered to pay.

After scratching his signature on the receipt, he took her hand. A tingling coursed through her body. She couldn't quite ascertain if she was pleased at his touch or at herself for being so incredibly awesome.

The mysterious package hadn't arrived, obviously, so Nicole boldly invited herself upstairs. Inside his apartment, like Jack did often in the hotel room visits, Justin didn't wait long before he released his affections.

With her back against the door, he took her head in his hands and breathed. "For your information, I don't make it a habit of picking up strangers on the street and luring them up to my apartment hours later."

"Well, it's not my habit either—" She was glad he pressed his mouth into hers because she'd run out of cute and clever things to say. Her teeth gently took hold of his lower lip, slowing his powerful kiss just for a second. She reached and undid the button and the zipper of his shorts. In a move that always drove Kirk crazy, she slipped her finger along Justin's belly beneath the elastic of his boxers, teasing and working her way down.

His breathing increased. "You are the hottest woman I think I've ever met."

Certainly not the first time she'd heard that line.

She said nothing, but allowed his hands to move under her shirt and explore. His kisses weren't as sweet as Jack's and his body didn't cause hers to tremble like Jack's did, but the heat created was intense. She could feel the crescendo of an orgasm before Justin tugged off her panties. She was about to get in bed with Jack's attorney, she thought with pleasure. Was there anything she could not accomplish? She gasped at his touch between her legs.

She fantasized about Jack, wishing she were in bed with him instead. If Jack Winston someday took the oath of office of the President, she would be the one standing by his side. Nothing would stand in her way of getting what she wanted.

Hours later, since they both had plans, they said their goodbyes. She sat in her car and her body reacted in a way that betrayed her. She shook, and then she cried. She didn't know exactly why. She missed Jack. She missed Kirk. For a moment, she felt like the soiled woman outside the hotel before Jack sent a town car for her. All of her sins were heavy like a musty wool blanket. Once this lawsuit was behind her, she would be happy. If Jack loved her, she'd be happy. If Kirk told her he couldn't live without her, she'd be happy.

Maybe a quick stop in the confession booth might help her feel better. *God, help me be happy*, she pleaded out her windshield. *Why aren't you bringing Jack back to me? Why does Kirk hate me so much? God, are you even there?*

Nicole told herself the road to victory was never an easy one, clearing her face of any tears and streaked makeup. She smiled at herself in the mirror, erasing away signs of defeat. She would win and get everything she wanted. Even if she had to sustain some bruises along the way.

God, forgive me for the bruises I am about to inflict.

Chapter 25

With both hands, I pushed my hair behind my ears in an attempt to control my curls. I wished I'd worn a ball cap to the game. "Sorry they lost," I said, with a tilted head and half grin.

"Not your fault. But, I had fun regardless." Kirk smiled and took my hand.

Strolling past the vendors with tables of souvenirs, I slid my hand out of Kirk's and hooked my arm around his. This day had been a vast improvement over the last time I had visited this ballpark with my brother. Other than the sprinkling of rain on the way into the ballpark, which made my hair expand, the day had been perfect. No red flags or heaviness burdened me. Highlight films replayed in my mind of making love to Kirk into the night and again this morning. The thought of reconvening again in his bedroom shortly made me tingle a bit.

My ankle lightly throbbed and I could no longer suppress my limp.

"Oh, let's sit. I forgot about your ankle," Kirk said.

We took a seat on a bench on the platform to wait for the train. I spoke, facing him, "So, I have an idea. I think I'm going to hold a fundraiser to help fund a memorial to those who died in the crash. I feel like doing something for the ones who weren't as lucky as we were. What do you think?"

"I think you've got a good heart, Jezebel Stone," he said, not looking at me, but instead gazing down toward the floor.

"Or, I'm still struggling with survivor's guilt, guilty for not rescuing anyone, for not—"

"Let's stick with good heart." He looked up at me with a smile.

We boarded the Metro and took the second seat on the left. "Hey, it's our seat," I said.

"Excellent."

Small talk had evaporated along with the day's light, and all that remained were touches and quick kisses aboard the subway train. I rested my head on Kirk's shoulder and yawned.

"Jezebel…"

"Yeah?"

"I like you. I like you a lot…"

I picked my head up to face him, wondering what had caused him to sound so intense. A flinch of panic hit my stomach. I hadn't considered getting dumped the day after sex, but this sounded like it could be heading in that direction.

Tension gripped his words. "I'm sort of worried…about things."

"Kirk, what are you worried about? Does this have to do with your divorce not being final yet?" I made a note to ask him when that exact date would be.

"Um, well…"

"Oh crap, you're dumping me! Sex with me is driving you back to your wife, isn't it?"

I forced a smile to make my statement appear as if I was joking, but I wasn't joking.

"No, no, I'm not going back with my wife." His

hand squeezed my knee as he looked off.

"Okay, so what's your worry?"

I sat up and looked intently into his eyes as he spoke, "I just like you a lot. When I started this whole thing, I didn't have any intentions of this lasting. I was sort of doing it for fun, a casual date or a friendship. I just didn't intend for this to happen…"

The brakes on the train locked before the intended stop, causing us to brace against the seat ahead of us. The train then started forward again.

"Do you want it to keep happening?" I asked, my voice creeping into a high pitch.

"I do. I really do. It's just, I'm not so sure you know the real me yet and I think you'll run when you find out."

"Are you like a serial killer or something? Kirk, you're scaring me now." My mind heard Ken's pinging.

"No, I just…I just hope you still like me as you get to know me better. That's all I'm saying."

"Kirk, you're a nice guy. I think your wife may have killed your self-esteem just a bit, that's all."

"So, you're not going anywhere?"

"Just back to your place to have my way with you."

"Perfect." He kissed my cheek. "Okay, I'll stop worrying." His half smile still appeared hesitant. He turned his face toward the window, blackened by the tunnel wall.

I leaned against him again, but this time my mind was not as relaxed. Just like with Michael, I had most likely jumped into bed again with a guy I wasn't sure I completely knew. Too afraid to ask a serious question, I asked, "When's your birthday again? And what's your middle name?"

****

Tuesday morning, I scurried out of the office elevator, trying not to reinjure my tender ankle. As I passed the wooden reception desk, I delivered a smile to the receptionist.

"Jezebel. This was left for you by the security guy." The receptionist handed me a white envelope. "Inside is your security pass. Someone found it on the sidewalk this morning by the front door."

"Oh my. I dropped it Sunday night? The building could have been broken into."

"Sunday? And it wasn't found until this morning…strange," she said.

"Yeah, strange. Well, at least some honest person turned it in. I really need to be more careful. Thanks."

My mind flashed through the walk from the rooftop fireworks to the Metro. How could I have dropped it?

As soon as I stepped into my office, I sensed something was not right. My desk was messier than I had left it, a file drawer was half open and a file lay open on the floor. I paused, wondering which attorney had hurried through my office in a desperate search for a document. Straightening my desk, I noticed a note from Justin asking me to join him for coffee downstairs. Had Justin made the mess?

Before meeting Justin, I poked my head in to see Ken. "Hey, good lookin', how was your holiday?"

"Fantastic! How about you?"

"Well," I said, taking a seat, "I slept with Kirk. It was great, really great…"

"Wow. But, TMI. And I do not mean too much information. I'm saying Three Mile Island, baby—"

"I'm well aware of your favorite disaster reference, my dear friend, and why do you do this to me?"

"You're right. I'm being harsh, but slightly joking too. It's just…ping, ping, my damn radar won't shut up. I'm happy for you, really, I am."

I smiled and then softly voiced frustration, "Damn you and your pinging and your TMI." I pointed at him and then fell, defeated, against the back of the seat. "He's awesome and we had terrific sex, but then yesterday he started telling me he's worried and that I don't know the real him."

"Look, you slept with him, yes it's a big step, but you didn't agree to marry the guy. Did you?"

"No. Quick reminder—he's already married."

"Right. Right. Details." Ken tapped his finger against his chin. I waited for him to refer to himself as Lucy and to call me Charlie Brown and demand I put a nickel in his tin cup. "Just take a few steps back, until you feel you know the 'real Kirk'. Slow it down. Guard your heart."

"How are you so wise yet still single?"

"I'm single because I'm wise."

After the Charlie and Lucy session, I headed downstairs to meet Justin. I spotted his smiling face across the coffee shop. Standing in line to order a coffee, I waved at him. With a hot coffee in hand, I joined him.

"Glad you came," he said, standing.

We exchanged obligatory small talk. "So, your boyfriend seems nice." His voice trailed off and I wondered if he was sincere.

"Oh, yeah, thanks. We had a good weekend."

"What's wrong? Is he bad in bed?" Justin smiled a

crooked grin, picking up his coffee cup.

"He's great in bed. I mean, things are fine." Blushing, I wished to change the topic, but my mouth spewed, trying to explain. "It's, I don't know, I'm just concerned we went too far too soon... Sorry."

He smiled, appearing uneasy, resting back against the leather booth.

I smiled back. "How was your weekend?"

"Well, if it makes you feel better, I think I went too far, too. I met a hot woman at a coffee shop and we had lunch and drinks and went back to my place. Now, I can't reach her. The number she gave me either isn't hers, or I wrote it down wrong."

"Oh, ouch. So you were bad in bed."

"No! Top of my game. I feel so used... I'm a man-slut." He laughed, running his fingers through his hair.

"We're both sluts. Oh my gosh, we're both Jezebels."

He laughed and changed the subject. "So, we need to get ready for D'Angelo."

"Yes, we do. Hey, did you tear through my office in a hurry looking for something? My desk was a bit out of order."

"No, I had stopped by my office after fireworks to pick up my laptop and left you a note, but your office looked fine. I left no mess, promise."

"Okay, strange. Well, let's talk D'Angelo. I think the questions look great. You successfully used the info from the tape, without using the recording. I think it will baffle her. She'll wonder how we know she met Winston at the hotel. I don't get it. Let's just use the recording and get this case thrown out."

"We have to do what the client wants."

"Feels slimy."

"Definitely. I think they're both a bit slimy," Justin said, sipping his coffee with his eyes still on me. "He deserves to lose money, but the partners at Crosby don't. They're getting screwed. That's why we need to get this case thrown out on summary judgment, for the innocent people involved."

"I hope he decides not to run for office. I'll feel compelled to rat him out. It doesn't feel right representing a cheater."

"We don't know for sure he's a cheater and besides, we're just doing our job. Our job is to provide him with a defense. Provide his firm with a defense. We're not here for moral guidance. Plus, if he is a cheater, does that necessarily make him a bad senator?"

"Once a liar, always a liar and an affair is a big lie. Who knows what he'd be capable of lying about."

"So liar is worse than slut? I confessed truthfully that I was a slut, so that's okay?"

"You're not married. You got played. But yes, lying trumps all other sins in my book. Well, maybe murderer is worse, and child molester, and rapist…"

"What about extortionist? This D'Angelo's extorting."

"I think they're playing some sort of sick game with each other and we're stuck in the middle."

He lifted his coffee in the air, "Well, here's to gaining lots of billable hours from the crazies and their game playing. No harm to us. Just doing our jobs."

"Cheers to the crazies."

His head tilted and his eyes peered into mine, stopping my laughter. "Something good did come out of this crazy case, Jez. I enjoy winning our friendship back."

"Cheers again."

His smile made me forget about pinging, about a boyfriend who held a secret, and about a mysteriously disheveled office. My focus today would be winning a case, a case that in my opinion, held no good outcome for either defendant or plaintiff.

Chapter 26

Nicole agreed to meet Kirk for lunch. He'd chosen a restaurant that was a good distance from Olive Oyl's office. She was sure he was preventing a run-in with her. Although he wouldn't tell her what he wanted to talk about, she guessed he most likely missed her. Maybe sex with Olive Oyl repulsed him, and he craved a real woman. Still her stomach tossed a bit with nerves, which surprised her. She didn't like feeling nervous.

He was seated in a corner table of the small restaurant. As she approached, she anticipated that he would stand, and pull out her chair like usual, but he didn't. He just snapped out her name in a huff.

"Well, Kirk, you seem to be in a pleasant mood today," she said, sliding out her own chair. His glance moved down her body, and rested on the table in front of her.

"Nicole, I'm not here to play your games. You betrayed me and I want you to make things right."

She ordered a diet Pepsi and a salad, and she let what he said sink into her mind. "How did I betray you, Kirk? You kicked me out—"

"I know you slept with Winston. Just admit it, and stop lying to me. Please." He slapped his hand against the table for apparent emphasis.

"Kirk, I did slip. I was weak, and I'll admit, I was

coerced into having sex with Jack. I felt guilty and wanted it to stop. He said if I stopped I'd lose my job. And look what happened, I got demoted and moved to another floor. That's why I'm suing. Kirk, I love you but I'm weak."

"Shut up, Nicole, you're so full of it. You're the furthest thing from weak. I also know you were in love with him. Damn it, can you for once, just be honest with me?"

As she tapped the straw on the table to release it from its wrapper, she rolled her eyes. He must've read the same damn transcript in Olive's office as she had. She licked her lips, composing her words thoughtfully. "Kirk, believe it or not, I can be weak, and I was lost and confused. Things weren't going well with us and I fell for Jack's lies when I needed an ego boost. I regret it. You were the one who told me about Jack telling his attorneys that we met at a hotel, so maybe you also heard that I said some things to him about loving him. I was simply trying to get him to settle the suit. All I want is my job back, and to stop all this craziness."

"Things were going poorly with us because you were sleeping with someone else. You're lying. You're playing me for a fool—"

"What reason do I have, Kirk, to play you? Huh? Seriously. What's my reason for stringing you along if I don't still love you?"

"Your fear of being without a man. Your ego. Maybe the fact that I'm with someone else, and you have to keep your nose in it. I don't know and I've been wondering the same damn thing, Nicole, exactly what motivates you to do anything you do. Why don't you tell me?"

"Love. Love motivates me, Kirk."

"Love for yourself."

She tweaked out a tear right then to soften his blows. It did hurt to hear him say that.

"What do you want me to do, Kirk, to make things right?"

"I want you to settle the suit now, before the deposition. Drop it. Or maybe I can make some money selling the future Senator's story to the tabloids—"

"You wouldn't do that, Kirk. I know you and you wouldn't do that to me or to yourself. You'd just humiliate yourself. And you'd make Olive lose her job. Imagine what her bosses would think if they found out she was sleeping with the plaintiff's husband? And that he shared info with me, and gave me the security pass to her office, and—"

"What security pass?"

"Your little girlfriend's careless, it's not my fault."

"Unbelievable. What did you do, Nicole?"

"Oh, nothing. I'm harmless. Just stop attacking me."

"Listen. Drop the suit, before your deposition." His elbow rocked the table as he shook his finger at me. "I'll take the risk of collateral damage, but I will expose Winston."

"It's in your best interest to let me do a fantastic job at the deposition and make them nervous so the settlement is huge. Thanks to your assistance, the deposition is going to go very well, Kirk. I promise you this. So, what I'll do for you is this. I'll go whining to my attorney that I want her to request minimal staff in attendance at the deposition. I have a fear of crowds, blah blah blah. Attorneys only in the room. So, that way your little skinny lover won't be there. I'm sure they'll go for it or I'll threaten a delay. I'll think of something. And, I have another plan already in the works to ensure the attorneys want to settle quickly afterward—"

"Yeah, you're so weak, Nicole." Kirk's sarcasm hurt.

"Be nice, Kirk. This is all very painful to be caught up in. I want it over as much as you do."

Kirk rolled his eyes and pulled his body closer to the table. Nicole continued. It was her turn to attack. "By the way, you think you're so innocent in all this. We weren't even separated and you were hooking up with Olive Oyl, so you're no saint, Kirk. And you haven't been honest with this woman, so you're a big liar, too. Get off your high horse."

"Stop it, you started this, you got this mess rolling. You did this."

"Well, then let's stop it. I'll settle my suit and you will agree to go counseling."

He flinched. He stared, sitting still as a statue. Finally, he broke the silence. "You honestly believe this marriage is salvageable?"

"Yes, at least schedule one counseling session, Kirk. I'm not going to be the one to give up."

"Fine. You settle the case and give me half of the money and we'll go to one session."

"Perfect." She crossed her arms, and sat back in triumph. She was a genius.

****

As if seeing Kirk for lunch wasn't stressful enough, Nicole got an urgent text from Jack to meet him at his house around nine o'clock that night. His wife was out of town, so it was safe to go there. Her insides quivered at the thought of being alone with Jack in his beautiful home. Completely thrilling. She'd have plenty of time after work to make herself gorgeous.

In his usual manner of treating her like a prostitute, he sent a town car to pick her up on her corner. Before exiting the car, she removed her cell phone's password, making it one step easier to access covertly.

Before she knocked, the front door opened. Jack pulled her inside. His hand on her arm stimulated her entire body, buckling her knees. The sleeves of his white dress shirt were rolled up to his elbows, his tie was loosened. His eyes appeared drained, and his face was sunken and aged. She didn't like the vibe she was getting. He hugged her. Very odd.

"Jack, what's wrong? Why am I here?"

"I need you, Nicole. We need to talk."

She followed him into the formal living room and sat next to him on a large sofa that faced the bay window. Papers and a laptop covered the coffee table in front of them.

"You're scaring me, Jack."

He handed her a glass of white wine. She took a sip and watched his eyes stab into hers.

"We need to finish this game, Nicole. Things are a bit out of control right now and we need this case to end, and end now. Something's happened."

"What happened? What's going on?" She held her clutch on her lap, her body tight with tension. She took another sip of wine. Her insides trembled, but she tried to appear calm. Her phone was poking out of the back pocket of her clutch. She'd record this in case he said something she could use in the future, just like dear old Justin suggested.

He inhaled and leaned his elbows on his knees. He turned his head toward her but did not make eye contact. "Nicole, I know a while back, before things got so ugly, we had something special. You know we connected and became friends. I want that now, I need a friend."

"I want that, too."

"My marriage is in trouble. My wife is causing the trouble. My chances of being senator are in trouble…"

"What's up with your marriage?" A wave of excitement hit her.

"I had suspected that my wife was being unfaithful. Different clues, different things, so I started snooping."

The thought of her picking up the pieces of his shattered marriage exhilarated her. She sat upright. After taking a sip of wine, she set the glass on the coffee table and reached over and touched his leg.

"What I found could impact many people's lives. She is definitely having an affair. I've been snooping in her email since figuring out the password wasn't hard. She uses our dead dog's name for everything. I found this in the trash folder."

He handed her a printout of an email chain. She glanced through it and it was certainly proof of an affair. Arranging meeting places, exchanging affections, it was damaging. "So who is 'Blue Sparrow'?"

Jack turned his body and looked her in the eyes. "That's the Secret Services' nickname for the President of the United States."

She gulped and could not believe what she was hearing and recording. "What?"

"That's the account he gives to a few family and

friends. Yeah, all these times she was visiting the First Lady, she was getting closer to her best friend's husband. Or, the sorority sister thing was a cover. I can't tell how long it's been going on."

"Jack...that's crazy, it's so... What are you going to do with this information?"

"Nothing. If this gets out, I'll look like a fool. The media will dig into me and even before I get a chance to run for Senator I'll be ruined. Plus this will destroy the President. Not that I don't want to see him go down, but it will be harmful to our party and to his reputation. He planned to endorse me. His ratings are high right now. The economy is finally improving. I need him to stay on top so I can be on top. I want to use this to blackmail him to make sure he really sees to it that I'm successful, if you know what I mean." He glared into her eyes, making sure she was understanding him.

"So, you're not going to leave your wife?"

"No, I'm going to let the whore know that I know what's going on. Then, I'll make sure she ends it and helps get me my Senate seat. I'll remind her that it's in the President's best interest that she cooperates. I really don't care at this point if her heart's not in it. I just need her public smiling loyal face for the next year. I will scare the living hell out of her when I let her know what I'm capable of doing to her if she doesn't cooperate. She loves being wealthy and living the lifestyle she lives."

"What about me? Where do I fit into all this?"

"You, my dear," He turned and looked at her with a smile that pleased her, "are going to settle this case, quickly and quietly." He stood and paced in front of the window.

She pulled her phone out and hit the stop button while his back was turned, then tossed her purse on the floor. Inhaling a deep breath, she needed to be strong and make sure he wasn't screwing her again.

She glided behind him and brushed her hand along his back, stopping to exhale against his neck. "Jack, I love you. I want to be there for you. But don't mess with me. Why not dump your wife and let me be the smiling face by your side?"

"Too risky. I need the wholesome family picture."

She slipped her hands around his waist, pressing her breasts against his back. Her thumbs cruised inside his waistband. She could tell by his breathing he enjoyed it. "I'd do anything for you, Jack."

He turned around, wrapping his hands slowly around the base of her neck. "Anything?" He snapped her neck toward him, yanking her against his body. Her breath halted.

Her eyes cemented into his, neither of them wanted to release the other's stare.

Unlike with any other man, she was completely feeble inside of his arms. But she couldn't let him know this. She pushed him away with her hips. "Didn't I say I would do anything, Jack? But I won't let you abuse me. You need to treat me right, Jack. She completely screwed you. I will be loyal to you—"

His mouth pressed into hers, sending a shock wave through her limbs. To show she was still in control, she grabbed the back of his head with her one hand and his backside in the other. With both of his hands around her neck, he shoved her away and out of his kiss.

"Nicole." He wiped her lipstick off of his lower lip. "I want to trust you. Can I trust you?"

Panting, she answered. "No one on this earth does to me what you do to me, Jack Winston. If you're loyal to me, I'll die being loyal to you."

"Nicole, I'm sorry about Rebecca."

"Really?"

"Yeah, I'm sorry. It was a fling. I've always been sorry about Rebecca."

"Jack, she messed everything up. She's what made me crazy."

"I know. I'm sorry."

The power of his kiss pushed her backward, so she dug her nails into the back of his shirt to steady herself. The taste of him satisfied her more than his touch. She wanted to consume him, every piece of him. Having other men want her was exciting, but having Jack love her, was the pinnacle of all things pleasurable. If she could grow old next to one man, it would be Jack Winston.

Her back pressed into the living room wall as his lips sank into the skin of her neck. Her shoulder caused a family photo to rock. His hands slid beneath her shirt, resting on the sides of her bare ribs.

"Jack, what your wife did was awful. I would never betray you."

She watched his hands push her shirt up, and then his lips pressed into her cleavage causing her head to roll back and slam against the wall. His forefingers teased beneath the top of her bra.

"Jack, can we go upstairs?" she asked into his ear.

Surprising her, he lifted her off the ground and he carried her up the steps. This was more than she'd expected and her head was ready to explode.

The cool, silky comforter wrapped the sides of her

head as her body collapsed into his bed, his wife's bed. She wondered if the president had been here. Jack hovered above her for a moment as his hand teased, sliding up her thigh. Although she'd had his hand there plenty of times before, this was more than she could handle. As he slid her lacy thong over her knees, she screamed his name. He brought his body back on top of her and kissed her hard. She reached between his legs, tearing open his zipper, forcing his pants over his hips.

He tilted his body on his side next to her. Caressing her cheek, he looked into her eyes.

She was on top of the world. There was nothing standing between her and victory. Jack was hers. Well, there was one more thing she wanted in order secure her grips on Jack Winston.

In a breathy plea, as if she were his subconscious instructing him, "I want to be with you every day. I want to work next to you again."

Equally as breathy, as if completing mile ten of a marathon, he said, "We'll let our lawyers negotiate, but you must," His thigh slid on top of her pelvis pressing her into the mattress, "you must keep quiet."

His attempts to weaken her into submission were transparent. She was about to agree to play the role of the mistress while he ran for Senate and eventually president, with his wife by his side. Of course, she'd be quiet, but she wouldn't let him take advantage of her. She imagined in order to make his wife also submit to his plan, he'd be doing the same thing to her.

She shoved him off of her and onto his back. In one swift move she straddled him, but before she let him penetrate, she pushed his hands onto the mattress. She flipped all of her hair to one side and said, "I'll do anything for you, Jack, as long as I feel I'm getting something out of this too. Make room for me in your offices, all of your offices, Jack."

He smiled, perhaps not in agreement, but most likely at her body gliding on top of his. She knew she had him and she knew no other woman had the power to please him like this.

After a while, he rolled her onto her back, slowly, supporting her head in a tender gesture. His kisses and his movements were slow, deliberate, comforting. She returned his affection with an equal amount of giving. This was the first time in a long time that she had made love.

Hours rolled by, accomplishing the passage of an entire night. They captured a few moments of sleep, but resumed lovemaking. Before the first rays of morning broke into the room, she disappeared downstairs while Jack slept. First she called for a cab to meet her on the corner. Then, she took out her phone and snapped pictures of the print out of the email exchange between the president and Dara. She needed the insurance.

She finished dressing and kissed Jack on the cheek. Without opening his eyes, his hand caressed her arm.

"I called a cab to meet me down on the corner. I'm going to leave before the sun rises. Need to be safe and smart, Jack."

"Good girl."

As she walked up the sidewalk, she replayed their conversation. His wishes to settle the case quickly weren't in her best interest. He needed to first see her performance at the deposition so she could show him that he shouldn't mess with her, ever, and that she was not a pushover.

On the corner, she didn't feel filthy like she usually did after their encounters. Instead she smiled with delight, basking in the glow of victory. She held secrets in her purse that were powerful enough to bring down the leader of the free world. She had just left the bed of a man who held the potential to someday be the leader of that free world. How could a woman in her position feel anything less than triumphant?

Chapter 27

"Really? Are you kidding me?" Cursing the sky, I hustled to retrieve the contents of my briefcase from the sidewalk. I spoke aloud to myself, to my guardian angels, or whoever was assigned to me today. "I do not have time for this. I really do not have time to be a klutz."

"Let me help you." A calm voice pulled me out of my argument with a higher power while a hand reached at some papers being tossed by a breeze. It was not a guardian angel, just Justin.

"I didn't know you were there." Embarrassed, I babbled. "Justin, thank you. The more I hurry, the more I stumble. Are you running late too?"

"No, just stepped out to grab Starbucks."

"Thanks," I said, taking the papers from Justin's hands. He smiled, seemingly entertained by me. "I won't hold you up anymore. D'Angelo in two hours. Are you nervous?"

"No, I'm ready. I'm not doing the questioning, so I'm good."

"So, can I sit in on it?"

"Don't think so. Apparently D'Angelo's attorney made a stink about a small audience being present. No paralegals."

"Oh, okay. Just call me if you need anything during it."

"Will do. Do you think you can make it to your office in one piece?"

I squinted my eyes at him. "Funny, Justin. I can make it from here."

He laughed, waving to me as he turned.

Once I reached my desk, I got right to work, upset for starting the day covered in perspiration. I dug through the pile of work in front of me, losing track of time. As I finished replying to an email, Ken poked his head into my office.

"Hey, didn't see you this morning. Busy?"

"Hey, Ken. Yes, I got a late start."

"Coming in from Metro Man's condo slowing you up?"

"Ha. Funny. No, in accordance with your wise advice, I imposed a no sleepover rule during the week. I do miss him though, but like you said, I'm keeping things slow and safe."

"And hot and heavy on the weekends?"

"Hmmm, maybe…" I stared off in the distance, pretending to imagine a future love scene.

"Oh you pretty little tramp, you." He laughed hard at his own joke.

"Sounds like the pot calling the kettle black."

"Touché. Ta ta, Jezebel, queen of seduction…" He continued to laugh at his joke as he moved down the hall. The Jezebel joke never got old with Ken.

I smiled at his echoing laughter, and then bolted out of my seat when I saw the time. Pulling two files into my arms, I hurried down the hall toward the large conference room near the reception area. The etched glass windows made it only possible to see silhouettes. I noticed at least one figure moving inside the room.

This could be my chance to catch a glimpse of D'Angelo.

I pushed open the door and saw a blonde woman at the head of the table.

"Hi," I said.

"Oh, hello, I'm Sarah, your court reporter for today."

"I'm Jezebel, nice to meet you. I'm the paralegal on this case, so let me know if you need anything."

"Thanks. I'm all set up."

"Good, the attorneys should be here soon. Justin Moorehead and Jonathon Green are the attorneys for the defense. I've got their cards here for you."

"Thank you. I'm going to run to the restroom then, since I'm ready."

"Down the hall on the left."

I followed, disappointed to not meet the plaintiff or observe an interaction between Winston and D'Angelo. Justin took the door from my hand. "Justin, the court reporter will be back in a couple minutes. Good luck."

"Thanks, I'll call you if we need anything."

Oh, how I wished I could hang out and watch the show. Instead, I zoomed back to my office, hoping there was still a chance to see the characters in this case later.

My cell phone rang from inside my briefcase. I hoped it was Kirk. It wasn't.

"Hi, Mom."

"Oh sweetie, I thought it would go to voicemail. I was going to leave a message. Sorry to bother you, honey."

"No problem. What's up?"

"Well, I just made a call. I have the wildest plan for

a little bachelorette party for your old mom."

"Oh, Mom, I am so not smoking weed with you."

"No, nothing like that. I hired us a psychic to do readings on you, your sister and me on Saturday—a week before the wedding! We'll have some wine and some take-out and get a reading done. What do you say? I haven't done one in a long time, and I really want to."

"Oh, Mom, I don't know…"

"Come on. It will be a scream. Maybe we can get your sister drunk."

"Mom, she's not going to get drunk with all her IVF stuff."

"Please?" my mother begged. I was pretty sure my mother was jumping up and down.

"It's your party, Mom. Okay, I'm in." As I stuck some papers into a file, I smirked at the thought of Cala letting lose, getting hammered, and buying into the clairvoyant powers of a psychic.

"Thanks, sweetie. This is going to be a blast. I promise."

As I finished the conversation with my mother, I wondered what my reading would show. Had I found a true love? Would another near death experience lurk in my future? Or, would the psychic see nothing but boredom lying ahead for me?

To better create my own happy future, I sent Kirk a quick "I miss you" text before tossing my phone away into my briefcase. I felt a wave of power at the thought of controlling my own destiny.

Chapter 28

Nicole's stomach panged with a nervous spasm at the thought of seeing Justin. She hadn't planned out all she would say to him, but she was confident her mere presence would shock him into a stupor. She had been so preoccupied with thoughts of seeing Jack and wondering how he would react to her and her answers, she'd given Justin very little thought. She'd even toyed with the idea of messing with Jezebel, but decided to keep that little token of fun in her back pocket just a bit longer.

The elevator doors opened and she entered the reception area of Harrington & Paulson, along with Silvia Anton, her attorney. The contemporary décor was much nicer than Crosby's. She liked that Jack could afford the expensive attorneys. She scanned the area and noticed the backs of some suits disappear into the adjacent conference room. The receptionist instructed her attorney to go inside the same room.

She took in a cleansing breath and asked God to get her through this day successfully. When she entered, she first made eye contact with Jack, who immediately re-engaged in conversation with his attorneys. All she wanted was to walk up to him, wrap her arms around him and whisper in his ear how she could make everything better, make his life perfect. Sadness slithered across her heart as she imagined him discussing strategy to bury her. She had to stay strong. Jack liked his women strong.

Justin's back was facing her, but she recognized him. His hands were in his suit pants pockets, pulling them tight against his backside. He turned his head, probably in curiosity to take in the sight of the plaintiff who just made her entrance. Nicole looked right into his eyes. His eyes appeared to squint and strain, as if attempting to adjust to a sudden burst of sunlight. She smiled. His face slipped into a frown. His skin turned an ashy gray, and then crimson filled his cheeks. His mouth opened slightly as his eyebrows crinkled. She could only imagine what his poor brain was trying to process, his heart racing faster as he connected the dots. Especially once he realized she didn't return his stare with a shocked expression, but with a look of satisfaction.

Stay on top, Nicole. Stay strong, she lectured herself.

Senior Partner Jon Green for Harrington & Paulson stood directly across the table and nodded, introducing himself. Along with her attorney, they reached across and shook his hand. Of course, his eyes hit her cleavage. Next to the partner, across from her attorney, Justin pulled out a chair. He leaned across and shook her attorney's hand. His eyes pierced Nicole's and he said, "Nicole D'Angelo." It seemed to take a long time for him to spit every syllable of her name across the table. "I'm Justin Moorehead."

Nicole smiled, never removing her eyes from his. "It's a pleasure to meet you, Mr. Moorehead."

His hand squeezed hers so hard she thought a bone would snap. She attempted to squeeze back, and had to fight hard to not show the pain on her face. Perhaps she should have yelled, "Ouch!" to embarrass him, but she couldn't look like a wimp. She pulled out a chair and took a seat, crossing her legs with self-assured poise.

Jack sat on the other side of the partner, so she was able to keep him in her periphery. She wondered if he could smell her perfume; she wore his favorite one. He jotted notes on a yellow legal pad as Nicole answered the first hours of standard mundane questions. Like a seismograph measures earthquake waves, she wished there were some way to measure the tension in the room. She couldn't help but feel a bit proud for creating it all.

Throughout the dull parts, she'd purposely trace a finger down her neck, bite playfully on a fingernail, or tug open her jacket. She wanted to keep the men distracted. It was in these moments that she knew God had intended for women to be the superior sex.

"Ms. D'Angelo, on the night of June 19th, you met Mr. Winston at a hotel, did you not?"

"Absolutely, I did."

Jack's eyes shot up off his legal pad.

"You went willingly to meet the man who you accused of sexual harassment and discrimination?"

"Yes, I did."

"Did you tell Mr. Winston at this meeting that you loved him?"

"Yes. Mr. Winston was once a wonderful boss and dear friend. I'll always love Mr. Winston. Even though I'm suing, I'm not a hateful person."

"Did you say you were in love with Mr. Winston?"

Her attorney interrupted. "I'm objecting to this line of questioning-"

Nicole looked at her, touching her leg. "It's okay, I want to answer this." Silvia's face was red and her beady eyes wide. Nicole looked back at Mr. Green. "If he told you that, he misunderstood."

"So you never said the words, 'I was in love with you'?"

"I knew what Jack Winston was doing. He called me purposely to the hotel to trick me, to seduce me, to coerce me into sleeping with him so I'd drop the suit. I may have played along with him a bit to get out of there with my pride intact, but I knew he was most likely recording me, trying to trick me into saying something damaging. Truth is, I was hoping he had asked me to the hotel to negotiate a settlement. When I felt he had other intentions, I fought back."

"Did you say you would do anything to get him back?"

"Yes." She heard air blow out of Silvia's mouth.

"Yes, you said you wanted him back?"

"Yes, I do want him back in my life. I want my job back and I'll do anything to get it back—within reason and within my moral standards, of course. When he moved me to another job, over sex, it shattered me emotionally. Damaged me. I was so distraught at this unfair treatment that I had no choice but to sue. Now, I want to make things right between Jack Winston and me. I want my job back." She shot her eyes right into Jack's. He didn't flinch. She wanted to make love to him.

"If you're so damaged by him, why would you want to work for him again?" Jon Green's smugness was no match for her own.

"This kind of position within a law firm is rare, to

work for the most senior partner in one of the most prestigious firms. No one will disagree that Mr. Winston is one of the best. I want and deserve the opportunity to work for him and follow his promising career. I believe in second chances and I think Mr. Winston knows how to make things right between us again and to behave professionally. I think Mr. Winston has learned his lesson."

The Harrington & Paulson partner flipped over two pages of his notes. Perhaps she'd just ended their line of hotel questioning.

When they recessed for lunch, before heading to a deli with Silvia, Nicole excused herself to use the restroom. She felt surprisingly calm, given the circumstances. As she turned into the vestibule before the women's and men's room doors, Justin stopped her, his body blocking her from any type of escape.

"Listen, Nicole, I don't know what you're trying to do here, but our little outing never happened. Got it? Keep your mouth shut or—"

"Or what, Justin? You'll tell your boss on me? That you slept with a plaintiff on a case you're working on? No, you listen. You negotiate on my behalf one hell of a gorgeous settlement. Or I go to the D.C. Bar with one juicy report. I tell them you told me to tape record the defendant in my case and get info on him. Which I did, by the way. You can say I tricked you, but by then, your career will be over. What was the term you used, Justin? I just need to 'ring the bell'? Well I got a whole lot a ringing to do my friend, so serve me well. Okay?"

She patted his chest and he swatted it away. She could almost feel the fire in his breath and behind his dilated pupils.

She threw in one more jab. "Oh and Justin, the paralegal you work with here? She's messing around on the wrong side of the case too, just to make you feel better."

With a hand rummaging through his hair, he turned and disappeared.

Her stomach growled, reminding her she had a lunch to attend to with her attorney. She was certain Silvia had some glowing compliments for her.

Chapter 29

Mid-afternoon, after a request from Jon Green to create a new exhibit for the deposition, I hustled up the hall toward the conference room. I was anxious to open the door, and get a smile from Justin, indicating all was going well. As I approached the reception desk, the receptionist spun in her chair, startling me. "Jezebel! Steve is looking for you—he's frantic. He needs you to help him file something ASAP."

With an eye-roll, I groaned. My usual joke was how some of the attorneys acted as if a heart or kidney had just become available for transplant. Really, was any civil pleading that urgent?

"Can you take these into conference room C for me?" I handed the exhibits to the receptionist.

"Absolutely. Run, before Steve has a coronary."

I finished with Steve and his "kidney transplant" and returned to my desk expecting to hear about the D'Angelo case at any moment. Ken popped his head in my office. "Your plaintiff is super hot. Smokin' hot."

"You saw her?"

"Yeah, everyone was leaving the conference room when I passed. I lingered. A blonde bombshell came out whispering to a frumpy looking woman. I assumed Bombshell was your girl, Frumpy was her attorney. The attorney looked a little Kathy Bates-ish, if you ask me…"

"Interesting... Oh, Justin!" I called into the hallway over Ken's shoulder.

Ken waved goodbye. "Gonna run and let you two dish."

Justin paused in the doorway. "Hey, Jez, I'm in a hurry. Can we catch up in the morning?"

"Fine. Leave me hanging."

He looked at me with apparent sadness and defeat.

"Oh, you don't look happy," I said.

"Yeah, I gotta go. She was tough. Ugly. Hard to crack," he said with a tired voice, looking into the papers under his arm.

"Let me know if I can do anything," I said.

He flashed me his hand in a quick farewell gesture.

Odd, I thought. As of late, Justin never turned down an opportunity to chat with me. His demeanor was unsettling. And that was the first time I had heard D'Angelo described as "ugly."

****

The next morning I didn't wait for Justin, but burst into his office after one warning knock on his doorframe and sat in his guest chair.

"So, what has got you so bugged about this plaintiff?"

Justin kept writing, never looking up from his notepad. "Good morning, Jezebel. I have a lot to do before the depo resumes in an hour. Can this wait?"

"You suck. Give me something."

My smile faded with his huff. The slam of his pen flattening against his notepad startled me. "Honestly, it was bad yesterday. And, I didn't sleep last night. I'm proposing to Green to suggest to Winston when this deposition is through that he settle. Settle fast. I'm sorry, Jezebel, but I'm going to have to ask you to leave."

Without a word, I did as he asked. And the last months of easy friendship were suddenly erased. I felt like his low-life assistant who was again paying the price for rebuking his holiday party advances. Needing some coffee and Ken, I slowly sauntered down the hall.

Ken assisted in lifting my spirits with our Lucy and Charlie Brown session, and then I headed off to work. As much as I tried throughout the day, I couldn't shake the ghost of my conversation with Justin. It hovered around me, saddening me.

Knocking the ghost out of my head, Kirk called. "Hey pretty lady, I'd like to get you out of your office today. What do you say? When does your deposition break for lunch? You're going to want to escape before the attorneys catch you and make you work through lunch."

He had an amazing knack for remembering my schedule. "Oh. Sure, I'll escape."

"Can you leave before noon? Meet me at the Corner Bakery again?"

"Um, sure. See you then."

Due to another emergency, I headed to the elevator in my usual rushed manner at a couple of minutes before noon. I decided to go out through the main elevators instead of the back ones, to see if the deposition had retired. Walking past the reception desk, I heard the familiar squeak of the conference room door swinging open, slowed my stride and glanced toward the door. Justin exited first. His eyes met mine. Still irritated by his treatment this morning, I turned and moved toward the elevator. He didn't stop me.

It had been days since I'd last seen Kirk, so his quick kiss outside the restaurant and familiar scent made me prickle with pleasure. We bantered and collected our meals. Our trays touched as we sat in a small table, facing each other.

"So, the deposition was getting out just as I left."

"Oh? Is it over, or just a lunch break?"

"I'm assuming lunch, but I didn't stick around to talk to anyone—"

"Good. I mean, glad you weren't late."

"Well, I was Jezebel-late, as my sister likes to say. A few minutes anyway…"

"That reminds me, I bought you something." He leaned toward the floor and opened his briefcase.

Excitement and embarrassment battled to be my main emotion. Excitement won as he handed me a rectangular box with a small silver bow.

"Oh, what's this for?"

"Today is the three month anniversary of the day we met."

And the three month anniversary of the scariest day of my life.

"Thank you. How thoughtful." I pulled off the bow and opened the box to reveal a silver Movado watch. "Wow, it's beautiful. Thank you, Kirk. A watch? Are you trying to tell me something?" I smiled and slipped it on my wrist.

"No, actually, the opposite. If you hadn't been late that day, we would have never met. So, I know I tease you about your lateness, but I'm grateful for it."

A tear stung at the back of my eyes. No one had ever been pleased with my flaws before. "Thank you, Kirk." I couldn't say anything else, fearing a flow of tears would embarrass me.

"You're welcome."

"So, is this to make up for freaking me out with your post-ballgame speech on the Metro?"

"Um, yeah. Sorry if I scared you. I didn't mean to."

"It did concern me a bit. Do you want to elaborate?"

"Um, well, maybe tonight? Not in Corner Bakery."

The sentimental tears had been chased away. Tired of being put off by the men in my life, and feeling fearless, I surprised myself by saying, "I'd like to talk right now. What won't I like to know about you?"

Kirk's eyes widened and then shot down to watch his fingers fiddle with his fork. He paused and fidgeted long enough to convey his uncomfortable presence in the spotlight. At first I wanted to give him a way out, to tell him it was okay if we waited to talk, but I sat there and did nothing. I wanted to hear what he had to say. Right in the middle of Corner Bakery.

"Well, it's just that I wasn't fully forthcoming the night I met you about the true state of my marriage. And I want to apologize." His eyes met mine.

"Oh? What do you mean?" A panicky sensation filled my body.

He leaned forward, taking a deep breath. His body rocked a bit, probably from a bouncing foot. "Um, we were in a state of planning the separation, not fully separated. We have since moved into separate places and are officially finished."

I twisted the watch around on my wrist, thinking, replaying the last three months. "I see. Kirk, when we ran into your wife that day after lunch, she was wearing her ring. Were you still together then?"

"She was in the process of moving out."

"Oh, okay."

"I'm sorry, Jez. I should have told you sooner. Things progressed with us unexpectedly and I never wanted to ruin what we had going. I'm sorry."

I didn't feel like letting him off the hook quite yet. "So, you had mentioned once that you would consider counseling if she wanted to. Is that still the case?"

"I feel like I'm the one being deposed now." He laughed a forced laugh, stopping when I didn't return it. "I suppose I deserve it. No, that's no longer the case."

Relief cascaded over me as I folded up the remaining red flag, and packed it away, turning down the volume of Ken's pinging. This answered many questions that had lingered, quashing doubt. So starting off with lies wasn't the best way to begin a relationship, and come to think of it, neither was a concussion and a sprained shoulder, so today we would start anew. With truth and a silver watch.

"Are you okay?" he asked.

"Yeah, I think so. I'm sure it was a hard time and we had just met, so I couldn't expect you to divulge all the details to me about your crumbling marriage."

"Thanks for understanding." His wide smile conveyed his relief.

"So that's it? Anything else you need to confess?" I couldn't help but smile back.

A passing customer apologized for bumping our table, causing the drinks to teeter. We steadied our glasses. He looked down and with one more fork fiddle he exhaled and said, "Nope, that's it. I'm clean. Thanks for listening."

The table, now steady, was still coated in a thin

layer of awkwardness. I spoke to try to cut into it a bit, "So, it's really been three months? Time flies. Wow, that reminds me. I did more work this week on getting the memorial done. The Metro wants to help, but their budget is tight and said if we could get some outside donations, it would help move things along, maybe get a bank to sponsor it or something. So, I've decided to start shopping for a sponsor and also maybe do a fundraiser. Maybe get some other survivors involved? What do you think?"

"Like I said before, you've got a big heart Jezebel Stone."

I twisted the watch again around my wrist and looked at the time. "Thanks. Just don't break it."

****

When I got to my desk, I stopped before sitting. A small brown paper bag from Au Bon Pain rested on my chair with a note that said, "Sorry for being a grump. Here's my peace offering. -Justin." Inside the bag was a chocolate chip cookie. Wow, two gifts within an hour. I took a bite of the cookie and grinned.

Chapter 30

Nicole's legs wobbled, her stomach twisted with sickness. Her shoulder ached with the weight of her briefcase and she wanted to throw her pumps into the street—or at someone, anyone. After saying goodbye to Silvia, she wished that she could run to her car and drive far away, but she had to make a brave appearance in the office.

She headed to her floor, glad not to see Jack on the elevator or in the lobby. Once there, she faked a grin to Dana and a few others who looked her way in curiosity. A ball of tears pressed against the insides of her cheeks.

She escaped into the ladies' room, dropping her briefcase to the floor. Her body betrayed her. She fell against the cool tiled wall. It could no longer bear the weight of what her heart had been carrying all day. Tears, stupid weak tears, covered her face. She wiped her nose with the edge of her sleeve. Stop, just pull yourself together, she begged to herself. Watching Jack's glares all day, Justin's narrowed eyes, intimate questioning and painful lying, had all brimmed into a bucket of stupid weak tears.

Growing up, she was scolded for crying. "Toughen up, Nicole. Stop the damn crying," her father would say. She was never able to wrap him around her finger like other little girls could do with their fathers. Her father treated her like her brothers, yelling at her after an injury, "Rub some dirt on it, Nicole. That couldn't have hurt." She heard his words now, and instead of feeling resentment for them, she welcomed them. She wanted her father to yell at her right now.

The restroom door opened not far from where she braced against the wall. She covered her face and headed toward a stall.

"Nicole."

"Jack, what the hell?" She wiped her cheeks before facing him.

"I went to your desk, someone said you came in here." He reached behind him and locked the restroom door's deadbolt.

She tried to release the strong Nicole, the powerful Nicole who slept with Jack in his wife's bed, but she couldn't find her. His eyes, his touch, released the beaten-down, weak Nicole who she held captive inside. Her back collapsed against the same tiles that supported her minutes ago. Her knees buckled and she crumpled into an embarrassed heap of sobbing mess on the floor. He joined her. His back against the tiled walls, side by side, they sat without words.

She swallowed up her emotions and breathed shallow breaths so she couldn't feel any pain. His arms rested on his knees, an inch from her.

"So, your deposition went amazingly well. Not sure what all the tears are for. In fact, one of my attorneys actually had the audacity to suggest strongly that I settle. I'd almost hazard a guess that you got to him." Jack paused, watching her. "Hmm, you didn't flinch. I'm thinking I'm right. I'll have to figure out what to do about him."

She wiped the back of her hand across her nose

like a child. "Do you remember your campaign fundraiser at the Mayflower that I worked so hard on last year? After dinner, you were mingling, talking with some party big-wigs while I spoke with some wives about twenty feet away. You took your eyes off the person you were talking to and our eyes connected. You smiled at me. From across the room you thanked me for helping you, for being with you. I loved that look you gave me. Today, your eyes hurt me. You threw hate at me. It's the reason I can't stand up right now. The truth is—I love you, Jack. I know that I love you. And I'm sorry."

He sighed and stood, straightening his pants and jacket, his dress shoes clicked on the tile floor. He extended his hand down toward her and helped her stand. Her hand was happy inside of his. Gently, he leaned into her face and kissed her. A slow, soft kiss that weakened her legs again.

"Let's settle then. End this mess."

"Okay."

"You can have your job back. No huge money amount or I'll look guilty."

"Okay. I'll sign whatever. I just need this to be over. As long as I have my job back, I'll be happy."

"But Nicole, we really have to cool things."

"I'll try." She lied. "What's going on with your wife?"

"She agreed to cool things, too. With him. She wants me to win. At least that's what she says. I'm sure she wants to protect *him* and keep herself away from media scrutiny."

Ignoring his request to "cool things," she placed her hands on his jacket lapel and stepped into his warmth. He took hold of her forearms, kissing her forehead, he whispered into her hair, "Not now Nicole, not now."

Those were the words he said to her after their very first embrace and kiss in his office. He wasn't saying "no", he was saying "later."

Chapter 31

Late Friday afternoon, I strolled through the hallway of the firm, looking forward to heading home. Startled by a voice calling to me, I darted into Jon Green's office.

"Jez, can you check the conference room for an iPhone with a pink and silver case. Has a rhinestone N on it, I think? The plaintiff thinks she lost her phone, or it was stolen from her office or something...anyway, she's checking to see if she lost it here. The receptionist is gone, but check her desk too," he asked with a smile, resting his phone receiver on his shoulder.

"Sure."

I looked around the conference room, on chairs, under the table. Nothing. After checking around the receptionist's desk, I stopped by Justin's office to see if he found anything.

"Knock, knock, can I come in?"

"Sure, yeah, come on in," Justin said.

"Did you happen to find an iPhone in a pink and silver case? D'Angelo lost her phone, but not sure where."

"Ah, no, I didn't find a phone. But, good news, settlement talks started. This case is going to soon be behind us."

"Darn, I was hoping for a big dramatic trial. All the juicy ones settle." I plopped down into Justin's guest chair, deflated. "Oh well, maybe the next one. You seem to be in a much better mood than earlier. I'm glad you're not stressed anymore. I didn't care much for stressed-Justin."

Leaning back in his leather chair, he grinned. "Sorry about that, Jez. I'm in a great mood now. Want to celebrate? Join me for a drink?"

"Sure. Just one, I'm meeting Kirk for a late dinner."

He leaned forward, placing his palms on his desk, preparing to stand. "Let's get out of here. We also need to talk about our trip to New York next week."

We selected a nearby restaurant, moving through the happy hour crowd toward the bar. Beer seemed to taste so much better on Friday evenings.

"So, how much is D'Angelo getting?" I asked, licking the foam from above my top lip.

"They're not close to a number yet. She wants her job back with Winston, primarily."

"Can you imagine suing your boss, accusing him of awful things, and then working for him again? Awkward." We moved into a newly abandoned booth, thumping our mugs onto the wooden table.

"I hope he makes her work life miserable. I want her to suffer," Justin proclaimed, partaking in a swig of his beverage.

"Justin! That's not very nice. I don't like her, but your feelings are a bit strong, don't you think?"

He wiped his mouth with the back of his hand. "I hate her. She's made my life miserable for the last few weeks, so I want her to suffer. Karma."

"She was suing Winston, not you. Thereby, helping your paycheck."

"I still want her to be miserable. I want Winston to make her life miserable."

"Maybe she's hoping he takes her along on his political ride," I suggested.

"Well, then, I hope they both lose."

"I've never seen your vindictive side before."

"Certain people bring it out of me. How's Kirk?" he asked.

"Things are going well. He bought me this." I held up my watch proudly, but pulled it back onto my lap when Justin's eyes narrowed at the sight of it. He pulled himself upright in his seat. Apparently vindictive Justin was still here. Or was this jealous Justin?

"Nice. So, what's this Kirk guy's last name?"

"Flynn. Why?"

"Oh, no reason, just curious." His eyes floated up over my head and around the room. He then looked at me, delivering a transparently forced smile.

"What's wrong? You don't like my boyfriend do you?"

"No, don't know him so I have no opinion. Just be careful—"

"Why does everyone feel the need to tell me to be careful? It's becoming a bit exhausting. Just say, 'nice watch, Jez, I'm happy you're happy.'"

"Nice watch, Jez, I'm happy you're happy." I watched him strain to smile.

"Your sincerity is overwhelming. Speaking of being careful, ever hear from one-night-stand bimbo?"

"No, and I hope karma gets her too."

"If I didn't know better, I'd think you had PMS, Justin." I giggled and smoothed the napkin on my lap, a bit uncomfortable with his aggressive mood.

"Sorry, I'll lighten up. So, do you want to meet at the office before our flight and Metro to National together?"

"Only if non-vindictive Justin accompanies me."

"I promise you'll get good-mood Justin. Just don't be late."

"It's a deal."

Chapter 32

Kirk had just exited the elevator of his apartment building, relieved to be home after a long work week. His phone rang.

"Kirk. It's Nicole, I got a new phone, new number. The case is over. We settled. I'm getting $20,000 and my job back. Aren't you proud of me?"

"That's excellent news. I'm very happy this is over." Her voice caused his pulse to quicken, but he welcomed her words.

"But don't get all cozy with Olive Oyl just yet. You promised me a counseling session. I need to know you don't hate me, Kirk. Even if we end our relationship, we have things to discuss. We will need closure, right? And I'm sure you don't want me saying anything to Olive that will hurt your chances with her."

"Clearly we need closure, Nicole. One session. That's it."

"I made the appointment after you originally agreed to it. It's July 28th at 6. Thank you. I knew you could never hate me, sweetie."

He had to keep her happy just a bit longer, until he somehow found the right way to tell Jezebel about the connection. He needed to build Jezebel's trust and love and then find a way to tell her that it was all a big coincidence. He'd think of something.

He and Jezebel met at a Rockville restaurant for a

late evening meal since she was spending the next night with her mom and sister. The restaurant was within walking distance of her apartment. The sight of her simple beauty, flowing white skirt and her hair draped over one shoulder, painted an innocent picture of peace. It enveloped him, and he breathed with relief. With a hug, he attempted to pull the peace into himself. He held onto her a moment longer, trying to press down the guilt. Ugly guilt. He wanted to tell her the truth, but the truth was not pretty. He needed her to fall in love with the Kirk he was today. The Kirk of three months ago no longer existed. That was the whole truth, but how could he make her see that? In time she would. But did he have time?

"You are the most beautiful sight I've seen in a very long time, Ms. Stone."

"Why thank you. Is there any color that you don't look good in, Mr. Flynn?"

"Well, aren't we both just full of compliments. Shall we sit? I'm starving."

"Yes, and me too."

The waitress took their orders and they toasted the end of the work week.

"So," she shared, "my crazy case settled today. I would have liked a trial, or summary judgment victory, but at least it's over."

"The sex harassment case?"

"Yes, over."

"Wow, good news. Very good news."

"And I'm traveling to New York on Monday, so it's nice to have something off the plate. The attorney I'm traveling with was on the same case. We'll be celebrating."

"Oh, that Justin guy?" He tried to contain his jealousy, but his tone may have divulged his feelings.

"Yes, the one you met."

"Oh, great. That's great. So, when will this plaintiff start working for her boss again?"

"Um, not sure. Did I tell you that? Man, I have a big mouth."

Shit, he had the big mouth. "Oh, I just thought that was part of her settlement, you had said in the past, that's what she had wanted."

His face burned and guilt controlled his demeanor.

"Right. Yeah, I'm such a bad paralegal. I need to shut up. Okay, new topic. You're still my guest for my mom's wedding, right?"

"Of course, I'm looking forward to meeting your family. What time should I pick you up?"

"Well, I'm actually going to be there quite early to help set up. So, why don't you meet me there?"

"Sounds great. Can't wait to meet this Cala I've heard so much about and see her spectacular home."

"Oh, you won't be disappointed. On either front."

He calmed in her presence, yet worried he would lose her. That once again, they'd feel a jarring jolt, a crash, and be thrust into darkness. In one swift motion, she'd be taken from him, without hearing his side of the story, or believing it.

Back inside her apartment, he held her close, smelled her hair, kissed her face, enjoyed her body. During the night, when they separated, he reached through the blackness in search of her, taking her hand that rested against the mattress. He held onto her and kissed her fingers without waking her. He couldn't lose her inside the darkness again.

Chapter 33

"Things are actually going really well with Kirk," I reported to Carolyn, my cell phone nestled between my ear and shoulder as I reached to turn down the car radio's volume. "I think we are close to saying the L word, maybe. Maybe not. I don't know. All I know is things are heating up."

"That's fantastic, Jez. Who would have guessed you would ever find love on a Metro. I guess it can happen anywhere. I'm kinda jealous of you right now being in that fun falling in love phase. Very exciting."

"Thanks. Gonna have to hang up here in a minute. I'm outside my mom's. She's got a wild bachelorette party planned."

"Oh, your crazy mom. She's gonna offer you a joint, I just know it."

"I told her my law firm does random drug testing and that Cala would definitely stick to merlot. Get this, she hired a psychic."

"What a nut. Love her. Have fun, Hon. Let me know if the psychic thinks you're gonna marry Train Guy. Oh, we could have your wedding at a metro station."

"If you recall the Metro does not hold fond memories for us. I think I'll pass on the Metro wedding, as lovely as it sounds." I snickered, parking my car. Not believing I was discussing marrying a man who was still married to someone else.

We exchanged goodbyes and I retrieved an overnight bag from the backseat. My mother insisted on a sleepover.

My mom opened the door before I had a chance to grab the doorknob. "Let the party begin!" she bellowed, smacking her hand against her billowing skirt.

"Wow, look at this place." Candles flickered on every table and plates of appetizers covered the coffee table. "Mom, you cooked all this?"

"No, your sister did."

Of course my sister did, I thought. And all I brought was a small gift—a negligee wrapped in pink paper, stuffed down inside my overnight bag. I reached inside and pulled it out, re-fluffing the mangled bow. I placed it next to one of the dishes of food.

"I did make the brownies, though," my mother shared.

I wondered with a chuckle what surprises were in the brownies.

"Hi, Jez," Cala said, emerging from the kitchen with flowered plates from her own kitchen. "Try that crab dip. It's a new recipe and it's divine."

"I'm sure it's wonderful," I said genuinely, touching my sister's shoulder.

With arms reaching in front of each other, we ate, dipping and crunching and chatting with mouths full of food. Seated on the floor in front of the coffee table, I relished the crab dip more than I intended to. It was indeed divine.

"Okay, girls. So, Ms. Charlie will be here soon."

"Ms. Charlie?" Cala asked, tipping her wine glass back to her lips, eyes rolling.

"Yes, that's her name. She's wonderful. My friend Nancy had the best reading of her life with this woman. Told her she was going to lose her job, but would quickly get a better one and it came true. Nancy thought she was going to retire from that first job. Crazy, I tell you, just crazy. From what I hear, this Ms. Charlie is never wrong. Never."

I tensed. Did I want to know my future with Kirk? Did I hold the power to change my future if I did hear something bad? I had almost wished to hear that Ms. Charlie was only right half the time. Would my mother let me chicken out? This was the crystal ball I had hoped for, and now I no longer wanted to get a glimpse of my fate.

The doorbell rang, and in walked my crystal ball in human form. This crystal ball was indeed round, but had a pleasant dark brown face and wide grin. She appeared to be about sixty years old, and held the appearance of wisdom in her almond shaped eyes. She waddled side to side as she moved into the room, her beaded necklaces clanging like a wind chime. I stood to greet the guest my mother was already hugging. I shook the woman's rough, plump hand.

"Well, hello there. I'm Ms. Charlie," she said the words with a raspy low voice that sounded like a song spilling sweetly from her red lips.

I introduced myself in a matching sing-songy voice. I suddenly froze, feeling as though Ms. Charlie was already reading my thoughts, seeing my future, dodging through possible warning signs of dangers lurking in my coming days. I yanked my hand out of Ms. Charlie's, releasing myself from a perceived electrical current and assumed my seat on the floor, allowing Cala to take my place.

"Well, let's get started. I'll bring you one at a time into the other room. Your energies and auras will overlap if you stay in the same room and listen. I'll record the readings so you can listen to each other's later, if you wish. You will need to hand me an item that you wear all the time, a ring or something. Who wants to go first?"

"Mom, you go, it's your party."

My mom eagerly trailed behind the waddling psychic into the dining room. Cala and I resumed eating and quiet small talk.

About a half hour later, my mom bounced into the living room, arms spread out as if she was going to say, "Ta-da!"

"Girls, Miss Charlie sensed joy in my future. And, she saw a lot more bikes in my future. Maybe Joe is going to buy another Harley store? Oh, she said all good things. Okay, Cala, you go next."

I wondered if my mother had the capability of viewing any news as anything other than perfect.

Cala stood with a sigh, but held a small smile on her lips, still attempting to appear a skeptic. She disappeared into the dining room, while my mom recited her reading to me, finishing off the crab dip.

Another half hour slipped by and Cala emerged.

"How'd it go?" I asked.

"Good, she also saw joy in my future." She smiled, but I could sense a tinge of cynicism in her tone. "Although, she thinks I'll suffer a loss before a gain. She also saw rain falling on a big party at my house. Mom, that's your wedding."

"Oh, no bother. A little rain never stopped a party.

Rain's good luck for a bride!"

Her words again confirming for that indeed my mother was an incurable optimist.

"Well, it told me to order a bigger tent and definitely clear out all the downstairs furniture in case the reception is inside," Cala said.

"We may have just discovered Cala's new planning tool. You can consult a psychic before every event. You will now have the ability to control every detail, even the weather." The wine made me a bit punchy and teasing Cala came easy.

"Very funny, little sister. But you are onto something here..." Cala smiled at the ceiling as if heavily considering this new planning option, taking the teasing with ease. Perhaps the wine had kicked in for Cala as well. Although, Cala had said she was only allowing herself one glass of wine, she seized the wine bottle and poured herself a second glass. Wine and a psychic, I now knew the recipe for getting a more easy-going sister.

"Miss Jezebel, it's your turn." Ms. Charlie stood in the doorway holding one of her hands inside the other, like a butler announcing that dinner was served. Ms. Charlie nodded and smiled in my direction, inviting me to follow her into my future.

A bit of nerves danced inside my belly as I pulled out a chair, but that didn't keep a smile from crossing my face. My mother and sister had had happy readings and I would, too. I had heard that psychics would rarely tell you the bad stuff. I handed Ms. Charlie my watch.

"Miss Jezebel. You have a light around you. I like your energy." Ms. Charlie closed her eyes and smiled, her chin lifting up toward the ceiling. "You live with a cat."

"Yes." Not that difficult of a guess. Part of Furry was always on my clothing.

Ms. Charlie's smile faded, and I panicked. Where'd the smile go? Where's the joy in my future? Oh, maybe the chubby psychic had picked up on my skepticism.

"Hmm. Well, I don't want to alarm you but I see fire. It's very strong. You are safe. You are free and safe from it, yet I see fire."

"I was in a crash a while back—"

"Shhhh. Let me see."

I swallowed my words. My eyes darted to the dancing candle's flame in the middle of the table. Was Ms. Charlie seeing the fire because it was still so much a part of me? Would I ever escape that damn crash for good?

"You rescued someone."

No, I thought, I rescued no one.

A smile again crossed Ms. Charlie's face. "You are a hero, Ms. Jezebel."

No, I was not a hero.

"Does a white dangling wire mean anything to you?"

"No, I'm afraid I don't know what you mean." Was it the faulty switch that caused the crash?

"It's all right. It might not be related to the fire. I just see you near a white wire. A gray t-shirt."

The topic of the crash made me shift from side to side in my seat, just the way the psychic had waddled into the room. "The man that rescued me was wearing a gray t-shirt. I thought you were supposed to read my future, not my pa—"

"Shhh, this is just what I am seeing around you. Not sure what it all means yet."

"Any love? See any romance? See me with a man?"

"Relax, my dear. I'm seeing a few men who love you in a romantic way. A few."

A few?

Ms. Charlie chuckled with her lips closed, her breasts slightly jiggling against the tabletop.

Why did Ms. Charlie giggle?

"But you will only love one. Your time with one man will be cut short."

Maybe she was seeing Michael, my first true love. Since she was seeing so much of my past, perhaps she was seeing Michael, or maybe Justin. Maybe that was it, I would only love one man, and it would be Kirk. Would my time with Kirk be cut short? This woman needed to give me some names.

"Don't fret. Things will work out."

How could I not fret when I had no idea what in the world she was talking about? This was all so vague. Perhaps that was the trick to being a psychic.

After Ms. Charlie left the party, I reported my scattered reading to Cala and my mother. They just shrugged their shoulders, appearing to be unable to decipher my reading any better than I had. Averting the attention away from my future, my mom tore open the tiny package from me and screeched in delight. "Oh, if only I were 20 years younger, I would look great in this little number."

"Joe will love it, Mom. And, you still look like you did 20 years ago," I said.

"Well, aren't you sweet, my dear Jezebel," my

mother said, cupping my cheek in her hand. Her eyes seemed to twinkle with a genuine love, or from too much wine.

We then played the recordings from each of our readings. I speculated on whether we would someday look back at this and laugh at how wrong Ms. Charlie had been. Perhaps it would be under the hot sun and vast blue sky during our mother's wedding in Cala's backyard. We would point to the oversized dry tent, laughing and wondering what else Ms. Charlie had gotten wrong.

****

I was excited to meet Kirk for Sunday brunch the next day, even though my head ached a bit from the wine. The downtown hotel we had selected was brimming with guests enjoying the final moments of their weekends. Tinkling piano music filled the high-ceilinged restaurant while the scent of fresh cut flowers sweetened the bacon-scented room.

We grazed on the buffet. Breakfast food seemed to be curing my mild hangover.

"Ready for your trip?" Kirk questioned, stabbing a piece of waffle with his fork.

"Suitcase is packed but I need to get to the office early tomorrow morning to gather some things I need. I'm meeting Justin at the airport."

"Why do I feel a bit jealous that you're going away with this Justin guy?" He smiled, staring at his plate.

"Aw, that's sweet you're jealous."

Kirk chuckled, still not making eye contact. "Well, you better at least call me twenty times a day so this Justin knows you're with me."

"You don't need to worry about Justin. But I do

enjoy you being jealous."

We exchanged bashful smiles, Kirk's cheeks reddening and my stomach leaping with bliss. Changing topics, I shared the reading from Ms. Charlie. "She could see the crash. I can't believe she saw that I was in a crash."

"Maybe she had read about the crash and your mom had mentioned to her that you were in it. I always think these psychics do a little research before their readings." He made air quotes around the word readings." and slid into the back of his chair, indicating he was finished with the buffet.

"I don't know. My mom said she told her nothing."

"I don't believe anyone can see the future. It hasn't been determined yet. We have the power to control it. So how could anyone see it? Or, maybe by her making suggestions, we choose a path based on what a psychic says?"

"Perhaps. But, I'm a believer. I believe it. However, she did say I rescued someone and was a hero. That didn't happen."

"I know I didn't rescue anyone. Just tried to save myself," Kirk said, looking down.

I could no longer discuss the crash. Thinking of the incident still drained me. This reminded me to return a call to one of the potential sponsors for the crash memorial. I'd do that on the way to the airport tomorrow.

We grasped hands as we exited the hotel, evading cabs zipping up to the curb.

"Kirk, would it be okay if I met you back at your condo later? I think I'd relax more if I went by my office for a while this afternoon and got ready for my trip. You know the way I am, I'll probably be running late tomorrow morning."

"Okay. I have some errands to run, so meet me back at my place when you're ready."

His lips met mine with an unhurried, tender kiss. We parted, heading in opposite directions. He called my name, and I whipped my head in the direction of his voice.

Through the clamor of city activity, he spoke to me as if we were alone. "Jez! You rescued me that day. You rescued me." He smiled sweetly, hands in his pockets, turning back toward his destination, leaving me speechless.

Inside my office, I gathered the necessities for my trip quickly, anxious to return to Kirk. Realizing some of what I needed was in Justin's office, I hurried down the hall. I loved being inside the firm when it was quiet and still, void of hustle and stress. Where I—not the others—controlled my itinerary.

As I entered Justin's office, the scent of his cologne lingered lightly, making me wonder if he'd recently been there preparing for the trip as well. I sat in his chair, the window's light providing the desk's illumination. The folder I needed rested in front of me so I grabbed it. When I spun the chair around to exit his desk, my eyes were drawn to a white cord leading from an outlet into a file cabinet. Curiosity seized my actions. I opened the drawer. The white cord was charging a phone lying inside the files. Holding the iPhone in my hands, a small gasp left my lips. It had a silver and pink case with a rhinestone N. Was this the plaintiff's? It had to be. It certainly wasn't Justin's, but why was he charging it? Perhaps he had found it and was holding it for her? I hit the home button, lighting up the screen. No security code had been activated, so nothing stood between me and invading this person's privacy.

I selected the icon that said "setting," and followed it through to find the name of the phone's owner. Nicole D'Angelo. I should stick it back inside the drawer and pretend I never saw it. This was wrong, but I couldn't stop. I opened D'Angelo's pictures, hoping she was in her own pictures so I could see what she looked like. The first pictures were a series of snapshots of an email print out. I spread my fingers across the screen to enlarge them. Who was Blue Sparrow? Who was D.W.? The bodies of the email contained graphic details of a relationship. Flirting...plans to meet secretly...an affair? Why did D'Angelo have these pictures of this email exchange?

Stop, Jezebel! I yelled in my mind. *Put the phone back!* I pushed my fingers against my lips at the sight of the next photo—Justin asleep in a bed. Why on earth was a picture of Justin sleeping on the plaintiff's phone? My fingers fell off my lips and pressed against my queasy stomach. I flipped through more photos. A little boy at a birthday party smashing a cake. A one year old boy's birthday party. A shimmering body of water full of boats. Looked like Annapolis.

With one flick of my thumb across the screen, my breathing halted. A picture of Kirk. Kirk holding the boy. Another flick of the thumb, Kirk and a blonde woman holding the boy. The beautiful blonde wife I had met on the street and seen in pictures at his condo. Why were pictures of Kirk and his wife on the plaintiff's—

I shrieked, shaking. What was going on?

My boyfriend. The man I was falling in love with was smiling back at me, standing next to his wife. How could this be? Kirk was married to Nicole D'Angelo. The "blonde bombshell," as Ken had described her. This had to be a mistake, a crazy mix up. An explanation had to arrive soon. Kirk's wife's name was Nicole. My mind flashed to a previous conversation when he mentioned his wife had not taken his last name.

A throbbing pulse beat against my forehead as everything started adding up, replaying in my mind like a horror movie. My lips moved, mumbling, "No," with each passing picture. The photos documented the day Kirk spent in Annapolis on the day his battery had allegedly died. My thumb pushed the pictures faster, backing through time. These pictures documented Nicole's life for the past months.

Kirk would have known the name of the law firm representing his wife's defendant. He knew the day he met me on the Metro that I worked for that firm. That's why he wanted to see me, that's why he had asked probing questions about just this one case. He had touched documents on my dining room table, seen briefs pulled from my briefcase. That's why he lied to me about where his wife worked. I had told him about the recordings. I confided in him, never thinking my secrets would leave his mouth. Or that he would care. The stories I'd relayed to him were just for his entertainment, or so I thought. Never that they were information to be used by someone close to him. I heard his words, "you won't like the real me." The real Kirk had used me. The real Kirk shattered my heart into oblivion.

I had blatantly looked away from the red flags, the signs of danger. I chose to stay on the ill-fated ride. The red flags were taunting me now, as if announcing the start of a parade. A sick parade.

Justin, Kirk, Nicole. What nightmarish montage of horrific images had I just witnessed?

My body had slid onto the floor without realizing it. Trembling hands still gripped the phone, holding the truth I was forced to face. My fingers opened everything on this woman's phone. I searched Nicole's text messages, scrolling down to find Kirk's name. I skimmed through short texts between the two of them; my pained mind only able to read every other word, but I steeled myself. This was my chance to learn the whole truth. My eyes caught the word "paralegal." Nicole had threatened that he better not be with "that skanky paralegal." So even Nicole knew what he was doing. Hot humiliation cascaded over me, encompassing me. A shroud of sadness seized me. Spilling tears formed droplets on the phone's screen.

There were texts between Nicole and Jack Winston. They'd arranged meetings at hotels throughout the period of the lawsuit. My head shook in utter disbelief.

Pulling myself off the floor, my head buzzing in an unfamiliar lightness, I jogged back to my office, panting. Yanked open a heavy file drawer, thrusting it into my gut, I snatched a folder, "D'Angelo HR file." I collapsed into my chair, flipping through the pages. Due to the mundane nature of the documents in this file, I hadn't read it with any thoroughness. Tax forms, all the stuff completed on the first day of a job, bearing no significance on the lawsuit. I pulled out an employment form filled out by the plaintiff. A document that listed the name of Nicole D'Angelo's husband. Listed twice, under beneficiary of her life insurance and as an emergency contact—Kirk Flynn. How had I missed that?

Tears trickled off my chin as I ran back to Justin's office. I couldn't keep myself away from the tiny rectangular piece of technology that had just become a window to the truth. Holding the phone, I fingered the long white wire charging the phone. A white wire. Was this what Ms. Charlie saw? The white wire that led to a crash and burn?

I couldn't stop scouring every corner of the phone, opening doors to this woman's life, my own life. I touched the icon for "Calendar." What could I find on the calendar? And there it was, tucked inside a tiny square allotted to a day in late July—it said, "Counseling session. Me & Kirk. 6:00 pm."

Crashing, jolting, smash-against-the-seat-in-front-of-me pain wracked my body. I experienced every piece of agony I had felt after first meeting him. A fire burned in my stomach, wafting a smoky darkness throughout me.

Our ride was over.

I never would have guessed that Ms. Charlie's predictions would have come to fruition just one day later. My time with one man would be cut short as predicted. Perhaps it should have been cut short following that first crash. But, I had forced it and it broke. What had Kirk just said at brunch? That "our future is not determined yet. We have the power to control it."

In a foggy trance, I meandered back to my office. I didn't know what to do now. All the people warning me to be careful would say they had told me so. I had to talk to Justin, maybe he too was a victim. His picture was inside the phone, trapped like a fly in a spider web. Had Nicole been his one night stand, the reason for Justin's foul mood lately? My mind didn't want to believe it, but after what I had just learned, anything was possible.

From my own phone, I sent Justin a text asking if he could meet me at the restaurant where we had shared a drink on Friday. Placing "911" at the end of the text triggered his instant reply: Be there in 20 minutes.

My briefcase was heavy with materials for the trip, but light compared to the amount of weight elsewhere. Although I knew I must be a hideous sight, with swollen eyes and the look of a woman beaten, I didn't take any time to fix myself.

I flung my body inside a private booth and waited for Justin. Staring blankly, my mind unable to form any complex thoughts or solve any more mysteries. I shut out any replaying of the last few months.

In a gust, Justin entered and, with large strides, joined me.

"Jez." His chest heaved, evidence he had hurried. "You look…terrible. What's wrong?" Something in his eyes, in his tone, told me he had an idea.

Full of dramatics, I tossed the pink and silver cased phone between us on the table. Both of us looked at it, like it was a ticking bomb, holding our fate.

"You were in my office?"

"Obviously. Why do you have this?" I questioned with irritation.

He pushed a hand through his hair, his eyes inspecting his surroundings. With a gush of air from his lungs, he looked down at the phone, avoiding my gaze. "I took it."

I paused, waiting for him to continue.

"She left it on the table after a deposition break. Went to the restroom. So I took it."

I slapped my hand on the back of the phone and slid it onto my lap.

"Going to explain or do I need to guess?"

"She's the woman that I had the one night stand with. I didn't know who she was." He spoke so softly, I strained to hear. I hoped he wouldn't cry. "She threatened to end my career if I didn't get her a good settlement. She said she was going to turn me into the D.C. Bar. She told me she had taken a picture of me, so I just wanted to see what she had on her phone. I wanted to get revenge."

"Did you go through all the pictures?"

"I did."

The realization that Justin had betrayed me also, by not warning me that Nicole was married to Kirk, pushed another wave of disgust into my gut. "So you saw his picture? Kirk's picture?"

"Yeah. Jez, I saw his picture but I wasn't sure what to do. I planned to tell you on our trip—to show you the phone."

"Good Lord. Justin, you knew when we were here for a drink on Friday and you didn't tell me?" I questioned in a desperate tone.

His eyes looked into mine with sympathy, pleading for me to understand. "I wasn't sure... You had just told me his last name, so I wanted to confirm it first."

"You weren't sure of what? You met Kirk—"

"I wasn't sure what that was a picture of. I wasn't sure if she had seduced your boyfriend to get to you. I was still putting it all together. Saturday I was in the office and checked her HR file to see if I could find Kirk Flynn's name. I did. I didn't know how to tell you that I stole a phone, was duped and seduced by the plaintiff. I'm really sorry, Jez, I planned to tell you. I knew on Saturday you were having a fun night with your family. Forgive me, but I was feeling like a big fool."

"Well, we have something in common." I leaned back against the booth in weary defeat.

"I'm sorry. I'm sorry that Kirk wasn't what you thought he was."

"I'm still thinking there has to be an explanation…"

"The explanation is all in that phone."

"What revenge were you hoping for?"

"To prosecute her for perjury, for bringing about a false lawsuit, or something. But I thought of something else."

"What?"

"She has evidence on her phone that we can prove she had an affair with a future senator. I can kill that dream for him and for her, since I believe her goal is to follow him in his career. I could blackmail her. Also, did you see the email pictures on the phone?"

"Yeah, what is that?"

"Blue Sparrow is the Secret Service's name for the President of the United States. D.W is Dara Winston, Jack Winston's wife."

"What?"

"Winston's wife is friends with the First Lady. Jack had shared that with us once."

I turned on the phone's screen and looked again at the photo of the email. "How can you be sure?"

"D'Angelo was stupid enough to record a meeting between her and Jack where he tells her about finding the email exchange between his wife and her lover. The president's having an affair."

"Wow."

"Yeah, wow is right. I have some ideas of how to torture her with that as well."

My eyes looked far beyond the faces crowding the restaurant, gazing out the window at a tiny piece of visible sky, registering all I'd learned in the last few hours. "So, inside that phone, D'Angelo held the power to bring down a future senator and the President of the United States."

"Yes." He paused, smiling a sinister smile. "And now, so do we."

Chapter 34

I took a cab straight to the airport, avoiding the office. In my zombie-like state, there was no way I could face Vanessa or Ken, or anyone else for that matter, and not have them detect my world was in shambles. I couldn't even begin to tell the story without turning into a blubbering mess. And how could I ever tell the full story to anyone? I couldn't. I successfully avoided Kirk the night before by texting him that I was ill from apparent food poisoning, and wanted to be alone. Even though the tainted brunch allegation was a lie, my body did feel like it had suffered a debilitating poisoning. Exhausted from a lack of sleep, my over-caffeinated body trembled slightly and my stomach gurgled and churned. Ironically, my final meal with Kirk at the Marriott had been the last time I had eaten anything of substance.

My eyelids felt like garage doors, heavy and thick. I wished I could shut them tight and hide inside a dark room, but that was impossible. Life refused to stop just because my world came to a screeching halt. I sustained movement by assuring myself that being with Justin—my partner in being deceived—would provide a bit of solace.

I had chosen not to say anything to Kirk yet because I didn't want to tell him how I uncovered his secret. I wanted to tell him exactly how I felt when I saw his face in a picture next to his wife, the plaintiff. I wanted to say I had read their texts, saw their counseling appointment on the calendar, and saw the pictures of his nephew. I wanted him to feel as violated as I felt. But I didn't want him to inform Nicole about Justin having her phone. Justin held knowledge and power. And that needed to remain intact for as long as we could hold on to it.

I felt my body careening through the stages of grief. Currently I sat firmly in the anger phase. I was overcome with the desire to hurt Kirk, to hurt Nicole for what she'd done to me, and to Justin. They were awful people and I wanted them to feel pain. I wanted my pain to end.

As I moved through airport security, I barely had the strength to drop my carry-on bag on to the conveyor belt. As I stepped inside the body scanner, I chuckled to myself, imagining what horror the security people would see if only they could get a true glimpse of my insides, the jumbled broken disaster of what rested under my skin. Luckily, it only checked under clothes, typically this would be enough to cause me angst.

I arrived at the gate ahead of Justin and celebrated this achievement by purchasing a caramel latte. More caffeine was needed to fuel me through this day.

"Jezebel!" Justin called from behind me.

"Hey, want a coffee? My treat."

"Sure. Thanks." He wheeled his suitcase next to me, rested his hand on the counter, delivering a weak smile. "You okay?"

"I'm just great." My attempt to speak without overt sarcasm failed.

"Sorry. Maybe some document review will

brighten your day?" His attempt at the same was also unsuccessful.

The two of us chuckled, shook our heads, smiling, communicating in a silent mutual declaration that we could not believe what had transpired, but that we would get through it together.

Seated next to each other in a row of aligned chairs outside of our gate, we sipped our coffees and discussed our New York client and the case. Having difficultly focusing on one topic, I interrupted Justin in the middle of a sentence. "Justin, I need to know why we can't have her prosecuted for perjury." My voice dropped into a whisper.

Justin held my gaze, his mind apparently flipping through a file folder of information. "Because although perjury in civil cases is a violation of the law, it is rarely prosecuted. It'd be tough to prove, and our firm wouldn't be on board with it. It would be ugly. I want to handle her myself. In my own way."

"If she has the capability of doing what she's already done, aren't you afraid to mess with her more? Talk about getting ugly."

"Well, I already started the revenge-ball rolling, so I can't stop now."

"Justin! What have you done?" I questioned, looking over both shoulders to see how close possible eavesdroppers were. We were safe to whisper.

"Probably better you stay out of it."

"I'm already in it. Justin, this is just as much my revenge as it is yours. Spill."

He pulled himself closer, shifting his weight onto his arm that lay on the armrest between us. I could smell the coffee on his breath and the scent of his shaving cream.

"I made up a fake g-mail account for Nicole, from a computer in a public library. I emailed the president and threatened him with the information—"

"Justin! No, you didn't." My eyes spread wide, no longer weighted by heavy lids and I was sure he was now smelling my coffee breath rushing in his face.

"Yes, yes I did." A pleased grin crossed his lips. He continued, "I just said I, or Nicole I should say, had a copy of an email exchange and would go to the press with it. Mentioned that Nicole worked for Jack and she was getting revenge on his behalf." Justin shifted in his seat and glanced around. I did too.

Justin continued, whispering, "My hope is that the prez will say something to Jack, and Jack will want to make her life miserable. Jack needs the president to win in order for him to win his Senate seat, or so Jack said in the recording D'Angelo made. Jack can't have Mr. Family Values fail, if he plans to ride the wave of his current success. He can't be humiliated and proven weak because he's not man enough to keep his own wife in line. Then the press would presumably dig up dirt on Jack and Dara, exposing his lawsuit, dooming his career." We both glanced around us again. "Neither Jack nor Nicole could handle the ramifications of this. How great would that be if the prez hired a thug to rough up Nicole?"

"Justin. That's awful. This is scaring me. You're playing with fire. If they connect you to this, you'll be the one getting roughed up by a hired thug."

Justin snickered, appearing thrilled to play this game, but I wondered if he understood that this wasn't a game. This had world-wide implications.

"Look." Justin's face grew serious. "Do you want a president who behaves this way and gets away with it?"

"The whole country will suffer if this gets out."

"Exactly. That's why I'm killing two birds here. I'm not really going to go to the press, but am making him nervous, letting him know that at any moment, his world could collapse. He'll feel guilty and maybe shape up. Maybe he'll actually do something good for the country and do some work instead of screwing his wife's best friend."

"You're playing God."

As if God Himself had decided to speak, the loud announcement overhead caused us both to jolt. "Flight 5433 to New York will be boarding in five minutes."

"I'm going to visit the ladies' room before we board." I stood. The floor moved from side to side as if I had stepped onto a boat. The lights dimmed around me.

"Jez, are you okay?" Justin had maneuvered in front of me and held onto me by my forearms, his face inches from mine.

"I just got dizzy standing up so fast and I haven't eaten. Sorry to scare you. I'm good now."

Still not letting go of my arms, he spoke, "I'm going to buy you a muffin. You like chocolate chip right?"

I wiped imaginary sweat from my forehead, embarrassed to have become so needy and weak. "Thanks. I need some sugar."

While no longer dizzy, my head still spun with dismay. How had being late for a Metro ride three months ago landed me in the middle of a presidential scandal? Life was truly a trip.

Late for Fate

I entered the stall, plopping myself down on a well covered seat, too weak and exhausted to squat. My head felt heavy. I let out a quick sigh, clutching my forehead in my hand, resting my elbow on the tiny steel garbage receptacle. The simple act made me think about my cycle, remembering that I thought I would have my period during this business trip. My head bolted upright. In fact, I should have had my period days ago; it should have come on Friday. It always came on a Friday. Like clockwork, ironically the only part of me that was never late. Every fourth Friday it came. Today was Monday.

Exiting the restroom, I forced my hair into place and pulled myself together with a large breath. I needed to gather myself and keep moving through this nightmare that had now become my reality.

Justin handed me the handle of my suitcase and a brown bag carrying a muffin. I followed him onto the plane.

Perhaps the stress of the last 24 hours had caused me to be late. But what about Friday? All was happy and stress-free on Friday. And Saturday.

Justin sat next to the window and I sat in the aisle seat. Instantly the cologne of the man across the aisle irritated me. I panicked thinking this meant I was pregnant. I had heard of pregnant women being bothered by smells. The back of my head smacked against the seat and another sigh left my lungs. There simply had to be an explanation for my being late other than pregnancy. A thyroid issue, maybe that weird pituitary gland did this. I had no idea the purpose of the pituitary gland, but was desperate for something to blame. Settling on a uterine tumor, I relaxed just a bit.

"Jez, you okay? You didn't eat your muffin."

"Oh, yeah, Justin, I'm fine. Thanks for the muffin." I opened the bag, picking at the muffin's top with my fingers, and forced the food into my system.

"We have to head straight to the Boeing office from the airport. I'll send our bags ahead to the hotel. You okay with that?"

That would delay my pregnancy test purchase. "Sure. Sounds great."

"Jez, you've been through a lot." He had no idea. "I promise you a fun night out." I just wanted to crawl into bed.

A bump of turbulence scrambled my thoughts. I really wouldn't be surprised if the plane crashed right now, given my luck. But then I thought, perhaps I was meant to suffer a bit longer—that was more consistent with my current luck. Suspended above the earth, I was trapped inside this big machine, unable to buy a test that would give me an answer, unable to receive or place a call or a text from Kirk. In a way, hanging in the clouds for this brief hour provided me a temporary reprieve from the world below. A break from time.

"Everything's going to work out, Jez. You'll get over this guy in no time and be right back to your old self."

"Thanks, Justin. I'm sure you're right. I probably just need a good night's sleep."

I reached into my briefcase for a magazine to distract me. My fingers fumbled with my keys, my thumb caressing my Magic 8. In this fragile state, I couldn't handle whatever answer he displayed, so I chucked my keys toward the bottom of my briefcase.

I excused myself to use the bathroom, hoping my

long lost "friend" had arrived and my worries could dissipate. Inside the tiny locked closet, I looked up at the ceiling and mouthed a quick, "Please, God, please." Since I was floating in the clouds, did I really need to look upward to talk to God? Where was God anyway?

My pleas were to no avail as my friend was still AWOL and my worries still front and center. I yearned for that crystal ball to peer through to tell me all would be fine in a few days, a few weeks. A stabbing pang rammed my chest at thought of being pregnant. I pressed my palms into my eyebrows, rubbing the thought away. I had jumped ahead, way ahead. A test would give me the answer.

I moved with an awkward amble up the aisle, my hands moving from seat top to seat top. A man stood, blocking the way, instantly apologizing. In my brief pause in the aisle, waiting for the man to step aside, I looked down into a seat next to me. My eyes connected with a blond baby, sitting on his mother's lap. The smiling baby squeezed his fingers into his palm, appearing to grab the air. It seemed to be his primitive attempt at a wave. I smiled at the boy and waved back, my panging chest pain softening for just a moment. Kirk's child would have similar features. I looked at the mother, wanting to spread my smile to her as well. The mother looked tired, without the energy to muster a smile. Sweet moment over.

The plane landed without incident and Justin and I worked diligently through the afternoon hours. Submerged in document review, I forced my mind to focus on my work and not the possibilities of what could be cooking inside me. Uterine tumor, it had to just be a uterine tumor.

After adjourning from our work for the day, we strolled up the frenzied New York streets. They mirrored my whole life, I thought, chaotic and noisy. I needed to think of a way to ditch Justin and make my way to a pharmacy.

"Justin, I forgot some of my makeup and I'm going to duck inside this pharmacy here. Mind if I meet up with you later for dinner?"

"Sure. You want me to stay with you?"

"No. No, you go back to the hotel and freshen up and let's meet in an hour for dinner. Okay?"

"Okay. Call me if you need anything." His eyes narrowed with concern.

I patted his arm to let him know I would be fine.

I walked down the aisle past the feminine hygiene products, and then past the condoms, arriving at the pregnancy tests. An ironic selection of products in this aisle, I thought with a sneer. If only my trip could end at the beginning of the aisle, or the middle of the aisle, but today I was forced to walk to the end. What brand should I pick? Every woman who made the trip to this end of this aisle would be at one end of the extreme emotional spectrum. Either giddy with hope and anticipation, or plagued with gloom and dread.

I purchased the package promising to deliver the clearest answer and bolted from the store. I found my hotel room and flung my suitcase onto the floor. With my backside against the wall, I read the instructions, deciding it would not be possible to wait for the morning to test. I would take my chances now.

I peed on the stick and rested it on the bathroom counter. Focused on the tiny stick's window, my eyes remained glued on my new crystal ball. Was motherhood in my future?

Yes. The answer was yes. A moan left my body and my head rolled back and then forward into my hands. Tears fell into my palms.

My mind knew that I had done this to myself, being neglectful with birth control, sleeping with Kirk, but I still sent a curse word toward the sky, so God would hear me.

I washed my hands and face and then collapsed on the bed, ignoring my sister's warning to never lie on a hotel bedspread. I didn't care. My world was polluted right now, so what did a few more germs and pesky microscopic critters matter?

My easy decision to break up with Kirk had now become more complicated. I couldn't raise a child alone; I could barely handle a cat. Should I marry him if he asked? My God, I squealed, rolling onto my side, the man was still married. Nicole D'Angelo could be my child's stepmother. The thought caused my body to jolt upright.

I stripped off my clothes and turned the shower to its hottest setting. I scrubbed my body, washed my hair, rinsed and repeated. My blood was coursing through my body again and any remains of a zombie-like feeling dispersed. I painted my face with make-up, unable to cover my paleness, and wrestled my damp hair up into a tight knot behind my head.

Faced with a new reality, I would have to make some decisions. But for tonight, I could escape them for a bit, eat dinner and have a glass of wine.

Nope, no wine.

I sat on the edge of the bed, acknowledging that there was no ignoring what was happening inside me.

Carolyn's favorite quote about parenthood rang loudly in my ears, "It's not great all of the time and it's not bad all of the time, but it is—all the time."

This child would now be present in every single part of my life, from this day forward. Which meant Kirk would forever be a part of my life—all the time, from this day forward. I had to call him, to tell him, but that would also mean telling him all of the truth that I had learned in the past twenty-four hours. My heart thumped in a cruel reminder that it was working harder now, pumping for two.

Could I lie? Could I never tell him and just pretend the baby belonged to someone else? I pushed my hands along the sides of my head in disgust, wondering at what point in my life I had turned into a soap opera character.

The knock at the door shocked me back to my real life. "Jez, you ready?"

"Ah, sure, yeah, I'm ready. Just a sec." I sucked in a breath deep down into my toes, pulling strength into my body.

I opened the door, forcing a smile.

"Hey, you look nice, Jez." Justin moved around me carrying a six pack of beer in one hand and a box of crackers in the other. "Brought us a happy hour cocktail. I couldn't get us reservations until seven."

"Oh, okay. Thanks." Could I just pretend to drink? Would one beer hurt? Most women wouldn't know they were pregnant this early. But, I did. Although, God knows what my mother had consumed during her three pregnancies.

"So, I talked to Jon. Looks like the settlement is completely finalized in the D'Angelo case."

"Good. I guess…"

"Did you see the Nats won big last night against the Red Sox?" Justin smiled as he focused on the removal of the two beer caps. Still smiling, he opened up the box of cheese crackers.

"Justin, you seem pretty relaxed for just having sent the President a threatening email."

Still smiling, he handed me a beer bottle. "I didn't send it. D'Angelo did." He clinked the top of his beer bottle to the top of mine and took a swig. His arrogant smile and eye-twinkle made me cringe, as his self-pride was evident.

"Justin, it could get traced to you and the consequences could be worse than D'Angelo going to the Bar."

"Relax, you worry too much. The prez isn't going to want to dig into this. He has no reason to think it's anyone other than D'Angelo. And digging requires involving others. Involving others and calling me out, requires his story to be revealed. I'm good, trust me. She slept with me and used me, doesn't she deserve this?"

"I'm not saying she doesn't deserve to be punished, but I'm not sure she deserves to be punished—like roughed up punished, as you put it."

"We all have to live with our decisions and choices. Again, relax and drink that beer. You need it."

"I can't. I'm pregnant."

In mid-swig, Justin's arm slowly lowered, his beer resting next to his thigh. His mouth hung open, words seemingly unable to take shape. "Jezebel… Really?" A quiet sorrow filled the only two words he spoke.

"Yeah. Really." A burn hit my eyes, and the sight

of Justin's shocked face faded as tears blinded me.

He placed his beer on the desk, and gently drew me into a hug. It was the only comfort, besides the airplane baby's wave, that I had felt in two days. I pulled my hand away from Justin's side and wiped the tears off my nose. With his hands on my shoulders, he stepped back to give me space.

"How long have you known?"

I turned from him so I could wipe my face privately. "Suspected all day. Confirmed thirty minutes ago."

He placed his hands on his hips and said, "Wow."

"Yeah. Wow."

"What are you going to do?"

"Go see a doctor? Die? I'm not sure, really. What does someone do in this situation?"

"You probably need to start by telling the father."

A disgusted grunt left my body. "This sucks so bad."

He stretched out a hand to caress my arm. "I'm here if you need anything."

"Thanks." His touch did feel nice.

"Do you want to be a mother?"

I remembered a conversation I had had on one of my first dates with Kirk. How I told him it was something I hadn't given much thought to. And how he said he had a fear of being a lousy father. "I guess it would be nice, to be one someday. I just didn't expect to be one now, when I'm single. Oh, God."

"You don't have to have the baby. Or adoption is a possibility."

Silence coated the room, as I paced along the edge of the bed. "I suppose those decisions aren't totally up to me. What am I going to say to Kirk? Hey, found out our relationship started out as a big scam to get info for your wife and oh, yeah, I'm carrying your child."

"Well, that does sound about right."

Still pacing, I said, "Wow. Think of it, on that day I could've ended up in the first Metro car and died. I've been thanking God that I chose the second car. Yet, I still suffered a hellish fate."

"You don't know that yet. It could still be leading somewhere good."

"Doesn't feel like it right now."

"True. But just finish out the ride and see where it leads."

"You're getting a little deep, Justin." I softened for a moment, trying to push away the cynicism, the bitterness. "The journey is still not over yet, is that what you're trying to say?"

"Yep."

"That only frightens me more."

"Everything's how you look at it, I suppose. This could turn out to be the best thing that's ever happened to you."

"Right now, it's the worst."

"No doubt. Telling Kirk may be even worse, though."

"Thanks, that's helpful," I said with an eye roll.

"You guys could both raise the child without having to stay a couple."

Another grunt escaped me. "This is all so unbelievable. Why am I so irresponsible? How could I take my pills without any consistency and not expect for this to happen?" My arms flew upward, feeling again like an actress portraying a role on stage.

"Beating yourself up now isn't going to do any good."

"I just feel…scared. Scared and alone."

"You're not alone. You have a great family and, if you need a birthing coach, I can step in, if need be." A smile crossed his face, breaking the tension.

I couldn't help but laugh. Justin laughed too.

"That'll be slightly awkward. How do I go back to working with you after you've seen me give birth?" I continued to laugh. It felt good.

"I won't look down there. Promise." He held up his hand as if taking an oath, his smile easing my angst even further.

I wiped away a tear, this one caused from laughter. "You're being very sweet, Justin. Thank you."

He grinned and took a step toward me, rubbing both of his hands on my upper arms. "You're going to be okay. Everything will work out. Promise." His eyes were more convincing than his words. "Jezebel Stone, you are stronger than you think."

I looked down, not able to believe that everything would work out. Shame, fear, and dread weighed firmly on me. Justin's finger pulled my chin up, his lips tenderly resting on mine. Another piece of warm comfort had been delivered to me. I allowed his kiss, and met his with my own. For a moment I forgot about my pain, my future decisions and the hard days ahead, and allowed myself to swim in this consoling peace. Maybe this bit of solace was my crystal ball telling me that things would be all right someday. Maybe this was God's way of giving me a little rest from my hurt.

My hands moved along his back, welcoming the intimacy of the moment. It wasn't sexual, it wasn't hungry. It was tenderness, it was a life jacket. It was a sanctuary. His hands gently held my head, thumbs caressing my cheeks. He pulled his lips from mine. He looked into my eyes, appearing shocked at what had happened. "Jezebel. I'm really sorry."

He dropped his arms to his sides, while I remained frozen like a mannequin. I couldn't even answer. I wanted the comfort back.

Justin turned away with crimson cheeks, his eyes no longer connected to mine. "We should go eat. You need to eat, Jez."

"Justin." My mannequin arms and legs unable to move.

He looked at me, his gaze embarrassing me. "Yeah?"

"It's okay. Really, it was okay. It was nice." I smiled.

He moved toward me again. "Your life is complicated enough. I'm sorry. Let's just forget about it and eat a big juicy steak." He hugged me quickly, and asked with his eyes that I not make a big deal about what had just happened.

"Sure. Let's eat."

During our dinner, we reverted to light banter, like we had done before this past weekend. It was a fleece blanket resting around my shoulders on a cold snowy day. Everything about being with him brought me tranquility.

I fantasized for a moment that tonight I would sleep with Justin, somehow making the child become his. If Kirk found out I had had a child, I would tell him it was Justin's. I would have my revenge. I would rob him of ever knowing his child. I wanted to roll my head back and let out a laugh. But, was delivering pain to another, even if it was deserved, setting me up for more horrendous pain in the future? Should the sin of one be rectified by the sin of another?

Chapter 35

Nicole wondered how it could be so blistering hot at eight in the morning, as she scuttled through the Wednesday morning sidewalk traffic. Even the hand holding her new cell phone against her ear was sweaty. She despised perspiration.

"Kirk, you're all hyper and yelling at me. Calm down." She was stressed enough, with this being the first day back as Jack's secretary, so she would not tolerate his hysterics.

"I'm sorry for yelling, Nic, but I need to know if you said anything at all to Jezebel. If she saw you, or if she knows who you are."

"Relax. Olive never saw me, not that I'm aware of anyway. I never ran into her."

"Okay. She's just been acting strangely since the weekend, since the case settled."

"Not returning your calls, Kirk? Well maybe your little relationship has just run its course. Move on. Maybe she knew all along your involvement with me and she was actually using you."

"Your sensitivity is heart-warming, Nic."

"Hey, don't forget we have our counseling session next week. You better not blow me off."

"I wouldn't dream of it. I'll see you then."

Sweat was forming on her back. So unattractive. She stopped and removed her jacket, tossing it across the top of her briefcase. Fear pricked at her belly as she imagined what it would be like transitioning back in as Jack's secretary. Would he be kind or cold? How would others treat her? And, did she really care about anyone other than Jack?

At her old desk, she settled in, rearranging objects the way they had been before she left. A stack of files sat next to the computer with curt instructions on post-it notes as to what she needed to do with them. The writing was Audrey's, the woman who had replaced her for the past couple months. She wasn't surprised not to find any warm notes from her, wishing her good luck back at her job. Instead of being irritated, Audrey should be grateful because her reassignment got her a nice raise.

Mid-lipstick application, Jack's door flew open. "Nicole. I need to see you."

That answered one question—he was going to be cold. At least in public anyway. She straightened her skirt and smoothed her jacket, fluffed her hair. Her hands were shaking, so she needed a few deep breaths to steady herself.

"Yes, Jack," she said, closing the door.

He stood behind his desk, straightening papers, avoiding eye contact. "Sit," he demanded pointing at the guest seat.

She did. "Jack, I know this is going to be a bit awkward at first, but I'm hoping we can resume—"

"Nicole, what have you done?" Still standing, the tops of his knuckles pressed into the piles of papers in front of him. His eyes were burning into her soul.

"What do you mean?" her voice quivered.

He sat, appearing to soften somewhat. "Nicole. I

was hoping with this settlement, we could end the game playing. But, it seems you've taken this disturbing game to a higher level."

She slid to the edge of her chair. Her eyebrows, she was sure, were pressed together making unattractive creases in her forehead. Her ability to appear collected diminished.

"Jack, what the hell are you talking about? I'm done with games and so happy to be back—"

"I got a call from the President today about you, my dear."

Nicole's hands pressed against her mouth. The silence felt like a third person standing in the room.

Jack stood and moved in front of her, resting his backside against his desk, his leg touching hers. With his arms crossed in front of him, he continued in hushed tones, "You can imagine, based on the current state of our relationship that things were a bit strained. He acknowledged his personal failures in sleeping with my wife, but of course I'm in no position to assert moral authority over the man. We agreed that we despised each other, but politically and career-wise, we need to work in tandem."

Entranced by his every word, she didn't move. She let their legs remain together.

"He brought to my attention, that he received a threatening email from you—"

"What?" she shrieked. He held a finger up signaling for her to quiet her voice. "Jack, you need to believe me, I did no such thing!"

"Well, the email is from a Nicole D'Angelo and it claimed to have an email exchange between him and my wife. Enough details were given to prove to him that it was legit. It claimed that you were going to take it to the press. This is unbelievable. I'm now legally bound to keep you as my secretary, and all I want to do is strangle you." His face was so close, she felt his rush of warm breath against his face.

"Jack, I never sent him anything."

"Well, you were the only person I confided in and the only person I showed that email printout to. You were the only one."

"I understand, but what would I gain from ruining his career, and ultimately your career for that matter? Jack, that would be stupid and insane of me. I have everything I want right now. Why would I screw that up?"

He held his hand up to calm her. "Then who else would do this?"

She rubbed her temples and left her seat. She needed to move toward the windows, as if the light would give her clarity.

"My phone. I lost my phone. Someone must have it, or someone stole it."

"What was on your phone, Nicole?"

She spun toward him, sighing out loud. "Don't be angry, Jack, but I took a picture of the email printout. I wasn't sure what you had up your sleeve and how you were going to try to hurt me next. I hadn't planned to use it, but just to have it as insurance, if you threatened to hurt me."

His face reddened, his lips pursed, he rushed a hand through his hair. "But how would anyone know who it was from, based on the email?"

Bile crept up into her throat. Who had her phone? "I taped us, too. I had hit record, thinking we were going to talk about the case. I never imagined I was going to tape what you had told me. Jack, I'm sorry. It was before we made love that day. I forgot to delete it."

"Forgot, my ass." He huffed and walked toward her. His jaws and fists clenched, his chest heaving. "Who has your phone, Nicole? And why didn't you deactivate it?"

"I did. But the person must have still looked at the pictures and everything else."

"You had no security code on it?"

"I forgot to reset it. I retraced my steps, called over to Harrington and Paulson but no one found it, or so they said. I kept thinking it would show up. The battery was close to dead, so I assumed it was fine. I assumed it was dead, gone."

His eyes squinted. He wasn't believing her.

Olive! Was this why she was being cold to Kirk? Was Jezebel the person behind this? Of course she was. Or Justin, or most likely both.

"Jack, I can fix this. I think I know who stole my phone. Someone involved with Kirk. It might be just a little game she's playing. I can talk to her and convince her that Kirk is all hers—" She kept quiet about Justin.

"No, you're going to pay her. You are going to shut her up and keep her happy." He reached into his desk drawer and handed her an envelope, thick with a wad of cash. Had he planned to pay Nicole with this, to shut her up?

They stood face to face with just the envelope separating them. "I'm sorry, Jack. I was caught up in our game and I crossed a line and got you in trouble. But I'll fix it. I promise you, I'll fix this."

His eyes narrowed, his breathing still heavy. He

pressed his lips together hard, appearing to hold in a scream.

He hissed out words, restraining, "When you're sure it's been taken care of, I'll call the President."

The man standing inches from her was going to call the President. She felt like an important character in a movie. She had to save the presidency and country from ruin. Only she had the power to do it.

In an unexpected move, Jack's hand reached behind her neck, under her hair, pulling her toward him. His lips were a welcomed reprieve from the stress of the morning. A cool breeze in the morning's heat. His kiss was like aloe on sunburn. His hot breath then rushed in her ear. "Fix it and there will a reward for you, my dear." He was angry, she could tell. He was delivering a threat wrapped inside affection.

The sweat reappeared on her back, but she held herself together, pivoted, and exited his office.

Damn you, Olive. What the hell were you thinking?

No one messes with me, she thought, and survives.

Chapter 36

After five days of absorbing the idea of parenting, the thought still hadn't become any less terrifying. I arranged my desk, trying to push the thought of purchasing maternity clothes out of my head. Before maternity clothes, I would somehow have to face Kirk. In fact, since he was to be my date at my mother's wedding in twenty-four hours, I'd have to face him soon.

His voicemail and texts had become more stern and anxious. I had told him I was going to stay longer in New York, so he had no idea I had arrived home two days ago. I wouldn't have been able to handle a surprise visit from him at my apartment.

I had made the dreaded call to the doctor, and the nurse's response to my request to see me sooner added to my anxiety. "Hon, if the test is positive, you're pregnant. We'll see you at eight weeks. We'll see you sooner if you experience any issues." Issues? This whole pregnancy was an issue. My appointment was set for the day before I was to leave for Niagara Falls.

Denial was no longer possible. This was real. Since I was not suspended high in the clouds anymore or in a city miles away, I had to face reality. I had to face Kirk.

I bundled a stack of files into my arms and headed to Justin's office. Even though a bit of awkwardness hung between us since we hadn't discussed our hotel kiss, there was still comfort in his presence. He remained the only person who knew my secrets.

"How are you feeling? Here, let me take those, you shouldn't be carrying heavy things." Taking the files into his one arm, Justin pulled out a guest chair for me with the other.

"Relax, Justin. I'm fine." I sat. A part of me enjoyed his attention. I hid my smile.

"I'm worried about you. Have you told him yet?"

"No, but I have to tonight. My mom's wedding is tomorrow and he was supposed to meet me there. I want to enjoy the day. I need to get rid of the unpleasantness tonight and be done with it."

"Have you decided…what you're going to do? With the baby?"

"No. Honestly, I'm just taking it day by day for now."

"So," he said, sitting behind his desk. "I got a response from…to my email."

"Really? What did it say?" My eyelids could not open any further.

"Just simply that he was going to speak with Jack. And, that going to the press would mean dire consequences for everyone. And, that was it."

"Wow. You need to delete that email account now. You're done, right?"

"I don't know…" He turned in his seat and gazed out the window. An evil smile crossed his lips.

"Justin! Really, you need to stop. This is getting dangerous."

He spun back toward me. "Okay, I'll stop. But this has been so much fun."

"If he really is going to talk to Jack, then you

achieved what you wanted. Nicole's life will be miserable."

"You're correct. But what am I going to do with her phone? Should I toss it in a dumpster?" He pulled the pink and silver cased iPhone out from his briefcase.

An evil smile now crossed my lips. "May I have it?"

He smiled back. "See, revenge is fun, isn't it?"

The rhinestone N felt like it burned as it rested in my palm. "It's not revenge. It's justice. But we need this whole thing to end now."

"I'm done, but it looks like for you, it's just beginning."

"Is the battery charged?"

"Charged and ready, Ms. Stone."

I grabbed an empty file from Justin's desk and stuck the phone inside, tucking it beneath my arm. "I'm just going to use it to put an end to something."

Before I could disappear into the hallway, Justin called my name. I turned to see him smiling at me and I smiled back. "What?"

"I was thinking of the irony of this situation. This Nicole uses sex and seduction to get what she wants. She holds the power to bring down men and kings. She actually is a Jezebel."

I thought about it and let it all sink in before allowing a broad smile to cross my lips. "Wow, you're right. A living breathing Jezebel is in our midst. Hmmm. We almost let her take us down, too."

****

As eagerly as I had expected, Kirk agreed to meet me for lunch. It may have been the growing life inside me, the fact that I had to end a relationship, or that I carried a phone so full of secrets it felt radioactive, but my body nearly combusted with nausea. Nonetheless, I felt strong.

I passed by the glass windows of Corner Bakery and saw him standing inside. His body stood erect at the sight of me.

I tried to muster a smile, but it felt like a grimace.

"Jez, it's so good to see you. I've really missed you." He grabbed me by the shoulders and pecked my cheek. I wished he knew there were three of us now. "What's wrong? I sense you're upset with me. Are you?"

"Kirk, can we sit please?" I motioned to an empty corner table.

We sat, his eyes never leaving my face. "What's wrong? You're scaring me."

"Kirk, when we had lunch here last time, when you gave me this watch…" My eyes glanced down at my fingers fondling the silver wrapping around my wrist. A new habit of mine. "You told me about how you misled me in the beginning of our relationship, that you had still been married to your wife. I accepted your apology for that and I asked if there was anything else you needed to share with me. You said no, and I went on believing what we had was real and that you were being honest with me."

"Jez, what are you saying? What have you heard?" His cheeks were red and his eyes were blinking, as if I were the sun.

"Does this look familiar?" With my lips pressed together tightly, I slid the phone—N side up—across the table.

He looked at it, still and silent.

"Well?" I asked, feeling like an attorney in a movie who had just showed a witness a damaging piece of evidence.

"It's my wife's, my ex-wife's, phone."

"And it tells quite the story. From pictures to her calendar, it told me the story you withheld from me." A rush of queasiness reminded me of what I was withholding from him.

"Jezebel," he screeched in an un-manly fashion. Both of his hands grabbed my hand resting on the table, covering the token he had gifted me. "I want to explain. I want to explain everything. I'm so sorry."

I pulled my hand away but allowed him to speak. "My wife, my ex-wife, well, she had been hard to deal with and she cheated on me, and she drove me insane. I'm sorry you got pulled into this unfairly. She truly made me go crazy. It's almost abusive how she treated me. And my initial reaction after meeting you was to use you to make her jealous, but then I got to know you… I fell in love with you, Jezebel." He appeared to swallow emotion. "You've changed me, helped me. I made a bad decision in the beginning, but like the crash, it turned into something great."

"Let me ask you something, Kirk. For a very long time after your initial 'bad decision,' you continued to ask me probing questions about her case. It was my fault to share with you, but I thought it was an innocent way to entertain you and make conversation about my job, thinking that the information would be going nowhere. But you knew names that I hadn't disclosed to you. You probed, but I thought it was just you showing interest in my work. And, Justin and I have reason to suspect that you shared this information with her. She was way too comfortable with our questioning. In fact, I also have reason to suspect, after thoroughly reflecting on some strange occurrences over the past few weeks, that she, or perhaps you, snuck into my office."

"I assure you I did no such thing," he said with a look of shock spread all over his face. "Jezebel, I'm sorry and I want to make it up to you."

"Then if you didn't do it, you allowed me to become a victim of her manipulation. My office was messed up and my security pass was found on the street. If you didn't do it, then your lovely wife did." I purposely omitted the ex before wife. "What you did, Kirk, by continuing to lie, to use me, to allow me to put my job in jeopardy, solidified for you that this relationship is not real. It was all based on a lie. I do take responsibility in that I did see red flags along the way, but I continued with the relationship, not trusting my gut."

"I can fix everything—"

"You slept with me, allowing me to believe that you cared for me."

"I do. I do desperately."

"Enough to agree to go to a counseling session with Nicole next week, without telling me?"

"It's her. She wanted closure."

"I wish I could get closure too, and for this nightmare of a relationship to end, but it can't because I'm pregnant. Pregnant with your child. And it makes me so sad to know that this baby was conceived not out of love, but out of manipulation and your greed to win back a deceitful wife and get money from a trumped up lawsuit."

"Jezebel. My God, you're really pregnant? My

God." His hands rubbed his face. The phone still rested on the table between us, its rhinestones catching the sunshine and making tiny circles of light dance on Kirk's hands and face.

I stood again, swallowing my nausea. My hands and knees shook uncontrollably. "I need to get back to work."

"Jezebel, this changes everything. We need to work together here and fix things, for the baby."

"I haven't decided what I'm doing with the baby, Kirk." I felt superior, relishing the power I held as I gazed down at him.

"Jezebel, what are you saying? You can't make a choice you'll regret."

"Speaking from experience, Kirk? You know what? For months, I haven't been in control of this relationship. It's my turn and you have nothing to say about it. How does that feel?"

"Jez, it's my child, too. We can work something out."

"Go to Hell, Kirk. Go to Hell."

Streams of tears streaked my cheeks as I walked through the city streets. The summer heat did not register with me, because inside I felt cold and numb. I let the tears roll down my neck and onto my blouse. Heads turned toward me when I let a few gasps and sobs escape uncontrolled, but I didn't care. The tears fell for the man I thought I had known, but who all along had been just a stranger. Tears rolled for time wasted, for poor decisions, choices that not only brought me pain, but affected people around me, like Justin, and now this innocent child.

The day of the crash, I had blamed God, wondering

how He could let disaster happen. How could a loving God let lives be placed in harm's way, blood spilled, psyches scarred. But what chain of human decisions, poor or otherwise, had led to that disaster?

In my own life, I could have ended the relationship, not had sex with a man I barely knew, or in the very least, taken my pill on time. I could have chosen to not share privileged information carelessly. I had held the power to stop a train from careening out of control. Maybe for me, God had been on the train in the form of a skinny man in a gray t-shirt, pulling me away from disaster, away from Kirk, out of harm's way and through a door, easily opened. Maybe a loving God had sent me a message in the form of a crimson flag, maybe in my friends' pleas to be cautious, but I chose not to listen. After being rescued, I made the choice to turn around and walk, head on, back into the fire.

Wind whipped my hair, a gust unexpected, lifting the collar of my shirt upward, brushing along my tear-stained cheek.

Chapter 37

I wasn't one hundred percent thrilled with the dress I had selected, but during my New York trip, my mind hadn't been focused on shopping. Cala had made the unilateral decision that we would wear simple black sleeveless dresses as our mother's maid and matron of honor. So, I did as instructed.

I slipped on my heels, grabbed the white paper wrapped wedding gift, and headed out the door. I was at least pleased with my gift purchase—an engraved silver frame for the couple's wedding portrait.

On my way to the elevator, my cell phone rang. It was Cala.

"Hey, are you on your way?"

"Yes, I'll be there in fifteen minutes."

"I probably should have told people not to wear spikey heels, my landscaping is going to get destroyed."

"Cala, you can't tell people what to wear to a wedding. Your landscaping will survive."

"Can you stop by the florist? I forgot a boutonniere for the pastor. They said they'd make another one quickly for me."

"Sure." I was secretly pleased that Cala allowed a small detail to slip through the cracks.

"Have you been watching the weather?" Cala continued without waiting for an answer, "Rain and wind from that stupid hurricane is moving faster north than they predicted. It better stay away from Bethesda until this wedding is over. Say a prayer it slows down."

The hurricane had flooded many towns in Mississippi and Louisiana, leaving hoards of people homeless. I felt a twinge of guilt at wishing it to slow and deluge another city so our event could stay dry. Cala referred to the "they" who had predicted the weather; presumably she meant the weather forecasters, but had she forgotten that Ms. Charlie had been the one who predicted this?

I completed Cala's errand and arrived at her house, nearly getting run over by a catering van. Men and women in white shirts, black pants and ties, whisked by me with trays and boxes. I couldn't help but smile, thinking this was all for my mother.

A gust of wind knocked me slightly off balance as I reached for the door. My attention was drawn upward at the passing cluster of clouds polluting the baby blue sky. Amazing how a storm hitting the southern states was reaching me right now in Maryland, tying thousands of people together in an ominous way.

Cala greeted me as I entered the foyer, her hair neatly arranged atop her head in a professional up-do. My sister's eyes assessed my own hair, and her face registered disapproval of my amateur attempts at hairstyling.

"Jezebel, where's your date?"

"He's meeting me here."

"I'm looking forward to finally meeting this mysterious man from the train."

"Um, I sort of changed my date. Kirk and I called it quits."

"Oh, I'm sorry. But I feared that wouldn't last."

She shook her head and luckily her attention was distracted by an incoming guest. "Damian!"

"Well, look at my two gorgeous sisters. And you both remember Paula, right?" He swept his hand behind Paula's back and led her into our sibling circle.

Cala and I greeted Damian's date with a hug. She too had her hair arranged pristinely atop her head, exposing a pencil-thin long neck. I couldn't help but picture her tiny body getting carried away by a hurricane gust during the ceremony.

"Where's Mom?" I asked, looking around.

"I hired a hair stylist to come to the house. They're up in my bathroom. She could work on you next, Jez, if you'd like? Damian, really? Those old nasty shoes? Couldn't you have at least cleaned up a bit for your mother's wedding?" Cala was apparently not embarrassed to be scolding her brother in front of his date and a foyer full of workers.

"Mom loves my fashion sense. Relax. I'll make sure the photographer doesn't capture my feet in any pictures, so not to ruin the wedding." He flashed his charming grin to Paula and me. I giggled harder than intended.

"I've worked hard, you two. Do not make fun of me." Cala placed her hands firmly on her hips, nearly poking a caterer in the gut waiting close by to speak to her.

Placing the guitar case on the ground, Damian nuzzled up next to Cala, wrapped an arm around her shoulders and kissed her cheek. "Place looks fantastic, sis, we're only having fun."

Cala allowed a faint grin, clearly enjoying his affection. She then turned to answer the caterer's question.

Wind tossed my unprofessionally styled hair, drawing my attention to the opening door and the man walking through it. "Kirk!" I squealed as a rush of hot queasiness rocked my body.

"Jez, I know you said you don't want me here, but please just let me talk to you for a minute." His fingers wrapped around my bare arm and felt like fire on my skin. He attempted to lead me into the living room away from people, but I yanked my arm away.

"Kirk, this is my mother's wedding. This is not a place to talk."

"I'm the father of your baby, I deserve to be here."

"Baby?!" Damian and Cala bellowed in unison.

I couldn't even look in their direction. "Kirk. Leave. Now." I knew his loud announcement of my pregnancy had been intentional.

He didn't budge. "I'm your date. You asked me here."

"I have a new date."

As if on cue, the front door slammed closed. A soothing voice made me smile. "I'm here people! Let this party begin!" Ken's hands waved in the air as if waiting for applause. His gray suit was impeccable, solid aqua tie and all.

"Ken!" Cala and I exclaimed in harmony.

"Cala, this place looks fab." He kissed both her cheeks as if he were European, and then did the same to me. For the first time since Kirk arrived, I exhaled.

"Kirk," Ken said, as if long time friends, "shall I escort you to your car?"

Ignoring Ken, Kirk pleaded, "Jezebel, can we talk before I go?"

"I have nothing more to say to you and I'd like to enjoy my mom's wedding, please."

"Jezebel. I love you. I'm sorry. And, I won't stop trying to win you back." Kirk left, pulling the door closed behind him.

My eyes connected with Ken's. He stood silent, not pinging or singing, no jazz hands or dancing fingers, just a friendly gaze that brought me comfort. On Friday after my breakup, I confided in Ken about my situation, leaving out the presidential scandal. Ken didn't judge or say I told you so. "I'm here for you, my love. Whatever you need. I'm here," was all he said. And he had given me the same warm gaze he was giving me now.

He reached and hugged me, and to make me laugh, he whispered in my ear, "Your brother looks hot. Is he definitely straight?"

Before I could even answer him with a laugh, Cala was pulling me away. "Jezebel. I need to talk to you."

Alone in my sister's formal living room, Cala faced me with her hands on her hips. There had to be indentations on those spots. "Are you really pregnant?"

"Yes. I just found out." Full of shame, my eyes hit the carpet avoiding my sister's glare.

"How could you be so irresponsible? This is unbelievable."

Shame was replaced with fury, and my eyes raised and dug into my sister's. "Thanks for your support, Cala." Like a child, I rolled my eyes and huffed.

"I'm in hell right now trying everything under the sun to get pregnant, but careless you gets the baby!"

A hot lava rose inside me. "Cala, this pregnancy has absolutely nothing to do with you. Your fertility issues did not come into my mind when I slept with

Kirk. Or, when I forgot to take my pill. I'm really sorry, Cala, but for once, this is not about you." I knew my words were like knives digging into Cala's chest. I had never before seen my sister speechless. My instinct told me to say I was sorry. But, I wasn't sorry.

Cala slowly turned and headed to the kitchen. Ken cackled in the distance. I, wiping a few stray tears off of my cheeks, jogged up the steps to look for my mother. I sought a security blanket.

I slowly opened my sister's bedroom door, and the sight of my mother's long, off-white dress spinning in front of a tall mirror caught me off guard.

"Mom, you look like an angel."

"Oh, sweetie, you're here." My mom joined me in two quick strides and engulfed me in a hug.

"Mom, I love your hair, and your dress. You're gorgeous!"

"Oh, a trained professional made me look this good." Her laugh filled the room. "Did you see Joe down there?"

"No. I didn't really mingle much. Do you need anything?"

My mom paused, and silently stared at me with a contented grin. "Jezebel. I want to tell you something." She took my hands in her own. "I'm just so proud of you. You've always made me so proud. Each of my children has unique strengths, and you've always been my sweet girl with an understated beauty and brains to boot. I know, I know, I'm emotional and sappy today, but I want everyone to know how happy I am. I'm a lucky woman."

"It's not luck, Mom. You're a good person and you deserve to be surrounded by good things." I softly kissed my mother's cheek. "I'm happy for you. I just hope it doesn't rain."

We both glanced out the large bay window overlooking the garden and the pool. A white trellis stood in the center of a grassy patch surrounded by an array of flowers, dancing in the breeze. A stage was set for the impending nuptials.

"I'm not worried about rain. I did have to laugh though at the rain being caused by Hurricane Charles. That Miss Charlie is something else!"

"Oh, I didn't even make the name connection. That is something else."

We tipped our heads back, letting loose boisterous laughter.

I joined the family downstairs and busied myself with last minute preparations. Guests began to arrive and Ken and I made sure a waiter handed each of them a glass of champagne and offered them a tray of hors d'oeuvres. The seats in the garden filled. I instructed Ken to sit up front and to take pictures with my camera. The wind had calmed and not a drop left the sky.

Damian strummed his guitar and sang a ballad as I closed the patio door behind me. Cala handed me a nosegay of pink roses—an olive branch of sorts—and smiled pensively.

"Thanks, Cala. Everything is beautiful. It looks like the rain is going to hold off." Cala smiled wider. I looked at my mom. "Joe looks terrific. He can't wait to have you meet him at the end of that aisle."

My mom laughed, and then appeared to suppress a cry, pressing her lips together and blinking tears away. "Your dad would have been so proud of you girls. And your brother. As awkward as it would be to have him at my wedding, of all things, I wish he could see you three today."

I laughed lightly. "He is here, Mom. I don't believe he has ever left us. And I think he'd really like Joe. Maybe he even brought you Joe."

Cala turned her head away, appearing to privately wipe a tear away, but she couldn't hide a loud sniffle. She took a step and opened the French doors. "Are you two ready?"

"Yes," we said together.

Cala walked down the aisle first to the sounds of violins and flutes, and I followed. We stood together at the end of the aisle, smiling at a beaming Joe who nervously stroked his freshly slicked hair. In unity, we looked up the aisle. Everyone stood to watch my mom make her way toward Joe. With the exception of a few bashful glances to the ground, she never took her eyes off him.

No breeze blew, no rain fell, not even a flying bird disturbed the scene in front of me. This was the picture a crystal ball would have held many years ago on the night my father had died. Hope, and of love reborn, albeit in a different form, with a different person, but love was born again. Smiles and laughter were allowed to resurface after sadness. Sunshine to radiate after a storm.

While music played, the couple exchanged vows and rings, and a minister pronounced them husband and wife. A chorus of cheers burst from the audience as Joe swept his bride into his arms, kissing her with zeal. His hug pulled her from the ground and her heels kicked upward with joy. A strong gust of Hurricane Charles pushed through the crowd with a sudden force, knocking the white trellis backward onto the ground, but it failed to disturb the bride and groom's bliss. I glanced at Ken, happy to see he had captured the moment with several snaps of my camera. That would be the new photograph my mother could place in the silver frame for her dining room. The definition of joy, of love, of contentment, frozen forever.

Chapter 38

After leaving Cala's house, Kirk drove around the posh Bethesda neighborhood for an hour. Fearing someone would call the police about his stalker-like behavior, he stopped at a nearby diner to eat. He nibbled on a sandwich, telling himself there was still time and a possibility he could fix this situation.

His head throbbed. He should have gone back to his condo and climbed into bed. Instead, he drove back to Cala's house. He parked around the corner behind the last wedding guest's car. Without a plan, he cut between two large bricked homes, walking past tiny signs warning of a security system in use, and climbed a knoll that overlooked Cala's backyard. Enough trees and shrubs surrounded him so that he remained camouflaged. He'd wait until the wedding was over and meet Jezebel at her car, show her how serious he was at making this work. Tell her he'd be here for her throughout her pregnancy and after. He'd beg her to have the child, and tell her they'd be good parents.

She had asked him on the fourth of July, if he'd ever camp out on cement, if there was anything he felt that passionate about. He knew the answer now. He'd do it for her.

His chest ached in a way that was unfamiliar. He'd experienced intense pain at the hands of Nicole, but this was different. Nicole brought him sadness, but it was always accompanied by anger, resentment, and jealousy. But this pain stood alone as pure heartbreak.

Crouching between the shrubs, he felt like a criminal but was mesmerized by the scene below him. He barely breathed. Jezebel mingled, hugging guests and relatives. After a hug, the guests held onto their smile long after the embrace. It was a testament that everyone around her enjoyed her presence. Her insides must be a mess, full of confusion and perhaps, he hoped, sadness over their breakup. But, she smiled and laughed. Her laugh carried through the crowd, over the band's music and greeted him on the hillside. At first it stung to hear her voice, but then it brought him happiness. She was the occasional ray of sunlight poking through an overcast day.

Guests migrated to their seats and the best man took the microphone to make a toast. The crowd laughed at the man's jokes, made oohs and aahs at his sentimental remarks, and tapped each other's glasses with enthusiasm. Next, Cala took the microphone.

"I received many compliments today on the decorations, the food, the gardens, and many commented how perfect everything looked. I'm not going to lie, that made me happy. But when I look at my mother and Joe, I see a perfection that cannot be created or planned. It's the picture of pure love and happiness. Just looking at the two of you together brings me joy and I'm sure everyone here agrees. I spend a great deal of time trying to make my family into a neat orderly image of what I see as perfect. But, really, you each are remarkably perfect just as you are. So, family, forgive me in my attempts to change you. I love you the way you are. To Joe and Juliana, may the love and joy you radiate today last for all eternity. Cheers!" And the crowd yelled out the same.

Cala walked immediately to Jezebel and hugged her, saying something in her ear. Jezebel hugged her again and they seemed to be sharing a secret, keeping their faces close, hands still touching each other's arms. He hoped that some of the love and elation floating around this backyard would reach him, too.

He deserved to be hated by Jezebel and clearly he could see the error of his ways. But through his original deception, he got to know Jezebel and fell in love with her. Although his original reason for calling her was wrong, his feelings for her in the end were pure and good. Jezebel taught him what it was like to feel love and to be loved in a healthy way.

A rustling in a nearby bush made him jolt and look around. How had he been reduced to an animal in the shrubbery? He glanced back to the crowd, slightly nervous that his movements may have caught the attention of a guest. But he remained undiscovered. Invisible.

The band played and Jezebel danced in the center of the crowd. People surrounded her, like a protective ring keeping her from harm.

He laughed when he saw Jezebel take the stage and join the band with her harmonica. She was actually quite talented. Unlike Nicole, whose superficial gifts were only apparent the moment you met her, Jezebel's gems were infinite and nestled among many layers. The longer you took to get to know her, the richer and more beautiful she became.

It was an odd, sickening feeling to have a part of his flesh, walking around inside another human being, far away. Jezebel held the power to take this baby away from him. Was it fair? No. But he couldn't fault her for wanting to end the pregnancy. She claimed this baby was conceived out of manipulation. But Kirk knew the truth. It was created out of love.

Chapter 39

I opened my eyes, so nauseous I couldn't lift my head off the pillow. If only this could just be a hangover I could cure in a few hours. After a half hour of trying to convince myself to make my way to the kitchen to find a box of crackers, I finally sat up. Furry leapt onto my lap.

"Oh, Furry, it all wasn't a nightmare, it's really my life." I had a wonderful time at my mother's wedding, but afterward, Kirk was waiting by my car. Luckily, Ken had walked me out and threatened Kirk with a call to the police if he didn't leave. Before leaving, he told me that he would never give up on me. I anticipated more surprise visits from him.

Looking forward to my mother's wedding had been my week's distraction and kept me moving forward. Today, I faced nothing. No plans to see friends or family, no boyfriend to have lunch with, nothing. Nothing but the reality of a child growing inside me, and that decisions had to be made.

The ginger ale and crackers settled my stomach, so I went directly into the shower. If I sat on the couch and grabbed the remote, I feared I would waste the entire day. After my shower, I noticed a voicemail alert on my phone. I had no idea how long the new message had been there. I listened and it was the minister I had met on the train the day I had fainted. I had contacted him about helping me with a fundraiser for the Metro memorial.

In a spontaneous move, I dressed and headed to the minister's church. I didn't know what time the services were, but perhaps I could see him afterward. At least this was getting me out of my apartment. I had a purpose.

As I entered the massive church vestibule, I could hear a booming voice and followed it into the sanctuary. It was more like an auditorium, and didn't resemble any church setting I'd ever been in. I took a seat in the back and listened to the minister complete his sermon. I sang with the congregation, and was entertained by a full band on the stage.

After the service, I kept my eyes on the movements of the minister so I would not lose him in the crowd. Finally, I caught his attention. "Pastor Stevens? Hi, it's me, Jezebel. Jezebel from the Metro." I felt foolish introducing myself like that.

"Oh, my! Hello Jezebel-from-the-Metro. I'm so glad you came to the service." He shook my hand and squeezed my opposite shoulder with a firm but tender grip.

"Well, I was a little late, but enjoyed what I saw."

"Well, late or not, I'm glad you're here. So I talked to my son, he's in the band here and in another band outside of church. He would like to help with a Metro memorial fundraiser. He has some thoughts on putting on a concert. Here, come with me, I'll introduce you."

The pastor led me up the steps next to the stage. The stage crew were placing instruments in cases and binding up wires and microphones. "This is my son, Evan."

I extended my hand and a current of electricity bolted through it as we connected. His eyes met mine and lingered as if trying to retrieve information. Our handshake stopped, but our hands remained connected.

"Were you on the second car that day?" he asked. It was a question delivered with purpose.

"Yes."

I liked his eyes. They lit up as his mouth moved into a smile. "You were on the ground and someone pulled you up, correct?"

It was him. Evan was my crash-savior. "Yes. That was you? My gosh, it was you who pulled me up, wasn't it?"

"Yes. Yes. You were seated in front of me before the crash. I could never forget that curly hair of yours." He smiled with one beat of a laugh.

Awkwardly we looked at each other, still holding hands. We released our hold, but I felt an urge to reconnect with him. I stepped toward him, a bit too eagerly, and yanked him into a hug. "For months, I've been wanting to thank you. Thank you, Evan."

"You would have done the same for me."

The pastor, a forgotten participant in the conversation, excused himself to speak with a church member.

I couldn't take my eyes from Evan. "I don't know. I don't know if I would have. I didn't try to save anyone that day."

"Here, come with me." He guided me toward an empty room down the hall from the stage. He shut the door and motioned me to take a seat.

"So, I'm Jezebel Stone, by the way. I don't even know if I introduced myself or if your father introduced me. Or, if he told you about me…"

"I know. I knew your name from the day of the crash. I overheard your conversation with the guy next to you." He spoke with a confidence and a calmness that gave me a chill as if he were talking about his experience seeing a ghost. It reminded me of sitting across the table from Ms. Charlie. Evan knew things, like Ms. Charlie, that made me uncomfortable.

"Oh." I felt embarrassed, trying to recall the conversation I had had with Kirk. A conversation I had relived before many times, but never in the context of someone else overhearing.

"You had told the guy your name and explained the Jezebel story to him. It made me laugh."

"Oh, so you were there the whole time?"

"Yeah, I saw you get on. The seat was open next to that guy and also a seat was open next to me. You chose him. I wasn't offended or anything." We laughed again together.

"So, I have to ask you something I've always wondered. How did you get that door open? The guy I sat with, Kirk, said he and another guy had tried prying open a door and couldn't. No offense, but you're not that, not that—"

"Muscular?" We both laughed again.

"Well, yeah. But two big men couldn't get it open, and you…"

"Well that's something I actually think about quite often. Nothing made it open. I barely touched it and it slid open. I can't explain it."

"Wow. You didn't bolt though. You turned and grabbed me off the floor. Through the blackness and the smoke, you came back for me. Why?"

His eyes sparkled as they met mine. He definitely had pretty eyes and a pleasant face. "Can't really explain that either actually. But I wanted to find you. This is personal, but I've been wanting to talk to you, to tell you about that day."

"Really?"

"My dad told me you had talked to him about a fundraiser and he told me your name. So, I knew we'd eventually meet. I guess it was fate."

"So, tell me your story. About your ride."

"I pictured us doing this over a beer, but okay, here we go." He straightened, and then leaned forward, resting his forearms on his knees. He looked up into my eyes. "I had had a rough few months. I live in a constant battle with depression and it had hit an all time low for me. My father and I had been fighting. He wants me to go back to college. Actually he'd love for me to become a minister and take over the church. It's been his dream, his very vocal dream."

"And it's not your dream, I gather."

"No, not at all. I'm 26 but he hasn't given up on me becoming a minister. I want to pursue my music career, but he sees that as foolish. I feel like I constantly disappoint him. Anyway, I hadn't slept in days before the crash. I have times when I sleep all the time and this had been a time of insomnia." He ran his hand through his thick, dark hair as he let out a quick sigh. He rested against the back of his chair and continued, "I was heading home after meeting my band downtown. I was feeling low, like wanting-to-hurt-myself-low. I wanted to kill myself. Sometimes I thought about taking pills, or something quiet like that."

"Oh my God, Evan. That's awful."

"I know. Probably the insomnia hadn't helped my dismal mood. But on the train, I listened to you and that guy talk. You told him you were happy being a paralegal and he was pleased with his job. That you didn't need to be lawyers to be important in the legal world, every role was important. Lawyers couldn't do their job without you two. It made me think. I can serve the church as a musician and I can make a living as a musician. I don't have to be a minister to serve this church, or God, or my father for that matter."

"Wow."

"Yeah, wow. It brightened my otherwise gloomy mood. And then the crash happened. And that door slid open. Something was trying to tell me that my life mattered and that I wasn't…" He appeared to swallow the lump in his throat, and then composed himself with a grin. "I wasn't supposed to die that day. My way of thanking you, was to take you out the door with me."

"I wasn't supposed to die that day either."

"Nope. Clearly." He smiled, his eyes twinkling again, and we laughed again. Two souls forever bonded because of a fate missed, or a fate found.

"I struggled with the fact that I never saved anyone that day," I confessed.

"Well, struggle no more my new friend, because you saved this sorry guy." Grinning, Evan pointed at his chest with his thumb. He crossed his legs showing off his ripped, yet stylish jeans and boat shoes.

In our brief conversation, I could tell he had a sense of humor that was familiar and pleasing, like Damian's.

"Do you still think about…suicide?"

"No. I never did again. Not going to say it's been

easy, or my depression is kicked, but suicide? No."

"You could probably help many people by sharing your story."

"Yeah, maybe you're right. There's a reason for everything."

"Yeah, I think you're right."

"So, let me ask you about your ride. Ever see that Kirk guy again?"

A burst of laughter left my body. "Yes, unfortunately yes. We dated and it ended badly. He was using me to get to his wife and things got a bit…twisted." My face contorted with the word.

"You definitely should have picked the empty seat next to me."

I was becoming addicted to his sweet eye sparkle and laugh. "Yes I should have. Or, like you said, maybe it happened the way it did for a reason." My eyes wandered off in thought. "I've also thought a lot, since the crash, about fate and what causes bad things to happen. Free will or divine plan? What do you think?" My hands were flailing a bit more dramatically than I liked, and I quickly pulled them into my lap.

"Free will. We're not a bunch of puppets being controlled, but is there a plan? Yes, I believe there is some plan that we aren't aware of yet. I think we make choices, good or bad, and enjoy or suffer the consequences."

"You're sounding quite minister-like to me. Keep going please," I invited with a hand gesture.

"Well, I believe when we choose to ask God for help, He helps. God, Satan, they're both there for us to call upon. It's our choice, I feel. And, maybe God helps, even when we don't ask. Like with a sliding door, perhaps."

"Or a conversation that we overhear."

"Angels come in all forms. Even those named after an evil queen." We filled the room with laughter.

"I'm pregnant." The surprise announcement even shocked me. Evan's eyes didn't sparkle, but bolted open. I rose and paced behind my chair.

"Oh. Oh, wow."

"Yeah, and I don't know what to do. I hate Kirk. I hate him. But I can't have this baby alone. The disastrous repercussions from the crash continue." I paced the room, holding my arms around my stomach, embarrassed to be spilling my soul to a stranger. But this man seemed the furthest thing from a stranger. "Sorry, you were sharing, and I decided to share. Sorry for dumping on you."

"No, no you shouldn't be sorry. I told you I wanted to off myself. So pregnancy? Yeah, not so terrible and not nearly as psychotic." The sparkle and laugh returned.

"I don't know what to do. What in the hell should I do? I guess hell isn't a good word to use in a church."

"It's probably said more in a church than anywhere else."

I laughed, releasing my arms from my stomach.

Evan stood too and faced me, halting my walk. "Don't worry today about what you should do. The answer will come. And maybe someone will help you when you least expect it."

"Like an angel? Is there an angel that can take care of my child while I'm at work?"

"The answer will come. You'll figure out what to do."

His simple confidence and calming voice this time brought me peace. "I guess I don't need to make any decisions right this very minute."

"Not about your baby. But how about this fundraiser?"

"Yes, that sounds much better."

"My band could play and hold an event downtown. I think we'd draw a nice crowd."

"Does your band need a harmonica player, by chance?" I held a hand in the air.

A broad smile crossed his face. "I was just saying yesterday, 'boy could this band use a harmonica player.' Yes, indeed we need a harmonica player, musically-talented-biblical-queen-Jezebel."

Both our faces smiling, together we laughed, as if we'd known each other forever.

"Why does everyone have so much fun with my name? So tell me, what is the meaning of the name, Evan?"

He looked down, his face blushing, and then he met my eyes. "God is gracious."

Chapter 40

I slipped from the elevator with an unexpected vigor, given my state of nausea. Meeting Evan had given me a crisp new outlook on life. I would take each day as it came and tackle each problem as the answer to the problem arrived.

But when I checked my work messages, there were no answers but yet another problem. Three messages from Nicole D'Angelo. I had left early Friday and had neglected my messages. The first message was from Friday: "Jezebel, this is Nicole D'Angelo. Please, I need to talk to you. Please, please, I beg you not to tell anyone. If you do, you will put yourself in grave danger. Trust me, I've gotten death threats, and you'll be next. I need to meet you briefly and talk. I'll explain everything. And, get us both out of trouble." She rattled off her phone number so quickly and breathy, I had to replay the message several times.

The next one on Saturday: "Jezebel, please call me back immediately." Same breathy, quick number rattling. And this morning: "Jezebel, meet me after work. I'll leave my office at 5:30 and meet you at my red BMW which is parked outside the McPherson Metro station. We can talk inside my car, privately. Don't be late and come alone. I'm going to keep calling you until you text me that you're coming."

To keep Miss Crazy at bay, I sent her a text

confirming our meeting.

What the hell? I pushed my hair behind my head and let out a caveman-like grunt. When would this all end and when would Nicole D'Angelo be out of my life?

I couldn't imagine what had gotten Nicole in a tizzy but I was certainly intrigued. Had the email from Justin caused her to really get death threats? A smile crossed my mouth and I quickly swallowed it. I could not find pleasure in another women's demise. Or could I?

As I shoved files into my file cabinet, I stopped. What if Kirk had told Nicole that I had had her phone and Nicole had assumed that it was me who faked the email? Ignoring Nicole's suggestion to not to tell anyone, I immediately told Justin.

Justin smiled at the papers in front of him, as if I was sharing a joke. "I got messages too and deleted them. I was out of town all weekend, but I'm sure she was slithering around my apartment building. I'm sure she's just blowing smoke. Go see her. I'm sure it's nothing." He finally looked up at me. "In fact, tell her it was definitely not you. I want her to know it was me." His eyes narrowed. "Just make sure she's not recording you."

"But then we are done with this, right?"

I would also tell Nicole that the game was over. Everyone could go back to their corners and play nice.

Justin put his hands up. "I'm totally finished with that bitch."

****

As I hiked toward my meeting location, I was unable to decipher nervousness from nausea. It all felt the same, and I wanted to vomit. My ringing phone distracted me from my queasiness.

"Carolyn, hey."

"Girl, what's up with your crazy voicemail? You're scaring me. What's up?"

"Just want to have dinner and catch you up on a few things going on in my life. Tomorrow good?"

"You are going to keep me in suspense until tomorrow?"

"I can't talk right now. I'm meeting someone."

"Fine. Tomorrow at 6:30 then, at our usual spot."

I caught a glimpse of D'Angelo snaking through the crowd in the distance. "Gotta run."

I stopped walking, put my phone away and steadied myself for my impending encounter. I was moments away from talking face to face with Kirk's ex-wife, or current wife, or whatever she was. I wondered if Nicole knew I was pregnant.

I spotted the red BMW parked across from the Metro entrance. Walking toward her car ahead of me, Nicole swung her arms with determination, her high heels leaving permanent marks on the pavement. Even from a distance, I thought her hair looked a little too puffed and perky after spending a day at the office.

I, feeling dizzy, decided I could not wait for Nicole to open her car, so I sat on a bench near the Metro escalator. There was no way I was passing out in front of Nicole.

"Jezebel," Nicole called out.

"Nicole."

She took the seat next to me, both pivoting to face each other.

"Look, I know you took my phone," Nicole

snapped

"I did not take your phone. I only returned your phone."

"Whatever. Well, you had my phone and you snooped all through it."

"Thank goodness I did."

"I can understand why you hate me, but putting me in danger, was a bit uncalled for, don't you think? Emailing the President?"

"Nicole, I did not take your phone. I did not send the President that email. I do know who did and he's promised to stop."

"Justin." She hissed his name.

"It doesn't matter. The game is over. I returned your phone and the emailing has stopped."

"You need to send one more email. Please. To the President saying it wasn't me. Here. Here's a little incentive." She pulled an envelope out of her purse and placed it on my lap. "A thousand now and a thousand more once the President receives the email. Ask him to call off his goons who keep harassing me. Tell him all traces of evidence about the affair have been destroyed. And, you and your little cowardly sidekick promise to keep your mouths shut. It benefits us all, if we all stay quiet."

I held the money. I won the lottery without playing. Pausing for only a moment, I then handed it back. "I'm better off with the President thinking it's you, and not anyone else."

Nicole pushed my hand away. "You're going to be a single mom. You need the money. Kirk told me, and I'm sorry to hear you two broke up." My face flamed with hot embarrassment and I squinted my eyes at

Nicole, trying to read her, to detect a con, a plan, an agenda. Nicole continued, "You and Justin stay quiet about the President's affair, and about anything you learned about me and Jack, and I'll keep the money coming. Promise. And when the death threats stop, we'll give you more money. Jack promises that you and Justin will be taken care of, as long as you keep all our secrets."

I looked down at the envelope resting in my hands. I refused to believe Nicole was the angel Evan had referenced when he said, "Someone will help you when you least expect it."

Nicole touched my shoulder. "I know you don't owe me any favors, but if something happens to me...well, you're the only one who knows about the threats. So, anyway, I'm not sure what I'm saying, but maybe you'd want to share your information if I get whacked. Not implicating Justin, but you can tell authorities that I had information on the President and he wanted me dead."

"Nicole. This is crazy. Really." I paused, looked into Nicole's defeated eyes and continued, "Can't Jack protect you? Can't he call off the threats? I mean doesn't the President kind of owe him a favor after sleeping with his wife?"

"Shhh." Nicole quieted me. "Jack needs the President and he's already promised Jack all kinds of favors. I'm not sure Jack totally trusts me yet. My game got out of hand, I admit that. But I don't want to die. And, I need him to trust me, to know I didn't send that email."

I noticed Nicole's hands were shaking. She needed me, and this made me sit up a little straighter and enjoy the control I now held. "Fine, I'll tell Justin to send the email, without revealing our identities. Then, we'll stay quiet for all eternity." My voice took on a sarcastic lilt. Then, relishing my moment of control, I continued, "Nicole, my life has been a nightmare since you entered it and I want to be done with you. I'll do as you asked so we can all put you behind us."

Nicole paused, swallowing the appearance of any weakness, and smiled a superior grin. The weakened Nicole evaporated. The bitch was back. With a patronizing pat on my shoulder, she stood. "Good girl." She started to walk away and then turned back toward me, bending down close to my face. I could smell a fruity scent emanating from her glossy lips. "It would be so easy for me and Jack to tell the President your name and Justin's name and get you both knocked off too, but I'm not going to do that. I trust you'll do the right thing, stay quiet and tell the President this whole thing was mistake and it's over, for good. Let him know his secret is safe and that your beef was with me, not him."

I stood as well and watched Nicole walk to her car. I hoped it would be the last time I saw Nicole. Ever.

Something caught my eye at the base of the driver's side door of her red BMW. A white wire dangled to the ground.

A white wire.

"A white wire that led to fire," Ms. Charlie's voice announced loudly in my head.

I gasped. Something inside of me lifted me, propelling me forward. My legs forced my body toward Nicole's. I attempted to get between Nicole and her car to stop her hand from touching the handle, but Nicole's

French-manicured fingers reached for the red door, as her face turned toward my screaming voice.

"No! Nicole!"

As if the explosion had already happened, I flew through the air, pushing Nicole, but it was too late. Nicole's hand released the car door handle. Intense, angry heat and a deafening boom pushed our already propelling bodies to the ground. I covered my head with my arm and rolled away from the flames and flying metal and shattering glass. Faint screams penetrated my deafened ears.

The first thing I saw when I opened my eyes was my arm covering my face and the shattered watch on my wrist. I was alive. At least that's what I assumed. I felt pain in my limbs and in my head. Yes, definitely alive. A piercing pain ripped at my lower abdomen, an intense cramp seized my stomach. My arms wrapped around my stomach and faces appeared above me asking me in muffled tones if I was all right. The pain stopped my breathing and words wouldn't form. I just shook my head. My baby was not all right.

I looked to my left and saw two men turning Nicole's unconscious body onto her back. Her face, the once beautiful face, was unrecognizable in a bloodied mask. Her hair, now stained red and black, clung to the wounds on her forehead.

"Ma'am, ma'am, can you hear me?" voices yelled at Nicole.

Sirens roared as the sound of gushing water doused the now indistinguishable charred vehicle. I pulled my head up slightly to see if there were other victims, but only Nicole and I lay helpless on the ground. I then saw two men in charred suits, stunned, resting against a building. One moved and sat in the bench where I'd been sitting. The bench I had chosen to rest on instead of getting inside Nicole's car. Reminding me of why I sat, I touched my belly.

In a burst of hysterics, I pushed the bodies from my personal space. "I want to sit up. I'm okay, I'm okay." I sat up as hands supported my back. I held my stomach, squinting to the sky. "You've got to be kidding me? Really? Again?" I hissed quietly.

"You saved that lady's life. I saw you push her before the explosion." A man muttered as he wiped something off my face. "How'd you know it was going to happen?"

"A psychic told me." I knew I sounded insane, but what did it matter. I was nearly blown to oblivion by the President of the United States. "I need to see a doctor. I'm pregnant." I needed to most likely see Dr. Dennison, too.

Two paramedics rushed at me, pulling a gurney behind them. In a daze, I let them strap me to it and pull me inside the ambulance. My vital signs were being taken, when another horrific cramp caused my knees to lurch toward my chest. Voices said, "Relax." Hands tended to my wounds.

This pregnancy that had appeared so unexpectedly, so unwanted, so grieved, was now being taken from me. Maybe, like Evan had forewarned, God, or an angel, or the universe, was taking care of me, providing an answer, a way out. I wouldn't need to decide what to do with the child, decide how to parent with a man she hated. God was taking care of the situation. My cheeks were drenched in tears. The smell of antiseptic made me gag.

I sat inside another ambulance, smelling of smoke, stained by fire, my head pounding in pain. This time I was not saved, but had done the saving. "Sir, the other woman, is she okay?"

"She got knocked out and banged up, but she was conscious and talking last I saw her. A good friend of yours?"

"Um, yeah." So now I was bonded to another person as a result of a traumatic event. Bound to Nicole D'Angelo for life.

"Here's your briefcase. And this envelope was under you. Is it yours?"

I took the envelope in my hands. My blackened, sooty hands trembled. The chain of events of the past hour, of the past three months, had not fully been processed yet by my mind, but my body was well aware. I pressed one shaky hand over my contracting abdomen and with the other, wiped my wet cheek.

Chapter 41

Three weeks later

My neck was still a bit sore from the explosion, but otherwise, I felt like I had recovered from the events of that crazy day, so I hoped to enjoy my Niagara Falls trip without pain. I hadn't ever traveled alone before, but this solo trip came at the perfect time. I needed this time by myself, to meditate, to contemplate, to enjoy the peace I'd finally found. To savor the miracles of Mother Nature. Ironically this show by Mother Nature was an abundance of water. Perhaps a great symbol to contemplate after being involved in two fires. Fires that changed my life.

And, technically, I wasn't alone on this trip. I reached down to release my pants' button underneath my long t-shirt. It was certainly time to graduate to maternity pants, I thought with a smile. There were probably some that fit in the countless number of gift boxes Nicole had sent to my apartment. Her gratitude for saving her life was now occupying the entire spare room of my apartment.

Since I was surprisingly early for my flight, I sat near my gate after buying a decaf latte and checked my phone. Evan had just texted a picture of the flyer he'd designed to hang all over town today promoting our concert that was taking place next month. The sketch of the memorial cement bench with all the victims' names turned out to be the perfect logo for the fundraiser.

Just as my smile faded from reading Evan's message, a text flashed across my phone's screen from Justin: Have a great trip!

Replying with a simple "thank you," I smiled again. Justin had taken me out for a pricey steak dinner two nights prior. It ended in a sweet kiss. He asked to go out again after my trip, but I'm making promises to no one. I would simply see who would be left standing when my life's explosions had cooled and quieted. There would be no forcing and breaking, just seeing who was tough enough to stand with me after the fires were extinguished. Besides my sturdy Magic 8 ball, of course.

I smiled again at my growing tummy—at the strongest blast survivor. If he or she could withstand being blown up by a car bomb, I was sure he or she could handle the zany life of a single mom. As soon as the ambulance had pulled away from the sight of the car bomb, my cramps stopped. My baby refused to give up. Seeing the tiny heartbeat fluttering on the sonogram screen yesterday was a sight I'd never forget. My mom already lovingly nicknamed her grandchild, Phoenix, since he or she rose from the flames. I guess he or she really came as a result of that first fire, but rose also from the second. As much as my mother stunk at picking names, this nickname stuck.

Once Kirk realized there was zero chance of me ever taking him back, he said he wanted nothing to do with our child, "doubting it was even his," he said. I had no doubt he was the father, but I did have doubts he'd be a good dad. Since he'd just accepted a job promotion in Atlanta, I figured he wouldn't change his mind.

Nicole let me know in her most recent thank you note that she was following Kirk to Atlanta. So, in the end, he got exactly what he had wished for.

After Jack's arrest, I was certain that Nicole cried many nights on Kirk's shoulder. The one goon who'd been threatening Nicole, confessed to knowing who had planted the car bomb. The planter, and the confessor, had ties to Jack—not the President. Jack would most likely survive this by cashing in on more favors and if he did end up in prison, he could probably count on conjugal visits from Nicole—even if it meant she'd have to travel from Atlanta to do so.

I had hopes that Nicole's concussion, twenty forehead stitches, six broken ribs, a punctured lung, and singed hair, would have changed her in some way, in the very least, change her manipulative ways. Maybe Nicole could find the good in herself and summon that, and not the side of her that got her into the explosion in the first place. Could people really change? I thought they could. I wanted to believe that there is more good in people than bad.

I also wanted to believe that something good came from my time with Kirk, and that good was growing inside of me. Like the train cars all tied one to the other, I guess we all are in some way connected. Whether we liked it or not.

A voice boomed through the terminal announcing that my flight was boarding. I pulled my suitcase behind me onto the plane. My stomach twisted slightly at the familiar airplane odor and at the memory of my last flight, when I had realized I was most likely pregnant. The fear of an unknown future had terrified me. This flight would be different. I was heading off on a relaxing vacation.

"Excuse me, Miss? May I help with that?" A soothing male voice spoke over my shoulder, grabbing at my suitcase. "May I put this overhead for you?"

"Oh, that'd be great. Thank you," I answered without turning to see the face matching the voice. I pushed the retractable handle down and picked the suitcase slightly off the ground to hand it to him. The nice voice had a pleasing face and bright white teeth to match. His dress shirt sleeves were cuffed once, revealing a shiny silver watch and no wedding ring. He appeared dressed for a business meeting perhaps. His cologne was light and sweet, just the right amount not to cause any new waves of nausea.

"You're quite welcome. Are you heading to Buffalo for business or pleasure?" The man with the soothing voice asked, placing the suitcase overhead.

I turned to answer, but my eyes were at his belt buckle and noticeably flat stomach. My eyes fell to my lap in embarrassment. "Pleasure. Going on a solo vacation to Niagara Falls."

"Nice," he said, maneuvering awkwardly between me and the seat in front of me. I probably should have stood to get my long legs out of his way, but he moved in before I could act on that decision. He sat by the window and adjusted the shade to reveal the outside. He leaned back toward me. "I'm Decklan, by the way. Happy vacation."

"Thank you. I'm Jezebel." *Here we go. Bring on a name comment.*

"Pretty name," he responded with a sincere lilt as

he pulled his laptop from his briefcase.

Shocked, I answered, "Thank you. Heading to a business meeting?"

"Yes, in Buffalo. I'm an attorney and we have a client there."

Great, could I ever get away from lawyers?

"I'm a paralegal at Harrington and Paulson."

"Oh, great firm. I could not survive without our firm's paralegals. They've saved my life many times."

I laughed. Really laughed.

We taxied to the runway and prepared for takeoff. Then, the captain's voice interrupted our conversation. "Excuse me ladies and gentlemen, there seems to be slight issue in the cockpit and we need to get it checked right away. We are returning to the gate immediately. We apologize but will keep you informed."

"You've got to be kidding me," I whispered to the plane's ceiling with a loud sigh.

"Well, your adventure begins," said Decklan leaning toward me with a smile. "Looks like this is going to be an interesting trip."

I smiled back. "Aren't they all?"

They certainly were. Every trip, every adventure—however disturbing the journey—was interesting indeed.

A word about the author…

Lori M. Jones is an award-winning author from Pittsburgh, PA and writes women's and children's fiction. She's the author of *Renaissance of the Heart* (romantic women's fiction) and children's books, *Riley's Heart Machine* and *Confetti the Croc*. Her debut novel won the 2015 Silver medal in women's fiction by Readers' Favorites Awards.

Lori is a mother of two daughters. Her youngest daughter's heart defect was the inspiration behind *Riley's Heart Machine*. Lori is currently on the national Board of Directors for the Children's Heart Foundation and the president of its Pennsylvania Chapter.

She travels to schools and libraries delivering assemblies on writing stories from the heart. She is also on the writing team at North Way Christian Community Church. Her other passions are rooting for her Pittsburgh sports teams and hanging out with her dog Disco, bunny Opel, and last but not least, her husband Mark. She holds a bachelor's degree from the University of Pittsburgh at Johnstown and a paralegal certificate from Duquesne University.

http://www.lorimjones.com

Thank you for purchasing
this publication of The Wild Rose Press, Inc.

If you enjoyed the story, we would appreciate your
letting others know by leaving a review.

For other wonderful stories,
please visit our on-line bookstore at
www.thewildrosepress.com.

For questions or more information
contact us at
info@thewildrosepress.com.

The Wild Rose Press, Inc.
www.thewildrosepress.com

Stay current with The Wild Rose Press, Inc.

Like us on Facebook

https://www.facebook.com/TheWildRosePress

And Follow us on Twitter
https://twitter.com/WildRosePress

Made in the USA
Middletown, DE
03 June 2016